TIDEWATER

Also by Joss Kingsnorth

The Journey In

TIDEWATER

Joss Kingsnorth

First published in 1995 by
HEADLINE BOOK PUBLISHING

A HEADLINE REVIEW hardback

10 9 8 7 6 5 4 3 2 1

British Library Cataloguing in Publication Data

Kingsnorth, Joss
Tidewater
I. Title
823.914 [F]

ISBN 0-7472-1536-7

Typeset by
CBS, Felixstowe, Suffolk

Printed and bound in Great Britain by
Mackays of Chatham PLC, Chatham, Kent

HEADLINE BOOK PUBLISHING
A division of Hodder Headline PLC
338 Euston Road
London NW1 3BH

AUTHOR'S NOTE

Many people have generously helped me with the factual information relevant to the background of this novel, though the characters, incidents and some of the locations are imaginary. I am especially grateful to: Alison Noice, Janet Horton, Trevor Bartlett, Marjorie Chetham, Dean Johns, Chips Barber and Luke Atkinson.

CHAPTER ONE

'I suppose there'll be no stopping Desna now,' Nell remarked. Gingerly she removed the somnolent mallard from the sofa and examined the cushions for feathers and droppings. It seemed as clean as she could reasonably expect in the circumstances so she sat down. The brown speckled duck, one wing held in a grubby bandage, waddled off, protesting with sotto voce quacks.

'You realize we shall hear nothing but wedding, wedding, wedding for the next six months? Good old Desna, she'll love every minute of it.' Emmet, her head bent over the starling she grasped in her hand, crammed a mess of dog food and soggy dog biscuit into its open maw with an artist's paintbrush. 'To make up for having such a quiet wedding herself, I expect.'

'Do you realize that must have been at least twenty years ago? God, Emmet, where does the time go? Yours must have been ten years ago!'

'Eleven,' Emmet said meticulously. She gathered up more food on the paintbrush and inserted it into the starling's gape. Behind her a grey hen dozed on the Rayburn rail; below the cool oven something wrapped in an old jersey stirred in its sleep. Emmet's kitchen drove Desna to distraction, and although she was not excessively houseproud like their older sister, Nell nevertheless found the pre-eminence of sickly animals unnerving and upsetting. She could never have lived with it as Emmet did.

'There you are, you greedy beast. That's all you're going to get for the moment.' Emmet opened the door of an empty cage and shoved the starling inside. She turned to her sister. 'Now, how about some coffee?'

'No, thanks, I'm not staying.' Nell never quite trusted Emmet's

1

domestic arrangements, fearing always that she might find droppings of some kind in her coffee mug, though she never actually had. 'I just called in on my way back from this woman who can't decide if she wants her house redesigned in the Shaker tradition or if she prefers something more Gustavian.'

'My heart bleeds! What's Gustavian, when it's at home?'

'Never mind. Drake's Farm is in no danger from it,' Nell said with a laugh. 'So how did you hear about Harriet's engagement?' Nell attempted to fend off one of the cats who was anxious to sit on her lap and so deposit as many of its hairs as possible on her trousers.

'Mo rang to tell me. Are you sure you won't have coffee?' And when Nell shook her head, 'I think I'll have some. I didn't have much lunch.'

Nell watched Emmet as she opened the lid of the Rayburn, moved the grey hen along the rail out of the way and hauled the heavy kettle on to the hotplate.

Nell observed her sister, in the very middle of all the apparent chaos, her pale, frizzy hair tied up anyhow and wearing her usual odd medley of oversize jerseys and old jeans picked up from charity shops, calmly orchestrating the needs of what looked like a private zoo. On the uneven flagstones at her feet lay a pile of assorted dogs, all smelly and all clearly devoted to their diminutive saviour. Around the walls bags of feed were stacked; dog biscuits, mixed corn, flaked maize. In the cupboards containers of glucose, antibiotic and hypericum ointment. On the worktop a box of mealworms.

'What does Mo say about the engagement?' Nell asked. Their mother's opinions were always unpredictable.

'She thinks Harriet's too young.' Emmet fetched a mug and the jar of coffee. She propped herself casually against the Rayburn rail next to the grey hen as she waited for the kettle to boil; looking ten years younger than she actually is, Nell thought.

Next door to the kitchen was what had once been a scullery. Through the open door Nell could see the shelves and old pine tables were full to bursting with cages as usual. The cages contained birds and various small mammals in the early stages

2

of their recovery, having been victims of every possible kind of accident and who would later, if their luck held, join the noisy occupants of the pens and aviaries out in the yard. The menagerie wasn't confined to the scullery; on the far end of the kitchen table a cardboard box contained a writhing and vocal heap of kittens watched over by their feline foster mother, one of the many cats that stalked, dozed, washed and squabbled or just sat on every available surface. At first glance it looked as if every sick creature in the county had been brought to Emmet's door.

'Might as well be comfortable,' Emmet said, though comfort was not a word Nell generally associated with the Darby household. Emmet heaved a pile of children's jeans and tee shirts, and some yellowing bills from a nearby chair and, when the kettle boiled, made herself a mug of coffee, pouring the milk from a half-empty bottle on the table. She sat down with a sigh and propped one trainer-clad foot on the other knee. The slightness of her body lent the posture a degree of elegance, like that of a dancer, perhaps bequeathed to her by the Joubert genes. As her half-sister, Nell had inherited more height and the dark glossy hair of another father, a father who had made himself scarce soon after she was born.

'So,' Emmet said, 'do we know what Harriet thinks of all the hoo-ha? Since it's *her* wedding?'

'Whoever knows what Harriet thinks? She'll go along with it in that vague dreamy way of hers. Poor Harriet.'

'I wonder why everyone always says "poor Harriet", but they do, don't they? Most girls would kill to be in her position. Rich mummy and daddy, no need to strive, a generous allowance...'

'Though I don't know what she spends it on. She looks as if she gets her clothes from jumble sales.'

'Like me, you mean.' Emmet's eyes gleamed with humour over the rim of her coffee mug.

'Oh you! You don't care anyway, do you?'

'That's true. Besides, it's not absolutely mandatory to wear a Jasper Conran or an Issey Miyake when defleaing a hedgehog.'

'Don't! You're making me feel itchy.' Nell pushed aside another mangy-looking cat that was attempting to move in on

3

her from the arm of the sofa. 'And how are Tom and Beth?' she asked dutifully.

'Thriving, thank goodness.'

Nell felt pangs of both envy and amazement at the casual manner in which Emmet accepted motherhood, as if her children were just another brace of abandoned kittens or puppies to be cared for, though Nell had to admit they looked well on it. She had no children of her own, a state of affairs she constantly and with melancholy resignation, regretted. Now she was thirty-seven and it was probably too late.

'And how does Beth like school now the novelty's worn off a bit?'

'Adores it. And she'll be in seventh heaven if Harry asks her to be a bridesmaid.' Emmet groaned. 'I'm afraid my daughter likes everything that's mega soppy.'

'She will be asked, of course. She'll look like an angel!'

'I just hope Tom's not required to be anything,' Emmet said. 'Nine is not an age known for its co-operation over this sort of thing.' She sipped her coffee and scrutinized her sister. 'Your looking rather the biz yourself today. How on earth do you manage it? I like that jacket you're wearing. Is it hand-knitted? Those licheny colours suit you.' She sipped her coffee. 'So what's new with you? Have you had any more lucky snips at auctions?'

'I did in fact. The other day I went quite mad and bought a beautiful little putto holding a bunch of grapes. The real thing, not a concrete copy. Fortunately the dealers who would normally have snapped it up weren't there and I got it for a decent price.'

'You must be doing all right in spite of the recession.'

'Yes, I suppose I am.'

'You've always had a wonderful artistic flair. Anything else new?'

Nell hesitated, wondering if she dare tell Emmet that Daniel had phoned. All Nell's family disliked Daniel. Then, 'Daniel phoned,' she said, and regretted it immediately. She felt her colour rise.

'Daniel! I don't believe it!' Emmet put her coffee mug on to the floor with a decided clunk. The tabby cat that had tried to colonize Nell took the opportunity of jumping on to Emmet's lap and proceeded to butt its head against her hand. 'After all this time! He's got a bloody cheek, hasn't he?' Emmet exclaimed. 'What the sod did *he* want?'

'He wanted me to meet him. Flick has left him, apparently.'

'What do we do now, cry?' the usual tolerant Emmet said crisply. 'In any case, Flick almost certainly had good cause. I can't imagine for a moment that Daniel hasn't been playing the field. He's too attractive for his own good.'

'I must say he sounded desperately low,' Nell said, ignoring Emmet's gibe.

'So he rang you. Good old Daniel. I'll say this for him, he's got more nerve than a dog's got fleas! But then he always had, hadn't he?' Even to spare Nell's feelings Emmet found it hard to watch her words. Nobody likes to admit that they had once made a colossal error of judgement; after all, she had made one herself, hadn't she? She thought of Maurice, incommunicado like an anchorite, bent over his word processor in his wooden shack. However, she regarded her own mistake in an altogether different light. She and Maurice had separated by mutual consent. Nell had been cheated on, betrayed and deserted in an all-too-public fashion.

'Why do you have to bring fleas into everything?' Nell said, irritated. She already very much regretted mentioning Daniel and was relieved when she felt something scraping harshly against her legs. Glad of the distraction, she bent to discover that the creature that had been asleep in the cool oven had emerged and was roaming the floor, dragging the old jersey in which it had been wrapped, behind it. Emmet pushed the cat off her lap and scooped the hedgehog up.

'Poor old Houdini,' she said fondly, cradling it with regard to its prickles. 'He only has one eye. He lost the other to maggots. And he's a heat junkie like every other hedgehog I ever met. Come April and he'll have to be weaned off it.'

'Maggots! Oh my God! And teeming with yet more livestock I'll bet!' Nell's skin crawled in faint alarm.

'That's where the defleaing comes in. Don't worry, they

5

wouldn't stay on you anyway. Hedgehog fleas are very particular. Sorry, we keep getting back to the same topic.'

'Don't we just!'

Emmet laughed and returned the creature to the floor. 'Run along, gorgeous. Go back to sleep like a good hedgehog. I adore them, don't you?'

'Well . . .'

'Naturally you told him to sod off? Daniel, I mean?'

'I didn't word it quite like that.'

'Of course you didn't. I expect you were more polite. All the same . . . how long has it been?'

'Four years.'

'Four years seems to be about his limit, doesn't it? Why d'you think he wanted to see you again? Surely he didn't imagine for one minute that you'd agree to that?'

'No, I don't think he did.'

'It's a pity that you couldn't say that there's a "significant other". There isn't, is there?' But she need hardly have asked. For months after Daniel had left, Nell had worn a look of total desolation. Now her demeanour was reserved and guarded, not at all like the spirited and witty person she had once been.

'Perhaps we're loners, you and I,' Nell said. She looked towards the scullery. Even from here she could see that in one cage a couple of baby rabbits rustled in a bed of torn up newspaper, tweaking their noses against the bars; in another a solitary crow gave sudden harsh squawks; in a third a pigeon with most of its feathers missing sat looking understandably glum. On the floor the dogs twitched in their sleep. 'Not that you can be said to be alone. You have the children, and I'm dead certain half these cats come to bed with you,' and with a momentary return of her old, dry humour: 'There simply wouldn't be room for a man as well.'

'He'd have to take his chances like all the rest,' Emmet grinned.

Nell stood up and retrieved her shoulder bag from the floor. 'I must go,' she said. 'I don't like to leave the shop closed for too long. Anna wasn't free to step in today.'

'Why don't you hang on? The sprogs will be back in a minute.'

'I could fetch them if you like, save you getting the car out.'

'Thanks, but it's Dinah's turn today. It shouldn't be necessary really with the village only just down the lane but what traffic we do get always seems to come down it at ninety miles an hour! And lately there's been the rabbits. They find the rabbits too upsetting. *I* find the rabbits upsetting, for goodness' sake!'

'Yes, I saw one or two as I came. Myxomatosis again, I suppose?'

'It's a foul disease.' Emmet sprang up from her chair. 'Did Desna mention Easter to you?'

'She said something about it. I think I switched off about then. After half an hour of wedding-itis.'

'She wants us all to go on Easter Sunday.' Emmet picked up a small tortoiseshell cat and began to stroke it absent-mindedly. 'I said it would rather depend if I could get someone to look after the animals. There's an unemployed youngster in the village who seems quite keen.'

'You mean you can't leave them even for one day?'

'It depends,' Emmet said, appearing to bear such responsibilities lightly. 'It's not too bad at the moment but we're coming up to the busy season. Well, you know what it's like. Fledglings and infants of every kind. Folks bring them from far and wide. I'm afraid it's largely due to that piece I wrote for the *Evening Echo*.'

'Have you done any more articles lately?'

'I'm working on one now for one of the glossies.'

'I don't know when you find time for it all. I think you're an absolute bloody marvel,' Nell said. She had once seen her sister neatly stitch a minute tear in the pulsating side of a damaged thrush. The next time she had visited Drake's Farm the thrush had recovered and been set free again. There was no doubt about it, Emmet had a very special gift when it came to animals.

They heard the sound of a car stopping, voices and slamming doors, heralding the arrival of Beth and Tom. The two women were at the door as the children erupted into the yard, scattering the dozen cats and causing a small commotion among the occupants of the outside aviaries. In the kitchen the dogs woke up and waited with thrashing, or in the case of the bull terrier, Earwig, twitching, tails. In the yard Beth immediately picked up a compliant long-haired cat and cradled it in her arms, trailing her school bag behind her. 'Darling, darling Mogsy.' She buried her face in its fur. 'Did you miss me, darling Mogsy? Oh hallo, Nell! Did you notice Mogsy waiting for me? She does that every day, don't you, Mogsy?'

Tom brushed past everyone and stomped angrily into the kitchen where he flung his school bag on to the sagging sofa. 'I hate this world,' he said bitterly. 'I just *hate* it.' He disappeared upstairs.

Emmet and Nell exchanged glances.

'I'd better go and see what that was all about,' Emmet said, pulling a face. She kissed Nell. 'Goodbye, darling. Take care as you turn into the lane.'

Beth came to see her off, still clutching the long-suffering Mogsy. Its legs had fallen through her arms and dangled in space but it registered only mild discomfort. This treatment was as nothing compared to what it had once endured at the hands of human beings before its felicitous arrival at Drake's Farm.

'What's the matter with your brother?' Nell asked, touching Beth's spun-gold aureole of hair. Its springy tactile quality made it almost impossible to resist. Tom's hair used to look exactly the same; Nell remembered Emmet's agonies of regret when she'd cut it off before his first day at school. Even with this concession he had still been teased for his unorthodox clothes.

'I don't know. He wouldn't tell me,' Beth said. 'Anyway, he's always cross about something.'

'Why's that?'

Beth shrugged, losing interest in Tom and his problems. The cat subsided slowly to the ground and escaped, sitting a little way off and vigorously licking its flank.

Nell got into her white Renault van. It was a recent acquisition and had her logo painted on the side in dark blue and gold: *Alfresco – designs for living.*

'When are you coming again?' Beth asked as Nell started the engine. Beth admired Nell. She represented everything Beth aspired to; her clothes were nice, not muddy like Mummy's or too posh like her other aunt, Desna's. She was not yet very much aware that her own appearance was somewhat quaint, causing old ladies to stop in the street and make comments like, 'Charming!' or, 'Poor child!' according to their own predisposition. As far as Beth was concerned Nell's main attraction was that she had a *shop* of her own with lovely things in it. 'And when can I come and help in the shop again?' she added hopefully. Her idea of heaven was to spend Saturday morning helping Nell.

'I'm not sure, just at the moment,' Nell hedged. 'I'll let you know.'

'Soon,' Beth pleaded.

Nell fastened her seat belt. 'Soon,'she called, waving as she went.

She felt a heel as she inched carefully into the lane. Normally she would have set a specific date, knowing how much Beth counted on these treasured days out; but she just couldn't commit herself, not as things stood.

She had been less than honest to Emmet about Daniel's telephone call and her own reaction to it. Of course she had been indignant and hurt that he should get in touch with her as casually as he had once left her. Of course she had, and naturally she had said as much to him. Indeed, she had been on the point of putting the receiver down as soon as she realized who it was but he had seemed genuinely remorseful and almost pathetically grateful and she had, in the end, listened to what he had to say.

'My God, Nellie, you don't know how good it is to hear your voice. You sound so wonderfully sane and normal. I seem to have been surrounded by nutters for so long I'd forgotten what it was like.'

The thought of all the pain he'd caused her prevented her from saying that it was good to hear *his* voice again. But even at the end of a telephone it still had the power to stir her to her innermost part. She'd had to steel herself to maintain an icy exterior.

9

'What is it you want, Daniel?' she asked, cutting through his blandishments.

'I want you to come out to dinner with me.' He evidently remembered her well enough to come directly to the point. She had no patience with waffle.

'Why should I want to do that?'

'I know, I know. No reason on earth. I just hoped you might, that's all. No strings, no games. Just two people enjoying each other's company. We always did that even when things were rough.'

'What a short memory you have, Daniel.'

'Look, Nellie, you've every right to be absolutely pissed off by what happened. I understand completely—'

'You don't understand. You never did understand . . .' She could hardly believe that he was speaking of the experience that had torn her apart.

'I'm trying to now. I'm not the insensitive bugger I used to be, believe me. I think you could say I've grown up a bit. And I want to talk . . .'

'I'm sorry, Daniel.'

He had pressured her to change her mind but she had held out. When she had put the receiver down she was shaken but at least she had been able to cling to some rags of pride. All the same, she knew Daniel; if he was really set on an idea he would not take no for an answer. She was by no means sure that she would be able to hold out against the sort of tenacity she knew him capable of. This reminder of her weakness filled her with an anxiety shot through with excitement.

The lane she was driving down wound tortuously round and between humpy, wooded hills, closely following the brook that skirted Drake's Farm before it hurried down to join the River Dart. Earlier that day it had sleeted and every now and again an astringent gust shook icy drops on to the windscreen, but now a citreous sunlight percolated through the tree branches and scattered itself on the surface of the wet tarmac. Just before the lane joined the main Totnes road, a crow flew up from where it had been picking at what she hoped was the carcass of a rabbit.

Sometimes the rabbits weren't dead before the crows found them but had blundered into the road, perhaps hoping for a swift end. Unlike Emmet she felt herself to be helpless in the face of such grim facts of life and death, reminders of mortality in a pastoral Eden; for this particular part of Devon seemed almost untouched by the twentieth century.

She passed a low wooden bungalow that dated from some time in the thirties. It was at the furthest end of a narrow strip of land that still belonged to Drake's Farm; the rest of the estate had been sold off as grazing land many years before. When Maurice and her sister had first acquired the farmhouse the idea had been to do up the bungalow and let it as holiday accommodation, but soon after Beth had been born Maurice decided to move into it himself. Except for rare occasions when Maurice remembered his paternal duties and took the children to an art gallery or museum, it appeared that he and Emmet hardly communicated and in effect, maintained entirely separate lives. In the farmhouse Emmet lived her apparently chaotic existence, surrounded by children and animals, while half a mile away Maurice crouched over his word processor, smoking endlessly, and painstakingly fabricating the tortuous prose of his latest novel. Nell had once tried to read one of her brother-in-law's books but she had not been able to get further than page five. Nevertheless, since they got published she imagined that someone, somewhere must not only read them right through but possibly understand them as well. What never ceased to amaze her was that Emmet gave every indication of finding these domestic arrangements entirely satisfactory, and what was more, appeared to be perfectly happy. Happier certainly than she'd ever been in the years that she and Maurice had lived together.

Emmet insisted that she managed better without Maurice than with him but there was a world of difference between Maurice and Daniel. Maurice was focused somewhere inside himself. Nell guessed that for him other people remained strictly on the periphery; they were and ever had been several removes away from what appeared to be the more absorbing reaches of his imagination. Daniel, however, was a man constantly on the alert to other people; how to react to them, how to assess them, what were their needs and aspirations and – Nell had no illusions about this – how to use and manipulate them if necessary. He set out to charm and continued to do so until he lost interest or it became clear that there was nothing in it for him. Even though she had been perfectly aware of the unreliable nature of his attraction she never could stop herself from responding emotionally to him. There was at the same time something charmingly candid, almost naive about him, once one had come to terms with the fundamental capriciousness of his character.

In four years she had at least acquired some sort of perspective on what had happened. She'd had plenty of time to reflect. If she ever agreed to see him again as he asked, if she could just forget the hurt and bitterness she had endured and forgive it, she would be better able to handle him. The success she had single-handedly made of her business had given her a sense of her own power and worth, but it had never for one moment banished the conviction that if he ever came back into her life his presence would make all the past suffering and pain worthwhile. They would both be more mature. This time their happiness would be on a firmer foundation.

The small town of Totnes lay on the River Dart between its source high up on the moor and its estuary at Dartmouth. Nell's sister Desna lived on its banks further down where the river widened but Nell herself rented a flat over her small shop which was situated in a narrow alley just off the High Street. Alfresco sold old pine and genuine country artifacts for the decoration of house, conservatory and garden.

At the rear of the shop was a minute yard, just large enough to hold the van and a few of the garden ornaments that had become quite a lucrative sideline. She parked, locked the van and turned towards the covered flight of steps that led from the yard to the door of her flat. Daniel was sitting on the bottom step with her large black and white cat, Morgan, on his lap.

'I thought you had to open the shop sooner or later so I thought I'd wait,' he said.

* * *

Emmet found Tom sprawled on his bed picking at the wallpaper where a small patch of damp had made it loose. He was red in the face from tears he'd considered too babyish to shed. Emmet sat down beside him under the hanging flight of Tom's model aeroplanes: a Bristol Beaufighter dangling threateningly above a Mig and a Vulcan bomber apparently confronting a Hurricane.

'What's the matter, sweetie?'

Moodily he went on with his wallpaper picking.

'Please don't make that patch any bigger, Tom. We can't afford to have your room done just yet.' She leaned over him. 'Now tell me what's up. Have you been in trouble with Mrs Webb?'

He shook his head.

'What then, tell me?'

There was a silence, then, 'Adam Gear said that we were hippies and that my dad was a weirdo!' he blurted out.

'Is that all? What Adam Gear thinks about us shouldn't upset you too much, should it?'

'It wasn't only him. They all said it.'

'Were they bullying you?'

'Not bullying exactly . . .'

'Because you're not the sort to get bullied as a rule, are you?'

'No,' Tom said gruffly. 'They just called us hippies and said Dad was a weirdo.'

'Look, I think it was just that they were in a silly mood. I think it will all be forgotten tomorrow. I think *you* should forget it.' Emmet sometimes found it difficult to understand her son. Here he was, with well above average intelligence and reading skills, able to understand such mysteries as the workings of computers and space rockets, fazed by the infantile taunts of a few witless kids. She had tried her hardest to see to it that the children conformed to the sort of unwritten dress code that prevailed among the young, even though she herself detested it. Beth appeared to be largely unaffected as yet – she would be too dreamy even to notice anyway -but Tom was another matter. Obviously she would have to try harder.

Tom looked doubtful. 'But I don't think they will forget it,' he said dolefully.

'Listen, darling, if it happens again I'll speak to Mrs Webb, eh? How does that sound?'

'I don't want you to talk to Mrs Webb.'

'I won't unless it happens again. You *will* tell me, won't you?'

Tom nodded. 'You think I'm stupid,' he muttered.

'No, I don't. I think you were very sensible to tell me. And don't worry, we'll sort it out somehow.' She got up. 'Now, how about some toast and peanut butter?'

Tom agreed to that and Emmet went downstairs to make it. Every now and again Tom would tackle her about their family's choice of lifestyle and every time she was at pains to emphasize that it was not because he didn't love them that their father lived apart. She tried to stress the particular nature of Maurice's work but she was afraid that this cut very little ice with Tom at least. Beth was far more philosophical about it. Sometimes Emmet thought that Tom would have been better able to accept a father who had absconded completely, which apparently was not considered 'weird' by his peers.

She sighed as she cut bread for the toast. Tom would always ask questions and she rather fancied that the answers were not going to get any easier. She would have liked to have asked Desna how she coped when Rupert was nine years old, except that Desna wouldn't know. By that time Roy had seen to it that Rupert was away at boarding school. Maurice might have his faults but all the same, Emmet thought, not for the first time, she would far rather be married to him than to Roy. No. She could not find it in her heart to envy Desna.

CHAPTER TWO

Harriet left before the papers arrived. Desna, faintly dismayed by her daughter's apparent lack of interest, picked up *The Times*, the *Telegraph* and the local paper and for once appropriated them before Roy came downstairs. Spreading them on the half of the large polished table not laid for breakfast, she turned eagerly to the announcement pages.

> The engagement is announced between Philip Nicholas, son of Mr and Mrs G. H. Emmerson of Dartmouth, Devon and Harriet Lucy, daughter of Mr and Mrs R. Hindmarch of Upper Ash, Devon.

So there it was, she thought with satisfaction, all official. Nell and Emmet would probably laugh at her for being hopelessly stuffy and conventional but it was just that she hated anything that was haphazard or unsystematic. As for her mother . . . well, Mo would doubtless continue to argue that Harriet was too young and didn't know her own mind. However, it had been a long time since Desna had heeded what her mother said. In any case she herself had married at the age of twenty and neither she nor Roy had experienced a moment's regret; besides, her mother's record in the marriage department could hardly by called a roaring success.

Desna was downstairs before Roy, as always, and had seen to it that both the grapefruits were neatly sectioned, that four pieces of toast were slotted into the rack, three for Roy and one thin slice for herself, and that the coffee machine was switched on. The aroma was already percolating enticingly through the room.

She had smoothed the sleep from her morning face with a film of moisturizer and had applied a little pale lipstick. Her hair, which was as abundant as Nell's, but not, like Nell's entirely unaided by artifice, was slightly damp from the shower; she had tied it back with a peacock-blue ribbon that matched her dressing gown. Roy was particular about his appearance even when he was wearing casual clothes and had no patience with laxness in others. In any case Desna took a pride in being highly organized; her morning routine unfailingly included time spent on herself even though it meant getting up half an hour earlier. Laying a proper breakfast was another part of the ritual; in winter, as now, in the dining room, while in the summer they moved to the huge conservatory with its view over the terrace and the lawn.

'It's in,' she said as Roy appeared. He sat down. He was in shirt sleeves with a grey and maroon patterned silk scarf at the neck. Later he would add his navy-blue guernsey and a navy and white waterproof sailing jacket, his normal gear for when he was working in the yard and he had no formal meetings. Desna poured his coffee.

'Spelling all right?' he enquired, drifting brown sugar sparingly over his grapefruit. His gourmet appetite had unfortunately to be leavened with caution; he was a large-framed man who could easily run to fat now that his way of life was less exclusively physical than it had once been.

'Seems fine,' she said, offering *The Times* folded to the appropriate page. 'Don't you want to see?'

He waved it away. 'Darling, you're making a pig's ear out of those papers.' The irritation in his tone made it perfectly clear that last night still rankled. It was too much to hope that he had forgotten. 'I'll look at it later. What we'll have to think about straight away is the date,' he continued. 'We'll have to get on to Peters about booking the church. You know what it's like in the summer, every bloody girl in the county wants a summer wedding. Just make sure it's not in Cowes week that's all, or the damned church will be half empty.'

'I thought the middle of July.' Delicately Desna prized out a section of unsweetened grapefruit and put it in her mouth.

'Suits me.'

'Good.' She glanced at him. 'Roy, it's going to be expensive.'

'Damn the expense. We've only got one daughter, for heaven's sake,' he said expansively. 'Besides, I thought you intended using your father's bequest for Harry's wedding.'

'It might not cover it completely.'

'We'll manage. At least we won't have to fork out for Rupert when the time comes, if it ever does, the young blighter.' As usual when speaking of their son he used a tone of hearty tolerance as if the two of them were engaged in some exclusive male conspiracy. Rupert, at sixteen, was still at boarding school.

Desna smiled. 'So we can have a slap-up do?'

'A slap-up do,' Roy agreed, drinking his coffee.

Desna felt a bubble of relief break inside her and the tension of the last twelve hours softened into smiles. She had been so hoping that Roy would not plead the exigencies of the recession as an excuse for a small affair for Harriet. Roy had all the ruthlessness on occasion of the successful man of business but as a rule had never counted the cost when it came to his own family. It was a matter of pride to him that he was generous to her over her own personal allowance and, in the past, to Harriet over hers. Even now that Harriet had the job in the gallery he continually pressured her to accept money for clothes. It was not his fault that she was not particularly interested in clothes or for that matter, in spending money at all.

Roy had come from a background where money had always been in short supply. Perhaps this was the reason why he was so attentive to all aspects of it – its acquisition, its management and its disposition.

Desna watched him covertly as he finished his grapefruit and thrust the empty shell to one side, helping himself to toast. All his movements were precise and decisive. His hands were strong and tanned even at this time of year, with just a hint of dark hair on their backs. When she had first met him twenty-three years before, the hair on his head had been even darker than her own; it still grew as vigorously but now it was a handsome silvery grey. There was no doubting the fact that he was still an attractive man. She had always been aware of the immediate impact he had on other people, both physical and psychological; it was like a force field that could both attract and repel with equal violence. The years had enhanced rather than diminished this quality in him.

She cradled her coffee cup in both hands. 'What do you think about a marquee in the garden?' she said. 'Because I don't see how we can keep the guest list under a couple of hundred at the very least.'

'Instead of an hotel, you mean?' Roy bit into his toast. 'Sounds like a good idea. You couldn't have a better setting, anyway. But do exactly as you want, I leave it to you.'

Desna was not deceived. Every decision she made about the wedding arrangements would be carefully scrutinized, though only a few of them questioned. Nowadays he claimed to trust her organizational flair implicitly though he also said he could never understand how she had acquired it, given the collection of unreliable genes she had inherited from her unconventional parents.

'It's not what *I* want, darling,' she said. 'Not entirely. It's what Harriet wants that really counts.' However, neither of them really believed this.

'Good God! Harry doesn't know what in blazes she does want half the time. Leave it to her and she'd join the queue at the registry office on a Saturday morning, kitted out in her usual God-awful heap of cast-offs.'

Roy took another piece of toast and began to butter it aggressively. 'Sometimes she strikes me as being more like Emmet's kid than ours.' Roy treated Emmet with a kind of affectionate contempt. A poor relation. 'You know, as Philip's wife Harry'll jolly well have to wake her ideas up.'

'I'm sure she will,' Desna said soothingly. 'It's just that she has a lot on her mind at the moment. And her clothes are nothing unusual these days, you know. Most girls dress the way she does.'

'Only art students like her friend Faith.' Roy finished his

coffee half standing. 'All the same she doesn't strike *me* as being the very picture of the ecstatic bride to be.'

'You know Harriet. She keeps it all inside.'

He grunted. 'Two things,' he said as he touched the side of his mouth with his napkin before tossing it on to the table. 'I think it would be as well to get old Peters on to booking the church right away. Today. And,' he paused, 'while you're about it I think you should make an appointment to see Sally Bright.' Sally was their doctor, with a surgery at Upper Ash, the nearest village.

'I don't think that's really necessary.' She looked away, avoiding his gaze. 'I feel perfectly well.' No, he had not forgotten last night.

'I mean it, Desna. Yesterday evening was most untypical of you. But let's face it, it wasn't the first time, was it?' So he *had* noticed those other occasions. 'I expect she'll say you need a course of vitamins or something, that's all. Perhaps you should try HRT or whatever it's called.'

'I suppose I could ask her.'

'You *must* ask her. And don't play it down when you get to the surgery. With all that there is to do in the next few months you'll need to be pretty fit, believe me. After the wedding we'll have to think of ways to cut down on your workload.'

'I haven't got a workload. I don't call looking after Mount Huish a workload!' Impatiently she reached across to help herself to more coffee. 'I'm sure Sally will think I'm making a fuss.'

'We don't pay huge insurance premiums for her to think that.' Roy stood at the door, implacable until she agreed.

'All right. I'll make the appointment.' She sighed.

He left punctually at eight. Just because his success was established he saw no excuse for the slightest relaxation of routine, since work was second nature to him. It always had been. Soon after he left school in Gloucester he had joined the marines. Based in Devon, he had fallen under the spell of the sea, of boats, sailing and all things nautical. He had left the marines and started a small boat repair yard with a loan from the bank. He had met Desna and they'd married a few years later. Since then he had never looked back, expanding the business into both chartering and yacht brokerage. Now the office in a Portakabin had been replaced by smart accommodation in a white painted building on the waterfront in Kingswear, across the river from Dartmouth. Hindmarch Marine had expanded to swallow up two neighbouring properties and was at present bursting at the seams with expensive yachts laid up for the winter or undergoing refits. Even the recession had not materially affected the business. There always seemed to be individuals or companies who could afford the services of Hindmarch Marine.

As the Merc disappeared down the drive, Desna could see from the window that Roy was already on the telephone, thoughts of Harriet, the wedding arrangements and, no doubt, even her unfortunate lapse of last night already dismissed from his mind. And thank goodness for that at least, she thought.

She took her coffee, black as usual and sugarless, into the conservatory. The conservatory was heated and contained a few large glossy-leaved plants and some substantial wooden chairs upholstered in dark green cotton drill. The original floor tiles had been in too poor a state to keep when they first moved in, damaged from the leaking roof and other misfortunes, and she had had them replaced by slabs of reclaimed French limestone; their pearly glimmer in the early morning light was half obscured by a large geometrically patterned kelim. As in the rest of the house Desna had asked Nell's advice on almost every aspect of furnishing and decoration, from the warm earthy colours of the conservatory walls, as of some Tuscan villa, to the Cretan pithoi. Without her sister she would have gone in for cane and chinz with eau-de-Nil paintwork, which she now saw would have been a mistake.

Even in its previous state of neglect and disrepair she had loved Mount Huish from the moment she had walked into it, clutching in her hand the estate agent's somewhat optimistic blurb; in fact the estate agent could hardly have been more surprised when the Hindmarches had returned to the office that very afternoon with what was, all things considered, a very respectable offer. The place had been empty for five years and it had been expected to remain so indefinitely, this being before the era when every waterside property of any description whatever was snapped up for huge sums of money.

Mount Huish was built in the 1920s as a country retreat for a wealthy industrialist and his film star mistress. The style was vaguely classical though well seasoned with Art-Deco detail, the proportions generous. Then it must have looked an incongruous and slightly vulgar intrusion on the wooded banks of the river but time had done its work of mellowing and softening and the surrounding planting had matured; Mount Huish was now considered to be a positive asset to the area. The rich industrialist and his mistress occupied it sporadically, using it for lavish house parties until he had come to grief off the Skerries in his yacht and drowned, to the general amazement of the locals. Amazement, that is, that he could have got as far as Start Point in his inebriated state before disaster struck.

After that Mount Huish had been bought by a famous playwright, then during the war it was taken over by the Special Operations Executive, to which many locals attributed the beginning of its disintegration; afterwards it became a home for delinquent boys who were luckily not in residence long enough to complete the process. Since the fifties one or two brave individuals had acquired it and made short-lived and ultimately futile efforts to restore it to its former glory before running out of money. Fortunately one of their achievements was the overhauling of the roof, which had at least preserved the house from the worst ravages of the weather. Then, twelve years ago, the Hindmarches had bought it and rescued it from the brink of ruin.

Desna drank her coffee and gazed out on to her favourite view; a slice of lawn, a stone balustrade and a screen of trees that allowed glimpses of the river running secretly between wooded banks. In the evening the water betrayed its presence with a million fragmented points of light; at this time of the day and at this time of the year all was peaceful, no outboards, no pleasure craft bound between Totnes and Dartmouth and no trippers to disturb the herons and cormorants from their silent vigils. When Roy had suggested a few days ago that Mount Huish would soon prove to be too big for them and that they might consider selling, she had immediately panicked.

'I was absolutely convinced that you loved this place as much as I do!' she had cried. 'How can you even think of it?'

'I had an idea that you might like something a little easier to run, that's all,' he had said soothingly. 'It was just a thought.'

'I love the work. In any case, how could we manage the entertaining in a smaller place?'

'I didn't mean smaller necessarily. Anyway, forget it. If you're happy—'

'I most certainly am happy. You know I am!'

So no more had been said. All the same, the notion that Roy could even consider moving was not easily forgotten.

A squirrel ran along the branch of a holm oak and executed a perfect mid-air arc to the trunk of a nearby beech; a green woodpecker stabbed the lawn for grubs. Gusts of a cold March wind shook the branches of the trees, some now misted with pale green. In a moment Desna would dress and her day would begin. Already most of it was accounted for; telephone calls to the Reverend Gerald Peters of Upper Ash, to the caterers, the photographer, the florist and, of course, to the wonderful little dressmaker in Totnes who had made such a good job of Nicola Wakeham's dress. And then, inevitably, the doctor's. Roy would make a point of asking her if she'd seen Sally. There was no getting round it.

It was all such a fuss about nothing. It had been a small dinner party by her standards. Harriet had asked for it to consist of as few as possible; just the family, Philip, his parents Isabel and Giles, and his sister Tessa, who was a year older than Harriet. Desna had also asked Helen and Kit Wakeham since it was more than likely that Nicola's two younger sisters would be bridesmaids. Desna had hoped for more lavish engagement festivities altogether but Harriet had protested and she had given way. They had agreed to split the celebrations, since Emmet found dinner parties difficult with the children and Roy refused to entertain their friends *and* Mo at the same time if it could be avoided; so it had finally been arranged that the whole family would come for the day at Easter.

Perhaps in the circumstances it was just as well, though nothing else had gone wrong. The food was perfect. The new recipe for the consommé had turned out beautifully, the lamb parcels were succulent and tender, the crème brûlée a great success. It was when they moved to the sitting room for coffee, when the wine had mellowed them and when the conversation was at its liveliest that she had fallen into a deep and peaceful sleep. All she remembered was the descent of a soothing darkness, the voices round her nothing more than the distant pounding of surf. The next thing she knew was that Roy was standing over her, looking thunderous, with brisk reminders about more coffee. If they noticed it, nobody remarked on her minor lapse, but Roy's expression left her in no doubt what he thought about it.

The trouble was that it was not the first time it had happened. Two weeks before, when they were guests of the Farquarsons, she had nodded off over the chocolate marquise; she had been too embarrassed to check if her nearest neighbours at the table had noticed, she had merely picked up her spoon and continued eating as if nothing had happened. Roy, however, had noticed; he was still as vigilant as ever of her behaviour even though she had never given him real cause of anxiety until now. She supposed he was right; she would have to do something about her recent propensity for nodding off.

A sound from the direction of the kitchen reminded her that Carol had arrived and that she had spent too much time brooding. This kind of introverted activity was not a habit of hers either.

Carol was putting on her striped apron ready for her morning's work. She lived in the village, had a seven-year-old son Davy, and a husband who did shifts in a bakery in Brixham. In between, she fitted in an OU course in sociology.

'Carol, I'm sorry but I haven't cleared the breakfast things.' Clearing the breakfast things was not one of Carol's assigned tasks. 'My morning seems to have got off to a slow start . . .'

'Don't worry, Mrs Hindmarch. Leave it to me.' Carol picked up a tray and moved to the door. 'How did the engagement party go?'

'Very well. Quiet, you know . . . not really a party.'

'I expect Harriet preferred that.' Privately Carol thought that Harriet was slightly weird, with her bedroom full of the oddest things, nearly all smelly: animal skulls, snake skins, seagulls wings and a collection of spooky-looking bones. All the same, she was at least friendly if rather shy, much nicer than Rupert who seemed to think that because he went to a minor public school he was really cool. Still, he was only sixteen and, thank God, away most of the time. And thank God too, she thought as she went to clear the table, Mrs Hindmarch was a meticulous employer, very fair and never, surprise, surprise, found herself out of 'change' at the end of the week, like some.

That morning Desna chose to wear a suit of rich tomato-red wool. In the bedroom she smoothed the skirt over her hips in front of the cheval glass. Could she have put on a fraction more weight since she'd last worn the suit? She adhered strictly to her self-imposed diet, but it didn't seem fair; Nell and Emmet never put on an ounce and Isabel Emmerson was a bag of bones. Last night Isabel had consumed three gin and tonics, accounting for at least a hundred and fifty calories, not counting the wine, whereas she herself had been as abstemious as usual. If she hadn't, if she had drunk as much as the others, her overwhelming drowsiness would have been easier to explain.

She went downstairs and spent an hour on the telephone. She booked the church for the 16th July, had a preliminary chat with a very pleasant woman at the caterers who said she would be prepared to arrange for the services of the florist, photographer and videographer too. That in fact her firm would take care of everything if necessary. Then Desna telephoned Sally and made an appointment for two o'clock.

Sally Bright was forty-two but looked younger. She was also brisk, businesslike and approachable. She took Desna's blood pressure and pulse and a sample each of blood and urine. She

24

questioned her closely about how rigorously she was dieting, and if she slept during the day.

'And how do you sleep otherwise?' she asked.

'You mean other than at dinner parties?' Desna said.

Sally grinned.

'I've never had any trouble that way as a rule,' Desna said, 'but lately I occasionally wake up and don't drop off again immediately.'

'How about mood swings, hot flushes, that sort of thing?'

'No, I'm not troubled by any of those. But surely I'm not menopausal yet!'

'Are you drinking more than usual? Water, I mean.'

Desna shook her head.

'Or alcohol?'

'If I had been I would be like a barrel by now, believe me!'

'And you're not worried about anything?'

'Not a thing. You know me, I'm not the worrying type.'

Sally looked at the display on her VDU. 'I think you were a little concerned about Rupert at one point. Has he settled down now?'

'I don't suppose we shall ever be able to claim that he has settled down exactly,' Desna said with a slight smile. 'He's never been an easy child, not for us and not for the school. He's not like Harriet. But I can't say I've been especially anxious about him. Not more than usual.'

'And how is Harriet now that she's a bride-to-be?'

'She's very well. Still working at the gallery.'

'I don't seem to have seen her lately. It might be a good idea if she arranged for a check-up.' Sally was slightly puzzled that Harriet had never consulted her about contraception; she hoped the girl's shyness wasn't preventing her from taking adequate precautions. She saw her so rarely that it had been hard to establish any kind of rapport.

'Now back to you.' Sally smiled, her straight wing of blonde hair brushing her face. 'I fully expect the tests we're doing to be completely normal but in any case I'd like you to make another appointment for next week and we'll have another think. If in the meantime you have any other worrying symptoms come and see me sooner.' She tested her patient's reflexes and asked her if she ever had any temporary muscle paralysis.

'Never,' Desna said. 'I'm sure it's all a fuss about nothing. Roy insisted I came,' she added, rising. 'I expect I need a tonic or something.'

'I'll prescribe something, of course,' Sally said, getting up from her swivel chair, 'but I think we should leave that until next week.'

Desna made a further appointment and left. By this time she was absolutely convinced that there was nothing seriously wrong. She probably had a virus. Just before she'd nodded off at the Farquarsons' she remembered a woman called Myra complaining about some virus she'd had that made her feel very tired besides sick and dizzy. In fact she had gone on about it at some length. Desna had either caught the bug from her or had fallen asleep out of sheer boredom. On either count, she thought, damn the woman. Besides, she had other things to think about. Arrangements for the wedding would absorb most of her energy and interest for the next four months. She looked forward to it with happy anticipation. Her own wedding had been a very quiet affair when what she would really have liked, at twenty, was a dress that swept the ground and a guest list of hundreds. But neither she nor Mo had had the money; it would be Harriet who would be getting the sumptuous dress and the huge reception. Not that Harriet had much enthusiasm at the moment. Though she would. Eventually. In the end she would thank her parents for giving her something lovely to look back on.

CHAPTER THREE

The pot was the texture and colour of toast, veined with lava flows of smoke grey; its form was vaguely bird-shaped with a vestigial uplifted beak and a rotund body. It was heavy. Harriet clutched it to her narrow chest as she heaved it from the glass display shelf, dusted underneath and replaced it. She moved on to a group of small pierced bowls; these were pale as the rabbit skull she had come across two days before, bleached milk white by the sun and salt air and wedged in a crevice between rocks. Her fingers had explored its bony protuberances and creamy concavities before she had slipped it into the pocket of her old navy donkey jacket. Later she had added it to the collection she kept in her room.

She took her time this morning; she was alone since the gallery was rarely busy this early in the year, unlike the summer when Dartmouth seethed with visitors and the Yardarm Gallery enjoyed, if that was the right word, its fair share of browsers. It was filled with light from the spots which bounced off the white walls and glass shelves; she sometimes had the sensation that she was on display herself, like a fish in a tank. But on such a wintry day few paused to gaze into the large plate glass window where she had placed three massive Caen stone sculptures, examples of work from the current exhibition. She had been employed in the gallery for three years and the arrangement of the displays was now mostly left in her hands. It was something she enjoyed doing and was at least one thing she knew she was good at.

Outside a woman in a grey tracksuit, a red baseball cap, trainers and a yellow fluorescent strip, was chaining her bicycle to the railings. A moment later she bounced up the steps and in through the door, bringing with her a gust of cold, seaweed-smelling air.

'Hallo there, Harry!' Mo greeted her with a peck on the cheek before removing her bicycle clips and whipping off her jaunty headgear. A long sandy-grey plait hung down her back and her complexion was tanned and seamed like leather.

'Hallo, Mo.' Harriet replaced the bowl she had been holding and looked about for somewhere to put the duster.

'Congratulations, sweetie. How did the dreaded engagement dinner go, then?'

Harriet shrugged. 'All right, I suppose.' Then, as if she realized the inadequacy of this response, added, 'Yes, fine, actually.'

Mo studied her granddaughter with eyes which were a peculiarly penetrating blue, her head on one side and wisps of her odd-coloured hair escaping from the braid.

Harriet was damned good-looking, she thought, standing there with her long legs encased in black, her short black skirt and her droopy jersey. Her hair was fairer than Desna's, a kind of bronzy brown, very long, and presently pulled back from her face and tied with a long silk scarf. She had huge eyes and a wonderfully translucent skin; it was no wonder that when Philip returned from bumming around the Caribbean, he had been knocked sideways by Harriet's newly emerged but fragile-looking beauty.

The trouble was, Mo thought, that there was something *too* breakable about Harriet; and it wasn't only her clothes that appeared to droop. Harriet herself tended to do so, a habit that might become a permanent physical attribute if she allowed it to. But one didn't have to look far to discover the reasons for the child's defensive stance, it was all too apparent. In Mo's opinion, Roy had a lot to answer for.

Mo looked round the gallery, jingling her cycle clips in her pocket.

'You know, you should have been a painter, like me,' she said. 'The way you've set this place up shows genuine creative flair.'

'You know I haven't the talent. Not like you. Not like Faith. She got an A at A level. I only got a pathetic C.'

'What a good job I never took A levels! Or School Certificate for that matter. It could have blighted my life!' Mo turned her back on Harriet and inspected a row of impressionistic landscapes. 'As it was, nobody told me I was any good but then nobody told me I wasn't either. I just decided I wanted to be a painter and that was that.' Abruptly she spun round and came over to Harriet, held her arm in a rather painful grip and looked at her searchingly. 'Now about this engagement. Is it what you truly want? I mean, you're not just marrying to escape, are you?'

'Escape! I don't know what you mean?'

'Oh yes, you do. Because, if that's the case I think you should reconsider. Now! Before your mother really gets the bit between her teeth. You know what she's like: wind her up and off she goes . . .'

Harriet moved away defensively and began to search for the duster she had discarded earlier. 'Of course I'm sure! I adore Philip. You know I do.'

'Naturally you adore Philip. Who wouldn't adore Philip? He's bright. Well, he's quite bright, he's well educated, he has a good job with Hindmarch Marine, thanks to your father, though I'm sure he could have done extremely well for himself anyway. He has no conspicuous vices and, of course, he is exceptionally good-looking. It doesn't necessarily mean you have to marry him. Couldn't you just have a bit of an affair – sleep with him or something?'

'I sometimes think you say these things on purpose to shock people, Granny.' Harriet put special emphasis on the name she scarcely used in an attempt to point out the unsuitability of her grandmother's remarks. She wished Mo would stop probing into her affairs. A warm tide of embarrassment stained her cheeks.

'Nonsense, you young things don't shock.'

'You think he doesn't love me, don't you? I mean, with all his chances, all the great sailing groupies he's hung around with,

29

why choose me? That's what you think isn't it?' Harriet began to dust the counter vigorously but quite unnecessarily.

'Don't come the old soldier with me, my girl. You know as well as I do that you're well educated too. And bright. And have been far-sighted enough to have acquired the right sort of parents. *And* I'm absolutely certain that it hasn't escaped Philip's notice that you are a bit of a knockout!' Mo could have added that she was also the boss's daughter and likely to inherit a great deal of money in due course, but she desisted. She was trying to boost Harriet's self-esteem, after all.

At last Harriet smiled. 'You're biased.'

'Of course I'm biased but I think you should credit me with a little of the wisdom of old age.'

Harriet could hardly believe it when Philip suggested that they should get married. Compared to his, her life had been sheltered in the extreme; boarding school followed by three years at the gallery. But even while still in his teens Philip was off skippering dinghies in the Medway and Crouch. That was followed by a spell in the Mediterranean where he had skippered flotillas of Beneteaus before swanning off to become a boat bum in the Caribbean. There he had taken all kinds of jobs on a variety of yachts, including skippering, all valuable experience leading to his success in obtaining his Yachtmaster's examinations.

Harriet couldn't remember a time when she hadn't hero-worshipped Philip, but since he had asked her to marry him she'd had frequent spells of panic and depression when she became obsessed with the idea that he had made the offer only as a result of unspoken pressure from the two sets of parents. The arrangement would be all too convenient for everyone, after all. Philip had worked for her father for nearly four years now, though for much of the time he had been away from the yard delivering newly refitted boats to all points of the compass, or acting as skipper for wealthy charterers. Since Christmas he had worked mainly in the yard and it was during this time that he had suddenly become so attentive, as if he was seeing her with new eyes. In fact they both spent an inordinate amount of time just gazing into each other's eyes as if hypnotized.

Mo had fortunately released Harriet from a scrutiny of a different kind and was examining a watercolour featuring Dartmouth Castle.

'So don't let the young rascal break your heart, you hear?' she said. She tapped the watercolour with an enquiring finger. 'How much is Gordon asking for this dog's dinner?'

'That one? A hundred and eighty pounds. You're not interested are you?'

'Daylight robbery.'

'What's daylight robbery?' Gordon, one of the owners of the Yardarm Gallery had come down from upstairs where he had been unpacking a consignment of pottery. Polystyrene chips still clung to his hairy jersey as if he had just plunged through a silkworm colony.

'Hallo, Gordon,' Mo greeted him, unfazed. 'How's business?'

'Good morning, Mrs J,' he smiled with exaggerated formality. 'Business is quiet just at present. But it'll pick up at Easter. Thank you for asking. And how are you?' He began to rummage underneath the counter. 'Harry, have you seen those orange-handled scissors anywhere?'

'They're upstairs on your desk.'

'*Are* they? That's funny, I looked there. Still, I'm sure you're right. What would we do without this girl, Mo?'

'You may have to do without her when she's married,' Mo said slyly.

Gordon looked shocked. 'You said it wouldn't make any difference, Harry!'

'Of course it won't. That's Mo's idea of a joke.'

'I can't do with jokes like that this morning. I'm feeling far too fragile. I've just had this beastly letter about the new business rate.' He moved over to the stairs again. 'Are those paintings you promised me finished yet, Mo, dear?'

'I'm waiting for them to dry completely before I varnish them.'

'Not too heavy-handed on the varnish, I hope.'

'What d'you take me for? All the same, they're taking ages to dry, drat the things.'

'I'm not surprised; down there by the water! It must be chronically damp.'

Gordon referred to Mo's riverside cottage at Papermill Quay. 'Anyway, you never said how you are.'

'Bloody exhausted, if you must know. That lot next door had some sort of party going on last night. Chanting, they were. Kept me awake till all hours.'

'I told you before that you should buy a nice quiet bungalow up at Stoke Gabriel,' Gordon remarked, picking the white cocoons off his sweater and making a small pile of them in the palm of his hand.

Mo pulled a face. 'No, thank you, sweetie. I'd rather die. Number two, Papermill Cottages and I will rot away peacefully together.'

Of course her grandmother wasn't serious about dying, Harriet reassured herself. She didn't like to think about Mo dying. It seemed so unlikely that Mo would do anything so conventional for a start. Desna never spoke of such a possibility; but the trouble with her parents' generation was that they never thought about death, or if they did, they simply didn't speak about it. They behaved as if they thought themselves immortal, leading their lives restlessly, acquisitively, as if a mountain of material objects could act as a bulwark against oblivion. Like the Egyptians, except that the Egyptians were always too late, since they were dead already.

The door of the gallery burst open and Toby came in. Toby was Gordon's partner and as physically unlike Gordon as was possible. Gordon was of medium height, with his prematurely greying hair tied back behind in a neat pigtail and a permanently worried expression on his face. Toby was tall and rangy and booted like a football hooligan, with his red hair shorn to half an inch all over. His clothes would have suited the Pied Piper and, unlike Gordon, he was an optimist. He painted, though not very well, in Harriet's opinion. The gallery was, first and foremost, to have been an outlet for his work but the truth was that almost all their stock sold better than Toby's reckless daubs. However, he never seemed to give up hope of finding a rich sponsor. Under his arm he was carrying evidence of yet another scuffle with the Winsor and Newtons.

He dumped a bundle, wrapped in an old denim jacket, on to the counter.

'Mind the glass, man!' Gordon rushed forward to thrust a sheet of gallery wrapping paper under the untidy heap, scattering polystyrene chips as he did so.

'What d'you think of this idea, Mo?' Toby said, imperturbably, peeling back a fold of denim which was stiff with dry paint. 'I've decided to have a go on wood, like your original van Eycks and whatnot.'

Gingerly, Mo examined the collection of old chunks of timber adhering to which were great lumps of clotted paint.

'This is a new departure, isn't it?' Mo said. Toby's last offerings had been minimalistic, tiny markings on huge sheets of handmade paper, like the meanderings of a drunken spider. 'I don't think the van Eycks worked on driftwood, did they?'

'At least it's seasoned,' Toby said. He lifted one from the pile. 'Now this one was done on a piece I found on Slapton Sands. D'you see how I allowed the grain to become part of the finished effect?'

'They're great!' Gordon said stoutly, but he looked worried.

'You'll have trouble with the salt later on,' Mo said darkly.

'Who cares about later on?' Toby said dismissively.

Mo grunted. 'Unprofessional,' she said.

Toby turned to Harriet. 'You're very quiet, Harry.' He put an arm around her shoulders. 'Commiserations on the engagement. Are you sure you know what you're doing?'

'Don't you start!' Harriet said irritably. 'Why does everyone take it for granted that I don't know my own mind?' She grabbed her duster and started flicking it around. 'Gordon, you've dropped bits all over the floor!'

'Sorry, I'll pick them up.'

'No, leave it to me, for goodness' sake!'

Mo was amused to see Harriet asserting herself here as she never did at home. It was a hopeful sign.

Toby gathered up his paintings. 'I'll put these on the wall

33

upstairs so we can see them to the best effect,' he said, undaunted by the lukewarm reception they'd had so far. 'I think you'll see what I'm getting at when they're properly displayed.'

When Gordon and Toby had disappeared upstairs Mo prepared for her own departure. 'Why don't you call in tonight, Harry? If that young man can bear to part with you for an hour or two.'

'I *am* supposed to be seeing him tonight, as a matter of fact.'

'Of course you are. What d'you mean, "supposed"?'

'Well, you know how it is . . . if they have an unexpected client, Philip might have to stay late.'

Mo frowned slightly. 'You're not interested in boats, are you?' she said.

Harriet sprayed polish and rubbed the glass where Toby's paintings had left a drift of sawdust. 'It's not that I'm not interested in boats, Mo. I get seasick, that's all.'

'Yes, I know you do. I was just thinking that you won't expect to see much of Philip after you're married, will you? One way and another.' They both knew that Roy kept Philip fully occupied with the yard's business and that Philip himself was perfectly happy with this arrangement; it wasn't only that he expected one day to become a partner in the firm, he was and always had been fanatical about boats, about sailing and about the sea.

'We agreed we wouldn't want to live in each other's pockets.' Harriet rubbed harder.

'You'll carry on working here?'

'Why not?'

'Because there's no future in it, that's why not! You have a good brain if you'd only use it. You should either have a share in the gallery or get stuck into studying something sensible.'

'I wouldn't know what. I'm not as bright as you think I am. Besides, Gordon and Toby often allow me to share the decision making with them.'

'Darling, it isn't the same thing at all. You should think about what I've said.' Mo could have added that she trembled to think how Harriet would cope when she eventually become hostess for the firm of Hindmarch Marine, a position that Desna filled to perfection. Philip would certainly own the firm one day since Mo thought it extremely unlikely that Rupert would ever have the necessary application or interest.

Mo opened the street door. 'Well, I'm off. I may see you later if you've nothing better to do, eh? I'm cycling over to see Emmet this weekend. Shall I give her your love?'

'Please do. And the kids.' Harriet liked Emmet. Last time she had been at Drake's Farm Emmet had been burying a badger that had died from its injuries after being hit by a car. Harriet had been impressed by the respect the children had accorded the dead creature. She thought that in some ways children were more aware of life and death and had more veneration for these fundamental processes than adults. She would like to have made a drawing of the badger before its interment but Emmet said it was already quite smelly enough. Not that Harriet would have minded that.

There were few customers that afternoon and at five thirty she called up the stairs to Toby and Gordon. 'Do you want me to turn off the lights before I go?'

'I'm coming down in a minute so you can leave them,' came Gordon's disembodied voice from above. 'But lock the door as you go, there's an angel.'

Harriet changed her skirt for a pair of old jeans and wheeled her bicycle out from the storeroom. Conscientiously she locked the door of the still bright gallery and pedalled off, passing the ancient Butterwalk in Duke Street, and out on to the quay where the wind blew more keenly. She waited on the slipway for the higher of the two ferries, with several cars, a van and one or two foot passengers. Some daylight still remained but it was overcast and the lights of Kingswear, where she was bound, were already trembling on the surface of the dark water. The tide was running out quite fast, piling up blackly behind the mooring buoys and making extra work for the huge splashy paddle wheels that powered the ferry across the river.

On the other side she plodded up the wet slope to the road. Her father had offered to buy her a car but she had not yet managed to pass her test, partly through nervousness but mostly because she did not see driving as a priority; like her grandmother, she enjoyed cycling and saw no compelling reason to forgo it.

The lights were on in the yard and offices of Hindmarch Marine. Beyond the open gates, cradled and shrouded, were all the winter lay-ups and from a forest of masts came the continual clatter of wire rigging on aluminium.

A piercing whistle brought Harriet to a standstill, and Philip came towards her through the maze of props, oily engines, hoists, welding equipment and the coiled snakes of rope and cable. Every time she saw him she felt a tide of joy swelling up inside; it was probably both sentimental and corny, and perhaps it was what people meant when they talked of their hearts leaping up. In any case, she didn't want to analyse the feeling. It just happened.

'Hi there, face-ache,' he said, kissing her on the cheek, while at the same time wiping his hands on an oily rag. He was in oil-stained jeans, a navy sweater with a Arab-style scarf at his neck, his fair hair disordered by the keen breeze.

'Don't treat me like some kid,' she said accusingly.

'You are a kid.' He grinned. 'Want a lift? I can chuck your bike in the back of the Land Rover if you like.'

'I'd rather bike it, thanks. Shall I see you later?'

'That's why I wanted to catch you. Your dad and I have to check the work on the Oyster 66. This Italian guy is coming down to see her tomorrow and Roy is anxious that it's all spot on.'

'I know, he's always talking about it lately.'

'The Italian is some hotshot apparently. Seriously rich.'

'So will it take the whole evening?'

'Could do. Why? Do you want to do something special?'

'No. So if you don't come, I might go over to Mo's.'

'Good idea. I'll ring you.' He kissed her again, savouring her mouth which was wet and salty with the spray from the ferry crossing. She turned away. She didn't like him kissing her within view of the men in the yard. He wanted her to be grown up enough to enjoy his caresses while treating her like a kid at all other times. In this respect he was just as bad as everyone else. But it didn't make any difference to her feelings for him. She loved him; she always had.

She mounted her bike. 'Sure,' she called as she went. She pedalled on up the road. It would be pointless staying in waiting for him to ring, he'd be sure to forget once he got involved in working on the Oyster. Instead, she would spend the evening with Mo, watching the box and eating Turkish delight and stem ginger left over from Christmas. Her parents didn't approve of her spending time slumped on the sofa watching television; like their days, their own evenings were meticulously timetabled: guests to dinner or dinner out, social functions or business-related engagements. Her mother never seemed to stop preparing food: making preserves, cooking huge pies for the freezer, fussing over sauces, sticking cloves of garlic into dead animals, on and on as if she were expecting a siege. Then there were the special occasions. Parties, Christmas, summer lunches or evening drinks in the garden with anything up to a hundred guests, the preparation of hampers to take to boat shows or for entertaining on their own boat, a Moody 376 called *Eos*. The next thing would be Easter with the family, which Desna was preparing to make a major do. And as for the wedding! To say that she would be in her element was a mega understatement, but there was nothing Harriet could do about that. In fact, her father had taken her aside and given her quite a lecture about how mean and small-minded it would be to deny her mother the unmitigated pleasure of organizing the one and only wedding she was ever likely to get her hands on. It would be a tour de force. Harriet hadn't been able to stop thinking that it was also very much for her father's benefit and his standing in the community.

'Listen, Harriet,' her father had said emphatically. 'No one will expect this to be a hole-and-corner affair. They'll think you're pregnant or something. And I'm damned sure we can put on a better show that the Wakehams. No, on this occasion you'll have to be guided by us. It's the very least you can do.'

On this occasion! she'd thought bitterly. On what occasion

hadn't she given in to her father?

So it was to be the whole shebang – church bells, choir, morning dress, lace and ribbon, hundreds of guests, a flower-laden jamboree. Philip didn't seem to care one way or another, so she supposed she shouldn't either. It would keep Mummy happy and that was something, because she sensed that her mother had not been her usual buoyant self lately. Harriet could not have said precisely why she thought this, except that last night she'd noticed that her mother had actually nodded off at one point, but she could hardly be blamed for that; Harriet had nearly done so herself. The senior Emmersons were ultra boring and it was a mystery to her how they could have produced a son as absolutely exceptional as Philip.

She swung the bicycle off the road and on to a track which veered away through the trees towards the river. It was a short cut to Mount Huish.

She enjoyed every part of her daily routine, one she knew that most of her contemporaries would find boring. She liked the cycle ride, she enjoyed talking to customers at the gallery, arranging work, dusting and polishing, meeting artists and looking at the beautiful things they made. She was extremely fond of both Gordon and Toby and boiled with quite uncharacteristic rage when, the other day, her father had called them arse bandits.

'I don't know why you are so all-fired keen on working for those arse bandits when you could stay at home and help your mother prepare for the wedding. It is *your* wedding after all,' had been his actual words. And he'd even seemed surprised that she had flown at him, though it was true that demonstrating temper was something she rarely did. Especially not towards her father, because she was, in truth, afraid of him.

If only the wedding could be dispensed with, that she and Philip could just live together, like Nell had lived with Daniel. But it would never be allowed. Her parents never actually said as much but she knew that they would have disapproved of Nell's former arrangement even if they'd liked Daniel. Which they never had.

As soon as Harriet saw the lights of Mount Huish twinkling at her through the trees, the depressingly familiar fluttering began just below her ribcage.

CHAPTER FOUR

That evening Nell took particular care to look her best, as if she was anxious to demonstrate that she was the same woman Daniel remembered. Except that she wasn't. She looked what she was, a moderately successful, self-sufficient, though probably lonely, businesswoman. All the same, she would not have liked Daniel to know that the loose-fitting cinnamon-coloured suit was being reserved for the special, special occasion or that the ivory silk shirt had been bought that afternoon to go with her antique amber beads and amethyst and amber scarf. Daniel had always noticed what she wore. Though he made no comment, she saw that in this respect he had not changed.

'You see why I couldn't talk about it over the phone,' he said. 'There's too much I wanted to say. *That's* why I asked you out to dinner – to explain. How's your terrine by the way?'

They had reached the main course before Daniel switched the conversation from the wary small talk that had occupied them over drinks and a very fine Provençal fish soup.

'It's delicious.' Nell was determined to enjoy her very expensive meal. Cornucopia must be doing all right. 'How's Simon, by the way? I hope you're treating him well?' Simon had stepped in as Daniel's partner after she had left. He had inherited money and was anxious to invest it in something that would give him an interest. Nell had liked what she knew of him but feared that he was too naïve for his own good.

'Simon's fine,' Daniel said shortly. He didn't want to talk about Simon.

They sat at a window table in The Pig in Clover, an upmarket restaurant in Dartmouth. It overlooked the harbour and the lights of Kingswear, which spangled the hill opposite. Nell couldn't remember ever having patronized such an expensive restaurant when they were together – they'd been on a fairly tight budget. But Cornucopia had already been on the upward path when they had split up – or more precisely when Daniel had left her.

At the beginning of their passionate affair it had seemed natural, in view of their shared interest, to build a business of their own. Together they had chosen the site that would best lend itself to being converted into an emporium for antiques and architectural salvage; this had been an old bacon factory in East Devon. And it was Nell's skill at figures as well as her eye for unusual acquisitions that had given Cornucopia such a boost. Its two huge floors of intriguing and idiosyncratic antiques, as well as a line in cannibalized old pine furniture that Daniel started, had since become well known not only in the county but nationwide and even abroad.

Nell had first met Daniel at a country house clearance sale. At the time he was the owner of a small junk shop – it could hardly be called anything else – in Exeter. She had already been working for a dealer called Prettyjohn for five years who, since he had come to trust her judgement, let her have a completely free hand at sales and auctions. She had been after a satinwood work table and a walnut davenport; Daniel had run to earth some particularly fine linenfold panelling that had been relegated to an outhouse. She had caught him in the act of smothering it in even more dust plus a quantity of rotten sacking to hide it from rival dealers. She hadn't classed herself among them so she had been vastly amused. It had created a bond between them and after the auction, at which they were both successful, he asked her over to the pub for a celebratory drink. It had been the start of an incandescent affair.

'I'm sorry to hear about Flick,' she said, glancing at him as she guided some minute new potatoes on to her fork.

'You needn't be. I won't elaborate on what happened except to say that I think we both realized we'd come to a sort of crossroads. So I can't claim to have been very surprised when she suddenly announced she wanted to take off in another direction. Do her own thing, as they say. Flick is a bit of a feminist, you know.'

'A very small bit, I'm afraid,' Nell said drily.

He grinned. 'You always did have an ascerbic wit, didn't you? Well perhaps not, but she does hate the idea of being tied down. Tied down! With me! I ask you. I'm the last person to tie anyone down. All the same I wouldn't want you to think it was all her fault. I've been a bugger to live with lately. Regret is very insidious, you know, Nell.'

She grinned, determined to keep it light. 'You sound like Noël Coward.'

He frowned momentarily before he laid down his fork and reached across the table, resting his fingers just for a moment on her wrist. He gazed at her, his dark brows drawn together. She remembered his hazel eyes as lively, amused, alert, sometimes candid and confiding but never anxious and almost haunted, as now.

'It's wonderful talking to you again, Nell. So easy,' he said, taking up his fork again. 'I'd forgotten.'

'Daniel, I don't know why you're talking to me at all. If you're looking for a shoulder to cry on, you can forget it.

He managed a wry grin. 'No,' he said, 'that's not what I had in mind at all.'

'You're not being particularly intelligible.'

'I'm sorry. It's difficult.' He reached over and picked up the bottle of Lanson champagne. Daniel was certainly pushing the boat out tonight. 'More?' She shook her head. 'You're enjoying your meal?' he said almost accusingly. She noticed that he was making slow progress with the terrine of pork and guinea fowl.

'I don't often have the chance to dine so well,' she said. 'Besides, I missed lunch.'

'You should look after yourself.'

'So I should, shouldn't I? No one else will.' She laughed but there was more than an edge to her remark.

'As a matter of fact, that's what I was coming to . . . in a way . . .' He broke off while he arranged his knife and fork on

43

his plate with an air of finality. He subjected her to a searching gaze and she summoned up more of the defences that had so far helped her to endure being with him again. 'Look,' he said. 'There's no point wrapping it up in fancy speeches. What would you say to us getting back together again? And please give it a thought before you throw the remains of your dinner at me.'

What would she say to their getting back together again! As if she had thought of anything else for the past four years; four years when her whole life had been suspended in a time warp no matter how she tried to escape. Four years in which she and Daniel could have amassed a store of shared memories and intimacies, years that had been squandered on this and that, and when she'd begun to notice, if no one else had, that her skin was no longer so pliant, nor her eyes so bright. Vital years in which she could have had children, not just any children, for she was not the motherly type by nature, specifically Daniel's children.

She stared out of the window, hardly taking in the ghostly shapes of moored yachts out on the river. Daniel ducked his head in order to gauge her expression. 'Nell?' he queried.

She moved a hand as if to fend him off. 'Don't . . . please.' She could never bring herself to believe that, given Daniel's nature, there might also be a backlog of hurt, betrayal and deceit, of silences, rows and woundings. In the imaginary and parallel life lived by herself and Daniel throughout these years of separation nothing like that had ever occurred.

Daniel leaned forward and spoke in a near whisper. 'You look shattered. I'm sorry, I didn't mean to upset you. But I did mean what I said. I'd no idea that my suggestion would be such a no-no. Nellie, I am so sorry.'

She came out of a trance and glanced at the other diners, hardly believing that they could not have noticed what was going on. 'How could you?' she said in a fierce whisper. 'How could you bring me here and do this to me?' She lay down her fork. Suddenly she wasn't hungry any more.

'Look, I've apologized. I just thought for a moment that there might be something left, that you might feel something for me

in spite of my having acted like a shit. I see now that there isn't
and that you don't.'

The waiter came to remove their plates and to ask about
dessert. Nell shook her head.

'Just coffee,' Daniel said. When the waiter had left Daniel
reached across to cover her hand with his. He said quietly, 'Let's
forget it, shall we? I seem to have made my usual balls-up of
things, bull in a china shop and so on. Just because I've come to
my senses after a three-year aberration doesn't necessarily mean
that you still feel the same. Sod it! Of course you don't!'

She found speech again. 'What astonishes me is that after all
this time – it's *four* years incidentally, not three – you are prepared
to think of me as some kind of stopgap. What sort of colossal
arrogance makes you believe that just because Flick has left you,
and you're at a loose end, you can come running to me? I mean,
it's breathtaking . . .'

'Look, Nellie, sweetheart—'

'And for God's sake *don't* call me that.' That had once been his
favourite term of endearment.

The coffee came. It was good but they drank without
enthusiasm.

'I see that I've explained myself very badly indeed,' Daniel
said at last, putting down his cup. 'I'd like to tell you something
if you could just hear me out.' He leaned towards her. 'The main
reason that Flick buggered off was because I was becoming so
obsessed with what I'd thrown away when I left you. You see,
idiots like me take an awful long time to grow up but I think I
finally did, something Flick has not yet managed, to be brutally
honest. I was too immature to value you when I had you.' He
shook his head. 'I can't believe what an arsehole I was to leave
you!' He smiled at her, his eyes full of that special appeal that
had once never failed to melt her. To her dismay she found it
still could. 'And I can't believe I'm rushing in where angels fear
to tread now!' he said. 'But you know me: it's a habit of mine.'

'I think you'd better ask for the bill and drive me home,' Nell
said as briskly as she could manage. She was desperate to be
free of him. She had thought that she could cope with an evening

45

of Daniel. Now she saw how misguided she had been.

'Of course.' He signalled the waiter, paid for the meal with his credit card and they went out into the night. The air was cold and she wrapped her long woollen scarf more closely about her. A boat chugged up the river, almost invisible except for its lights, which moved stealthily between the dark shapes of vessels riding at their moorings.

As they walked to Daniel's car, a classic E-type Jag, they maintained a careful distance, not touching.

'Why do you drive a gas-guzzler like this?' Nell said as he opened the door for her. Inside it smelled expensive and leathery.

'You know what a sucker I am for anything antique.' He slid into the driver's seat.

'Including antique love affairs, apparently,' she said caustically.

He sucked in his breath. 'You've every right to put the boot in. I deserve it, don't I?'

They spoke very little on the way back to Totnes through the dark country roads, and when they arrived back outside Nell's flat she immediately made a move to open the door. She knew she would not be able to cope with much more in the way of intimate scenes with Daniel. He put a restraining hand on her arm.

'Nell, before you rush off, will you promise me something?'

He took her silence for acquiescence. 'I want to see you again very much indeed. I suppose I need hardly say that. Will you promise me that you will at least think about what I asked. I made a bad mistake when I left you. There's no going back to where we were, naturally, but couldn't we just give it a second try? If it doesn't work, then . . .' He turned to look at her. 'Listen, I know you never married but if there's someone else, someone special, then just tell me to get lost.'

Someone else. She could hardly call the intermittent relationships she'd had since Daniel someone else exactly. She sat very still and spoke with difficulty. 'You hurt me, Daniel. You hurt me very much. At the time I thought I'd never get over it. But now I have, at last I have. And I could never take that kind of risk again. Never. Don't you see that?'

He was silent and when she looked she saw that he had put his head in his hands.

'You do see that, Daniel?'

With a hand still to his temple he was shaking his head. 'Darling, Nell. Poor Nell. I should be kicked from here to Land's End for what I did.'

'Yes . . . well. I'm over it now.'

He put both his hands over hers as they lay in her lap. His touch sent a tumult of mixed messages flying through her system. He kissed her very gently on the mouth.

'I'll ring you,' he said, his voice full of gentleness and meaning. In a trance, she left the car.

Yes,' she said, 'yes.'

Inside the flat she threw off her scarf and coat and went immediately to the kitchen where she rummaged in a cupboard for a small bottle of cognac she kept there, poured herself a generous slug and took it back to the sitting room. She discovered she was trembling and tipped some of the brandy down her throat even before she opened the doors of the wood-burning stove and threw in another log. She kicked off her shoes and slumped into an armchair. Still clutching the glass she closed her eyes. How could one evening with Daniel have turned her into such a tacky mess? How could she have said 'yes' to him? She hadn't drunk *that* much, had she? In a moment of weakness, she had let him know that she was still susceptible; he would never let it go at that now that he knew. Persistence, at least in short-term aims, was something he was good at.

The cat flap clicked open and slammed shut followed by thudding footsteps. Morgan appeared, took a spring and landed heavily on her lap. He made one or two turns and settled down, but Nell was too preoccupied to notice that he was doing her best suit no good at all. She had opened her eyes and was sipping her brandy, gazing into the fire, her toes encased in black tights, held out to the gentle warmth. She hoped the brandy would blunt the edge of reality even if it failed to do anything about her confusion. Absent-mindedly she stroked Morgan's long black and white fur and he began to purr thunderously. Of course Daniel's remorse and his eagerness to try again could be perfectly genuine. He certainly sounded as if he deeply regretted having broken up their relationship. If only she could be sure . . .

They had never married, which certain members of her family had found suspect, but then it hadn't seemed important; many of their friends had similar arrangements which worked perfectly well. Besides, at some level she must have known that Daniel could not handle that much commitment, and in any case such a formality could never have held him if he'd wanted to leave. Which after five years of what had seemed like a wonderful partnership in every way, was precisely what he did.

She swirled the remaining brandy round in the bottom of the glass, watching it cling momentarily to the sides. Above anything, she wanted to believe him. After all, wasn't he offering her the very thing she had dreamed of for all the four years they'd been apart? Outwardly, her life during that time must seem like quite a success story. Intending to reduce the possibility of their paths crossing in the course of ordinary business, she had moved from East Devon to Totnes and eventually to the small premises just off the High Street. She'd painted the interior of the shop white, stripped the beams of sticky black stain, leaving them grey, covered the floor with rush matting and began to sell statuary, Cretan pithoi, unusual garden furniture, old kitchen furniture and a few rough-textured linens and robust cotton drills with ticking stripes. She also stocked a range of special organic colours for adding to limewashes. Advising Desna about the decoration of Mount Huish had led to further commissions designing interiors for those who admired her rugged country style. In fact she was discovering that this was now her major source of income.

From her armchair she cast her eyes round the sitting room. Compared to the bedroom and kitchen it was disproportionately large, having two triple-arched windows that looked out over one of the narrow side streets so typical of the town. She had worked like a Trojan on the flat over the shop when she had first moved in; stripping, scrubbing and painting until her arms nearly dropped off. She had painted the room with the special paints in a colour she had mixed herself, attempting to copy the uneven terracotta that she had found on some old Italian tiles. She had ripped out the 1950s fireplace and used the Italian tiles round the newly revealed original. Above it she had fixed a huge mirror, wonderfully spotted with age. She had painted the woodwork a pale grey sanded down until it was almost white; she had also sanded and polished the floor on which she put her precious Tabriz marriage-tree carpet. Between the windows a large stone bust of Aphrodite, with a broken nose, presided – a female deity in a female milieu.

Morgan could hardly be called female but he could hardly be called male either. He plumped out his cheeks, purred more loudly and dug his claws in briskly to secure Nell's attention.

'Get off, cat! You're ruining my skirt!' Nell exclaimed abruptly. She put down her empty glass and got up, tipping him off her lap. She hadn't really wanted Morgan but Emmet had insisted that she had a moral responsibility to adopt at least one of the many unwanted kittens that arrived at Drake's Farm. Now Nell had to admit that the flat would seem lonely without him.

In the kitchen she scooped out a huge dollop of cat food from the tin while Morgan caressed her legs with his substantial furry body. He knew better than anyone that, despite appearances to the contrary, his owner was a soft touch.

'Why can't I be content to bumble along like Emmet,' she asked him, 'and just be happy as I am?'

CHAPTER FIVE

'I'm Barney.' The stranger put one foot on the kitchen step as if prepared to spring across the threshold. The foot wore a grubby white trainer and was fixed to a jean-clad leg of exceptional thinness. If it came to that, Barney's whole body was notable for its lack of anything in the way of excess flesh. The effect was modified by a thick quilted body-warmer worn over a polo-necked sweater. Above that again was a narrow head, freckles, a grin and rust-coloured hair.

'Oh, hallo,' Emmet said. 'You rang about the job?'

'Right.'

'Come in.' Emmet's invitation was redundant. He was in already.

'Coffee?' she asked, but with the distinct impression that if she hadn't offered he would have taken the kettle off the Rayburn and helped himself anyway.

'Thanks.' He looked round, surveying his surroundings, glancing through the open door of the scullery, noting the birds in their cages; a crow, a jackdaw, pigeons, and the cardboard boxes of what looked like old sweaters, except for the one from which a heap of blue-eyed kittens were struggling to escape.

Emmet handed him a mug of coffee. 'Why don't you sit down?' she said. He lowered himself on to the decrepit sofa while Emmet sat at the table. The dogs roused themselves and came to inspect the new arrival. Immediately they heaped themselves about his legs and gazed at him adoringly.

'Well, it looks as if animals like you!' Emmet said. 'The point is, do you like animals?'

'Sure. That's why I answered your ad.' Emmet had put a

51

postcard in the window of the village post office stores.

'Have you ever had any yourself?'

'Only mice and guinea pigs. We had a dog once. Not much room in a council house, what with four kids.'

'Your brothers and sisters?'

'Right.'

'Do you live at home now?'

'How old d'you think I am?' He grinned and his face disappeared momentarily behind his mug of coffee.

She looked at him more closely. 'I've no idea,' she said truthfully.

'I'm twenty-nine, aren't I? And I live in a bedsit down the village.'

'Oh.' Emmet was nonplussed. 'I was expecting somebody younger, just to help out with the chores, you know.'

'I don't mind what I do. It's all money, isn't it?'

'You see I couldn't offer you full time and I couldn't afford to pay you much. Have you a job already?'

'I do bits of labouring. Painting, digging gardens. Sort of handyman stuff, you know. I could fit you in I expect,' he said kindly.

'Thank you very much,' Emmet said, but her irony was lost on him.

Beth appeared at the door holding Mogsy. From upstairs came a faint sound of running water and footsteps along the landing. Tom's friend Lee Arnold, whom Tom inexplicably admired and whose mother was currently in hospital, had come for the day and they had disappeared upstairs half an hour before.

'This is Mogsy,' Beth said, approaching Barney and holding the cat out for his inspection. 'And I'm Beth. What's your name?'

'Hi, there, Beth.' He stroked Mogsy's head. 'Everyone calls me Barney.'

It turned out that Barney was his surname and that he was slightly coy about his first name.

'I'm not very used to interviewing people for jobs,' Emmet said.

'I can see that,' he said, and winked – at least she was almost positive that he winked. 'I think you better ask me what my hourly rate is before we go any further.'

'No, before we go any further I think I better take you round and show you what I should want you to do. You may not like the idea of clearing out aviaries or chopping logs.'

'I'm not fussy about what I do.'

Emmet was becoming gradually more aware of ominous sounds drifting down from upstairs.

'Excuse me a minute,' she said and sprang up from her chair.

On the landing a garden hosepipe threaded its way leakily from the bathroom to Tom's room and subsequently out of Tom's window. Tom and Lee were leaning over the sill aiming the jet at various targets in the garden, most of which were feline. On hearing Emmet's squawk of rage both boys turned round, letting go of the hose which snaked back inside, liberally spraying Tom's bed, his model aeroplanes and most other things in the room.

'Go and turn off the water this minute!' Emmet yelled and Tom shot out of the door with all the speed of the cats he'd recently been targeting. The jet died to a trickle. Lee was cowering by the window as if he expected Emmet to hit him. Tom returned, looking sheepish.

'Tom! Lee! I want you to clear all this up, take the hose downstairs and hang your duvet out on the line to dry.' Emmet thought she was acting with commendable restraint. 'I'll talk to you later, Tom. I'm busy with a visitor just now. By the time I've finished I don't want to see one drop of water left. Is that clear?'

'I'm sorry,' Tom mumbled. 'We didn't mean—'

'I should hope not.' Emmet clumped downstairs crossly. Beth was showing Barney the hedgehogs in their cardboard box, now removed from the Rayburn.

'I'm sorry about that,' Emmet said briskly. 'Those hedgehogs were late babies. I'm putting them in the pen in the outhouse today, all except Houdini. I'll keep my eye on him for a bit longer. Perhaps you'd like to help me.' She picked one up and thrust it into Barney's hands. It rolled up, trapping his fingers inside.

'Wow! What a grip! Who'd have thought it?' Barney said, apparently unperturbed by close encounters of the prickly kind. 'Look, it's unrolling already.'

'We try not to turn them into pets but they get used to us all too quickly,' Emmet said. 'The idea is to return them to the wild, of course.' She had been observing Barney closely. He handled the creature gently. His hands were surprisingly small for someone who earned his living with them.

Tom and Lee arrived in the kitchen, lugging the hose. They hesitated when they saw the stranger.

Barney grinned at them. 'What's your game then? Thinking of joining the fire service?'

The two boys gave him a thunderous look, glanced at Emmet and disappeared rapidly out of the door without answering.

Barney helped to carry the box of hedgehogs outside. Emmet opened the door of an outhouse. Inside a section of it was partitioned off and its floor covered in a deep layer of bark chippings. There were no other hedgehogs visible.

'But they're all in there somewhere,' Emmet said. She allowed Barney to place the newcomers in the pen and they ploughed off through the chippings snuffling excitedly. Then she showed him the aviaries. There were some in the yard but most were in the old apple orchard beyond a high wire fence that excluded the cats. The mallard with the broken wing tagged along behind, hoping for food. So did Beth. Barney seemed to have intrigued her enough to abandon Mogsy for the time being.

'These are wild birds,' Emmet explained, 'so we try to move about quietly. D'you understand?'

'Sure, I get it. You'll let them go when you've fixed them up. Right?'

'If they recover sufficiently, yes.'

A few apple trees still occasionally bore small hard apples but their chief function now was to provide perches for the birds, since the aviaries had been built round them. There was a constant noise of cheeping, cawing and quacking. One of the blackbirds was even singing a sweet springtime song, although it was not yet quite spring – and in any case his chances of mating this year were still in the balance.

Barney wandered round the cages stopping occasionally to inspect a dozing owl or a one-legged seagull. Free, but apparently tame starlings, jackdaws and sparrows flew round his head. He came back to Emmet, Beth still following.

'Here, can I ask you something?' he said.

'If you like.'

'Why d'you do this?' He waved an arm at the aviaries.

'Someone has to.'

'Must cost a fair bit. Does someone pay you?'

Emmet laughed. 'I wish they did.'

'So you do it for love, right?'

Emmet bent to refill a pan of water for the ducks. They gathered round, quacking. 'I suppose you could say that, yes.' Her voice was muffled and embarrassed-sounding.

'You're a very kind lady.' Barney took the bucket from her hand. 'Here, let me fill this for you. Where's the tap?'

Beth took his hand. 'I'll show you.' She led him to the tap. Emmet watched them go. She thought, I think he'll do.

Returning with the filled bucket, he said, 'I've heard of you, you know.'

'I don't suppose much goes unnoticed in the village.'

'And there was that bit in the paper about you as well.'

'Yes, of course.'

'So what d'you feed this lot on, then?'

'I'd show you all that if you agreed to come. Mostly stuff like flaked maize, mixed corn, Vitalin, and dog and cat food, of course. I get stale bread from the bakers sometimes . . .'

'I reckon it's a full-time job you've got here, what with this lot and the kids and all.'

'I help,' Beth said stoutly.

'Of course you do,' Emmet agreed. 'And Tom.'

They reached the end of the orchard where a stream gurgled over its stony bed and where ducks slapped about on triangular feet and dabbled their beaks in the water. A pair of swans watched the humans approach. The cob fluffed up his wings at them.

'Some of these ducks are old customers of ours,' Emmet said with a grin. 'They live in the stream but they never stray far.'

'Now they bring their babies,' Beth chipped in. 'Last year there were eight!'

'I don't blame them,' Barney said. 'They know when they're on to a good thing. What about the swans? They don't look too pleased to see us.'

'His name's Sydney,' Beth informed him. 'Tom hates him.' All the same she was careful to put Emmet between herself and Sydney's businesslike beak.

'Don't take any notice,' Emmet said. 'He likes to show off. He's very protective. His mate had problems with a length of fishing line and is just getting over it, fortunately. They don't always.' She turned. 'Well, that's about the extent of the property. The stream marks the boundary,' she added as they made their way back through the orchard.

They came upon Tom and Lee struggling to hang Tom's duvet on the clothesline, not too seriously since they were both snorting with mirth. When the others approached they stuffed handfuls of duvet into their mouths and went red in the face.

'You're not making much of a fist of that,' Barney commented, grabbing the duvet and straightening it out with a few deft movements. Tom's mirth turned to outrage that a stranger should dare to comment on his competence. The two boys sloped off in surly silence. Emmet felt very slightly put out by Barney's unconscious incursion, unreasonably since he was only trying to help.

'All my brothers and sisters were younger than me,' he said with a grin, 'so I know all the dodges.'

They stood at the door in the wire fence that separated the orchard from the yard.

'So you see what sort of thing I should be asking you to do,' Emmet said. 'Mostly helping with the feeding morning or evening and chopping logs for the Rayburn. And then there are the chickens; in the field beyond the garden. Are you interested?'

'It looks like it's just up my street,' he said. 'It's obviously too much work for one.' Emmet could see an enquiry about Mr Darby's role in all this in Barney's eyes. She knew very well that all kinds of tales about the Darbys circulated round the village. *He'd* moved himself to the bungalow so that he could entertain a fancy woman. *She'd* kicked him out of his own home and what a scandal it was that he put up with it, he ought to let her know who was boss, et cetera, et cetera.

'It's a good job I came along, isn't it?' Barney added matter-of-factly.

'Hmm,' Emmet agreed faintly. 'Then you think you could spare a few hours morning or evening?'

'Either, or both if you like.'

'Splendid. But I suppose you'd better tell me what your rates are now.'

'Four pounds an hour all right?'

'Yes, I think I can manage that.'

He rubbed his hands briskly together. 'Right. Let's drink to that,' he said. 'I could do with some more of that coffee if you're making some.'

'Whose idea was it?' Emmet asked Tom. Tom was sitting on top of his still slightly damp duvet with *The Hitchhiker's Guide to the Galaxy* propped on his knees. Lee had gone home.

'It was Lee's,' he said defensively.

'Lee's?' Emmet repeated. 'I see. So Lee's the ideas man.' She gave Tom a long appraising look.

'No, it was mine,' Tom confessed. 'I wanted to see how far the water would go.'

'A perfectly legitimate experiment, Tom darling, but badly thought out. I wish you'd take time to consider before you embark on these things.'

'Sorry,' Tom mumbled.

'Let's call the matter closed then, shall we?' She kissed him.

Tom turned his head away. 'Anyway, what did that man want?'

'He's coming to help around the place for a few hours a week.'

'You don't need him. You've got Beth and me. We help, don't we?'

'Of course you do. You're very helpful, darling. But you see you're at school most of the time, don't forget.'

'Do I have to go to school?' Tom fiddled with the corner of a page.

'Yes, you do. It's the law. Besides you want to learn things, don't you? You like learning things. Mrs Webb said you had an enquiring mind.'

'I could learn things at home.'

'You know that's not possible. I don't know as much as the teachers.' Emmet stood up. 'You can read for a quarter of an hour, then lights out, OK?'

Tom grunted. 'Lee's mother has to stay in hospital for ages. Can he come again?'

'Of course, if you want him to,' Emmet said with forced enthusiasm. 'Who's looking after Lee and his brothers and sisters?'

'Some woman,' Tom said dismissively. He stood up on the bed and kicked the duvet back so that he could put his feet underneath it, then he slumped down on the pillow. 'What would happen if *you* got ill?' he asked without looking at her.

Emmet straightened the duvet. 'You know me. I never get ill.'

'But if you did?'

'I'm sure we'd manage. After all, there's Desna and Mo and Nell. And now we'll have Barney.' Naturally she didn't mention Maurice, and Tom wouldn't have expected her to. Nobody expected Maurice to do anything.

She hoped she'd done the right thing, employing Barney. Money was tight but what could she do? The animals just kept coming.

58

CHAPTER SIX

Harriet bumped her bicycle down the last few steps to Papermill Quay. Behind her came the sound of the leat gurgling its way into the river. The utter darkness was alleviated by the glimmer of one small bulb high up on a pole and from the faint light filtering through the curtains of the two cottages that were the only human habitation.

She chained her bicycle to the railings that marked out the minuscule garden in front of one of the cottages. It was beginning to rain; a fine, infiltrating drizzle, and the oil-black water made secret viscous noises as it crept ever higher up the quay wall. Next to the quay she could just make out the rotting hull of the ketch *Prudence*, which had been there ever since she could remember. Once, many years before, it had displayed on its wheelhouse a For Sale notice but that had long since vanished together with most of her planking. The smell of mud, seaweed and decaying timber filled Harriet's nostrils; it was a smell she rather liked; she associated it with her grandmother.

Papermill Quay was on the east side of the river, at the entrance of a small creek which dried out almost completely at low water; the creek and the quay were named after a mill that had operated there until the 1950s but which had since become derelict. The buildings, which she had passed on her way down, were now without roofs and been almost entirely recolonized by elder, sycamore and oak.

Next to her grandmother's front door a rope dangled from a bell which was blue-green with verdigris. Harriet rang it and pushed open the door.

'Anyone home?' she called.

Mo emerged from the kitchen into the sitting room, which, together with a tacked-on scullery, were the only downstairs rooms. 'Oh, it's you, poppet. Are you quite soaked?'

'No, it's only just started.' Harriet stood blinking in the light, clutching her bicycle lamps to her chest.

'Coffee, tea or something stronger?' Mo asked.

'Tea, please.' Harriet took off her navy donkey jacket, plumped down on Mo's sofa and at once, as always, felt at home.

Mo's cottage was tiny. It had originally been built for a fisherman's family but now two people at once seemed to constitute a crowd. There was the usual smell that always reminded Harriet faintly of potato peelings but it was quite overpowered by that of turpentine, linseed oil, new canvas and paint.

The ridged and scooped-out stone slabs on the floor were evidence of generations of feet and the thick stone walls, which had withstood occasional inundations over the years, had settled down to a comfortable old age; they had once been plastered and painted cream but that had been a long time ago. Now they flaked and blistered in peace, practically obliterated by a vast collection of objects, since Mo never threw anything away. Mo claimed to know where everything was but Harriet doubted it. Emmet's place by comparison was a model of tidiness, and as for Desna . . . Harriet's mother could hardly bear to spend more than a few minutes at a time here. The chairs and sofa were festooned with old shawls, paisley tablecloths, a carelessly discarded orange cardigan, an ancient blue coat. In the corner a pair of muddy wellies had subsided in a heap and the dresser, which took up most of one wall, was crammed with a heterogeneous collection of objects. Its shelves held china, some of which matched, but also jagged fragments of mottled mirror, ancient postcards and photographs, bottles of turpentine, curling brown envelopes clamped together by bulldog clips, unravelling balls of string, and here and there a jug of interesting twigs, pieces of driftwood and a lump of chain welded together by rust. In the middle of it all a black cat called Rose Madder slept peacefully. Shelves bursting with books competed for space against the walls with a miscellany of hats on a row of wooden pegs from which depended a landslide of well-worn garments. By the window an easel was set up on which a half-finished painting glowed wetly. Beside it a small table overflowed with rags, smeared with the colours of the rainbow, brushes and tubes of oil paint. A finished canvas stood next to it on the floor. Opposite the dresser, built into the wall, was a black, wood-burning stove which gave out waves of welcoming heat. Mo stood beside it and poured boiling water into a mug containing a teabag. She added milk from a cardboard carton and handed it to Harriet.

'Here we are, Harry. Drink up.' She poured tea for herself, black and strong, then sat down in the only armchair. 'So young Lochinvar hasn't ridden out of the West tonight, then?'

'Who?'

'Never mind. I don't suppose they do Scott in schools these days.'

'We did the First World War poets.' Harriet slumped down into the heaped sofa and sipped her tea. 'This is heaven. Philip and Daddy have got held up at the yard. Daddy's making a great fuss over this Italian, Botticelli or something. They've just done up his yacht. It cost a bomb.'

'Don't tell me, it's called *The Birth of Venus*!'

Harriet giggled. It was a sound Mo only ever heard here or at the gallery. 'I said I would be here if Philip manages to get away.'

'Let's hope he does. Meanwhile, what would you say to cheese on toast or has your mother filled you to the brim with game pie and St Emilion *au chocolat*?'

Harriet giggled. 'We had grilled fish of some sort.'

'Of some sort! Good heavens, girl. Don't you know?'

'I forget.'

'It beats me,' Mo said with a grin, 'how you came to be your mother's daughter.'

'Or how she came to be *yours*!' countered Harriet. 'Anyway, Rupert makes up for me. In greed anyway. All the same, I'd adore cheese on toast. I'm ravenous again after the bike ride.'

61

It was no surprise to Mo that her granddaughter was still hungry; she herself had enjoyed – it seemed insulting to Desna's cooking to say *endured* – enough meals at Mount Huish to observe the effect her son-in-law had on Harriet. She got up from her chair and went out into the kitchen where there was an venerable electric cooker, a pine table and an old Belfast sink with one tap, cold.

'One slice or two?' she called.

'Two, if you can spare the bread.' Harriet stood up. 'Shall I help?'

'There isn't room for both of us out here. You can tell me what you think of my painting instead, the finished one on the floor. But be careful, it's still wet.'

Harriet picked up the canvas that was leaning against the wall. It measured about one foot by two and was executed in Mo's usual highly impressionistic style with big juicy sweeps of the brush; hot gentian blue and a cool turquoise fading to a fine glaucous veil, some dark olive green, a suggestion of ochrous yellow and a hint of apricot made up the watery image of a swimmer together with the suggestion of a large fish.

'What are you calling it?'

'*The Girl with Fish*, of course,' Mo shouted from the kitchen whence also came a delicious smell of grilling cheese.

'You ought to do one called *Girl Eating Cheese on Toast*.'

Mo's head appeared round the door. 'That's a wonderful idea. You can pose for me.'

'I love *The Girl with Fish*. Has Gordon seen it?'

'Not yet. Not till I've finished the set. They're all for my exhibish later on.'

'Why d'you always stick to the Yardarm when you could try London?'

'Lay the table, will you?' Mo called. 'It's nearly ready. I'm too lazy to bother with trying London, showing locally suits me fine. I never was as ambitious as Persis. Anyway, I know my limitations.'

Harriet pushed aside a heap of objects that littered the table, including a basket that contained oranges, a second cat, this one a tortoiseshell called Polly Chrome, and Mo's bicycle clips. 'Are you eating?' she called, tickling the cat's ears.

'No, I had something earlier. If I ate this late I'd be awake all night. I'll be happy with a glass of wine to keep you company. How about you?'

'No thanks. But in that case do you mind if I have it on my lap?'

Mo came in bearing a large, steaming plate. 'Whatever you like,' she said. 'There you are, wrap yourself round that.' Sitting in her chair with her glass of supermarket red, she watched Harriet digging in with a sense of satisfaction. Casually she reached for a sketchbook and, taking Harriet up on her suggestion, began to draw.

'This is absolutely scrumptious,' Harriet said with her mouth full. 'Speaking of inherited traits and so on,' she continued, munching, 'what about your sister? How is it that Persis is so ambitious and you aren't?'

Mo briefly interrupted her drawing to reach for her glass. 'That's easy. Persis had, has, as you must know, a perfectly colossal talent and an even bigger ego. I was more modestly endowed. To be absolutely truthful I don't think I could have coped with the responsibility and sheer hard work that comes with that level of ability, never mind the emotional instability and the demands of fame itself. Besides, it surely hasn't escaped your notice that I had husbands and three kids to look after.'

'Some women artists manage.' Harriet cut into her cheese on toast and ferried a slice to her mouth.

'Most don't. At least in my day they didn't.'

'When you said emotional instability, did you mean that Persis is a bit of a fruit loop?'

'Depends on who you are comparing her to. For instance, your father thinks *I'm* peculiar, would you believe?'

Harriet grinned. 'Oh, Daddy. He thinks anyone who doesn't belong to the Royal Dart Yacht Club is a bit freaky.'

Mo put down her glass and went on with her drawing. 'Funny we should be speaking of Persis. I had a letter from her this morning.'

'You said she never kept in touch.'

'Neither she does. I haven't heard from her for years. Years!'

Harriet glanced at Mo. 'You look worried. What did she want?'

'She's talking of coming to stay, of all things.' Mo worked away with her soft, dark pencil with hands that were rough, stained and knobbly at the joints from a long and rugged existence. 'The trouble is that we were never very close, there's twelve years between us.'

'So why does she want to come here all of a sudden?'

Mo, intent on her work, frowned. 'I wish I knew.' The pocket of her baggy trousers still contained the letter, a single page that looked as if it had been torn from a sketchbook, covered in huge black writing. There wasn't much in the way of greeting or enquiries after Mo's wellbeing, just the bald announcement that for some weeks the Yorkshire studio would be undergoing some extremely inconvenient and boring repairs and could she, therefore, pay Mo a visit? There was no attempt to disguise the impression that Persis intended to make use of her. All the same, someone with her sister's money and connections did not actually need to stay with a poor relation just because of a little disruption at home, especially when to Mo's certain knowledge she had a house in Italy and a villa in Greece; unless Persis had changed out of all recognition, there had to be an ulterior motive and Mo had a shrewd idea she knew what it might be. For so many years she had counted on her sister's ruthless ability to expunge anything inconvenient from her memory. She hoped, she hoped passionately, that Persis wasn't going to rake up past history at this late stage.

Her first reaction was to tear up the abrupt and worrying message and consign it to the stove. How dare Persis scribble such an outrageously arrogant note after years of silence? For all her sister knew she and all their close relations could have moved away, emigrated or even died. And now she demanded a reply by return of post.

'But you will say yes, won't you?' Harriet pleaded. 'She sounds scary but I'd like to meet her, you know. D'you remember that exhibition of hers you took me to see at the Hayward when I was doing GCSE? I don't suppose I took in very much at the time but I do remember being frightfully impressed by those huge bronzes. They were like sort of desiccated figures, sort of menacing looking.' Harriet finished the last of her cheese on toast and laid her knife and fork together neatly. She picked up the bottle of wine that sat between them on a low stool and offered it to Mo.

'Yes, please.' Mo held out her glass.

'I think Persis is still making those figures,' said Harriet. 'I saw them in a magazine at the gallery.'

'Monsters I call them. You'd think to look at them that Persis was a tortured soul, wouldn't you? But to the best of my knowledge she's lived a life that has been entirely cushioned from any discomfort whatsoever. She's always done exactly as she pleased,' Mo said sourly.

'I rather like them all the same. I believe they're quite an accurate reflection of human beings, don't you?'

Mo gave Harriet a shrewd look over the rim of her glass. 'Do you *really* think we're as bad as that! God, how perfectly frightful! Harry, how can you face the future if you really believe that?'

'There doesn't seem to be much hope, though, does there?'

'Then you must surely be of the opinion that all this wedding business is nothing but a cynical charade?'

'If you must know, I do,' she said quietly. 'I'm going through with it for Mummy's sake.'

Mo gawped at her granddaughter. 'You don't mean to say that you're marrying Philip for Desna's sake! Goodness, I sincerely hope not!'

'Of course I'm not,' Harriet went on composedly. 'I love Philip and if I have to go through all this crap to get him . . .' she shrugged. 'But then they say that nothing worth having comes easily, don't they?' She gazed at Mo with her extraordinary, candid eyes and Mo saw that these words did not originate from a youthful desire to shock, she really believed what she was saying. 'I love Mummy and I don't want to upset her,' Harriet went on in that quiet, even voice that somehow sent a chill through Mo's veins.

'But you still believe that there's no hope for mankind in general?' she said.

'No, I'm afraid I don't. Does that shock you?'

'It certainly saddens me that someone as young as you are should think that way. Now, I could understand it if you were my age. Most old fogeys like me believe that the world has gone to the dogs.'

'*You* don't though?'

Mo bent down to take another piece of sawn driftwood from a pile and stuff it into the stove. It caught and flared with a greenish flame. 'No,' she said, leaning back and reclaiming her glass. 'I think there's always hope.' She glanced at Harriet who was putting her empty plate on the floor at her feet. 'Now, listen, I'm interested. Will you and that handsome young man of yours be bringing children into this big, bad world in view of what you've just told me.'

'I don't think it would be fair, do you?'

'You'll change your mind once the knot's tied.'

Harriet shook her head. 'I don't think so.'

'I take it that Philip agrees?'

Harriet looked away. 'We haven't actually discussed it, but he seems not to care if we have children or not.'

Mo leaned forward and grasped Harriet's wrist in a grip that was almost painful. 'Now listen, Harry. All young men and some young women talk like that before they get married, but you can bet your life it will be a different story if you suddenly spring your views on him when the honeymoon period's over. *If* you're really serious about this you will have to get it sorted before the wedding, d'you hear? Not afterwards.'

'I'm quite sure Philip doesn't care one way or another,' Harriet protested.

'And I'm quite sure you should thrash it out with him, pronto.' Reluctantly she released Harriet's arm.

Harriet squirmed inwardly. She felt uncomfortable with the subject. It presupposed sex, which she didn't mind talking

66

about in general terms like any grown-up person, but when applied to herself and Philip it became a source of anxiety and embarrassment. It wasn't that she didn't desire him – he had the power to turn her insides to jelly – it was just that she encountered a wall of resistance every time she attempted to visualize Philip and herself in bed together, intimately entwined. For some reason it was easier to imagine him in bed with one of his past girlfriends. All the same, Philip was becoming insistent and she knew she wouldn't be able to put him off much longer.

'Everybody fucks before marriage these days,' he'd told her. 'What's the point in waiting? Besides, they want to know if they're sexually compatible.'

She had no idea what he meant by 'sexually compatible' but she feared the worst. She would not be sexually compatible with Philip, she would be hopeless and he would call everything off. Besides, for many other reasons which she could hardly comprehend herself, she had the deepest suspicion that sex between people ruined things. And here was her grandmother asking her intimate questions and making assumptions about her that were stirring up all these troublesome questions.

'Yes, I expect you're right. I'll talk to Philip.' Then, dismissing the topic, said, 'Have you finished your drawing?'

Mo nodded. She had been too troubled by their conversation to do it much justice.

Harriet jumped up to look. 'You draw so well. Will you turn it into a painting?'

Mo put the sketchbook on the floor. 'Perhaps. Sometime.'

'Do you mind if we watch telly?' Harriet asked.

'Go ahead,' Mo said. 'If you can put up with the poor reception. I'll just clear these dishes. Help yourself to a chocolate brazil. I can't eat them, my teeth won't stand up to it.'

Harriet switched on the television, which was jammed on to a shelf between a tottering pile of art magazines and a stone figure of a bacchante which Mo had carved when she was at art school. A detective drama series flickered on to the screen. Harriet took the chocolates back with her to the sofa.

'I'll wash up in a minute,' she called.

There was a brief clattering of crockery and then Mo came to join Harriet. She glanced at her granddaughter unselfconsciously enjoying the twists of plot in a way she never would have done at home. As the gruff hero and his sidekick were within an ace of catching the villain the brass bell rang again, and there was a hammering on the panels of the door.

'Ask who it is before you open the door,' Mo said as Harriet went to answer it. 'Not all the baddies are on the screen.'

Before Harriet could speak a deep male voice came authoritatively from outside. 'Her Majesty's Customs and Excise here. Open up and come quietly. You're rumbled!'

Harriet opened the door. 'Come in, Philip, you berk.'

Philip came in on a draught of cold air and a flurry of rain. 'Just as I thought! Illicit consumption of chocolate brazils.' He helped himself to one from the box and gave each of the women a kiss. 'How goes it, Mrs Joubert?'

'You're too late for cheese on toast,' Mo said.

'Shit! Never mind. Actually I stopped off on the way for some fish and chips.'

'What would your mother have to say about that?' Although Mo was extremely fond of Philip, she had very little time for the senior Emmersons. She could never understand how two people she thought of as pretentious could have spawned a comparatively modest young man like Philip.

'She gave up trying to civilize me years ago,' he said, dumping himself down on the sofa beside Harriet. 'I do believe she's hoping that Harry will reform me.'

Mo grunted. 'Fat chance of that. She's worse than you are. Coffee anybody?'

'I'll do it,' Harriet insisted, making for the kitchen. It delighted her to be with her two favourite people – besides Mummy, that was. It meant she could relax, be herself without having to filter all her words and actions through the watcher who stood at the door of her brain.

They stayed until nearly eleven. Then Philip helped Harriet to hump her bicycle to the top of the steps to where he had parked his beaten up old Land Rover. Next to it the multicoloured van belonging to Mo's neighbours lurked in the shadows. Philip pushed the bicycle into the back as Harriet climbed into the passenger seat.

Before they drove off he took her face in his hands and drew her to him, placing a firm and exploratory kiss on her mouth, which tasted faintly of chocolate. After an evening when it had been possible to drop her usual defences, Harriet came to the conclusion that she might eventually get to like Philip doing this but when his hands crept under her baggy jersey to reconnoitre her breasts, she pulled away. Companionable kisses were one thing but he always expected more. It would only lead to a situation that she would no longer be able to handle.

'Aren't you ever going to let me touch you?' Philip said in her ear. 'We're engaged now, for God's sake.'

'Of course,' she parried. 'But not now. Not here.'

'I could ravish you right here . . . and now,' he said. Neither of them knew for sure if he was joking. 'There's no one around for miles.'

'You wouldn't do that. You're not like that,' Harriet said simply.

Philip sighed, disentangled himself and started the engine. 'No,' he said, 'you're quite safe.'

He did not despair. There was a girl he'd known when he was flotilla sailing off Bodrum who started out even cooler than Harry but once he'd broken the ice, as it were, she had turned out to be a tremendous goer. Too much so, because in the end it had turned him off completely. In any case he had never been in love with her, and he was in love with Harriet. As he pulled the Land Rover on to the road he glanced at Harriet's profile; the light reflecting back on to her face gave her that ethereal, almost insubstantial look that made his guts ache with the need to be near her, to touch her. And, he had to admit it, to protect her; although he would never have risked her scorn by suggesting such a notion. Of course she had always been there, ever since they'd been kids together. It made the whole outcome almost inevitable.

'D'you remember when I took you out in my Mirror,' he said

grinning in the darkness as he slowed down to negotiate the turn into the back lane that led to Mount Huish, 'and you were seasick?'

'It was rough!' she protested.

'On the river?' he laughed. The image of her stricken face and his own remorse at not having believed that she could be seasick on a river was still quite clear after all this time. He supposed that it must prove that he was crazy about her and probably always had been. It occurred to him, too, that for her to go on such a trip with him when she steadfastly refused to sail with her own father must mean that she had quite liked him as well, even when she was twelve.

If only he could get her to relax all the time as she had tonight, he felt that everything would be all right. But he would have to get her away from Mount Huish. He wasn't much of an amateur psychologist but he could see that her mother's accomplishments and Roy's powerful personality were sometimes hard for Harriet to handle.

CHAPTER SEVEN

The auction rooms dealt with the lower end of the market, a contrast to the elegant Regency salerooms Nell had more often frequented when she had worked for Prettyjohn. The chill from the concrete floor was seeping through the soles of her suede boots and the familiar compound of decay, mildew and damp raincoats filled the air. However, this was exactly the kind of place where her sort of bargains were occasionally to be had. Today she had struck lucky, at least she hoped so, for out in the covered yard at the back, marked as lot number 457, was a collection of garden urns. They were well down the list; even going at his usual brisk trot it would be an hour before the auctioneer got to them. Worth the wait, with any luck. Anna, who helped her out from time to time, was looking after the shop so there was no rush.

Meanwhile Nell made herself as comfortable as possible on one of a horrible set of plastic chairs (lot 93) while the auctioneer and his attentive following shifted about the echoing shed – rooms was a misnomer – from one lot to another. She only half heard the all-too-familiar stream of patter.

'. . . On we go, then. Lot twenty-five . . . metal filing cabinets . . . fifteen quid I'm bid . . . twenty from this gentleman here . . . twenty-five I'm bid . . . thirty if you like . . . there we are, thirty . . . name, sir? Now then, on we go . . . back to reality . . .' There was a shuffling of feet. 'Six boxes of welding wire . . . come along now, we've five hundred lots to shift today . . .'

Nell fished into her capacious bag and brought out a very superior stainless-steel Thermos, a find at a car boot sale, and poured herself a cup of coffee. The monotonous spiel of the auctioneer was reduced to a background mutter as she thought about Daniel. She was convinced that she wasn't being over-credulous – experience had taught her to be a realist, hadn't it? – but there was no doubt in her mind that Daniel had improved. His manner was less bumptious and arrogant. After all, he hadn't taken her apparent compliance for granted as he once would. And he had been honest about his failure to see through Flick right from the start and the immaturity that had left him open to her easy charm. Flick was not the kind of woman to grow middle-aged with, let alone old. Nell could well imagine her thirty years hence, seeking out toy boys half her age.

Daniel had rung while she was eating her breakfast accompanied by Morgan, who was eating his.

'Just wondering how you are this morning?' Daniel said. 'I lay awake thinking about you most of last night.'

'Liar!' she said, half amused. At the back of her mind a memory lingered of that exact word that had once burst from her in anger.

'Don't say that!' Daniel sounded hurt, as if he too remembered. 'I was going to suggest that I come round tonight. I could bring a takeaway to save cooking.'

'I'm not sure about that.' His telephone call had surprised her after all. She had not expected to hear from him so soon. 'Why so soon?' she said.

'I thought we'd wasted enough of our lives as it is. How often does one get a second chance?

'It wasn't I who threw away the first one, Daniel.'

'Don't rub it in, Nellie, for God's sake. I'm only too aware that it was all my bloody fault. Please say I can come.'

'I don't know . . .'

'What about sevenish? I'll bring something. Are you still partial to barbecued spare ribs?'

She relented. 'Okay,' she said, 'and yes I am. I haven't turned vegetarian like Emmet.'

'Darling Nell. I'll look forward to it.'

So she'd burned her boats. There was no turning back, and there could be little doubt as to what the outcome of the evening would be. She wondered how she was going to be able to concentrate on garden urns for the next hour.

'In sombre or in pensive mood . . .' A voice in her ear startled her out of her reverie. It was Hugh Daish; his spare, lanky form stooped towards her, his nondescript fairish hair falling forward to skim his eyebrows.

'Hallo, Hugh,' she greeted him. 'Where have you been hiding? I haven't seen you for ages.'

His lugubrious face cracked into a grin. 'Nor I you, unfortunately.'

'So what are you doing here? Slumming?'

'Just keeping my ear to the ground.' He slid into one of the execrable plastic chairs beside her. 'Anything interesting?'

'I'm not telling you. You'd send the bidding sky-high just for the hell of it . . .'

She regarded Hugh not as an amateur exactly, but as a dilettante with an shrewd eye for a good antique.

'You're a tough cookie,' he said. The would-be-Hollywood-cop twang superimposed on his particularly well-bred accent made her smile. 'As a matter of fact I'm just—'

'Seeing how the other half live?' she teased.

'I was about to say that I've found a fascinating item buried deep in the trash.'

Nell glanced down the list of lot numbers. She hadn't noticed anything that could conceivably interest Hugh but then she hadn't really been looking.

'You'll have to tell me. I can't guess. Then I'll tell you what I had my eye on, if you promise faithfully not to bid. Anyway, I don't think they're your sort of thing.'

'I already know what you're after. It's got to be the stone urns out in the yard. Reconstituted stone urns actually, so mind you don't pay too much for them.'

'Don't try to tell me my job,' she said with momentary irritation. She offered him coffee from the Thermos. 'Here, have some coffee and tell all.'

It had always been easy to fall into good-natured camaraderie with Hugh. She'd known him ever since the days with Prettyjohn when she'd encountered him occasionally in auction rooms, but she'd lost touch when she had shared the running of Cornucopia with Daniel. Then it had been Daniel who had scoured the salerooms, while she was mostly in the office. She realized that since she had been running Alfresco, she'd seen Hugh only at first. Lately he seemed to have entirely vanished from the scene. In the early days she'd had an idea that he fancied her more than a little but by then she had met Daniel and as far as she was concerned, no other man existed. She had heard that Hugh had inherited his parents' house somewhere in the Teign valley and she knew that he collected furniture, but what else he did, or even if he was married, she had never been sufficiently intrigued to find out.

She glanced at him now as he drank the coffee, cradling the mug in his large, rather bony hands. He was wearing a long leather coat battered and scored as if by immense age, over a greenish guernsey and a check Viyella shirt – the latter two items the traditional wear of the country gent, the former rather less so.

'So you're not letting on?' she said. 'That's not fair.'

He stood up and beckoned mysteriously. 'Come with me. My lot's just about to come up.' She stood beside him as he bid for a heterogeneous collection of worn-out cutlery in a pine box and a collection of old postcards. He got them for two pounds.

'Hugh, what are you up to?'

'All will be revealed. Now let's go and bid for those urns, shall we? What's your top price?'

They went and stood under the corrugated iron roof of a lean-to while various rusty lawnmowers and an ancient oil tank were knocked down to an inexplicably eager bidder.

Nell got her garden urns for near her top price. Unfortunately they were just the kind of thing that was attracting high bids. All the same she was pleased; selling them either separately or as a set she could probably get twice what she had paid for them.

'How do you intend to move them?' Hugh asked as the crowd thinned out and drifted away.

'I have a little man who'll shift them if I give him a ring.'

Hugh hesitated, wanting to ask if the man in question was Daniel Thorne. But then she would hardly have called Daniel 'little'. Since he'd been back in the country he'd realized that he'd lost touch, though a whisper had reached him that Nell was on her own again. In fact he'd rung Alfresco that morning and been answered by an unknown woman; it was she who had innocently told him where Nell would be that morning. He had managed to avoid giving his name.

'How about lunch?' he suggested.

'I'm sorry, Hugh. Some of us have to work for a living you know!' She smiled. 'Another time perhaps.'

His look of friendly nonchalance quickly replaced one of disappointment and she wondered for a fraction of a second if he still fancied her.

'I'll hold you to that' he said good-humouredly.

'Now, show me why you bought that awful load of crap,' she demanded.

They went to pick up his purchase. Outside again, he pocketed the postcards and abstracted one item from the old box before he tipped the rest into a litter bin with a tinny clatter. He held up a small blackish object.

'A basting spoon,' he said. 'Scottish silver, circa 1715. Not mint condition, unfortunately, but what can you expect?'

'You crafty old bugger. But not your line of country surely?'

'Not really, but it was the only item of any value here . . . apart from the postcards, which are always useful in my line of country. And the garden urns,' he added gallantly. He wrapped the spoon in his handkerchief and slipped it into his pocket. 'Now, let's shift those urns. I don't think we shall have a problem fitting them into the back of the Discovery.'

In spite of her protestations Hugh insisted on acting as delivery man and her purchases were duly transported and arranged in the walled and paved yard at the back of the shop. They enhanced the area that in the summer was bedecked with flowering plants, taking on the look of the terrace of a small country house.

After this Nell absolutely had to offer him a snack lunch, as he had hoped.

'So you're not running Cornucopia now?' Hugh said, leaning against the jamb of the kitchen door while Nell sliced bread and laid out cheese.

'No. Didn't you know? I haven't had anything to do with Cornucopia for four years.'

'That long! What happened?'

'Daniel and I split up. I thought everyone knew that. It was a pretty conspicuous event; but obviously the grapevine doesn't stretch to your part of the world.' She reached on to a shelf and took down some jars of pickles, managing a rueful smile.

Hugh looked away to disguise the surge of restored hope that he felt must be overwhelmingly obvious in his expression. He took in the attractiveness of his surroundings. The dresser that took up almost all one side of the room had been painted thinly with kingfisher turquoise, which had then been rubbed down and its shelves filled with white and terracotta pottery. The walls were a muted apricot and had been stencilled with an attractive leaf design in white.

'I've been rather busy. And I was in America for a time,' he said. 'I haven't been back long.' He scanned the kitchen for signs of a male cohabitee and was encouraged to find none. He wished he had the guts, or the cheek, to ask outright.

'Do you mind eating here?' Nell asked, reaching in a drawer for cutlery.

'Not at all. It's a knockout of a kitchen.' He stood by the window looking out. Below was the paved yard, now decorated with the most recent additions. He turned back to the room. 'You did all this yourself?'

'Looking back I don't know how I had the energy.' But she did know. It had been a way of expressing the anger and desolation she'd harboured for too long. 'I've lived here nearly three years.' For one whole year after she and Daniel split up Nell had drifted from bedsit to bedsit and from job to job without purpose or hope. After she had successfully helped Desna to redecorate Mount Huish, Desna and Mo between them had eventually nagged her into starting the business and putting her talents to use.

'I'm sorry about you and Daniel,' Hugh said, feeling a hypocrite. For he wasn't sorry. He was glad.

She shrugged. 'History, now,' she said, not believing it. She indicated that he should sit at the table. She wanted to eat and then hurry him away so that she would have time to clear up the flat, tidy the newspapers, vacuum the floor and plump the cushions. This afternoon she would be too busy in the shop and after that she wanted time to herself, to bathe and change.

'I'm so glad we ran into each other again,' Hugh was saying. 'Perhaps we could have an evening out sometime? A meal perhaps. What d'you think?'

Nell rummaged through her rag-bag of excuses and, feeling like a rat, said, 'That would be nice, Hugh. But I'm afraid I can't give you a very satisfactory answer. I'm booked up with one thing and another in the immediate future.'

He appeared unperturbed by this obvious fabrication. 'That's all right, Nell, I'll ring you in a week or two if I may?' He recognized her reply for what it was but something stubborn inside him refused to be fobbed off. Now that a second chance – first chance now he came to think of it – had unexpectedly presented itself he felt impelled to pursue it even beyond the point that seemed reasonable. All the same, he was not prepared to outstay his welcome on this occasion. Towards the end of the meal she was already showing signs of restlessness; sadly he didn't miss her well-disguised relief when he refused coffee, saying that he had to keep an appointment; a fictitious one as it happened.

He pushed back his chair and unfolded his long body from it with a sigh. 'That was a very fine meal, Nell. Just the type of thing I like.' He looked down his slightly beaked nose at her; she was of medium height but he seemed to loom. Six foot one in his socks.

'I'll be going then, Nell.' They shook hands solemnly, like casual acquaintances, which he supposed in fact they were. 'We must keep in touch.'

'Thank you for lugging those things back for me,' she said politely. 'Hernia material, I'm afraid. No ill effects, I hope?'

'None whatsoever. It was a pleasure after all these years.' He wanted to say that she had become more beautiful in his eyes; that the years had, if anything, refined her features. Creamy skin with a high rounded forehead, framed by dark hair, cut urchin fashion and bound with a twist of grey and white scarf, straight nose and a mouth that betrayed her sensitivity. He speculated on how her relationship with Daniel had ended. Had she seen through the man at last, or had he left her or had it been a mixture of the two? He would have to find out.

Of course he said none of these things. Instead he repeated his intention of ringing her soon and left. The door closed behind him a fraction too promptly to allow for optimism.

Inside the flat, Nell flew round tidying and vacuuming and then hurried downstairs in time to open the shop at two o'clock.

Daniel leaned back in Nell's Victorian sofa and stretched out his legs. His red braces tightened over a trendy black shirt. He put his hands behind his head, still an habitual pose of his, she was quick to notice. There was something proprietorial about the attitude. Whereas Hugh had sat on one of her kitchen chairs looking awkward and slightly ungainly, Daniel occupied space with absolute nonchalance. Morgan sat on one of the armchairs regarding the visitor through half-closed barley-sugar eyes; he had resisted altogether Daniel's perfunctory attempts to win him over. On a low table two plates contained the remains of the barbecued spare ribs.

'You'll never know how much courage it took to ring you the other day,' Daniel said. He reached lazily for his can of Fosters, wrapping it round with his long fingers. His hands were supple and dextrous. When he and Nell had first started Cornucopia the furniture they sold owed as much to his ability to piece together disparate chunks of old pine as it did to a genuine antique pedigree; later, with success, he had hired someone else to do it.

Nell said. 'I don't believe you. You haven't a timid bone in your body.' She was sitting at a safe distance on the other side of the fireplace. She was drinking tonic because she wanted to keep a clear head. Daniel, being Daniel, would want to rush things and now it came to it, a remnant of caution was making her critical and watchful.

'Perhaps I didn't three years ago,' he said. He seemed bent on pruning a year off the time since their separation. 'But getting one's fingers burned is a painful business, nothing like it for knocking the shit out of one.'

'I thought you said that you and Flick parted amicably, or at least that it was your fault?' she observed casually. Reports of Daniel and other women had come to her ears during the Flick era. She had not disbelieved them.

'Oh, right. Yes, undoubtedly it was my fault. My fault for being so lousy at reading character in the first place. You were always much better at that than I was. Obviously you had Flick sussed at once. Poor old Flick. She'll never be anything but a big kid in some ways.' To Daniel this was patently a startling discovery. He drank from his can of lager. 'But there you are. At the time I fell for that kind of flaky charm. I was wrong and I don't mind admitting it.' Abruptly he subjected her to a look of such intensity that she almost flinched. 'I have to say it again, Nell. How I ever came to throw you over in favour of Flick I shall never know. I must have been right off my trolley.'

His sincerity was so transparent that the cautious cynic who lurked at the back of her mind took a bad knock. She was silent, watching the bubbles in her glass fizz against the slice of lemon.

Daniel went on implacably. 'D'you know something? I believe you're better looking now than three years ago. You've actually improved . . .'

'Don't tell me! Like wine you mean?'

He grinned. 'You always did see through my shit, didn't you? Except that this time it's true. It really is.' A pause, while he scrutinized the new Nell. Still slender, a chic oversized shirt of rough silk under a slate-grey waistcoat, carved wood beads, hair bound in a plaited scarf of ochre and slate blue. She always had known what suited her. 'We were quite a team, weren't we . . . running Cornucopia together? Simon's OK but he hasn't your flair and Flick couldn't care less as long as the cash kept rolling in.'

Nell had met Simon once or twice and had quite liked the man. It seemed that the partnership he and Daniel had formed soon after she had left the business had proved successful. Probably Simon prevented Daniel from acting on some of his madder schemes, just as she had.

'But you've done well,' she said. 'You've expanded the business, I hear, in spite of the recession.'

'We've been lucky. We haven't depended on the UK market much. Most of our stuff goes to America or the continent. I know you were never very keen on that but needs must. Simon takes care of the business side and I'm the front man. Well, you know me! I've always liked meeting the punters. It's what I'm good at.'

Yes, he was good at charming the customers. Or bullshitting them. It depended on one's point of view, she thought. Whatever he said about his inability to understand character there was no doubt that he had a shrewd grasp of what a customer wanted or thought they wanted, or didn't even dream they wanted until he suggested it. He knew instinctively how to play on their acquisitiveness and social aspirations; and he seemed to have a sixth sense when it came to knowing the size of a customer's pocket. He had never been any good with money himself but then there had always been someone else to take care of that.

'You had a tremendous talent for figures, didn't you?' he said. 'A bit on the cautious side but it certainly kept me on an even keel.' He grinned and looked round the room. 'And it's obviously standing you in good stead now. I hear you're doing OK yourself.'

'It was a question of having to,' she said succinctly, 'or go under.'

He finished his lager and put the can next to the empty plates. He ran a hand through his black hair – it was as unruly as ever – in a gesture she was familiar with. In the past it had alerted her to the fact that he had done with one piece of business and was ready to move on to the next, or move on altogether. She wondered which it would be this time. Part of her desperately wanted him to stay, an almost greater part was desperately afraid he might not. Unable to remain still, she got up from her chair, offering him more lager, or coffee, perhaps a brandy. Morgan had given up hoping that *he* was going to be offered anything more to eat and had gone out.

Daniel tilted his head back so that he could continue to look at her. 'God, no, woman! I want to remember this evening. It's more than I could ever have hoped for, let alone deserved.' He dropped his voice, holding out a hand to her while remaining unthreateningly on the sofa. 'Come here, Nell.'

She approached him, conscious that her heart was thundering against her rib cage as if it would burst through. How stupid! she thought. How stupid! It's only Daniel, after all. Only Daniel!

He possessed himself of her hand as soon as it was within reach and held it in both his, caressing it. Then he pressed a kiss into the palm and she felt his tongue touch her skin briefly. Goose bumps rose up all over her body. Daniel! Daniel!

'Darling Nell,' he said very softly, and looked up at her. Still sitting he reached out and pulled her closer. Awkwardly, she stood over him holding herself rigidly straight. He kissed her palm again and this time his tongue was gently insistent. She made a sound which she desperately hoped didn't resemble a sob.

'Please, Nell,' he said, 'don't be too hard on me.'

Somehow or other they were both on the sofa, then propped against it, half lying on the Tabriz carpet with the marriage-tree pattern. The cynic in her brain had already lost but continued to nag faintly. If he wanted to touch her, let him. There was precious little good sex to be had these days, dammit, as she knew to her cost. And that was one thing Daniel was good at. In any case it meant nothing. It had no significance for her now. Besides, she wasn't cut out to be alone and celibate.

He kissed her, touching her in a gently exploratory manner, as if getting reacquainted with her body. At first she merely allowed it and then, with a suddenness that was absolutely overwhelming she relinquished all the former caution that would have held her back, and began to kiss him in return, pressing herself to him, feeling the wonderful familiarity of his body: the body that had given her such joy in that past remembered time. It was like coming home. It was human warmth. It was the end of a millennium of unresolved desire. She held his hands tightly against her breasts as they found their way under her shirt.

He stood up to lead her to the bedroom, if he could find it.

'I didn't intend this to happen,' she whispered against his shoulder.

'Neither did I,' he said. 'At least not yet.'

'It's too soon,' she protested weakly.

He half led, half carried her to the bedroom where he began to peel off her clothes and divest himself of his own. He was more patient than she remembered, but patience was not necessary. Her body was responding to his like a runaway fire and the climax was soon and fierce.

Later he supported himself on an elbow and looked at her naked body. Small rounded breasts, curvaceous hips – albeit slightly more so than when he'd last seen them – long thighs the colour of creamy coffee. He caressed her from breast to just above her knee.

'You're stunning still,' he said, allowing his hand to drift to her inner thigh. It was damp, warm and inviting. 'Better.'

'So are you.' She ran her hand over his stomach with its familiar line of dark hair down the middle. He had developed a slight paunch but she couldn't see that as an imperfection. Not now.

'I love you, Nellie, he said. 'Christ, I do love you.'

'I never stopped loving you. I tried, but it didn't work.'

He dropped a kiss on her forehead. 'Thank God for that,' he said.

And so it was that she allowed Daniel Thorne back into her life.

CHAPTER EIGHT

Desna stood next to Nell on the side of the pool, her long toes curled over the edge, the muscles of her thighs, which were ever so slightly puckered, braced before she plunged into the motionless blue water. It enfolded her like liquid glass. A neat dive.

Nell sat on the edge and let her feet dangle in the deep end of the pool, her back to the classical statuary mantled in its leafy bower. Having a rich sister had its advantages and this was one of them. Every Wednesday, as soon as she closed the shop, she drove up to Desna's and swam with her in the Mount Huish private pool.

Nell watched her sister as she struck out for the far end, aware of a feeling of supreme wellbeing that had been with her all day; she had hardly been conscious of the hours passing as she worked. Desna turned to swim back. She was wearing well for her age, Nell thought; but why shouldn't she? She had access to all the good things of life, had never known what it was to have sleepless nights over men, money or the future, had a successful husband, two great kids and a wonderful house in an exceptional setting. Of course she had worn well. She was taller and had larger bones than Nell but her figure was achieved at a price. Nell could eat what she liked without putting on an ounce but Desna allowed herself to indulge in only a fraction of the delicious food she prepared. It really wasn't fair.

Nell glanced down at her own body in its one-piece swimsuit (for serious swimming) and was glad that it had stayed young-looking. Would Daniel have bothered with her if she had let herself go? She didn't like to entertain such a notion.

Desna's head emerged at Nell's feet, sleek and dark. 'Aren't you coming in?' she asked sharply. For a moment she reminded Nell of an autocratic games mistress from whose attentions she had once suffered.

'What's the rush?' she said, slightly puzzled. Irritability was not usually one of Desna's faults. 'I'm acclimatizing.' Nell let herself down into the water, feeling full of pent-up energy. 'OK. Now I'll race you. Three lengths!'

They set off in a hectic swirl of spray. Desna usually beat Nell but she had the advantage of being able to swim every day. There had always been an element of competitiveness between them in which Emmet had no part. When they were children Emmet had seemed very much the baby – the product of a different father, and different in appearance with her mass of blonde curls – which Beth had inherited. She had lived in a world of her own, part fact, part fantasy, in which the animal kingdom from worms to elephants played leading roles.

Neither of Mo's husbands had stuck around for long. The first, Desna and Nell's father, had been an incurable womanizer, according to Mo. They didn't remember him and he had shown very little interest in either of them so it had been a surprise when, after he died four months ago, he had left Desna and Nell twenty thousand pounds each. Before she finally settled in Devon, Mo possessed perennially itchy feet and a preference for painting rather than housekeeping. With two children in tow she had been forever on the move; London, Dumfriesshire, then Norfolk. After that she had been obsessed by the idea that painters were better received in France; there she had met and married Claude Joubert. This had been less of a success than her first marriage and the inhabitants of the remote village where they'd lived a lot less tolerant of a female painter, with children to boot, than she expected. She had returned to England pregnant, without Claude but with Desna and Nell, to explore the possibilities of Cornwall. There Emmet had been born, jokily named after the Cornish word for 'ant' or in other words 'incomer' or 'tourist'. Nobody seemed to know what became of Claude in the end and it was hard to escape the impression that Mo was quite free of any regrets whatever about either of her failed marriages.

In adolescence Desna's older sister bossiness caused Nell to react with terrible passion but as adults they had grown closer, in spite of Desna's tendency to believe that she knew what was best for everybody. One such occasion had been when Nell and Daniel had decided to live together rather than marry, another when they split up. It irritated Nell that Desna appeared to assume that the added authority of having a successful marriage herself lent weight to her words; at those times there had been long periods when Nell had avoided her sister and her unwanted advice.

In a rush of white water Nell touched the edge of the pool a few seconds before Desná. This time she had won.

Showered and wrapped in large fluffy towels they sat in comfortable canvas chairs with drinks beside them. Desna's was mineral water from some exotic spa, Nell's was a gin and tonic.

'You're in good form today,' Desna said, towelling the back of her hair, her previous fretfulness apparently forgotten. 'Do you still go to that acupuncturist?'

'Only occasionally now.'

'She must have done you good. Has it made a difference?'

For some time Nell had suffered debilitating migraines. 'Put it like this. If I get a headache now I know it will be the kind everyone else gets.' Nell sipped her gin and tonic and leaned her damp head luxuriously on the canvas cushion. It was beautifully warm. Heating the place must cost a bomb, she thought inconsequentially. She wondered if having the same income as Desna, she herself would be as wasteful of resources. But then, here she was enjoying them, wasn't she?

'Sounds good.' Desna glanced at Nell's glowing face and filed away the existence of a proficient acupuncturist for future reference. One never knew. 'So life is looking up?'

Nell nodded. She couldn't quite conceal her animation. Happiness is not easy to fake or to conceal. Desna looked at her more attentively.

'Come on, Nell,' she cajoled. 'It's not just a good acupuncturist, is it? Admit it. There's a man in this somewhere. Has to be. I know you too well.'

Nell laughed and buried her nose in her glass. 'Actually there is.'

Desna leaned forward eagerly. She hadn't seen Nell look so... well, radiant for ages. It was what she always hoped for for Nell ever since that rat Daniel had vamoosed for good. 'Tell me. Who is he?'

Nell shook her head. 'No, no, no.' She was immovable. 'It would spoil it to tell anyone at this stage. It's too new.'

Desna's eyes narrowed. To punish Nell for not confiding in her she was snappish. 'I hope you're not getting mixed up with another devious devil. I don't altogether trust you not to fall for the same type all over again. I'm sorry, Nell, but I worry about you.'

Nell kept her temper. She was too happy to fall out with Desna over trifles. Instead she smiled. 'Well, for God's sake don't! I'm a big girl now, remember, so you can cut that out!' She finished her gin and tonic in a quick gulp. 'Anyway, how are the wedding plans going? Has a date been decided yet?'

Desna accepted the change of subject like a lamb. She couldn't resist a topic so close to her heart.

'July the sixteenth. You will keep it free, won't you?'

'Good heavens, I can't think that far ahead! But, yes, it goes without saying. So it's to be a church and all the trimmings?'

'And a marquee on the lawn, we thought.'

'It'll be a gorgeous setting. Harriet's agreed to the big splash, then?'

'She says she doesn't want any fuss but since it will be me doing all the work I'm sure she'll be happy to let me. She's such a dreamer. More like Emmet than anyone.'

'But she's happy?'

'It's never easy to tell with Harriet, though as you know she's always adored Philip.' Desna sipped her mineral water thoughtfully. 'I remember a hilarious occasion when she was twelve. Philip was taking his A levels and we were asked over to the Emmersons' for drinks in the garden. Naturally Philip breezes in, all tanned and gorgeous-looking and gave Harriet a sort of brotherly kiss. She went absolutely crimson, poor kid. Then she disappeared into the loo and I couldn't persuade her to come out for ages.' Desna turned a laughing face to Nell.

Nell's heart went out to her niece. She could imagine only too well the insensitive teasing that Harriet would have had to endure from Roy and the Emmersons. She had witnessed some of Roy's clumsy chaffing. No wonder the poor girl had problems.

Nell finished her drink and put her glass carefully on the slatted table beside her. 'Do you think you're doing the right thing,' she ventured, 'in planning a big wedding like this? I know you'll be in your element but one has to wonder how Harry will cope with it.'

Desna laughed. The sound was very slightly brittle. '*Harriet* won't have to cope with it at all. I told you!'

'But she'll be the focus of a lot of attention and she's terribly shy, isn't she? What if she refused to go through with it at the last moment through sheer nerves?'

'She's too smitten to do that. What a pessimist you are, Nell. I thought you were getting over that!'

Nell shrugged. 'Well, I hope Philip will treat her well. I'm very fond of Harry.'

Desna bridled. 'And you think I'm not! Good heavens, Nell, I'm her mother, not you. Don't you think I have her welfare at heart, for God's sake?'

'Sorry, Des. I know sod-all about children or how to bring them up. I never had a chance to find out unfortunately.' And never would now, she supposed. Unless . . .

Desna was immediately the understanding elder sister. She laid a hand on Nell's towel-swathed arm. 'There's still time, you know. Women are having their first babies much later these days. And who knows, if this new man, who you won't tell me about, turns out to be *the one* you might well be pregnant a year from now.'

'Pigs might fly!' Nell laughed. She would dearly have liked to be able to tell Desna about Daniel. If only Desna could be made to understand that he had changed, that he had matured, grown up at last. If only she could banish the last remnants of doubt within herself. The previous evening had been the sort of experience that she'd previously believed she would never know again. How could she explain *that* to her sister, say how naturally it had happened. It was as it had been when they had fallen in love at the very beginning, only much, much better. Deeper, more satisfying, more truly loving. How dare Desna presume to tell her, which she would there was no doubt, what she should or shouldn't do, who she should or shouldn't love! It was all very well for her; she had a stable marriage and, presumably, a satisfactory sex life. The two sisters had never discussed the intimate details of their sex lives, ever, though Desna was particularly reticent. She clammed up, almost regally, even about aspects of her relationship with Roy that couldn't matter one way or another. To Nell this verged on the ridiculous, as if Roy were God or something. It wouldn't have surprised her if Desna did not in fact believe something of the kind. She seemed to exist, capable and intelligent though she was, merely to be instrumental to the greater comfort of Roy Hindmarch, as an adjunct to his self-esteem. In Nell's opinion her sister was considerably more cultured than her husband, possibly more intelligent. It annoyed her that Roy took it all for granted.

As if conjured by her thoughts, Roy appeared at the other end of the pool, his reflection stretched and contracted grotesquely by the still gently moving water. Nell conceded that Roy was a very attractive man but he was most definitely not her type. Too obviously physical, too arrogant, too macho. She liked to be wooed, not bulldozed.

Desna leaped up. 'Oh God, whatever's the time? Hallo, darling. Are we late or are you early?'

Roy kissed Desna, one hand proprietorially on her bare shoulder. 'Hallo, darling. Hallo, Nell. Don't worry, I'm early. Good swim?'

The two women agreed that it had been wonderful. Nell rose from her chair in a more leisurely fashion. Others might jump when Roy appeared but she didn't see why she should.

'I must go,' she said, seeing that Roy was about to light one of his horrible cigars. Here she was, jumping to a different tune! Daniel may have called or rung the flat. She willed herself not to hurry.

'I'll ring you about the arrangements for Easter,' Desna said. She was standing next to Roy, his arm was round her shoulders. The message was, 'We are an established, secure couple sufficient to ourselves.' Desna said, 'I hope *that's* not too far into the future!'

Nell shrugged off the dig. In spirit she was already just one or two hours into the future.

Desna was back to her soignée self. She put on a midnight-blue, high-necked dress, a favourite since it combined a look that was both austere and dramatic. She liked strong colour, unlike Nell who went in for subtle neutrals or even rather sombre clothes; everyone remarked on Nell's flair for line and colour though she hadn't anything like Desna's budget. As for Emmet, Desna didn't consider she had what could rightly be called a taste in clothes since she usually threw on whatever was handy. She would have to make sure she had a serious talk with Emmet about what she intended to wear to the wedding. It was bad enough trying to keep Mo in line. Sighing, she swung round to view her back in the cheval glass. Why couldn't all her relations be depended on not to let her down?

Dinner was simple by Desna's standards since there would be just herself, Roy and Harriet; she had prepared French onion soup, a raised chicken pie and pears baked in wine with cinnamon. At the start of their married life it quickly became clear that Roy didn't know a soufflé from a sardine, though he had a healthy appetite and a determination that everything he had control over should be the very best. Before they married she had trained in catering and topped it up with a cordon bleu course which she'd paid for herself. Now Roy considered himself to be something of a gourmet. The only cooking he couldn't abide was anything in the way of nouvelle cuisine.

'I can't bear things in puddles,' he warned her.

Roy had already showered and changed and was in the sitting

room before Desna, established in one of the large, comfortable armchairs which she had had covered in a blue patterned Liberty fabric. An arched mirror over the fireplace reflected the rich creamy walls and the honey-coloured shades of the table lamps. A fire burned though it was not strictly necessary since the central heating was extremely efficient.

'I put your drink by your chair,' Roy said, 'with ice and lemon.' He had a hefty nautical almanac open on the arm of his chair but after marking his place, he closed it and put it on the table beside him.

She picked up her drink and perched on the arm of his chair where the almanac had rested. She could smell, faintly, his discreet aftershave. 'Thank you, darling. How was your day? Was Bonicelli pleased with the Oyster?'

Roy patted her bum and leaned back, letting out a breathy 'umph' like some large contented animal; a bear perhaps, she thought, or possibly something less cuddly-sounding.

'More than pleased. He was ecstatic. Can't wait to take her out and play with all his new gadgets!' Roy gave a deep chuckle.

'He must be absolutely rolling. What on earth does he do?'

'I never enquired too deeply into that, except to satisfy myself he could pay. Anyway he insisted on putting some of it up front.' Roy sampled his Scotch. He patted Desna again. 'I thought perhaps we could have him down at Easter.'

'You mean, when the family are here?' Desna said doubtfully.

'He'll fit in. He's a family man himself. Or was. And he'd like to meet you.'

'Well, if you say so. Yes, I'm sure that will be all right. Does he want Philip to deliver the Oyster?'

'Eventually, yes. If Philip can be spared. He'll probably want it over in BVI.'

'British Virgin Islands, you mean?'

'Hmm. He has interests over there.'

'Philip's turning out really well, isn't he?'

Roy grunted. 'He'll do. So we have a date for the wedding,

then? And you've sorted out the caterers. You're not using the shower who made such a balls-up of the Wakehams' wedding, I hope?'

Desna went to sit in her usual chair. 'Of course not. I'm using a newish firm called Bonne Bouche that I've heard good things about. The woman I spoke to sounded very nice, efficient too. She's prepared to undertake most of the arrangements, including contacting the marquee people. Shall I show you their brochure?'

Roy made a gesture of dismissal. 'After dinner.' A pause. 'You seem to be more on top of things today. When did you say you get the results of the tests?'

'Next week. I expect it was just one of these odd viruses that are going about.'

Roy drew his dark brows together, reserving judgement. 'What are we waiting for, as if I didn't know? Where is she?'

'She said she might be a bit late. They're putting up a new exhibition.'

'Well, I hope those two wankers pay her overtime.'

'Roy! I wish you wouldn't be so rude about them. I think they're charming. In their way, of course.'

'Bollocks. I've never made any secret of how I feel about her working for those two. They've probably both got Aids for all anyone knows.'

'That's ridiculous. And even if they did, how would it affect Harriet?'

Roy got up. 'You've led a sheltered life in some ways, Des. Come on now, I think we've waited long enough.'

Desna got up from her chair. It was no good arguing with Roy over Gordon and Toby. If Roy wanted to believe one could catch Aids simply by working with someone, nothing in the world could shake him.

As Desna ladled out the soup she heard Harriet's footsteps in the hall. Roy frowned as his daughter came into the room and slipped into her place at the table. 'What kept you?' he said.

Harriet glanced at each of her parents in turn. 'The exhibition took longer than we thought.'

'Well,' Roy said, 'I think the very least you could have done was to ring up your mother to say you'd be late. Do you think the food cooked itself?'

'It's all right,' Desna interrupted diplomatically. 'She did warn me she might be held up.'

Harriet put her spoon into her soup, capturing slivers of onion in the clear brown liquid. She liked soup because it was easy to eat; by the time they reached the main course she usually found her appetite ebbing away. All the same, she was much better than she'd been a few years ago. There had been some problems in her teens.

'Anyway, never mind that now,' Desna was saying. 'Darling, I think we should decide on the dress quite soon.'

Harriet's spoon stopped in mid-air. 'The dress?'

'The wedding dress, darling! You'll have to make a decision about that quite quickly. Have you thought about it?'

'No,' Harriet said, 'not yet.' She bowed over her soup, crumbling her bread with her left hand. On the third finger Philip's ring sparkled, diamonds surrounded by sapphires. His choice, not hers. She would have preferred smoky agate.

'Better get a move on if you're having it made.' Roy's voice became very slightly louder when he was addressing his daughter, as if she were hard of hearing.

'You could even design your own,' Desna said lightly, 'like Nicola Wakeham did. We could use the same dressmaker. I didn't actually like Nicola's dress, it was far too fussy, but no one could say that it wasn't beautifully made.' She was already visualizing Harriet in a slender column of silk, her head wreathed in flowers like a Pre-Raphaelite painting. At the same time Harriet was reluctantly abandoning a private dream of herself and Philip in normal clothes, having married quietly in a registry office, making a secret dash to a croft in the Highlands, a crumbling mill on Dartmoor, or a secluded fisherman's cottage in Cornwall. By now she knew that none of these would be vouchsafed her.

'And you'll need to choose bridesmaids too,' Desna said encouragingly. 'Naturally you'll have Tessa.' Philip's sister was a year older than Harriet in age but light years older in sophistication. At least, that's how it seemed to Harriet.

'I suppose so. And Faith.' She hoped Faith would be free. They kept in touch by telephone and the occasional postcard but Faith had another life now. She was in the final year of her Fine Art course in Bristol.

Harriet collected the soup plates, glad of something that would remove her from her father's critical gaze. During the conversation with her mother she could almost hear his impatient thoughts.

While Desna served the chicken pie she returned to the subject of bridesmaids. 'And I think we should ask Nicola's younger sisters. The twins are quite presentable.'

'But I don't want any more,' Harriet said, appalled into speech.

'Two isn't enough, darling. Nicola had six.'

'Six is pathetic.'

'Come on now, Harry,' Roy said, cutting into Desna's succulent pastry. 'Don't be wet! It'll be thought we can't afford more. If the Wakehams can do it I'm bloody sure we can!' He started off trying to sound placatory and patient but finished up angry.

'I didn't realize it was a competition,' Harriet said. 'Anyway, I hardly know the twins.'

'I do an awful lot of business with the Wakehams one way and another. Don't lose sight of that, young lady!' Roy boomed. 'I know you don't care a damn but they're folks to be reckoned with locally. I won't have them offended!' He had meant to leave all this to Desna but there were other issues at stake here besides frocks and flowers.

Desna said smoothly, 'I think we're bound to ask them. They did at least approach you about being a bridesmaid for Nicola, even if you refused. Look, ring Faith tonight. Who knows, she might even have the same views on being a bridesmaid as you have.'

Harriet's heart sank. She hadn't thought of that. If Faith refused to come it meant that the only other ally she could rely on would be Mo. Perhaps Nell. But while she liked Nell very much she was a little in awe of her too.

The conversation carried on without her: who was owed a

part in the wedding, or at least an invitation, who wasn't, whose feelings were to be considered, what business relationships were to be advanced, which dropped. None of it had anything whatsoever to do with her love for Philip. She chewed through her chicken pie and tender mangetout as if they were old potato peelings until Mo's name was mentioned.

'She's not completely poverty-stricken,' Roy was saying, 'so what foxes me is why the hell she can't afford to get herself a decent hairdo and some at least halfway presentable clothes.'

'Roy!' Desna chided him gently. Before she had met Roy, her mother's appearance had been an occasional embarrassment; since she had begun to see her with Roy's eyes it had become a continual thorn in her side too. All the same she felt she had to play down Mo's eccentricity. 'I'll try to speak to her again.'

'Well, you'll have to do something about it before the wedding,' Roy said, 'or she doesn't come. And that's flat.'

'All right,' Desna said despairingly. 'I'll see what I can do.' Why couldn't her mother be normal, like other people's?

'I think Mo should just be herself,' Harriet said so quietly that at first neither of her parents heard. 'She wouldn't be the same person if she looked just like everyone else. I like her as she is.'

'Making an effort for her granddaughter's wedding surely isn't too much to ask, is it?' Roy said sharply. 'If Harry had her way, the whole affair would be a right foul-up. Batty grandmother, no bridesmaids, what bloody next!'

'You don't trust me to do anything, do you?' Harriet said in a low voice.

'Do you wonder with your dodgy track record?' Roy put in, his tone harsher than he really intended. Desna shook her head at him almost imperceptibly, which he found irritating.

Desna thought it best to change the subject. 'Did you say something about Persis coming to stay?'

Harriet put her knife and fork together. Most of the chicken pie still remained on her plate. Roy handed his plate to Desna for a second helping.

'Yes. Soon, I think,' Harriet said.

'Mo's not thinking of putting her up at Papermill Quay, is she?' Roy said.

'It's out of the question.' Desna was firm. 'She'll have to stay here. Mo can't expect someone like Persis to rough it in that pokey spare room of hers. Besides, it's damp.'

'Is this the sculptress we're talking about?' Roy demanded.

'*The* Persis Dane, no less,' Desna said, waiting patiently for Roy to finish his second helping. 'You don't know much about the art world, darling, or you would understand exactly how famous she is!'

'I'm not quite as clueless as you seem to think. She was the one who did that thing for outside the headquarters of the National and Civil Bank in the city, the one there was so much fuss about.' He chuckled. 'They said it didn't accurately reflect the spirit of their organization.'

'I believe they accepted it in the end,' Desna said. 'Mo said they put it somewhere obscure inside the building instead.' She felt a sense of excitement that she might at last have a chance to meet her famous aunt. Not only meet her but have her to stay at Mount Huish. Mo had always shown a strange reluctance to encourage any liaison with Persis but now Persis herself had forced the issue. Desna's mind was already busy allocating rooms and planning special little dinners to introduce the great lady to a select circle of their closest friends.

Harriet skipped coffee. While her parents had theirs she piled the dirty plates into the dishwasher and went upstairs to her room. She was engaged on a detailed pencil study of a sheep's skull that she and Philip had found on Dartmoor. The drawing had been inspired by a large reproduction of a cow's skull by Georgia O'Keefe that hung over her bed.

She had once painted the room a dark blackberry purple with grey woodwork but a year ago she'd changed it. The purple had taken an awful lot of covering but she'd managed it at last; now the room was pure white. Beside it the sheep's skull looked yellowish. Her mother believed in letting Rupert and Harriet do what they liked to their own rooms, within reason of course;

Rupert's was currently black. The cow skull reproduction was not the only Georgia O'Keefe in the room. There were others elsewhere on the walls, mostly skulls but one or two of adobe churches in desert landscapes. All Harriet's furniture was simple and kept to a minimum, leaving big spaces in between.

Her efforts at drawing were a closely guarded secret, though there was no obvious reason for subterfuge; except that if her mother knew she would be bound to insist that she did a course, or ask Gordon and Toby for an exhibition or, worst of all, show her sketches to friends as evidence that her daughter had a talent in at least one direction and wasn't completely hopeless.

She wasn't as gifted as Faith, she knew that, but more importantly she wasn't as motivated either. Somehow there didn't seem much point in seeking personal distinction when it was patently obvious that she lacked the necessary qualities to achieve it. Besides, she believed that the planet was teetering on the edge of disaster. For all she knew, she and Philip would have scarcely more than a few years together. She had never tried to explain her inertia to her parents. Better they were infuriated by it than think her mad. Fortunately the prospect of marrying her off had for the moment satisfied them.

She reached into the wardrobe for that half-finished drawing, alert for any signs that Carol had poked around inside while she had been dusting. Carol might tell Desna.

Harriet went to some lengths to make sure the angle and the lighting were the same as before as she arranged the skull on her desk. Then she sharpened her pencils and bent over her work, deepening the shadow under the zygomatic arch and taking pains to achieve the look of fragility round the nasal cavity. She might have little in the way of ability and even less ambition but when she was drawing she felt a sense of utter peace, of being withdrawn from the world in a way which even sleep didn't offer.

Below in the sitting room Desna poured another cup of coffee for Roy. She herself stuck at one. In spite of what she'd told Sally Bright, she had not been sleeping as well as usual; a passing phase, not worth mentioning.

'What the hell does she *do* up there all by herself?' Roy asked testily.

'I think she reads, or listens to Enya or one of those funny New Age tapes,' Desna said. 'Besides, it's not every night. Just when Philip's tied up. Be thankful she doesn't go out clubbing all the time like some girls and gets mixed up with the drug scene.' She spoke more tartly than she intended.

'I just wish to God she'd spend more time making herself look presentable,' Roy grumbled. 'Setting her hair or trying out lipsticks or whatever it is they do. I'm sure Philip would appreciate a bit more glamour. I know I would.' He smiled kindly. 'I wouldn't have chosen you otherwise.'

Desna handed Roy his cup. 'And Philip wouldn't have chosen Harry if he'd wanted glamour,' Desna defended her daughter. 'He obviously likes her as she is. You have to admit she's a very attractive girl even without the gloss.'

Roy tasted his coffee. It was black and strong as he liked it. Desna knew his preferences precisely. Early in their marriage he'd had to lay down the law a bit until she'd understood his little foibles; there had been a few tears, even some rows, but she'd got the hang of it at last.

'She might be all right now at a pinch but give her ten years and she'll be a dowd. I can't see Philip standing for that. Not in the position he'll be in then, God willing.' Roy finished his coffee and stood up. 'I'm off to my study. A few phone calls I have to make,' he glanced at his watch, 'before it's too late.'

Sometimes his constant attention to business irritated Desna. Lately she'd imagined that it had become almost an affectation and that some of it was not really necessary at all. At one time, when they were not entertaining, he had made a point of keeping at least part of the evening free to spend with her; now there was a kind of restlessness about him that constantly sent him off to his study or to the yacht club.

She picked up the almanac he'd been studying. It fell open at the marker. The British Virgin Islands. Automatically she put it tidily on the side ready to be taken back to his study. She wouldn't dream of disturbing him now; long ago he'd given her to understand that the study was sacrosanct even when he wasn't in it.

At least he'd said no more about her falling asleep. In retrospect it seemed a lot of fuss about nothing and she'd had been greatly reassured by Sally's demeanour. Putting it from her mind, she opened a bookcase and searched through a stack of glossy magazines. There had been one particular photograph, in the cookery section as it happened . . . ah, there it was! A cut melon, almost translucent and of a colour that was not quite ivory, nor yet pink, but with a hint of warmth. If that could only be reproduced in silk; what a colour for a wedding dress!

She let out a sigh. How she wished Harriet could be persuaded to sit beside her on the sofa and discuss these things like other mothers and daughters did, planning for what even these days was still an important event in a girl's life. Goodness knows, she'd tried hard enough to encourage Harriet to take an interest. It looked as if she'd be lucky if she agreed even to make time for dress fittings.

So the wedding would be all up to her, Desna. It would be her unique creation, an occasion that would be talked about for a very long time afterwards. It was a pity she would not personally be able to do the catering, but given the right firm – and she thought Bonne Bouche was it – she could certainly amaze with the originality of the wedding breakfast.

With her mind full of the possibilities of such a feast and with the glossy magazine slithering gradually from her lap, she fell asleep.

Roy's study was quite unlike any other room in the house. It had a dark serviceable carpet and leather chairs. A black-shaded brass reading lamp stood on a fine oak desk, a gift from Nell and Daniel years before; next to the lamp was a fax machine. The walls were covered in maritime charts and on the shelves were copies of the Macmillan nautical almanacs, books on celestial navigation, weather and marine equipment together with stacks of old *Yachting Monthlys*. On the fireplace there were several silver trophies and above them hung an arrangement of tattered burgees, all mementos of voyages and races undertaken in his younger, more carefree days. What was visible of the walls was painted the colour of ruby port.

Roy picked up the phone and dialled Bonicelli's London number.

'Enrico. Roy here. I've given your proposition a good deal of thought and I'm ringing to tell you that I'm definitely interested.'

The Italian's expansive tones fairly bounced down the wire. 'Ah, my good fellow!' When he spoke English Enrico Bonicelli was in the habit of using a kind of dated slang which some found ingenuous and charming. 'I can't tell you how delighted I am! You would be doing the right thing, absolutely no doubt about that! We must get together and discuss some more.'

'My wife was wondering if you would like to join us at Easter, if you're still in the country. It will be a family party, you understand, but you're very welcome. It would be an ideal opportunity to thrash out the details.'

'How charming of your wife. A family party would be just what I like. As you know, I now have no family; it is a great sadness.' Bonicelli's marriage had ended acrimoniously two years before and his wife spent much of her time and substantial alimony trying to prevent Enrico from seeing his children.

'We'll look forward to it.'

When Roy rang off it was with a new sense of determination. He was perfectly certain that Desna would not like the changes that were in the air but ultimately, when he had explained the necessity for them, she would abide by what he said. She had always bowed to his superior judgement when it came to matters like these. In everyday things he pandered to her whims, but the big decisions were his.

Nell and Daniel had spent most of the evening in bed. There didn't seem to have been time for dinner or even a snack. Time had not had much significance.

Nell said dreamily, 'It's midnight. Do you think I should make us some supper?'

Daniel stretched. His bare chest, with its scattering of dark curly hair, gleamed in the dim illumination of the bedside light. 'Perhaps coffee. And I could murder a sandwich.' He turned to look at her, then cupped one of her breasts and bent to kiss the nipple. 'I haven't made this much love since God knows when.'

'You don't seem to have lost the knack,' she said ruffling his hair. It was still ink-black, without a trace of grey.

'Nor you, my darling Nellie.'

Lazily she dragged herself out of bed and went to the bathroom, then to the kitchen to make coffee and sandwiches. She took them back into the bedroom and they ate sitting in bed.

'There'll be crumbs,' she said. 'How disgusting!' and laughed.

'I wish we could share a bed all the time. I wish things were exactly as they'd been three years ago . . .'

'Four.'

'Four then,' he said. Then with sudden gravity: 'In fact I wish we were back in partnership . . . in every way.'

A pause. 'We could be,' she said, putting the sandwich she was eating back on her plate.

'What d'you mean.'

'What I say. There's no reason why Cornucopia and Alfresco couldn't amalgamate. Though I couldn't keep up the shop here as well, of course.'

Daniel looked at her steadily. 'I was thinking of something more personal, Nellie. I meant marriage. This time I wouldn't opt for anything less.'

The shock of his suggestion robbed her of speech, of all things the least expected. At last she said, 'This isn't the old Daniel I used to know, is it? Surely *that* Daniel couldn't be doing with anything as conventional as the ties of matrimony!'

'This is not the old Daniel you're dealing with,' he said with a slow smile.

'Obviously not.' She looked at him, frowning. 'So is this a proposal, or what?'

'It's certainly not an "or what".' He took her hand and laid it possessively on his chest. 'Nellie, darling, I want us to throw in our lot together. There's no other way to say it. I want you to marry me.'

'It's too soon,' she said, with a violent shake of her head because she so much wanted to say yes.

'It's not too soon for me. I want you back with me and back with Cornucopia. This time all official.' He laid a hand on her neck and pushed his fingers up into her hair. 'Think about it, won't you?' he whispered. '*Then* say yes.'

CHAPTER NINE

Lee appeared at the kitchen door while Tom and Beth were still having their breakfast. Beth groaned and hid her face in her hands; she hated Lee Arnold. Emmet was cleaning the cages of the indoor birds.

'Hi, Lee!' Tom's face lit up. He admired Lee's gruff nonchalance.

'Hallo, Lee,' Emmet said, trying to sound as if she had been expecting him. 'Did you walk or did someone bring you?'

'I walked, didn't I?'

'Are you hungry? Would you like some breakfast?'

'I don't mind.'

'Tom, get Lee a bowl. Sit down, Lee,' Emmet checked the half-bald pigeon for signs of improvement before she put it back in its cage. 'Does your Mum know you came? she asked Lee casually. From experience she knew that too many questions elicited only a stubborn silence. She'd heard that Mrs Arnold had returned from hospital the day before but the information could be wrong.

'Yeah. She told me to get lost.'

'I expect she's tired. Is the lady next door still coming in?'

Lee filled his plate to the brim with cornflakes and dumped in a vast quantity of sugar. 'Yeah,' he said, adding milk.

Emmet bundled up the detritus from the cages in newspaper and carried it outside to the dustbin. She supposed they were landed with Lee for the day, which was not terribly convenient. Mo would be arriving soon and she had a rather short fuse when it came to small boys. Since the Arnolds were not on the phone she would have to drive to the village to check with Mrs

Arnold that she did in fact know the whereabouts of at least one of her children. Emmet guessed that Mrs Arnold had reached the stage of resignation in a life that had long since slipped from her control.

'Hurry up!' Tom chivvied Lee, who was stuffing in cornflakes as if his life depended on it. 'I'll show you my Stealth Bomber. It's nearly finished.'

On her way to see to the outside aviaries Emmet called, 'Tom, don't forget to do the birds' water, will you? Beth, I've put the cat food on the draining board.'

Tom said. 'Yeah, yeah, yeah,' impatiently.

Beth called to Mogsy. It was her job to feed the cats and as a result they trotted after her morning and evening as if she were the Pied Piper. They were presently gathered in a small noisy crowd outside the back door.

'Come on, my darlings,' Beth called in a special piping voice. 'Breakfast, darlings. Now, Mogsy, don't push. You're very greedy! Let Natasha have some. Come on, Damian, don't be shy. Don't let the others be horrid to you . . .' She had named them all with her favourite names – even the scruffiest had an impressive handle. She doled out the food in three separate dishes as Emmet had shown her, lecturing her charges, sometimes picking them up and rearranging them in front of the dishes to suit her own particular seating plan, crouching over them to see fair play.

Emmet grinned. Sometimes Beth reminded her of Desna. At one time Tom had been just as enthusiastic about the animals but now his attitude had changed. Lately he got quite sulky if she asked him to do the smallest thing.

The outside birds greeted Emmet with excited twittering. She made a point of not encouraging them to approach her; she hoped that most of them could be returned to the wild. Tame birds were too often dead birds. All the same there was no stopping the jackdaws. They had no fear of her whatever and perched on her shoulders and worried at her hair, forever taking liberties. The wood pigeons, on the other hand, acted as if they had never seen her before, throwing themselves into corners in a welter of feathers.

A redwing lay mysteriously dead. She picked it up and examined it closely, blowing on its feathers, but there was no apparent cause of death. It had been very thin when it was brought in but she thought it had been recovering; a pity, but these things happened. There were always some failures. She continued with her usual feeding routine: seed, flaked maize, mealworms, crushed dog biscuit.

A squirrel attached itself to the outside of the bird cage and waited for titbits, his eyes bright as beads. Last year she had driven three miles to return him to the wild. Obviously not far enough; two days later he was back. It wasn't her aim to create an army of dependent creatures but to give nature a hand, repairing some of the damage inflicted by the human species: badgers and birds hit by cars, herons and buzzards with gunshot wounds, foxes with festering snare damage, swans poisoned and strangulated with fishing tackle. Few of her patients' injuries were from natural causes.

She closed the door of the last cage and locked it behind her. The squirrel, christened Jack by Beth, leaped on to her shoulder and she fished in her pocket for a handful of peanuts; he selected one and began to nibble, turning it in his dextrous paws. The dogs had wandered out into the yard following Tom, who stood watching her.

'Where's Lee?' she called.

'He's in the loo. He's been ages. Is Barney coming today?'

'He won't be coming at weekends, just Mondays and Thursdays. At least you won't have the water to do on those days.'

Tom pulled a face and went to fetch a bucket which he shoved under the standpipe, turning it on. The water came out in a rush and shot into the bucket splashing his feet. Emmet observed but said nothing.

'Must I do the swans?' Tom grumbled. 'I hate Sydney.'

'He won't hurt you. He just likes to throw his weight about. But you can leave their bowl if you like. I'll do it later,' she conceded. It was a nuisance. She wanted to finish early because of Mo coming. Tom stomped off into the orchard, closing the gate behind him as he'd been taught.

Lee emerged from the kitchen chewing something. Somehow he always managed to finish up with his food liberally smeared round his mouth like a baby. He was the oldest of the Arnold brood; could he be competing with younger siblings for attention? Emmet wondered. What a truly unattractive boy he was! Part infantile, part world-weary adult.

'Would you like to help Tom with the bucket?' she suggested.

'Where's he to?' Lee looked round helplessly.

Emmet pointed to the orchard. 'Right down the bottom.'

'With them swans?' Lee sounded wary.

'No, not the swans. But they won't hurt you as long as you don't annoy them.'

Lee was not at all sure what actions would constitute annoyance. His mother was sometimes as mad as hell when he hadn't been doing *anything*.

Emmet sighed. There he stood, looking bewildered in his baggy black trousers with their garish stripes, which drooped pathetically over his dirty trainers. She had thought Tom's hair was short until she saw Lee's. Lee looked as if he'd been put through a hedge trimmer that had deprived him of anything so unmanly as a shred of hair. He didn't even appear to have any eyebrows. Poor Lee.

'Did you have enough breakfast?' she asked softening.

'Yeah,' he said. He was not one for niceties.

Jack came back for more peanuts and Emmet crouched beside Lee. She pressed a few of the nuts into his hand and, putting her arm round him, showed him how to hold his palm upwards. Immediately he pulled away and stood apart, nervously extending his arm. Emmet felt sad. A country boy who knew nothing of the country, a little toughie who was frightened of a squirrel. A child who had not had enough cuddles. He probably thought she was trying to molest him in spite of having already spent so much of his time, had even slept, at Drake's Farm.

The squirrel perched on his hand, flicked its tail and took its time selecting a nut. For the first time Emmet saw an expression of wonder suffuse the boy's face.

'Cor,' he said. "'Ee's not scared, is 'ee?'

'He trusts you not to hurt him.'

The squirrel ran down the boy's arm, negotiated the baggy trousers and went back to sit on top of the aviaries.

'Cor,' Lee said again.

'Off you go and find Tom. Shut the orchard gate behind you, please.'

Lee went leaping off towards the orchard punching the air with his fist. For the moment Emmet had finished all the tasks outside; she had got up at six o'clock to begin her daily routine. Now she returned to the kitchen to a wilderness of crumbs and spilt milk. A hedgehog was wandering about under the table leaving a trail of black droppings like slugs on the stone floor.

'Not you again, Houdini!' she said, picking him up and putting him back in his commodious cardboard box. She'd discovered him in January, undersized and starving, trying to eat the remains of the cats' food in the yard – one of a late litter – with a bad eye infection.

'He's getting stronger, isn't he?' Beth said from the door. She was knee-deep in cats who hoped for more food.

'He'll have to go out in the yard soon but we won't be able to return him to the wild because of having only one eye, poor old fellow.' Emmet pulled on rubber gloves to tackle the washing up. 'Help me clear this lot, will you, darling? Mo will be here before we're ready otherwise.'

'Why can't Tom and Lee do it? They never do anything.' Beth coiled a platinum-blonde curl round her finger.

'Lee's helping Tom with the water. But I'll get them to do something else, I promise.' It was hard work making sure that she delegated the chores evenly, especially now that Tom was being difficult with the animals. It was all too easy to use Beth simply because she was there, and usually willing. Emmet despised mothers who brought up their sons as helpless imbeciles when it came to housework and vowed she'd never be one of them.

'Anyhow, I don't like Lee,' Beth reluctantly began to put marmaladey plates next to the sink.' He gave me a Chinese burn *and* he said I had hair like a milky doishel.'

Emmet smiled. She thought it unexpectedly inspired of Lee to compare Beth's hair to a dandelion, though she would never have said as much to her daughter. She was torn between feeling sorry for Lee and being anxious about his influence on both her children.

'Perhaps he won't be here so much when his mother is quite better,' she suggested, offering Beth a crumb of comfort.

'Good,' Beth said with feeling. She had hoped that Nell would have asked her to help in the shop today but at least Mo was coming instead.

They collected the last of the plates and Emmet ran hot water into the sink.

'Why can't we have a dishwasher like Aunt Desna?' Beth asked.

'Because we can't afford one. Besides, we haven't that kind of kitchen; and I would still have to wash all the birds' dishes by hand.' The birds' dishes got washed in the scullery.

'I'm glad we're going to Aunt Desna's at Easter.'

'Why have you suddenly started calling Desna, aunt? You don't call Nell aunt?' Emmet piled dripping plates on the draining board and Beth reached to put them in the rack. Emmet had an idea why Desna was afforded the more formal title. There was a kind of grandeur about the Mount Huish ménage that she supposed was awe-inspiring to a child. Tom and Beth always looked forward to going there but that might have been something to do with the swimming pool. What little materialists children were!

The washing up was done and Emmet had started on the vegetables for lunch by the time Mo arrived on her bicycle.

'Hallo, there! Anyone at home?' she called as she leaned her bike against the wall. 'Get out of the way, dogs!' The dogs greeted her enthusiastically and Beth ran out to join them.

Mo was wearing her usual cycling gear, a grey tracksuit with a red stripe and a red baseball cap perched on her head. 'Hmm, lovey,' she said kissing Beth. Beth hung round her neck then, dropping off, ran to find Mogsy whom Mo would be dying to see, she knew.

Mo kissed the daughter she felt closest to; of course she loved Desna and Nell and had always endeavoured to treat them equally but with Emmet she always felt absolutely at home.

'Did you know that those two boys are at the bottom of the orchard bunging water at each other?' she said, divesting herself of her bicycle clips and fluorescent strip. 'I saw them as I came by.'

Emmet groaned. 'Oh no! Not again!'

'I'll go and sort them out,' Mo said briskly. 'What can I get them doing instead?'

'There's the hoovering.' At least they weren't annoying the animals. She hoped.

The boys came back, looking damp but chastened. Mo set them to vacuuming the sitting room reinforced by dire threats if it wasn't done to her complete satisfaction. Emmet had a mug of coffee waiting for her when she came back. She perched on a stool with her own. Beth appeared with Mogsy and Mo put an arm round her, hugging her.

'If that cat gets any bigger, she'll be carrying *you* round,' she said. The cat purred like an approaching train and Beth giggled and played with the end of Mo's plait. Other grandmothers she knew who were as old as Mo had short, grey hair. But perhaps Mo was actually quite young, after all.

'Now, Emmet,' Mo was saying, 'have you got that husband of yours to pay for some extra help around the place?'

'I haven't asked him but I think I've found someone.'

'A nice little woman like Desna's Carol is just what you need.'

Beth giggled. 'Barney's not a woman! He's a man!'

'A man! Well, that's different, I suppose.' Mo cocked an ear to the sound of the vacuum cleaner.

Emmet tasted her coffee, then loaded another spoonful of sugar into it. 'I needed someone to help with the outside chores – cutting up the wood for the Rayburn and helping to clear out the pens. I can manage the housework perfectly well myself.'

'I hope he's reliable,' Mo narrowed her eyes, 'and hasn't got one foot in the grave.'

'I shouldn't think so. He's only about thirty. He's not what you called polished but he likes animals, that's the main thing.'

'You measure everyone by how they respond to our furred and feathered friends, my dear. He isn't some sort of weirdo, is he?'

'No he's not! And judging people by how they treat animals is a pretty good guide in my book!' Emmet took a big swig of coffee.

'He can do ironing,' Beth piped up, in tones of wonder. 'He told me he can do anything.'

'He sounds like a paragon of all the virtues,' Mo said wryly. 'All the same, I should keep a close eye on him, just in case.' She rolled her eyes significantly in the direction of her granddaughter. 'Besides he could be casing the joint.'

'You should be the writer, not Maurice!' Emmet laughed.

'And how's your own writing going?' Mo enquired. 'Not found a single moment for it, I'll be bound.' She drained her cup. Cycling made her thirsty.

'*Countrywoman* sent me a hundred pounds for a piece I wrote ages ago about looking after wild birds. I'd forgotten about it. More coffee?'

The sound of the vacuum cleaner ceased and Mo went into the other room to survey the results. Emmet poured her mother some more coffee and Beth let Mogsy go and turned her attention to the kittens, who had discovered that a wider world existed outside their box.

'They're going upstairs to Tom's bedroom,' Mo said when she returned. 'That child Lee's a funny little toad. Is he really Tom's best friend?'

'He's horrible,' Beth said, holding one of the kittens in the air with its paws dangling.

'Tom thinks he's pretty hot anyway,' Emmet remarked. She left the stool to continue the preparation of the casserole for lunch.

Mo started on her second mug of coffee. 'Heard anything

110

from Maurice lately? Has he seen the children *at all* in the last six months?' She made no secret about what she thought of Maurice's lifestyle.

'Of course. He took them to a museum of agricultural implements . . . by taxi.'

'It was boring,' Beth commented.

'And he says *you* waste money!' Mo sniffed.

'It's difficult living in the country if you don't drive. As you know he's always had this thing about not learning.'

'But you had to.'

'I didn't mind.'

Mo finished her coffee. Emmet was terribly loyal to her husband. Or was it that she was so tolerant generally? She certainly never complained about the extraordinary domestic arrangements that had the two of them living entirely separate lives within a stone's throw of each other. Yet there was no talk of divorce; how long could this situation go on? 'Why don't you divorce him?' Mo said aloud.

Emmet glanced at Beth; but Beth, bored by the conversation was on her way out to the yard where she was building a den out of logs and pieces of old carpet.

'There doesn't seem much point,' Emmet said. She had thrown a pile of onions and carrots into a massive frying pan and was jiggling it over the hot plate. The injured crow let out a gruff caw. The baby rabbits scuffled in their newspaper nest.

'What if you meet someone else?' Mo persisted.

'In the course of my hectic social life, you mean?' Emmet laughed, her small face full of pixieish merriment. She tipped the vegetables into a huge stoneware dish and put the lid on. 'No, to tell you the truth, I can't be bothered.'

'You're too like me. Self-sufficient.' Mo took her empty mug to the sink and began to deal with the new pile of washing up that had already accumulated there. 'What do you want me to do next?' she asked when she had finished.

'Could you be an angel and wrap up the glassware I put in that box? There's some newspaper next to it.'

'What's it for?' Mo asked, kneeling down and beginning to

111

wrap a cut-glass bowl in an old copy of the *Observer*.

'The jumble sale at the school. We're trying to raise money for books.'

'It's disgraceful having to do things like that. Isn't this glass rather too good for a jumble sale?'

'I never use it,' Emmet said, putting the casserole into the oven. 'Besides, I don't like it.' She chuckled. 'Do you know where I got it?'

'Well, you didn't buy it yourself, that's certain.'

'It was a wedding present from the Emmersons. It's been in the attic from that day to this.'

'The only really tasteful thing the Emmersons did was to have Philip. I don't know how they managed it.'

'It's like some wonderfully nice people who have ghastly children.'

The two boys drifted into the kitchen hoping for biscuits. Mo produced a packet from her bag and cocked an eye at Emmet. 'Elevenses. Do you mind, dear? They're only quite small chocolate bars.'

Emmet wasn't keen on her children snacking but she knew it pleased Mo and she didn't come often. She nodded.

'That's for hoovering the sitting room so nicely,' Mo said. 'And, Tom, take one out to Beth.'

Tom was about to say 'thank you', but aware that his friend would think he was crawling, mumbled something unintelligible. Lee said nothing but began to tear off the wrapping at once as if he'd been starved for a week. He dropped the wrapper on the floor as he went out. Mo called after him and made him pick it up.

'I hope that child's not going to be a bad influence,' Mo said, putting the wrapper into the stove.

'I don't think so. They're just growing up, that's all. Tom won't even let me kiss him these days. And Lee's mother *is* in a bit of a fix.'

'What's wrong with her?'

'In village parlance "she's had it all taken away".'

'Sounds like a complete evisceration, poor woman!' Mo put

the last newspaper-wrapped glass back in the box. 'What else would you like me to do?'

'Nothing for the moment but I'm afraid we shall all have to make a trip to the village to make sure that Lee's mother knows where he is.'

'You go. I'll stay and look after the children.'

As Emmet threw on an old Barbour she asked, 'Have you heard from Desna lately?'

'I rang her this morning. She was just off to see the caterers but she managed five minutes,' Mo said. 'She says Nell has a new man.'

'Thank goodness for that!' Emmet unhooked the car keys from the dresser. 'When she was here the other day she told me that Daniel had contacted her again. Can you imagine!'

'Oh, my God!'

'So I hope the new one's an improvement. In everything else Nell is nobody's fool but when it comes to men she's a complete dumbo.'

'I wonder if we shall be seeing this man at Easter?' Mo pushed the dogs out of the way and shoved the box of glasses into a corner. 'Don't these dogs ever go out?'

'Of course they do. Morning and evening. But they like the heat. They're softies.'

'I tell you *who* will be here at Easter,' Mo said portentously, 'and that's Persis.'

'Persis! Persis whom you haven't seen for yonks? *Aunt* Persis?'

'Exactly.'

'But she never has anything to do with us. She's always been too busy, or too famous or something!'

'Well, she's coming now. She wrote me a very rude note inviting herself. It's not at all convenient but it's no good telling *her* that, it just makes her more determined than ever. I don't like it at all, I'm afraid it will mean trouble.'

'What kind of trouble?'

'I don't know,' Mo said evasively, 'but trouble and Persis have always gone hand in hand. That's why I've been so grateful we've left each other alone all these years. I hope she doesn't start interferring at this late stage. Desna offered to have her at Mount Huish but I couldn't possibly allow that. It will have to be Papermill Quay or nothing.'

Emmet, on her way out, said, 'Funny not seeing one's own sister for years. I can't imagine it.'

Emmet left, leaving Mo brooding. Stump, the dog with only three legs, hobbled up pleading for attention with its strange light eyes. Eyes that reminded Mo of Persis. Except that the dog's were wholly benign.

CHAPTER TEN

'It was a total bog-up,' Philip said. 'Mo swore Persis would be on the six fifty and that's the one I met. How was I to know the old bat had changed her mind and caught the earlier one to Newton Abbot instead?'

'How did she get to Mo's from Newton Abbot?' Harriet asked.

'Taxi.'

'Didn't Mo tell her she was being met?'

'She says she did. Anyway, there I was waiting on Totnes station like a complete plonker!'

Harriet couldn't see Philip's face because he was standing on top of a ladder, but she could hear the half-amused exasperation in his voice. He was painting the top half of the Mount Huish boathouse. Harriet was busy with the lower half.

'This should have been done last summer,' Philip said, sloshing on undercoat with a six-inch brush.

'Daddy said he couldn't spare anyone from the yard at that time of year.' Harriet carefully replenished her brush from the tin at her side. She painted with great attention to detail and as a result was making slower progress than Philip. She was standing on the decking that surrounded the boathouse and through the cracks could sometimes catch a gleam of the secretly gliding river under her feet. Now and again it betrayed its presence with stealthy plops and gurgles. It was deep at all states of the tide just here because of the curve of the river bank; sometimes it was carried backwards by the invading sea. Now it was almost low water and fifty yards away, below the opposite bank, a beach of mud and stones had appeared on which lay the spiky skeleton of a long-dead tree. On it a heron sat, apparently

115

asleep but probably watching for fish. In twenty minutes or so the sea would once more begin its ineluctable thrust inland; the creeks and runnels would fill, the detritus left by other tides would refloat or be submerged; a level sheet of water would rise until it almost touched the overhanging trees, whose lower branches had been trimmed to a horizontal exactness by these regular salty immersions.

Although Harriet hated being on boats, the nearness of water was as necessary to her as breathing. Sometimes, when the river was in spate, she could lie in bed and hear its hollow thunder as the tea-coloured water rushed away from Dartmoor to the sea. She found the never ceasing ebb and flow reassuring even though she knew that the Dart was believed to take one life a year, as a kind of tribute, legend had it. Considering its length, depth and turbulence after heavy rain, the number of people drawn to work or play on it, one death a year was fewer than she would have expected; unless the river was, after all, more benevolent than it was given credit for.

'Mummy wanted Persis to stay at Mount Huish but Mo wouldn't hear of it. I think Mummy was quite disappointed,' Harriet said. 'I take it Persis arrived safely in the end?' She stood back to assess her handiwork.

'Mo said so. But it sounded to me as if Persis was going out of her way to wind your grandmother up. Mo certainly sounded pretty pissed off on the phone. Don't stand too close, you'll get covered in paint.'

Harriet glanced towards the only bit of Philip she could see without craning her neck which was his feet, in a dirty old pair of deck shoes.

'I have to. This bit right underneath you is all that's left to do.' All the same she stepped out of the way while Philip moved the ladder. She recharged her brush and began carefully to cover the last few feet of weatherboarding. Philip, having finished his section, leaned against the railings and watched her. Her hair was caught up, all anyhow, in a scarf which was now spotted with white paint; it revealed the graceful arch of her neck as she bent to her work. She wore jeans and scuffed trainers with a fisherman's smock that looked as if even the fisherman had given it up as a bad job. Philip never got tired of looking at her, even old clothes could not disguise the grace and delicacy of her body. Last year he had seen her in the briefest of bikinis but even that was not such a turn-on as Harriet was now. Last summer was, in any case, just the beginning of his obsession.

He longed to take her in his arms right now and carry her into the boathouse.

'I've had a card from Faith,' Harriet said.

'Eh?' Philip was still in the boathouse.

'Faith. She says she can come at Easter.' Harriet painstakingly applied the last few brushfuls of paint. 'She'll freak out when she hears that Persis Dane will be here. She said she wanted to see what I intended to dress her in before she agrees to be a bridesmaid because if it was something gross like pale blue frills I could forget it!'

'Good old Faith. Tactful to a fault,' Philip grinned, back with the conversation. 'She always reminds me of a Jack Russell.'

'How can you say that! Faith is terribly pretty.'

'I was thinking of her temperament.'

Harriet wiped her brush on the side of the can, then on a sheet of newspaper, then stood it carefully in a jar of turps. 'Actually I think she would agree to wear a pink tutu if she thought it meant she could meet Persis Dane.' She squinted up at Philip with a look that was almost mischievous.

'I don't know about Faith but I'd give a month's pay to see Tess in one!' Philip said. 'Well, at Easter you'll be able to bat the breeze all girls together.'

Harriet pulled a face and stood back to view their work. Nothing, not even the inevitability of Philip's sister or the Wakeham twins as bridesmaids, could spoil this time alone with Philip. Having him to herself, engaged in mundane tasks, was her idea of bliss; he was so occupied in the yard that these opportunities were rare enough. Sometimes she even managed to coax him into discussing deeper, more serious things, though he usually argued that he was too busy with the here and now to bother with hypothetical cases. He said she thought too

117

much, which was curious. How could you think too much? But Philip was a pragmatist. What he enjoyed most was solving practical problems, which he was never likely to run out of all the time he worked for Hindmarch Marine.

'Right. That's finished then,' Philip stood next to her to survey their joint handiwork. 'Not bad,' he said, flinging a careless arm round her shoulders. 'We'll make a painter of you yet.'

'It looks better already. I hated it that brown colour. White's much nicer for a boathouse. I suggested blue round the windows but Daddy wouldn't have it.'

Philip pulled her close so that her cheek rested on his denim shirt. He kissed her nose. 'You've got more paint on your face than there is on the boathouse.' He turned her round and held her against him.

Closing her eyes she was aware of a new sensation; it was as if something inside her stirred gently, like a small awakening animal. She was neither stupid nor ill-informed; she had listened to the other girls at her boarding school recounting what sounded to Harriet like exaggerated sexual adventures, but she had failed to understand why they should have caused such obsessive interest, such fevered low-voiced discussions or such raucous screams of excited laughter. She had come to the conclusion that sex and love were so rarely associated that to expect them to co-exist was quite unrealistic. Not that she had ever had any experience of either, apart from loving Philip. The very few occasions when a man had overcome her shyness and asked her out had been acutely embarrassing to both and never repeated. It seemed to her that sex was the domination of one individual over another and love the companionship of equals. Her parents were a prime example of the first; what she wanted for herself and Philip was the second.

All the same, being held by Philip like this, feeling his heart thumping just by her ear, and his skin against hers, his mouth gentle on her eyelids, smelling his smell, a mixture of sweat, paint and, faintly, aftershave, was the most blissful sensation she had ever experienced. Safe. Just as long as he didn't demand more. She supposed now would be the time to raise all those issues that Mo kept nagging her about. Sex. Children. The future. Philip hadn't mentioned children. In response to her mother's urging she had at last been to see the doctor about contraception. Sally Bright had been friendly and matter-of-fact and had suggested she give the pill what she called a 'trial run' to see if it suited her.

'Hallo, you two!' Her father's voice sounded loud and clear although he was still on the zigzag path that led down through the rhododendrons to the boathouse. 'Call that work!' he added, with what seemed to Harriet a clumsy and embarrassing attempt at bonhomie.

Roy arrived at the bottom of the path, relieved to see that Philip was making an effort to wake his daughter from what he, Roy, thought of as a sort of virginal sleep. Time she joined the real world and learned what would be expected of the wife of a successful man. For he was perfectly sure that Philip would be a successful man. He wasn't afraid of hard work or of taking responsibility. Roy had plans for Philip which he had not yet completely formulated in his own mind. Perhaps by Easter . . .

Harriet blushed but Philip was not in the least put out.

'Hallo, sir. Just finished the undercoat. Looks better already, doesn't it?'

Roy stood on the decking with legs apart and arms folded across his barrel-like chest. 'Not bad, not bad. I've wanted this place done up for years. Never got round to it. You'll have to give it two undercoats, you know. To cover the brown.'

'Yes. Right. I don't know how long that fancy bargeboard's going to last. It looked pretty rotten when I cleaned it off.'

How easily Philip gets on with Daddy, Harriet thought with wonder and envy mixed.

'It'll do for now,' Roy said equably. 'We'll think about replacing it later. You've done a good job, Phil. Must have worked like a black.'

Harriet winced and angry colour flooded her face. But she turned away and said nothing. In one sentence her father had managed to include a denial of her own part in the work and a racial slur. And he was quite unaware of it.

'Busy time of the year coming up,' he was saying. Owners would be wanting their boats ready for Easter: others were thinking about selling, moving into something larger, faster or more luxurious. A few whose businesses had been hit by the recession were looking for something smaller or were selling altogether. Whichever it was, Hindmarch Marine would profit.

'The invasion of the Birmingham Navy,' Philip grinned, referring to the local name for the upcountry businessmen who kept yachts on the Dart. 'And the last quiet weekend of the winter. The pleasure boats start again on the twenty-eighth.'

'I like to see it myself,' Roy said. The sight of the pleasure craft chugging up and down the river from Totnes to Dartmouth pleased him as the bird-watcher welcomes the first migrants of spring. He enjoyed seeing business thriving on the water, just so long as it didn't complete with his own. The only things that tried his patience were the amateurish bad manners and incompetence of some of the summer users of the river.

'Right,' he said, 'if you've finished here, get cleaned up. Don't be long. Your parents have arrived, Phil. There's a cup of tea waiting aloft and Desna's made a chocolate fudge cake, you'll be glad to know!'

Philip carried out a pantomime of dropping everything to get at the promised cake, a favourite of his. His own mother was not one for producing a constant supply of delicacies, her efforts were strictly limited to dinner parties. Harriet smiled, delighting in Philip's ability to be spontaneous and quite unselfconscious. Her father laughed and she realized that he had not addressed one single word to her while he had been with them. She might just as well not have been there. But there was worse to come. She'd been so happy alone with Philip that she'd forgotten that the senior Emmersons had been invited to tea.

Roy left Harriet and Philip to clean their brushes and put the ladder and paint pots back into the houseboat.

'Make sure those doors are locked,' he called as he went. 'We don't want a repetition of last summer.' Last summer vandals had come, presumably by boat since boat was the only unobserved means of access, broken in, stolen an outboard, and damaged the inflatable and Rupert's Mirror dinghy. Roy's yacht, *Eos* was moored down near the yard.

They dawdled up the zigzag path, Philip's arm holding Harriet close while he told her nonsensical jokes. She wished that this treasured time alone with Philip could stretch to infinity. In a minute he would metamorphose into the person who joked, talked shop and blended so effortlessly with her father's generation. She had offered to help paint the boathouse in order to have Philip to herself for a precious hour or two. Such occasions were rare gleams of gold in the unremarkable ore of her life. Philip was always so busy, sometimes even out of the country delivering a yacht or carrying out sea trials for a customer. She hugged to herself the knowledge that the boathouse would need at least two more coats of paint.

Back in her own room she got out of her paint-stained gear and threw on a grey skirt, black leggings and ankle boots. With them she wore a baggy jersy with a wide neck that sometimes skidded off one shoulder. The mirror gave back to her an image of herself backed by the Georgia O'Keefe skull, a jaunty rose placed just above one of the skull's blank eye sockets.

'I look absolutely pathetic,' she told her reflection scathingly. She wished she could stay in her room and finish her drawing, since she could no longer have Philip to herself. Reluctantly she dragged a comb through her hair and went downstairs.

Philip lounged on one of the sofas, perfectly at home. Her father was standing in front of the fire, her mother was bending over a tray of tea things. Isabel Emmerson cried out a greeting from one of the giant-sized armchairs and raised a pointed chin in Harriet's direction. Harriet kissed her dutifully.

'Hmwa,' Isabel kissed the air beside Harriet's cheek. 'Darling Harriet, lovely to see you.'

Giles returned Harriet's kiss far more enthusiastically.

'I've poured your tea, sweetie,' Desna said. She looked poised and elegant in a cream silk blouse, a skirt of crimson wool and, resting on her shoulders, a cardigan that exactly matched her skirt. Harriet noticed, with a sudden jolt, that the cardigan was inside out. Even so slight a disarray was so unlike her mother that for a moment Harriet froze, panicking about whether she should mention it and risk her father's displeasure with both of them or ignore it and know for certain that Isobel's critical and mocking eyes would not fail to take note of her mother's lapse.

Harriet took her tea clumsily, which wasn't difficult for her, and in doing so contrived to sweep the cardigan off her mother's shoulders. Unfortunately she also spilled most of the tea down the front of it which had not been her intention.

'Oh, darling! Look what you've done!' The exclamation escaped Desna before she could bite it back. She was so anxious to present her daughter in a good light to the Emmersons.

'For God's sake, Harry!' Roy exploded.

There was a moment of general confusion. Philip leaped to take the cup from Harriet's nerveless hand. Giles stepped forward, gesturing vaguely with a napkin while Desna bent to retrieve the cardigan from the floor.

'If you sponge it at once I'm sure you'll find it won't stain,' Isabel suggested helpfully from her chair. She had of course noticed that Desna had the garment on inside out but had already put down Harriet's gesture as just another example of her future daughter-in-law's cack-handedness.

'Of course,' Desna said. After the smallest hesitation she was in charge of the situation again.

'Harriet!' Do that for your mother!' Roy barked.

It was by far the best way, Desna thought, to commit her expensive knitwear to Harriet's tender mercies. It would get her out of the room, give her time to recover from the embarrassment that was almost as painful for her to watch as it must be for Harriet to endure. She handed it to her with a smile. 'Just a little cold water, darling,' she said, making light of it, 'as Isabel suggested.'

Harriet took the cardigan and fled to the kitchen where, in her confusion, she made it too wet and finished up dunking the whole thing in cold water. Why, she thought, do I have to make a mess of the simplest thing when I'm anywhere near Isabel and Giles? It was bad enough when it was just her father. In the gallery she was appreciated by Gordon and Toby partly because she never, ever, broke anything. She fussed with the cardigan for as long as she dared before joining the others. She sat on a chair a little apart.

'Cake anyone?' Desna was poised over an extravagant chocolate confection. She darted a worried glance in Harriet's direction.

'Rather!' Giles said heartily. He was a tall man, spare, and with the beginnings of a slight stoop. He had once been handsome but was now inclined to be florid as a result of weekends spent sailing and rather too many rounds at the bar afterwards. He had been fair, like Philip, but even skilful combing could not disguise the fact that he was going bald.

'Just the tiniest piece for me,' Isabel said. She sat with her legs together at an elegant angle. Harriet thought it would be possible to make a passably accurate drawing of a tibia and patella from Isabel's legs, so thinly was the skin in its fine covering stretched over her bones. Her shoes were burnished leather of Italian design, her suit was probably Chanel.

'Oh, Desna, that's far too much!' Isabel cried, as a matter of course as Desna, as a matter of course, put a minute portion on her plate. Desna cut larger slices for the men.

'And when is dear little Rupert due home?' Isabel asked.

'Little!' Desna laughed. 'It's been a long time since Rupert was little!'

'Nearly as tall as me,' Roy said with pride, sitting down in one of the blue-patterned armchairs with a sigh and placing his plate on a small table at his side. 'He's sixteen, you know.'

'Yes, I suppose he must be. We didn't see much of him at Christmas, did we?' Isabel said.

'He stayed with a school friend in Gloucestershire. The Youngs.'

'But he'll be here for Easter?'

Roy nodded. 'Young limb!' he said with a grin.

'Aren't they all at that age?' Giles conveyed a forkful of cake to his mouth. 'Hmm, Desna! This is death by chocolate and no mistake!' He turned to Harriet. Unlike his wife he was quite uncritical of his future daughter-in-law; in fact he found it difficult to take his eyes off her whenever she was in the room. He said,

'Well, then, young Harry, how are the wedding plans progressing? Got it all taped?'

'Well . . .' Harriet mumbled, Desna's exotic gâteau dry as dust in her mouth.

'Of course she hasn't!' Roy put in. 'But you can bet your life Desna has, haven't you, darling?'

Desna produced a stilted smile. She wished that Roy had the wit to see that if he continued to put down his daughter like this in the eyes of her future in-laws, they might have it in their power to dissuade Philip altogether from marrying her. Not even Harriet's looks and Philip's undoubted affection for her, not to speak of the business connections between the two families, would be able to save the match if the Emmersons set their minds against it. She saw Philip's love for Harriet as insubstantial, the sort of love one would have for a lovable stray puppy. 'We thought we'd get Harrods and Marks and Spencer to do the wedding present lists,' she said brightly to divert attention. 'I had the organist on the phone yesterday so Philip and Harriet will have to choose the music quite soon. And I still haven't finalized the guest list!'

'What a business it all is!' Isabel groaned. 'I'm absolutely dreading it when Tessa finally decides to settle down. Not that she's showing any signs of it at the moment. She seems absolutely set on a career in spite of all the boyfriends and the mad partying.' There was more than a suggestion in her tone that a girl without a career who married young was, by definition, a lesser mortal. Harriet chewed her lip, wishing the purgatory would end. From time to time she glanced at her mother to check for any other signs of absent-mindedness. In Mo or Emmet a garment put on inside out would be par for the course, in Desna it was worrying. Perhaps the wedding arrangements were proving to be too much even for her mother.

'Harriet's been lucky,' Philip was saying, grinning as he tucked into his second slice of cake. 'She found a real cool cat on her doorstep. Why would she need to look further?'

There was general laughter. 'You cheeky young bugger,' Giles said good-humouredly.

Harriet moved her chair closer to Philip, relieved by the breaking of a tension that had seemed to her almost tangible.

'Will you be inviting your famous relative to the wedding?' Isabel said, crumbling her chocolate cake into a mess on her plate to make it look as if she had eaten some. 'What's her name? I should remember, shouldn't I?'

'Persis. Persis Dane,' Desna said. 'Well, naturally, if she'll come. I asked her along today so that you could meet her but apparently the journey exhausted her and she's resting.'

'Don't think I'd know what to talk about to a sculptress,' Giles said in mock dismay. 'The only artists I know are Toby and that fellow who does those wonderful watercolours of old clippers. Toby's a nice enough fellow, for a queer that is, but I don't think much of his painting.'

Harriet pushed back her chair. 'I'll get some more hot water,' she said to her mother abruptly. She picked up the jug and escaped to the kitchen where Desna's cardigan still lay on a towel, damply accusatory. She refilled the kettle, leaning over the sink not knowing if what she was feeling was anger or misery. A pair of arms went round her, holding her tight. The kettle overflowed.

'Don't mind the old man,' Philip said, nuzzling her ear. 'He's a reactionary old bugger. He doesn't mean half of it.'

'That's the trouble,' Harriet said in a low voice. 'I'm afraid he does. So does Daddy.'

'Nah,' Philip said dismissively. 'It's the generation. They still can't get used to the idea that being gay's legal.'

'They're not that old.' Harriet switched the kettle on and leaned her back against the marble worktop. Desna had had the kitchen done up to look like that of a very superior country farmhouse (nothing like Emmet's, of course). It had two Belfast sinks, several old pine plate racks, and, suspended over their heads, a huge batterie de cuisine, which gleamed with efficient-looking stainless steel utensils. In spite of all the Victorian romanticism Desna had made sure that everything was highly functional.

'I tell you what,' Philip said, 'let's go and make a surprise

125

visit to Mo. Give this ancient relative of yours the once-over. What d'you say?'

'And she's not that old either,' Harriet said. 'She's quite a lot younger than Mo. More our parents' generation really.'

'Anyway, what about it? We could go to the pub afterwards. Get away from this drawing-room natter.'

'I'd love to. I was looking forward to meeting her.' Harriet glowed with pleasure. 'I hope she won't be too tired to talk to us.' She felt so great a surge of gratitude towards Philip for handing her the excuse for flight that she kissed him – the first spontaneous kiss that she'd ever attempted. He made the most of the opportunity before the kettle boiled and she broke away to carry the hot water back to the sitting room.

Perhaps with Philip's help, she thought as they made their escape, she might be able to survive the numerous rites of passage to be endured before that one final one in July.

'Roses, I thought,' Desna said. 'Masses and masses of roses. Banks of them. Harriet loves roses, we both do. And what's the point of having a wedding in July without roses . . .?'

'I couldn't agree more,' Isabel said, suppressing the tiniest yawn as she reached for the cup Desna was passing her. Her slender fingers bore a weight of gold that seemed almost too much for them, as if they should crack under it.

'And of course the church is gorgeous. A perfect setting, we thought.'

'Absolutely.' Isabel sipped her Earl Grey and her gaze wandered to the window where Roy and Giles stood looking out and discussing business. Her gaze lingered more particularly on Roy, whose powerfully physical frame seemed still to embody all that was virile, whereas Giles . . . She supposed that Roy must have been unfaithful to Desna, a man like that. Of course there had been that one occasion when she and Roy had been alone together on *Eos*. Desna and Giles had gone off into Dartmouth for some reason. There *had* been a moment then when she believed that Roy was about to turn a casual kiss into something more, but Desna and Giles had returned. Several times Isabel had attempted to contrive another opportunity but had the impression that Roy had thought better of it and was not willing to co-operate. Although he was patently a terrific stud, she mused, he was also a shrewd and ambitious man who would do nothing to endanger Hindmarch Marine in any way. No, she was afraid that if Roy Hindmarch wanted another woman he would take her from outside the circle of their immediate acquaintances. Isabel Emmerson sighed. But she had not quite given up.

'Don't you think it would be a nice gesture?' Desna said.

'I'm sorry,' Isabel said. 'What did you say?'

'That it would be a nice gesture if we all attended St Clement's on Easter Day. I think Gerald Peters would appreciate that.'

'If you don't think it would give him too big a shock. There would be at least a dozen of us, wouldn't there?' Privately Isabel hoped that Desna would drop the idea. She didn't fancy spending a large part of Easter morning in a cold church. She was very fond of Desna and Roy but there were some sacrifices that were too great even for friends. Once or twice a year at St Saviour's, for appearances' sake, was enough for her. 'By the way, darling, we must discuss outfits. We don't want a repetition of the Wakeham débâcle. Do you remember? Bride's mother wearing virtually the same outfit as the groom's. Puce, wasn't it? Something hideous anyway, but times two. What a hoot!' She shrieked with laughter.

Desna smiled. She suspected that it would not take much for Isabel to use her brittle mockery on *her*. Perhaps she already did, behind her back. She watched her friend's eyes stray towards the men. Isabel was happier in the company of men. Desna went to sit beside her on the sofa. Desna could only truly relax when Roy's eyes were not on her. It was he who had sprung from humbler beginnings but, even before her recent forgetfulness, he often treated her as if he expected her to let him down in some way. The trouble was, she thought ruefully, that she'd run Mount Huish so efficiently that it had, by degrees, raised his expectations ever higher. Poor Roy, he could hardly be blamed for his sensitivity on this point even though few people these days were snobbish about origins.

'I'm glad Harriet and Philip have pushed off on their own,' Isabel said. 'They get so little time together. He absolutely adores her, you know.' She sounded slightly surprised. 'Can't do enough for her.'

'And Harriet worships him. They do seem very much in love, and well suited. At least that was what the vicar said, and I think he's right.'

Isabel had her own ideas about that but maintained a tactful silence. It wasn't that she wasn't fond of Harriet, she always had been, but one had to think of Philip's future. There had been a girl called Vanessa whom he'd been quite thick with at one time; she'd been smart and ambitious and for a time Isabel had hopes that she would be the one. On the other hand Harriet's connections could be said to be almost more important than the girl herself. After all, Giles was intimately involved with the Hindmarch business, being their lawyer. And Hindmarch Marine offered reciprocal services, making sure that the Emmersons' yacht, *West Wind*, stayed shipshape.

'And how are *you* holding up so far?' she asked Desna. 'I'm afraid it's going to be a frightful lot of work for you. Even you!' she joked. She hadn't forgotten Desna's one or two odd lapses.

'I'm perfectly fine!' Desna was aware of sounding defensive. 'You know me. I thrive on it.'

Isabel lifted an elegant hand and let it drop as if the effort exhausted her. 'I don't know where you get the energy. You run this place like a five-star hotel anyway. I reckon you *could* run a five-star hotel with one hand tied behind your back.'

Desna laughed, pleased with the compliment. 'As a matter of fact I'd rather like to,' she said. She glanced across at Roy and Giles, their voices a rumbling counterpoint. 'Of course, Roy would never hear of me getting a job of any kind. I once thought I'd like to help in Sally Bright's surgery, just parttime, you know, but Roy was adamant though I could have done it easily without affecting him at all.'

'I'm sure.' Isabel admired masterful men but she wasn't sure if she could put up with being told what she could and couldn't do. Giles, of course, wouldn't have dared.

'I tell you, Giles,' Roy said testily, 'these new Department of Transport regs are going to cost a packet! Every bloody boat we charter out will have to be modified.'

'What are they asking for?' Giles said. He stood with hands in pockets looking out of the window. The sun had just put in an appearance from below a level bank of violet cloud from where it pierced the screen of trees, laying bars and lozenges of lemon-coloured light on the lawn.

'New cookers, stainless steel in the galleys, new fire extinguishers, nonflammable foam everywhere. It doesn't sound much for the individual but multiply it by a few dozen and you're talking serious money. The trouble with it is that it's extra outlay without any noticeable return. But it'll have to be done, bugger it, if we're to stay in business. And the owners are all bloody reluctant to shell out, I can tell you. Yet it'll be me who will have to chivvy them. Like a bloody sheepdog.'

'You reckon that the recession is really biting now? I thought you were weathering it rather well.'

'To tell you the truth I'm getting fed up to the back teeth with this country and its pettifogging attitudes,' Roy said belligerently.

Giles glanced at him. 'What will you do?' he asked, curious about the new tone of exasperation he detected in a man whose normal style was buoyant optimism.

Roy stood with his arms folded across his chest. He was not about to tell Giles of all people what was in his mind. 'Bite the bullet, I suppose,' he said. And then, following a train of thought, 'You know the liquidation job, the Oyster?'

'The one you were refitting for that Italian bloke?'

'Yes. Luxury job. He's pleased as punch with it. Like a dog with two bloody tails! Des and I have asked him down for Easter as it happens.'

'Just as well to keep in with the big spenders,' Giles laughed. 'He *has* paid I hope?'

'Without a murmur. I have a nasty suspicion that he thought it was cheap at the price. But I'm quite satisfied. Short-sighted to be too greedy.' Roy glanced back towards the two women. Isabel was looking rather foxy today. All the same he'd noticed lately that she was beginning to show signs of the stringy look of the older woman which he personally found repulsive. At least Desna managed to keep slim without losing that curvaceous sensuality that had first attracted him. 'What about another cup. I'm sure Des wouldn't mind making another pot,' he said.

Giles hesitated. 'Do you think it's too early for a bracer?' he suggested.

'Good idea!' Roy said heartily, making for the drinks. 'What's your poison?'

'My usual, thanks,' Giles said. He rubbed his hands together, anticipating the best part of the day.

The lane that led from the Mount Huish gate to the main road was little used and not particularly well maintained. Roy never complained about this; it deterred adventurous tourists. Philip drove too fast, as usual, scattering leaves and small pebbles in all directions.

On the main road he drove even faster; fortunately the Saturday traffic was light at this time of the year; by Easter it would be a different story. Harriet could never get used to Philip's driving. Nothing she said would influence him in any case. She knew he saw himself as carrying with him an aura of indestructability. It was perfectly clear that like most young men he saw himself as immortal in this respect, and certainly infallible.

She, on the other hand was painfully aware what a fragile collection of bones, blood and tissue comprised a human being; sometimes it seemed like a miracle that, as one slept, the atoms of the body didn't permeate the veil that held them together and become some sort of cosmic dust again. When Philip was at sea she deliberately tried not to think of him in case her fears should themselves become real and bring disaster on him. It was a relief to know that he didn't share her apprehensions; but then, if he did, he wouldn't so much as step into a boat in the first place, she supposed.

They arrived at the usual parking place, a narrow scoop in the bank at the side of the road, already partially occupied by the Wilds' disreputable van. There they left Philip's battered Land Rover, negotiated the stile and careered down the narrow path that plunged through the trees. The steps, that descended in a series of rickety angles beside the ruined papermill, were at this time of year slicked with mud,and the wooden handrail slimy to the touch from the drip of the overhanging trees. From somewhere to their right, hidden in the undergrowth came the rush and trickle of the leat and the air smelled dankly of rotting things, but there was now a distinct, sweet admixture of primroses. As the trees thinned the gleam of reflected light from the river grew stronger. The late sun shone levelly in their eyes.

On the quay several children belonging to Mo's neighbours, the Wilds, were playing a noisy game involving a car tyre. They were dressed in a curious collection of grubby clothes, apparently adult garments cut down, and all, both boys and girls, had long tangled locks. At the sight of Philip striding on to the quay, they abruptly stopped playing and watched the new arrivals with the deepest suspicion.

'Hi, there!' Philip said. He picked up the abandoned tyre and began to bowl it expertly along the quay. In almost no time there was a chaos of lank flying hair and flailing arms and legs accompanied by hoarse shouts and giggles.

Harriet became aware that there was someone standing at Mo's door. The figure had fixed them all with a penetrating gaze. She could well understand it when the children suddenly fell silent and slunk away, leaving Philip holding the dusty tyre.

Persis Dane, for it had to be she, was a formidable figure; her short, wild hair a pale halo round her head. She stood with her arms folded across her chest, her large hands clamped to her faded denim sleeves. She wore jeans thrust into cowboy boots and her weather-beaten features would have reminded Harriet of the craggy figurehead of some old trading schooner if a cigarette hadn't been jammed between her lips, destroying the illusion. Harriet knew her to be much younger than Mo but the first impression was that they were of an age. It must be the white hair; though even that had a kind of incandescent vigour all its own.

Harriet recovered from her surprise at this apparition and approached, shyly holding out her hand. 'Hallo, you must be Persis.' She coloured. Perhaps she should have said 'Great-aunt Persis' or even 'Ms Dane'.

Persis seemed not to have noticed her hand. 'I came to see what all the row was about,' she said in her gruff smoker's voice.

Harriet's hand fell. 'I'm Harriet,' she said. 'And this is Philip Emmerson.'

Philip's hand, though he had wiped the dust from the tyre on his jeans, was also ignored.

'You Desna's kid?' Persis asked Harriet abruptly.

'Yes,' Harriet said, though she had the impression that Persis wasn't listening.

'You better come in.'

They all trooped into Mo's cottage where Mo was setting out more mugs. The air was foggy with foreign-smelling cigarette smoke. Harriet kissed Mo.

'Hallo, you two.' Harriet detected more than a hint of relief in Mo's greeting.

'I hope you don't mind us coming,' Harriet said, 'and that Persis isn't too tired.'

'Tired!' Persis exclaimed, in spite of the earlier excuse. 'What bollocks!'

'Coffee or tea?' Mo asked.

'Tea for me, please.' Harriet had had scarcely more than a sip or two at home.

'And I'll have coffee if there's any going.' Philip kissed Mo. 'Just to be awkward.'

'No trouble,' Mo said cheerfully. 'So you've met?'

Persis was already lounging on the sofa, her cowboy boots, which Harriet took to be the genuine article, resting on the arm.

'So we have, at last,' Philip said. 'Sorry I missed you at Totnes, Miss Dane,' he added pointedly.

Persis shrugged, took her cigarette out of her mouth and

picked a crumb of tobacco from her lip. On her wrist was a colossal man's watch.

'Coffee for you, Persis?' Mo enquired, holding the kettle aloft over the four mugs. She had arranged them on an enamelled tray, painted with cabbage roses. 'Bugger the coffee, Mo. Get out the Bells, for Christ's sake.'

'There's not much left. You've drunk most of the bottle I bought yesterday,' Mo grumbled. 'Anyway, darlings, sit down. I'm sorry about the confusion at the station, Philip. I hope it didn't put you out?' She looked severely at Persis.

'Forget it. It was no trouble,' Philip said breezily.

Harriet glanced at Persis, who made no comment or apology but gazed at the ceiling, one arm behind her head, smoke trickling from her lips. She was taking up a large proportion of the seating accommodation but made no move to share the sofa. Philip took one of the chairs and Harriet perched on a small stool by the stove, which was a favourite place of hers anyway. She picked up Rose Madder and stroked her fur. The cat curled on her lap and went to sleep. Mo made the coffee and tea and dumped a glass and the whisky bottle down next to Persis, who out of long habit managed to help herself without shifting her position on the sofa.

'So what have you two been up to today?' Mo said, claiming the remaining chair; one she didn't normally use because its wicker construction was beginning to unravel.

'We've been painting the boathouse,' Philip said, helping himself to sugar.

'Shouldn't you be painting your new flat?' Mo said, smiling.

'It won't be vacant until July.' Philip had been rather against accepting help from Roy in the acquisition of the small flat in Dartmouth, but it was difficult to argue with a potential father-in-law who was also your boss. He glanced at Persis. He was even-tempered by nature but he found something challenging and faintly insulting about Mo's famous sister.

'Do you enjoy living in Yorkshire, Miss Dane?' he asked, more politely than he believed she deserved.

For some time Persis continued to smoke and stare at the

ceiling as if she were deaf or perhaps found the question deeply problematical. At the point at which Harriet was convinced that Philip was not going to receive an answer and was about to chip in with some remark of her own, Persis screwed up her eyes and, without removing her cigarette said, 'Enjoy? Well, there you are, aren't you? One has to live somewhere and Yorkshire's as good a no-nonsense place as any. To be honest, I don't notice my surroundings much.'

'Don't notice!' Harriet found herself exclaiming. 'But you're an artist!'

Persis turned her awful light blue eyes on Harriet, so like Mo's and yet so different, and for a moment Harriet thought she might faint. But perhaps that was just because of the smoke-laden air and her efforts to suppress a cough. She bent to stroke Rose Madder, who began to purr.

'Correction,' Persis said gruffly. 'I'm a sculptor. There's a difference. I don't mess with superficial appearances.'

'Well, that puts me in my place!' Mo snapped. She leaned forward to cram another log into the glowing maw of the stove. 'Me and my superficialities.'

It dawned on Harriet for the first time that Mo's easel and half-finished paintings were missing from the room. The last rays of the sun showed up the dust that veiled the miscellaneous heaps of objects on every surface. Artificial light was so much kinder to Mo's housekeeping.

'Don't pretend you don't know what I mean, Mo,' Persis said imperturbably.

Philip laughed. 'I don't know much about art,' he said, 'so I'll sit this one out.'

Persis let out a lungful of smoke. 'If only all the other motherfuckers who don't know anything about art would follow your excellent example,' she said.

Harriet glanced from Persis to Philip. But Philip evidently found the situation highly entertaining.

'But I don't know what you mean,' Mo persisted. 'Are you saying that sculpture has to be more meaningful just because it has three dimensions? Explain yourself.'

Persis emptied the last drops from the whisky bottle into her glass and grunted. 'Painting is all right in its way. Every once in a while it'll throw up something decent, but it's too fucking easy. When you have to slug it out with the essential physical bloody stuff of existence you have to be pretty damn sure of your conceptualization. Half-arsed notions are punished to the extreme limits of the law. And quite right too.' She threw back her head and poured the remains of the whisky down her throat. Harriet almost expected her to hurl her empty glass into the stove.

'You obviously know nothing whatever about painting,' Mo said, quite unmoved, 'if you think it's easy. Why d'you think there's such a dearth of good stuff?'

'And by the same token such an excremental landslide of the third rate!' Suddenly Persis turned her thunderous eyes on Harriet and said abruptly,' You look as if you might follow in your grandmother's misguided footsteps. Don't tell me you're a sodding painter too?'

Harriet felt colour stain her face. 'No. No, I'm not.'

'Thank Christ for that. What do you do then?'

'I work in a gallery.'

'You flog the frigging stuff, then?' Persis pulled on the last half-inch of her cigarette and threw the butt in the general direction of the stove. 'And getting cash and carried any minute now, eh?' To Harriet's immense relief she turned her gaze in the direction of Philip while at the same time reaching into the breast pocket of her denim shirt for a packet of Gitanes. She shook one out and cupped her hands over a match. Still looking at Philip and breathing out a great cloud of blue smoke, she said, 'Hmmm. Not bad. I was married once, believe it or not.'

'Twice,' Mo corrected her.

'Whose counting? They both buggered off anyway. The only thing that could be said for number one was he was stinking rich.' She opened her mouth and gave an uproarious laugh. Harriet saw that her teeth were good but stained yellowish by nicotine. The laugh turned into a spasm of coughing. 'Sweet bleeding Jesus,' Persis exclaimed between gasps.

135

Philip stood up. 'Come on, Harry. Time to go. Glad you're settling in all right, Miss Dane,' he said with more than a trace of irony.

'If you are going to insist on calling me that, young man,' Persis said, 'we are going to fall out. My name is Persis, right?'

'Right,' Philip said, grinning.

Mo saw them to the door, Persis simply waved her cigarette at them, without moving from her position on the sofa.

Mo stood beside them in the doormat-sized front garden. It was almost dark. The river as it approached high tide lay like a sheet of pewter stretching away to the furthest bank. A late flight of seagulls headed towards the mouth of the river and the sea.

'How are you going to bear it, Mo?' Harriet whispered anxiously. 'Will she be staying long? And did she say yet why she came?'

'Don't worry, sweetie. I can handle Persis. Other people may think she's the *crème de la crème* in her own field and perhaps she is, but I'm her sister, for goodness' sake.' She chuckled. 'Besides, it's difficult to be in awe of someone whose nappies you once changed!' Mo spoke more confidently than she felt.

'Did you really change her nappies?' Harriet said. 'I can't imagine that she was ever that young! Mummy wanted me to invite her over but I don't see how I can. Mummy wouldn't like the smoking and she'd hate the swearing. You see, Persis isn't quite what she expected. All the same,' she stopped frowning and began to smile, 'I'd love to see what Mummy and Daddy's friends make of her!'

Mo patted Harriet's cheek. 'Glad to see there's a spark of mischief there after all,' she said.

Back at the Land Rover Philip chuckled suddenly. 'What an amazing old dyke!'

'She's not a dyke. Didn't you hear her say she's been married. Her husband's pushed off . . . like Mo's.'

'In Persis' case, I'm not surprised,' Philip said with fine male arrogance as he started the motor. 'Seems to run in the family, doesn't it?' He eased the vehicle out into the road. 'Right, onwards to the pub.'

A cold hand seemed to twist Harriet's guts. She couldn't imagine what she'd do if Philip left her. But it didn't appear to dawn on him that his words could ever apply to them. She snatched in her breath. She was perfectly certain that she wasn't in the least like either Mo or Persis. Nor was Philip like their husbands. She hoped.

Philip glanced at her. 'Dreaming again!' he teased.

CHAPTER ELEVEN

Nell dived into her bag for her business card which allowed her into the antiques fair free. It was duly swallowed by the machine and she went inside.

She had not planned to spend Sunday here. She had found the leaflet about it after Daniel had gone, and remembered that she had originally intended to pay it a visit. But that was 'before Daniel'. Now she was here only in order to show him that in four years she had changed. She was an independent woman. Nobody's pushover. Besides, it was better than clock-watching, waiting for his return.

That morning was the third that she had woken up beside Daniel. She had stretched her bare arms above her head before turning to gaze at him as he slept. She could still hardly believe that he was here, in her bed. She studied his sleeping face and wondered at the vulnerability of it, even with the slightly villainous effect of his dark morning stubble. How many times had she woken up alone, having dreamed that he was with her, that they had made love as they used to, that they were together again as they had once been? The terrible emptiness and disappointment had sometimes been almost too much to bear. She could, she supposed, have taken refuge in tranquillizers or booze or endless and random sexual adventures. Eventually she had instead thrown herself into work with a single-minded determination to forget.

It had worked at a superficial level, and had certainly duped most people into thinking she had completely got over Daniel.

She studied his hand laying relaxed upon his chest, like the hand of Michelangelo's dying slave. She slid her own into it and

139

saw that his eyes were open, watching her quizzically. He always had the ability to spring from sleep into instant awareness.

'Hi there, Nellie,' he said.

She bent and pressed her mouth on his.

'What's the time?' he said.

'It's all right, it's Sunday.'

Suddenly he sat up. She fell back on the pillows. He reached for his watch and scrutinized it.

'God! I shall have to go,' he said, scrambling out of bed and searching for his abandoned clothes.

'Go? Go where?'

'I promised I'd meet this chap at ten thirty.'

'Today?' she protested. 'Why today, for God's sake? It's Sunday. I thought we were going to spend the day together.'

He bent over and kissed her. 'Darling. No can do. It'll have to be another time. What's the hot water situation? I need a shower.'

She rolled out of bed, pulling her dressing gown round her naked body. 'Daniel, you didn't tell me. Surely he won't expect you to see him today? Ring him up, why don't you?'

'Come on, Nell, don't get all possessive on me. Now what about this hot water?'

'There's plenty of hot water,' she said stiffly, unable to hide her hurt and disappointment. He'd said nothing of this last night, letting her believe that they had the whole of this day together. But now she remembered other times when his wheeling and dealing had taken account of neither the time, the day nor even previous engagements.

'How long will you be? When are you coming back?' She knew she sounded like a nagging wife but she couldn't help herself.

'I can't say. I may be some time, as the man said!' He grinned. 'Don't wait about for me, for goodness' sake. All right if I use the bathroom first?' He was already on his way.

She nodded. He came back and gave her a quick kiss. 'Darling Nellie,' he said, 'what about making us both a coffee? I'll be two minutes, literally.' He went out, she heard the bathroom door close.

When he had showered, dressed and drunk his coffee, he left her and she dawdled over a second cup before she too showered and dressed. Her plans for the day were in ruins though it was true nothing had been absolutely settled. She had evidently assumed too much, thought that because it would be their first opportunity for a complete day together he would have kept it free. Perhaps it was simply that he'd made the arrangement long before they'd met again, though she didn't really believe this. Arrangements could be unmade. He'd refused to be drawn about it and she hadn't liked to pursue him with questions. He had already accused her of being possessive and she wanted nothing to spoil these first few blissful hours of their reunion.

Instead, she decided that she would spend the time quietly, hugging to herself her new happiness, knowing that Daniel would be back, that they would have an intimate and voluptuous supper tonight instead of her usual scrappy Sunday evening snack. They could go out, or she could prepare something for a candlelit supper in the flat. Then bed.

She fed Morgan, who was pressing his substantial body against her legs, impatient for breakfast. It was as she tidied the sitting room and removed the empty glasses that she had noticed the leaflet.

The fair was taking place in a vast prefabricated building on the outskirts of Exeter. The interior had been transformed into an Aladdin's cave; stands displayed every kind of antique imaginable and some that could hardly be called antique at all. But all were nevertheless pored over eagerly by the crowd, which surged like a river round the overloaded islands of furniture, paintings, pottery, silver, books, bric-a-brac and a glittering assortment of collectables.

She didn't expect to find any bargains, especially none suitable for Alfresco, but useful contacts could be made, old friends and acquaintances in the trade met, gossip exchanged. Besides which, there was always something new to be learned.

The fair was a popular day out, and not only for the trade, so that an hour later Nell was scarcely halfway round.

She drifted, exchanging news, talking shop, browsing.

141

'Hi there, Nell!' A voice screamed at her from behind a draped Chinese shawl. 'Are you pretending you don't know me or what?'

Nell peered round the embroidered silk. 'Winnie!'

'Come and have a cuppa.'

Winnie Vivash had made herself comfortable on a battered armchair, her enormous bottom, swathed in yards of floral skirt, overflowing it on either side. A gypsy blouse, a wealth of beads, a knitted coat of many colours and a scarf tied bandanna fashion round her unlikely black hair, completed her ensemble. Above her numerous double chins an engaging smile left Nell in no doubt as to her welcome. Winnie patted the empty bentwood chair that stood beside her.

'Come you, you look shagged out! In a manner of speaking, of course.'

Nell squeezed herself past the table that served as a counter. It was packed to bursting with every conceivable knick-knack: odd Clarice Cliff cups and saucers, costume jewellery, lace fans, Victorian beaded bags, scent bottles, brass oil lamps, needlework samplers and children's plates painted with Mabel Lucie Attwell fairies. She sat down, glad to get out of the crush.

'This is nice,' Winnie said. 'Have some coffee.' She filled a beaker from an outsize Thermos. 'Here we are then.'

'Hmm, thanks.' Nell cradled the beaker in her hands.

'Well, what's new then, old chum?' Winnie's eyes were embedded in great rosy mounds of flesh. They could twinkle benignly or become calculating slits according to the situation.

'Nothing much!' Nell lied. 'How about you?'

Winnie's generous frame heaved with laughter. 'Got myself an amazing new stud!' she said. 'Just wait till you see him. Though, mind, hands off!' Winnie's affairs were legendary. There was something about her superabundant flesh and her corresponding largeness of spirit that was highly seductive to men and in fact to women. She never lacked admirers, some of them extremely ardent and extremely young.

'Don't worry,' Nell said. 'I don't think our taste in men coincides.'

'You speak the truth there,' Winnie admitted. 'Now I could never fancy that Daniel of yours. I know he fancied *himself*, still does as I hear it, but I don't like men who think they're irresistible.' She turned to Nell who had buried her nose in the beaker. 'You don't mind me saying so, do you? But I know that was all over years ago. I expect you've got yourself a decent fella by this time.'

'Whatever his faults,' Nell said, bridling, 'I never thought that Daniel was more conceited than most men.'

'Not still carrying the old torch, are you? Now you have to get yourself a really nice bloke. A looker like you, it shouldn't be too hard.'

'How d'you know I haven't?'

'Aha. Do I smell romance? Good for you! Go on, drink up.'

Nell sipped. 'This coffee has brandy in it.'

'If you think I'm sitting here on my backside all day without a little fortification, you've another think coming. Not for anybody!' She chuckled. 'Speaking of Daniel, I suppose you heard about the brouhaha at Cornucopia?' She glanced slyly at Nell, fidgeting with the clusters of rings on her pudgy fingers.

'You mean about Flick leaving him? Yes, I heard.'

'So you know *who* she ran off with?'

'No, I don't think he . . .' A pause. 'No, I don't.'

Winnie got up to attend to a customer who bought a silver-topped scent bottle. Then she turned back to Nell.

'Yes, there was one hell of a shenanigans up there. Flick went off with Daniel's partner, would you believe? Whatisname – Simon. Mind you, he's as naïve as they come where women are concerned, but fancy him falling for her nonsense and sending the whole setup down the tubes like that!'

Warning bells rang loudly in Nell's head. Daniel had said nothing about Flick having run off with Simon, of all people. Quiet, unassuming Simon.

'The guy who makes up their antique pine – you remember Arthur? – well, he told me that the partnership has broken down. Simon wanted to withdraw most of his capital, though I'm not sure if he did. I should think it would leave Daniel in a bit of a spot. Anyway, now he's left without a live-in woman and a business partner. Poetic justice if you ask me.'

'Poor Daniel,' Nell said, wondering why Daniel hadn't told her this. Wounded pride perhaps.

'Poor Daniel, nuts!' Winnie dismissed Nell's sympathetic response out of hand. 'You want to watch he doesn't turn up on your doorstep and try to sweet-talk you into picking up the threads again, my girl.'

Suddenly Nell saw. Her blood turned to ice in spite of the hot coffee and brandy. For a moment she thought she might be sick all over Winnie's collection of bric-a-brac. Her friend was so near the mark that for a moment Nell thought she must have heard something. The reasons for Daniel's sudden attention became blindingly clear. Hadn't he even suggested marriage and, by definition, that she should go back into business together? But why couldn't he have told her the truth? Why had it been necessary to lie or at least withhold the true facts? Unless he felt that his motives wouldn't bear scrutiny, that in spite of his apparent sincerity he'd contrived a renewal of their former passionate relationship to gain access to her business acumen and her capital. Besides, knowing Daniel he would have needed someone to share his bed: any port in a storm. Good old Nell, he would have thought. She would never turn me away. She'll drop everything and help.

'Drop everything!' Nell murmured to herself. 'How apt!'

'Did you say something?' Winnie enquired, offering more coffee.

'No nothing,' Nell said. 'And no more coffee thanks.' The feeling of nausea was wearing off but she didn't dare drink any more of Winnie's concoction.

'I thought you would have heard the gossip.' Winnie eyed her closely.

Nell shrugged. 'It's nothing to me now,' she said. How good at dissimulation she was becoming! How well she was disguising her shock from Winnie while inside she burned with rage and humiliation! Daniel's motives were now all too apparent. He wanted to use her.

'Tell me about the new boyfriend, Winnie,' she said, clutching at straws.

'See for yourself.' Winnie pointed but just then another potential customer claimed her attention. The only familiar figure Nell could make out in the direction Winnie's finger had indicated was Hugh Daish. He had paused at a stand that dealt in old postcards and was examining several of them, glasses perched on the end of his nose. For some reason the thought of Hugh and Winnie was not to Nell's liking even though she was fond of them both independently. Somehow she'd always imagined Hugh as a loner and had the impression that he just *was*; that his life between their rare meetings stood still, which was quite ridiculous. For some reason she couldn't imagine him with a woman, at least not with Winnie Vivash. Immediately she felt ashamed of the thought. Winnie finished with her customer and turned back to Nell.

'Not Hugh?' Nell queried.

Winnie shrieked with laughter. 'Hugh Daish! Darling, no! *Much* too posh and civilized for me. No, you idiot. See the guy standing behind him, the size of a mini-bus?' She waved a well-rounded arm. 'Yoo-hoo, Sean!'

An immensely tall young man shouldered his way through the crowd towards them. He looked out of place, as if he would have been more at home on a rugby field.

'There we are then, darling,' Winnie cooed as the young hero bent across the table, greatly endangering its contents. He planted a kiss on Winnie's lips.

'Nell, meet Sean.'

He extended a hand like a bunch of pink bananas. 'Hi.'

'Be a love and get us some of those super cream doughnuts from Walter's tea bar,' Winnie coaxed. 'Here, I'll give you some money. Get one for yourself. Get a dozen!'

'None for me, thanks,' Nell said quickly. The thought of eating anything, let alone cream doughnuts, made her feel queasy again. 'I must go anyway. I've only seen half the stands.'

'Must you?' Winnie said.

Sean said, 'Cheers,' and plunged off in search of doughnuts.

145

Nell stood up to leave. 'Another time, Winnie. Thanks for the coffee.' She looked in the direction of Sean's departing back. 'By the way, he's gorgeous. Where do you find these handsome hunks?'

'They find me, believe it or not,' Winnie's round face was wreathed in smiles. 'Like codling moths to a pheromone trap.'

Nell laughed. 'How unpleasant you make that sound.'

She left Winnie after extending a vague invitation to dinner. Normally she would have set a date but she was finding it hard enough to handle the here and now, let alone anything in the future. In truth, she had no intention of seeing the remaining stands, she was desperate to get away from the crowd whose noise and movement now only served to make her feel worse. Her anxiety to escape propelled her headlong into a tweedy jacket.

'Whoops! Sorry.'

'Not at all. Glad I was in the way. Hallo, Nell.'

'Hugh!'

'Lovely to see you again.'

'Yes, well I was just leaving.' Realizing she sounded rudely abrupt, she smiled. 'You always seem to materialize out of nowhere like the Cheshire Cat,' she gabbled, 'then dematerialize again.'

'I do in fact have an independent existence in between, believe it or not,' he said, smiling, 'with which you do not, unfortunately, concern yourself.'

His comment confused her. She was not sure how to take it.

He said, 'I'm sure you haven't been able to escape being offered some of Winnie's lethal brew but would a cup of Walter's more humdrum tea be acceptable? Or perhaps some lunch? I believe his sandwiches are usually quite palatable.'

She was dying to sit down somewhere, anywhere. 'Yes,' she said, 'perhaps it would. Thank you.' She hadn't thought he'd noticed her tucked away behind Winnie's shawls and embroidered firescreens. 'Winnie's coffee has left me with a rather strange taste in my mouth.'

'It's a wonder you've a mouth left.'

146

Walter's white plastic chairs and tables looked familiar, like the ones Nell had seen at the auction. Perhaps Walter had picked them up there. Hugh found a place under an inappropriate sun umbrella and went to the counter to fetch tea, sandwiches and some shortbread.

'Walter's own,' he indicated the sugar-coated shortbread while folding his long frame into the plastic chair as he had at the auction. 'I liked the look of the doughnuts but they were absolutely mountainous. What I really appreciate about Devon hospitality is that it is always assumed that one hasn't eaten for at least a week.' He poured Nell's tea for her as if she were an invalid. 'Is that all right?'

'Perfect. How did you know?'

'Have a sandwich.' He poured tea for himself.

She helped herself to an egg and cress one. Inexplicably her appetite had returned. 'These are good,' she said. 'You know he makes all his stuff himself? All his cakes are homemade.'

Hugh nodded. 'His father used to be the baker in my village until the multiples took over.'

'And which is *your* village?' she said, teasing.

'Anstey. I thought you knew.'

'No. Why should I? To me you're a man of mystery.'

He smiled. 'Not much mystery about my humdrum existence, I'm afraid. But why don't you let me take you out there some time and dispel the "cloud of unknowing"?'

'Thanks, but . . .'

He leaned forward. 'Nell, are you all right?'

She nodded. 'Perfectly.' To prove it she took a slice of shortbread and bit into it. For a split second his eyes focused on her fingers as she licked the sugar off their tips.

'Then why don't you come with me now?' he said.

'Where to?' Everything felt as if it were being filtered through a thickish blanket. Nothing felt quite real.

'To Anstey. If you've seen all you want to see here, that is?'

'Perhaps I . . .' If she did indeed go back with Hugh, she thought, then at least she wouldn't be at home when Daniel came back. It would put off the agony of having to confront him

147

until she'd had time to assimilate the bad news properly.

'That's settled then,' Hugh said, taking her vacillation as acceptance. 'Finish your tea and we'll get moving.'

'I forgot,' she said. 'There's my van.'

'That's not a problem. I'll follow you home and then we'll go on from there in my car.'

Obediently she drank her tea. The lingering taste of the spiked coffee with Walter's ginger-coloured brew made her feel distinctly peculiar.

As they made for the exit they passed Winnie, who closed one eye and held up a saucy thumb at her. Nell hoped that Hugh hadn't noticed the gesture. Sean was sitting next to Winnie with one arm round her, eating a large doughnut.

Nell and Hugh drove back to Totnes in procession. She left the van in the narrow lane next to the shop and transferred to Hugh's old Volvo. He had left the Discovery at home, he said.

'Are you warm enough?' he asked as they set off. 'The heater's not quite right at the moment.'

'Seems fine to me,' she said. Something about his vigilance gave her a feeling of security which she hadn't experienced for a long time. If only he could have been Daniel, but Daniel with a perfectly reasonable explanation for his lack of candour. What a luxury it would have been to be going to Daniel's house rather than Hugh's, to look forward to an evening of closeness in the place where he lived. As it was he hadn't yet suggested it, although he'd boasted about what a gem of a house it was. A perfect small Regency rectory, sensitively restored, he'd said.

But she would have to put him out of her mind. She should have known that his motives for seeking her out would be squalid. How could she have been so gullible?

She and Hugh made small talk, about the fair, about the situation of Anstey in the Teign valley – general conversation, nothing personal. After they'd passed through the village of Anstey, Hugh turned off into an unmarked lane, through an open gate and steered the Volvo down a short drive.

'Here we are,' he said. 'Welcome to Chapel Abbey.'

It stood on a small knoll, overlooking the wooded Teign

valley, a small unpretentious country residence built of squared grey moorstone, its doors and windows painted white.

The front door was encased by a neat portico which in turn was flanked by long windows and a trimmed magnolia. Inside the outer door was an inner glass door; Hugh stood back for Nell to enter. Beyond was a small square hallway with a floor of polished elm planks; directly opposite them an oak staircase rose to the floor above, its subtle patina a result of two centuries of wear and polishing.

Hugh threw his Barbour on to a fine seventeenth-century blanket box and helped Nell off with her jacket. She removed the peaked wool cap she was wearing and ran her fingers through her hair.

'Come in and get warm.' Hugh led her into one of the rooms that led off the hall which was, as she expected, furnished with good antiques but not lavishly. Its panelled walls had been painted a very pale grey and above them an extravagant cornice sported deeply cut oak leaves and acorns.

Hugh kneeled by the dying fire and piled on more logs. 'More tea?' he asked her, sitting back on his heels as the wood caught. 'Or something stronger?' He scrutinized her as she sat hunched on the sofa. For some reason her posture suggested an animal which, fearing attack, seeks to make itself invisible.

She was wishing devoutly that she hadn't come. It had been a mistake. But she could hardly insist on going home straight away.

'Nell,' he went on, 'you don't look your usual sparkling self. Are you all right?' It was the second time he'd asked her.

'Sparkling! Is that how you see me?'

'Yes,' he said, as if it were a matter of fact. 'You always seem so full of energy and enthusiasm.' Failing to receive an answer to his enquiry, he checked the fire and stood up. 'Would you like to come into the kitchen and choose what you want? I think we have a variety of things on offer.'

She was glad of the diversion. Anything was better than perching either side of the fire making small talk.

The kitchen looked functional but somewhat soulless, as if no one spent time there. It possessed a gleaming fridge, an expensive cooker, an old pine table and a Welsh dresser. The slate floor seemed to be original. However, apart from a few dishes left to dry by the sink, it gave her no sense that the place was lived in, in the way Emmet's or Desna's or even her own, emphatically was.

Hugh opened a few cupboards and the fridge, none of which was as well stocked as she'd been led to believe, and produced a slab of Sainsbury's fruit cake and some Earl Grey tea. He arranged them on a tray with cups and saucers, Minton bone china, she noticed, and carried them back to the sitting room where the fire was now blazing. From the window she could see part of the drive and a lawn punctuated with mature specimen trees; the lawn sloped away to woods already veiled in palest green; beneath their canopy the River Teign gurgled away from the great sponge-like bogs on the moor: the birthplace of the East and West Dart too, which flowed eventually through Totnes.

Hugh poured the tea and cut two slices of fruit cake.

'Why is an eighteenth-century house called Chapel Abbey?' she asked, making conversation.

'This part was tacked on to the ruins of a Cistercian abbey,' Hugh explained, sitting down and balancing his cup rather precariously on his bony knee. 'You can still see what's left of its walls in parts of the house. I'll show you afterwards if you're interested.'

'Yes, I'd like that,' she said, meaning it. Even in her present state of depression, history always had a particular fascination. She drank her tea and its mild bergamot aroma soothed her palate as the fire soothed her body and as Hugh's presence, she had to admit it, calmed her jangled nerves. He told her about the history of Chapel Abbey: of its dissolution and how it passed into the not unbiased hands of its accusing lawyer; how the house he'd built on the ruins had itself later burned to the ground. A new edifice had been raised in the eighteenth century and this had later been acquired by a successful neighbouring farmer, Hugh's great-great-grandfather.

'After that things didn't go so well,' Hugh said. 'Bits of the estate had to be sold off. Finally my father went into publishing and rented the land out. Fortunately he was better at publishing than his father had been at farming.'

'Is he still alive?' Nell asked. She ate a crumb of cake for appearances' sake. She wasn't at all hungry.'

'No. Both my parents died in 1988.'

'And you went into the antique trade.'

Hugh looked surprised. 'No. What gave you that idea?'

'Come on, Hugh! Why go to auctions? Besides, you're good at it.'

'It's only a hobby. I'm a publisher. I took over my father's business.'

Nell stared at him, astonished.

'You've heard of the Chapel Abbey Press?'

'Now you mention it, yes. Guide books, local history, that sort of thing? But isn't that *Matthew* Daish?'

Hugh's lugubrious face cracked into a grin. 'I never changed the name. I thought you knew what I did,' he said. 'But then, why should you? I keep forgetting we hardly know each other. It's just that I've always thought of you as an old friend.' This last comment he knew not to be strictly true. His feelings for her refused to be fitted into quite that category.

They finished their tea and Hugh led Nell through to the back of the house, beyond the kitchen into what had been sculleries and dairies in the time when the house had servants. Here the walls were not granite like the newer building, but massive blocks of dark red sandstone, quarried locally nearly a thousand years before by the monks themselves. The corners and details were blurred with age, the windows an arrangement of narrow slits that looked out on to a courtyard where a stalwart arch still stood, withstanding the ravages of time and King Henry's henchmen. All it harboured now was Hugh's Discovery, an anachronism in its surroundings. The courtyard was of mossy cobbles, originally brought weary miles from Budleigh Salterton by horse and cart.

'Now you must see the humble home of the Chapel Abbey

151

Press,' Hugh said. 'Then I'll show you the rest of the house, if you'd like that?'

Nell hesitated. It occurred to her for the first time that the house was miles from anywhere and she was alone with a man she hardly knew.

'Perhaps the press,' she said. 'Then I really should be getting back.'

The Chapel Abbey Press consisted of one room at the side of the house with a tranquil view of an orchard where a frosting of blossom was already apparent. The room itself was the most lived-in she'd seen so far, being crammed with shelves overflowing with files. Two Apple Macs stood on a large table, beside them a laser printer, a photocopying machine, something Hugh told her was an OCR and a cupboard that housed a large slide library.

'That's why I collect old photographs and postcards,' Hugh said. He reached into his pocket and drew out a collection he'd bought at the fair. 'Devon then and now,' he smiled, showing them to her. 'Set me back thirty pounds for this lot.'

'Thirty pounds for a few old postcards!' she said, looking at a picture of a crowded charabanc in front of what Hugh assured her was the Market House in Dartmouth.

'Worth it to me. Illustrations for the books. Some of my writers are too elderly to seek them out for themselves.'

Nell turned down any further exploration of the house. She was getting restless.

'Another time perhaps,' she said. 'I think I should be going.'

'So soon! I hoped you might stay to a meal. I mean a proper one.'

Nell made her excuses and Hugh reluctantly helped her on with her coat. There was a certain bleakness in her expression that was prompting him to ask again if there was something amiss. He almost spoke but was interrupted by the sound of a car outside on the drive.

Through the glass door Nell saw a large estate car pull up. It was full of Labradors and children. A stocky grey-haired woman struggled out of the driving seat and at the same moment the rear door was flung open and a small girl of about seven got out.

'Excuse me.' Hugh left Nell and opened the front door.

'Daddy! You're in!' The small girl bounced up the steps to meet him.

'Hallo, darling. I thought you weren't due home for ages yet.'

The grey-haired woman came up to the front door. 'Sorry about this,' she boomed. 'We dropped by on the off chance you'd be in. They've whipped Andrea off to hospital with a suspected miscarriage so I've been trying to deliver all the party guests home early. I do apologize, I hope it won't put you out.' She caught sight of Nell in the hall. 'Of course I'll take Laura back if it's inconvenient. She's no trouble, bless her. I'm afraid Henry's birthday celebrations came to rather an abrupt conclusion . . .'

'It's perfectly all right, Enid, I'm glad I was here,' Hugh said, resting his hand on the child's shoulder as she stood beside him, having claimed his other hand. 'I'm sorry about Andrea. I hope it won't prove serious.'

Enid was back in the car almost before he had stopped speaking. There were shouts of 'Goodbye', she reversed and then the car shot back up the drive, its rear window full of waving hands and tails.

Nell hitched the strap of her bag on to her shoulder. She was furious. Furious for allowing herself to be bamboozled with all that talk of old abbeys, monks, ancient family history, even the family business while small matters like children and presumably a wife were conveniently overlooked. Evidently Hugh hadn't expected the child back. How long would he have kept up the charade of being an unencumbered male? she wondered.

But Hugh appeared unconscious of any oversight on his part.

'Laura, come and meet Nell,' he said. 'Nell, this is my daughter.'

The child was slight but probably tall for her age, though Nell didn't know much about these things. She wore her blonde hair in a single plait, her pale skin was flushed with excitement. When she first caught sight of Nell a darker pink had suffused her small, pointed face.

She put out her hand politely. 'Hallo,' she said, shyly.

Back in the flat Nell kicked off her shoes and crouched by the gas fire, waiting for its heat to warm her. Morgan came and pushed his head into her hand, puffing out his whiskers and mewing gruffly to remind her that he hadn't had any lunch. The routine was that she would feed him only at breakfast and supper but he had never got the hang of it.

She wrapped her arms round him and held him against her chest. 'Why do you males have to be so devious?' she asked him. 'What's so hard about being open about things?'

Morgan struggled to get down. He was perfectly open about what *he* wanted; in any case, he had lost his claim to be of the male sex several years previously.

Hugh had explained about Laura on the way back, with Laura herself sitting behind them ostensibly reading *Ride to the Rescue*, but no doubt with her young ears tuned to what was being said. Nell supposed that Hugh's account of the marriage and subsequent divorce was being edited accordingly.

'Helen left us four years ago,' he said. 'Now she lives in America. I spent some time over there recently so that Laura could visit her mother.' He half turned in order to bring his daughter into the conversation. 'Otherwise we rub along quite well, don't we, darling?'

Laura said quietly, 'I like it better here. It was really boring with Mummy. Here I can go riding at Henry's.'

'Henry's mother, Andrea, runs a riding school,' Hugh said, 'so I can't claim to be the only attraction.' He laughed, an unexpectedly infectious sound. Nell couldn't remember having heard it before.

All the same, she was feeling sore. There was apparently no wife now but for Hugh to have suddenly produced a daughter like a rabbit out of a hat gave her the distinct impression that she was deliberately being made a fool of; the intimate chatter and shared jokes between father and daughter grated. Only once did she experience the slightest twinge of leniency towards Hugh and that was when she realized his presence at the antiques fair was because he'd been made redundant for the day, since Laura evidently had her own busy social life. He had been at a loose end. Just as she had been. All the same, she remembered that there had been clues at the house for anyone who wasn't too self-absorbed, to see: a child's book in the sitting room; a row of small vests and knickers drying on a rack in the kitchen. How could she not have registered them at the time?

She got up to feed Morgan. Hugh must have married soon after she had started living with Daniel and divorced about the time she and Daniel had split up. She wondered if it was too fanciful to believe that these events were connected in some way. Yes, it *was* too fanciful.

She turned on Classic FM and scraped cat food out of the tin into Morgan's bowl. The news came on – terrible wars, pitiless killings, genocides and famines of epic proportions. How could the human race bear the guilt? And here she was doling out precious protein to her cat and worrying about her love life. She put Morgan's saucer on the floor and stood gazing out of the window at the slate-hung wall opposite. Why especially should she hope to be happy in the midst of all this misery? It didn't add up. Yet she did; everybody did, didn't they?

In the other room, the telephone bleeped. Daniel. She took her time answering.

But it wasn't Daniel. It was Mo. Nell felt both disappointed and reprieved.

'Hallo, darling. Just rang to see how you are. I don't seem to have heard from you recently.'

'I'm fine. How are things going with Persis? Did she arrive safely?'

'After a few snarl-ups, yes.'

'Is she nice?'

Mo hesitated. With Nell she would have to watch her words. 'She's not easy. Rather selfish, in fact.'

'I thought all artists were supposed to be selfish. Except you, of course!'

'According to her I'm not a proper artist,' Mo said gruffly.

155

'Oh dear, Mo. It all sounds a bit of a disaster. When's she going home?'

'I've no idea.'

'Can't you farm her out to Desna for a spell?'

'Can you imagine what Roy would say? As you know, I've never quite cut the mustard as far as Roy's concerned and I'm damned sure Persis wouldn't! I always have this vague feeling with him that I've blotted the family escutcheon in some irredeemable way.'

'As bad as that!' Nell laughed.

There was a slight pause. Then, 'I expect she'll want to see you some time,' Mo said.

'We'll meet at Desna's if she's staying until Easter.'

'You *are* coming then?'

'I suppose I won't be able to get out of it. But you know I can't stand these family dos.'

'Don't underestimate the value of family, my girl,' Mo said briskly. 'You never know when you might need them!'

'Families are fine . . . singly. But there's something terrifying about them en masse.'

'Don't be feeble, Nellie. If you feel like that why don't you bring some nice man for moral support?'

Nell gave a sarcastic snort. 'Oh yes? And where do you suggest I find one? Gateway?'

Another pause. 'There isn't anyone special at the moment then?'

'I've decided to follow your example and be celibate.'

'But I thought . . .'

'Yes?'

'Nothing,' Mo said. 'Now listen, Nell. It's quite possible that Persis may drop in on you before Easter. I've told her you're very busy in the shop but she doesn't heed what I tell her, naturally.'

'That's all right. I don't mind.'

'I just thought I'd warn you.'

'What's the matter, Mo? She's not as bad as all that, is she?'

Mo was suddenly brisk. 'No, of course not.'

Nell's doorbell rang and Mo's faintly mystifying manner was

immediately forgotten. 'Look, I have to go. There's someone at the door.'

'Goodbye, darling.'

Before she could replace the receiver the bell rang again. She had been sitting on the floor, her boots kicked off. Through the glass of the door a shadowy figure waited. She padded across and opened the door.

'You took your time,' was Daniel's greeting. He stepped inside and took her in his arms. 'Darling, where on earth have you been? I've been hanging around since just after lunch.' He attempted a kiss but she avoided his mouth.

Undismayed, he went through into the sitting room and held out his hands to the fire.

'God, that's better. It's freezing out there now.' He held out one hand to her. 'Come here, Nellie. At least don't be stand-offish now that you *are* here.'

Instead she sat on the sofa facing him, appraising him as coolly as she could.

'Why didn't you tell me that it was Simon that Flick had run off with?' she said without preamble.

He took it well. 'I thought I had. Why? What difference does it make?'

'Quite a lot I should have thought. I understand he took his capital with him. Or that he wants to.'

'Who told you that?' Daniel remained standing in front of the fire.

'Never mind. Is it true?'

'He wanted to start up on his own somewhere else so as not to queer my pitch. North Devon, I believe. He's a decent bloke, you know, even if he did go behind my back with Flick. But I blame her for that. He's an ace with money but a bit green where women are concerned.'

'I'm sure Simon is a "decent bloke", as you put it, but doesn't it leave the business in a bit of a spot?'

'Cornucopia was doing well enough to survive without Simon, fortunately. In any case, I tend to roll with the punches, as you know.'

'How? No business can survive a knock like that, especially these days.'

'You underestimate me, Nell. In any case, Simon has agreed not to take everything out immediately. Not that he couldn't. Cornucopia is perfectly viable without him.' Impulsively, Daniel covered the space between them, flinging himself on the sofa beside her. He took her hand. 'For God's sake, Nellie! What sort of rat d'you think I am to expect you to come in with me if Cornucopia was on the skids? You know it's entirely up to you what you do with your money. I just want to marry you, that's all!' He took her head between his hands and looked into her eyes. 'To be perfectly honest, I couldn't care a shit whether you put your money into Cornucopia or not. What's important is that we make a fresh start together, and this time I wouldn't want anything – *anything* – to mess it up. Darling, I know it'll take a while for you to trust me again. I don't blame you for being cautious. But I'm such an impatient bugger once I've set my heart on something . . .'

He pulled her towards him and put his lips on her mouth. 'Understand this, Nellie,' he breathed against her skin. 'You don't have to do anything at all you don't want to. Anything you don't feel completely comfortable about. I leave that decision entirely up to you.'

Of course he was right. It was worth remembering that nobody was compelling her to act against her will. She was a big girl now. Dammit! Some would say that she was already practically middle-aged. In any case, she was old enough to make her own decisions. It had been a storm in a teacup. She was suddenly ashamed of betraying her lingering mistrust of him.

'You'll have to give me time,' she said.

'Not too much, Nellie, darling!'

CHAPTER TWELVE

It was eleven at night and Emmet sat alone in her kitchen feeling worse than she'd ever felt in her life. It was a very strange experience. She was never ill; Nell said she had the constitution of a herd of buffalo. She was well aware of the fact that she would be better off in bed but even standing up and walking across the room didn't seem to be an option.

The day had started badly. Tom had made a fuss about going to school and as a result she was late collecting Dinah's two, late delivering the four children at the school gates and late getting back. Hurrying to feed the dogs she had cut her hand on the tin. Blood poured from it in a copious stream and the tin of dog food crashed to the floor and rolled under the table. The dogs roused themselves to inspect its contents and the crow croaked hoarsely in its cage. The cats yawned in their sleep or hurried away from the scene of the disturbance.

At the sink Emmet struggled with the tap and allowed icy water to gush into the gaping wound on the ball of her thumb. She was not squeamish but she could see that it looked bad, would certainly need a stitch. She gritted her teeth against the pain as she watched the pink-stained water spiral away down the plughole.

With the blood still more or less streaming she wrenched open a cupboard and grabbed the first-aid box. Inside was cotton wool, which she formed into a vast pad and, using teeth and fingers, managed to tape into place. She looked at her watch, the strap of which was stained darkly, and guessed that she might just catch the nurse at the village surgery. What a sod that it wasn't Barney's day for helping or he could have driven

159

her; as it was she would have to manage by herself. At least she wouldn't have to worry about Tom and Beth. They had lunch at school, thank heaven.

She retrieved the tin of dog food – it wouldn't hurt them to wait an extra half-hour for their breakfast – and struggled into her shabby green Barbour. Taking a fresh pad of cotton wool, she swept up the car keys and slammed out of the back door.

She was away an hour while she had her hand stitched, with dire warnings about tetanus jabs from the nurse.

'No need to preach to the converted,' Emmet complained. 'You know I'm well up to date with those. God, I do feel lousy though!'

'It's shock,' the nurse assured her. 'I'll give you some painkillers. But do try not to get that hand dirty. I'll do another dressing for you tomorrow.'

Emmet drove home cautiously, changing gear with the tips of her fingers, thankful that it wasn't her right hand that was damaged. The cut throbbed painfully, in fact she didn't feel at all good. Now that she thought about it she had woken up that morning feeling distinctly peculiar. Back in the kitchen she made herself a strong cup of tea and, reluctantly, took two of the painkillers the nurse had given her. She didn't approve of taking tablets. She sat at the table sipping her tea, her left hand an amorphous white lump in her lap. It wasn't such a cold day but she felt frozen to her bones, unusual for her, for she *never* felt the cold. She dragged her chair nearer to the Rayburn and leaned tiredly on the rail.

The mallard paddled back into the kitchen. It was supposed to have been banished to the yard but it availed itself of every sneaky opportunity of returning to the pleasant warmth of its convalescence. It settled down under Emmet's chair. Earwig, the bull terrier, laid his head on Emmet's knee, gazing at her soulfully with his pink-rimmed eyes as if sympathizing with her plight. He knew about bad times, having been beaten and starved when he was young and finally shut up by his owners while they went away on holiday. Emmet fondled his tattered chamois leather ears.

'I'll feed you in a minute, old chap,' she told him. 'It serves me right for being in too much of a hurry. How could I have been so stupid?'

She fished in her pocket for a tissue. 'Now I'm getting a cold into the bargain. Bugger it!' The tissue came out and with it an unopened letter which had been there since yesterday and which she'd forgotten. She knew it was from Maurice, an impeccable product of his expensive laser printer. Maurice never came to see her when a letter or the telephone would do. He would have faxed her if she'd had a machine to receive it on.

She opened the letter with difficulty and spread it on her knee. It was short.

Emmet, my dear,

I wonder if you consider it absolutely necessary to enlist the services of a handyman to sustain what I believe is, always has been as I understand it, a non-profitmaking hobby? [How on earth did he know about Barney? she wondered.] If your singular variety of animal husbandry can be considered in these days of market forces and private franchises, to be a gainful occupation and no longer a drain on our joint resources, I will, of course, wholeheartedly withdraw my implied criticism and offer my apologies. However, if this is not the case, I look forward to hearing some justification of this additional expense, or perhaps that this was a purely temporary expedient. I hope the children are well. I will call for them on the Tuesday after Easter as arranged at about 10.00 a.m.

Yours, as ever, Maurice.

Emmet allowed the paper to drift to the floor where the duck pecked at it hopefully. In spite of the pain in her hand and, now she came to think about it, several other places, she let out a groan of incredulous laughter. Dear old Maurice, she thought, what a bad day that was for you when you convinced yourself, or were convinced by others, of your own importance, believing your single, undisturbed existence was the pivotal point of the universe. She might answer the letter or she might not, but certainly not while she felt as ill as she did just now.

That morning she went about her tasks in the orchard, the yard and the kitchen as if she were on automatic pilot; feeding, cleaning and tending the injured animals with her bandaged hand stuffed into a rubber glove, which didn't make her tasks any easier.

Feeding the patient dogs at last, she thought about Maurice, perhaps to take her mind off how miserable she was feeling. She had imagined herself deliriously happy in those early days when she had been in love with Maurice rather than simply loving him, as she did now. He had changed, of course – perhaps she had too. Once he even had a sense of humour, albeit mordant. She had been in her second year at the university when they met; he had been teaching in the English Department and she had admired him remotely from the perspective of the lecture hall and group tutorial. He was known for distancing himself from the crowd, certainly not one for sharing a pint after lectures with either colleagues or students. Privately she considered him to be rather shy and defended his character against criticism; he was said to be arrogant and elitist. He had never confessed to hearing that she had championed him in the face of these accusations but something, at any rate, had prompted him to overcome his alleged shyness and ask her out.

Her friend, a girl called Lizzie, had her own ideas. 'I'll tell you why,' she said dismissively. 'One: your beautiful blonde curls. Two: your particular brand of unthreatening femininity. And three: your renowned affinity with lame ducks.' Lizzie liked lists.

Maurice had been kind, yet tentative, had not jumped on her like the students she'd been out with, all anxious to lose their own virginity or deprive her of hers. With Maurice she talked of life, books and writing. At least Maurice talked and she listened, entranced. He had a beautiful voice. Mostly he talked of his own writing but where she was able to tease out meaning from his convoluted prose, she could see that his sympathies were of the right sort. Later she came to the conclusion that these were cerebral rather than visceral.

She was still convinced that she was one of the very few people who understood Maurice, or even bothered to try. Mo certainly didn't understand *her* when she suddenly abandoned her course and married him. His first novel was published very soon afterwards, to exaggerated acclaim in some quarters and violent hostility in others. At least it had not been ignored and it had showered them with more money than either of them had dreamed of. On the strength of it they had bought the run-down Drake's Farm with its few acres of land on which stood an amusing wooden shack. This was immediately designated as a holiday chalet, which would usefully augment their income. They hoped to refurbish the house and create a country idyll, an ivory tower where Maurice could write without the nuisance (as Maurice saw it) of having to teach a bunch of semiliterate students.

Unfortunately the money had run out sooner than they believed possible, and with the work on the farmhouse only half completed. Maurice's second book restored their fortunes sufficiently for them to survive Emmet's pregnancy with reasonable equanimity, but since there were no more funds for paid help there was nothing for it but for Emmet to do it herself, not only painting and decorating, but plumbing and carpentry as well. The original intention was that she would write too but her days were so exhausting that all she could do after them was to crash into bed like a felled tree.

But she had never once felt as bad as she did today. Normally she was so full of energy that she needed only a few hours' sleep a night. Giving birth to Tom and in due course to Beth, had turned out to be a breeze, no trouble at all. But by the time Beth arrived the kitchen at Drake's Farm had become a magnet for all kinds of injured, unwanted or stray animals. Emmet found that although she was incapable of turning away the creatures that came to her door in a state of need, she fortunately had a fearless knack of healing them. Maurice withdrew to one of the attic rooms. He said the pandemonium caused by the heterogeneous collection of babies and animals was insufferable.

'And you're beginning to treat me as if I was one of your bloody lame ducks,' he accused her, thrusting a finger against his torn jersey. 'I'm your husband, remember!'

'I have tried to see that you're not disturbed,' she said aggrieved. 'I love you. You're very special.'

'And you love the cats, dogs, ducks and God knows what with the same indiscriminate intensity.'

Emmet was puzzled. 'Of course I love them. Love isn't an unrenewable resource, you know.'

It was the nearest to a row they'd ever been. Soon afterwards, rain had poured through the attic ceiling on to Maurice's word processor and he had decided to move his study to the bungalow, returning only for meals and to sleep. A month or two later he made a bed up there for the times he worked late. Eventually he had a freezer installed in the minute kitchen and filled it with frozen roast turkey platter, seafood tagliatelle and chicken samosas so that his unpredictable mealtimes would not disrupt the household. There was never any bad feeling over these arrangements. They simply happened just as their sex life simply didn't. It had never been quite the overpowering experience that either expected anyway, so neither of them missed it.

Emmet was relieved rather than dismayed by their virtual separation. It was a strain having to conform to Maurice's exacting standards of intellectual dialogue while at the same time mopping up Tom's spilt cereal and breast-feeding Beth. It wasn't that Emmet wasn't extremely fond of Maurice or that she didn't appreciate his talent; it was simply easier when he wasn't around. She believed that real love made allowances, permitted people to be themselves; she would be the last person to interfere with her husband's right to function in the only way he knew how.

Now she was alone with her illness. It was midday before she finished the tasks she usually completed by ten thirty. Then she sought the comfort of the Rayburn again and collapsed on a chair. By lunchtime her throat was like a piece of cuttleshell and her body was firey and freezing by turns. She rang up Dinah to see if she could possibly swap turns for fetching the children.

'I'll be fine tomorrow,' she assured Dinah. 'I recover fast.'

'No problem,' Dinah said sympathetically. 'How will you manage with the animals?'

'More slowly than usual, that's all.'

'Take care. Let me know if there's anything I can do.'

Tom was thoroughly put out by the changed arrangements. 'It was your turn to fetch us,' he said accusingly. 'We were expecting you!'

'I know, darling. It couldn't be helped,' Emmet said patiently. 'It's just that the nurse said I wasn't to use my hand too much just for today.'

Emmet eased a rubber glove over the bandage and started on the accumulated washing up. Her nose was running like a tap and she sniffed sporadically to prevent drops cascading into the bowl, though some were falling on the piece of paper that Beth was flapping about just under her chin.

'Look, Mummy! Do look,' Beth repeated like a refrain. 'Mrs Bennet said my drawing was very good and you won't even look at it!'

'I'll look at it in a minute, Beth. Really I will. My hands are wet just now and I don't want to ruin it, do I?'

Beth stumped off into the sitting room to show her drawing to Mogsy. Emmet spoke to Tom in a tone she hoped would make him feel grown up and responsible. 'Look, darling. It looks as if you'll have to be specially helpful today. My hand is going to make things a bit difficult.'

'What have you done to it anyway?' Tom asked suspiciously, as if she had bandaged it as a ruse to get him to do more than usual.

'I cut it on a tin.' Emmet lifted her arm and let her nose drip on to her sleeve.

'Which tin?'

'Does it matter which tin?' Emmet was determined to remain cheerful.

'Did the doctor bandage it up then?' Tom was not slow to realize that it was a professional job.

'The nurse did.'

'Then you drove to the doctor's, right?' Tom said with withering logic.

'Yes, darling. I wish you wouldn't say "right" after everything.' He had got into the habit since he'd been friendly with Lee. 'Could you go and give the animals their water now? It's not much to ask.'

'So why couldn't you drive to school?' Tom persisted.

'I told you why! Now go and do the water. Please! Or nobody's going to get any tea!' Emmet shook the surplus water off her gloves irritably and picked up a drying-up cloth. She sneezed explosively, dropped the cloth and reached for a tissue. Tom stood his ground.

'Why can't Barney do the water?'

'You know as well as I do that it's not his day.' Emmet felt her face grow radish red. Sweat burst out of every pore. 'For goodness' sake!' she screeched suddenly. 'Stop arguing and give me a bit of help, Tom!' Her voice turned into a rasping whisper.

Tom went outside, murmuring rebelliously, the more so because such outbursts from Emmet were practically unheard of. The evening did not improve. The worse Emmet felt, it seemed, the more the children resisted all her attempts to get them to bed early.

It wasn't until ten o'clock that she finally managed it. She had some urgent correspondence that she knew would have to be attended to at once; applications to the Department of the Environment for the renewal of licences to keep wildlife (in particular the birds of prey), orders for veterinary supplies, a reply to an organization who wanted her to give a talk about the sanctuary (no fee offered). There was also the article she was preparing for a woman's magazine for which she had, as yet, to find a new, and if possible entertaining as well as serious angle. She had thought she might write about the night when Houdini escaped from his box, climbed the stairs and found a warm haven in her bed. She had been awakened by his prickles in the small of her back.

Normally none of this would have been a problem. She would

have worked until one or two in the morning, fitting in the checking and feeding of the more vulnerable of the rescued creatures as well. Tonight was different, which was why she was still hunched in her chair by the Rayburn at eleven o'clock.

Her head felt as if it were being pounded by a hundred malicious hammers, her nose and eyes were streaming, her hand hurt and every time she got up to make herself more coffee the floor shifted wildly under her feet. Sleep, she decided, would put her right, she was sure she would feel better in the morning if she could just get to her feet.

Summoning up her will she made the attempt. The room swam and she collapsed back into the chair. What on earth could be wrong with her? She put her head between her hands and was dimly aware that the back door had been flung open.

'I was passing and I saw the light so I came in on the off chance of a cup of coffee. I know you go to bed late. Didn't you hear me knock . . .?' She recognized Barney's voice but couldn't seem to do anything about it.

'What's up with you?' he said. 'You look like a dead dog.'

The live dogs were already greeting him with their usual enthusiasm in spite of having been fast asleep.

'I think I have flu,' she said. 'You better get your own coffee.'

'Never mind that! Shouldn't you be getting your head down?' He stood over her, his jeans and body warmer paint-stained as usual.

'Yes, I suppose so.' She remained where she was.

'Want a hand?'

'No!' she said as firmly as she could.

'Please yourself,' he said airily. He opened the lid of the Rayburn and dragged the kettle across. 'Look, you go and crash out and I'll bring you a hotty and a drink. Got any lemons and honey? My gran used to swear by lemon and honey.'

'Somewhere,' she said vaguely.

'You *are* in a bad way,' he said, laughing.

She crept upstairs to bed. Her bedroom looked out on to the garden and doubled as an office. In the corner there was an old desk piled high with papers. Next to it a bookcase overflowed with books, and cupboards she had built herself contained her miscellaneous collection of jeans, shirts and jerseys. The only mirror was insignificant and in an inconvenient place. Her bedside table held a lamp but had otherwise almost disappeared under a landslide of books, a great many of them on some aspect of animal husbandry.

She undressed, leaving her clothes in a pile on the floor, and crept into bed. She shivered. The heating in the bedrooms was not very efficient, a fact she'd never noticed before.

Barney arrived with a hot-water bottle and a large glass of lemon drink.

'Any aspirins?' he asked.

'They're downstairs,' she said. She wished he would go away. Instead he went to fetch the painkillers that the nurse had given her.

'What did you do to your hand?' he demanded to know, passing her a tablet to take with the scalding hot lemon and honey.

'Cut it on a tin.'

'Has the doc seen it?'

'Yes.' Then sarcastically croaked, 'My God, Barney, you'll make someone a wonderful wife.'

He looked hurt. 'I'm only trying to make sure you're all right since you didn't seem to be making much of a fist of it yourself.'

'Sorry. Yes, I'm being feeble, I know.' This was a very strange situation, she thought, hoping that he wouldn't choose this moment to make a pass at her. In any case, she was almost past caring.

He picked up her clothes, folded them and put them on a chair. She watched him out of the corner of her eye. It was as if he did this everyday. Perhaps he did. She had never enquired about a wife or girlfriend. Or boyfriend.

'I'll push off now,' he said. 'But I'll come in a bit earlier tomorrow.'

'There's no need.'

'It is one of my usual mornings, you know.'

'I know. But I'll be fine by tomorrow.'

'Pull the other one! Everyone's got this bug in the village and it's a bugger.' She felt slightly better already, just knowing that there would be someone to do the animals if by chance she wasn't fine by tomorrow.

CHAPTER THIRTEEN

'I'm going over to see if I can help,' Mo told Desna over the phone.

'Will you stay?'

'I'll see how bad she is. You know Emmet, she'll never admit defeat so I'm expecting the worst. I only found out about it by chance when I rang to discuss the arrangements for Easter. She could hardly speak, poor girl.'

'I'll take you in the car. I'd go myself but you know Roy and I are fetching Rupert this afternoon.'

'Don't worry. I'll bike it. Less complicated.'

'I do hope they don't all have flu over Easter. It wouldn't be the same without Emmet and the children.'

'I'm sure they'll be all right by then. Give Rupert my love.'

'Of course.' Desna felt an inner glow at the thought of having her son home again. The family complete. From the first she had hated the idea of sending him away to school but Roy had insisted. 'Make a man of him,' he'd said.

'What about Persis? Would she like to come here for lunch? I can easily fetch her and take her back.'

There was a pause. 'I think she's planning to go to Totnes to see Nell.'

'Nell?' Desna said. 'Why Nell?'

'Why not?' Mo replied testily.

'No reason at all. I just thought . . .' What she thought was that, as the eldest, she should have had the privilege of entertaining Persis first. It wasn't through lack of trying on her part. 'Look, I'll ring you when we get back this evening.'

Desna slid the aerial of her portable telephone back into its housing and replaced the handset. From upstairs came the distant sound of Carol hoovering. While she had been speaking to Mo Desna had wandered over to the window to look out on the small secluded terrace which the family thought of as Desna's private place. In the summer she frequently took cushions and her black coffee outside to sit on the stone bench, one of Nell's acquisitions, and think and plan in peace. She had planted a Pink Perpetue to swarm over the balustrade and a wisteria against the high wall that enclosed one side of the terrace; steps led down to a flower and herb garden and beyond that she and the gardener raised vegetables in the walled kitchen garden. She could just see the old greenhouses, now refurbished, which stood against a background of pink brick. Behind the wall the trees that screened the river were fuzzy with new green.

Part of her mind was busy with a scheme for softening the lines of the terrace still further with containers of summer flowers: pale yellow rock rose, anthemis and cornflowers. Here she had completely free rein for Roy insisted that the garden overlooked by the main rooms and the conservatory should be severely formal; the terrace and the lawns, with the trees and river as backdrop. She could see his point of view, especially now that the space would be needed for the marquee in July. All the same she was hoping that he would agree to some stone urns on the terrace itself which could be filled with cascades of flowers for the wedding.

This reminded her that now they were almost sure of the colours, she should make another call to Bonne Bouche to discuss flowers. At least she'd got Harriet to accompany her to Totnes yesterday evening to see the dressmaker, Sandra Gillimore. And at least there had been a provisional agreement about the colour and design of the dress.

'The straight lines would suit you, darling. And that exquisite warm ivory tint makes the most of your skin.'

'She certainly has the figure for these classic lines,' the dressmaker agreed. 'Not everyone can take them.'

'I think the colour makes me look washed out,' Harriet said

when Desna, holding a sample of pale silk against her daughter's chin, demanded a response.

'Not when you're wearing a warm foundation and a little blusher,' Sandra Gillimore opined.

'But I don't wear make-up.'

'But surely for such an important occasion . . .' Sandra abandoned what she had been going to say, warned by a glance from Desna. It seemed to say, 'Leave it to me. I'll bring her round in time.'

'Now all we have to decide are the bridesmaids' dresses,' Desna said.

Sandra did some little sketches, suggesting ideas. Fiddled with swatches of silk.

'I like the grey.' It was the only opinion Harriet had so far ventured.

'Grey!' Desna cried. Sandra screwed up her mouth and said, 'It's a possibility.'

'But grey!'

It shouldn't be too difficult to win Harriet round, Desna thought. They hadn't even finally agreed about who the bridesmaids were to be, except for Tess, Faith and Beth. She didn't know about Faith but at least Beth with her aureole of thistledown hair would make an angelic flower girl, even in grey. Tom would be an altogether different matter. When she'd tentatively suggested a role for Tom, Emmet had been quite forthright. 'Not a snowball's chance in hell,' were her actual words. Desna was still working on Harriet to take the Wakehams' fourteen-year-old twins as well.

Desna's second appointment with the doctor was at ten. She spent a few minutes cubing lamb and slicing onion before putting it into a bowl with wine and lemon juice to marinade. Rupert had specially asked for kebabs. He liked food that presented some kind of physical challenge. She had ordered lobster for tomorrow.

Carol came downstairs. 'Would you like me to do the sitting-room windows now?' she asked. It was part of their agreement that she cleaned the inside of the windows only. Naturally

173

Desna had a firm to do the outsides.

'Thank you, Carol. I shall be leaving in a minute. I'll leave your coffee things ready before I go.' Mrs Hindmarch was the only employer Carol knew of who provided real coffee rather than instant.

Desna thoughtfully enquired after Carol's husband, Mike, and Davy, the little boy, and how the OU course was going, before fetching her jacket and going out to the car.

Sally Bright looked up from her VDU screen, smiling reassuringly, as Desna walked into her office. For a moment she shuffled papers; her blonde hair swung. 'Good morning, Mrs Hindmarch. How are you?'

'That's what I want you to tell me,' Desna said with a hint of asperity.

The doctor grinned. 'Sorry. Automatic greeting. Right then, I have the results here and I'm happy to say that everything is absolutely normal. You're fighting fit. Your blood pressure's slightly up but it's nothing to worry about.'

'I see,' Desna said slowly.

'All the same,' Sally Bright continued, 'I think we should keep the situation under review. I believe I said last time that I saw nothing to be gained at present from HRT but that can change. Did I ask you if you were anxious about anything?'

'Yes, you did.' Desna tried to keep the impatience out of her voice. After all, the cat-napping had started weeks ago, long before last night when Roy had dropped his bombshell. In any case she didn't want to discuss *that* with her doctor, especially if it wasn't relevant.

'Any more nodding off in the evenings?' Sally went on when Desna didn't answer.

'No.' After all, it had happened only one more time, as far as she could remember.

'That's a good sign, anyway. No trouble concentrating?'

'Good heavens, no.'

'That's fine. And no difficulty waking up in the morning?'

'Hardly ever.'

Sally smiled encouragingly. 'Well, that all seems perfectly normal at the moment. But we'll keep an eye on things, naturally.'

'What d'you think about a course of vitamins?' Desna suggested.

'It wouldn't do any harm.' Sally smiled. 'With your reputation as a cook I would hardly think it necessary but you have been dieting quite rigorously, haven't you? Perhaps you should go easy on that for a while.'

As Desna got up to leave Sally asked after Harriet.

'She's well. Looking forward to the big day!' Desna had no idea if this was actually true. She hoped so. At least she'd been successful in getting Harriet to see Sally about contraception. It never ceased to amaze her that in these so-called permissive times, her daughter remained a virgin.

All the same, she drove away from the surgery feeling cheated. Not that she wasn't delighted to be reassured that there was nothing seriously wrong with her. It could just have been that she felt herself so close to Roy that she'd picked up his anxieties before he'd actually spoken of them. So she hadn't told Sally everything. There were certain aspects of her life that she could discuss only with Roy and some she could not discuss even with him. Both of them had come to a head the night before.

She had been sitting in bed, stroking on hand cream and resolving that next time she had her hair done she would have a manicure as well. The bedside light bathed her complexion, now innocent of make-up, in a flattering amber glow. The bedroom was their private haven, a place to feel nurtured and restored. It was large, and in the daytime had a view that corresponded to that of the sitting room directly below, except that at this elevation more of the river could be seen through the trees, especially in the winter, and beyond to the woods on the further bank. It faced southwest and she and Nell had together worked out a colour scheme of white, pale ochre and smoky blue; it was like a echo of the stronger colouring of the sitting room. The Emmersons no longer shared a bedroom and Desna had to admit that she would have liked a similar arrangement. However, she would never have dared so much as to suggest it to Roy.

She watched him as he tidied his thick hair, a silver-backed hairbrush clamped to his hand, and tried to ascertain whether he was in a receptive mood.

'I think we're making progress with the design of the dress,' she said, creaming her fingers in turn.

'Thank God for that,' Roy said, bending his knees slightly to see in the mirror.

'I've also been thinking about that dark area in the hall.'

'I didn't know the hall had a dark area.'

'At the back. I've always thought it seems rather cut off from the rest. I've thought of a wonderful scheme for it.'

Roy frowned at his reflection.

'By building shallow cupboards right up to the ceiling we could bring it forward and give us more storage space into the bargain. Kill two birds with one stone. What d'you think? It would be nice to get it done by July.'

Roy didn't answer immediately. He took off his short robe of thick navy towelling and laid it over a chair. His pyjamas were also dark blue; in silk with a narrow red edging. She'd bought both the dressing gown and the pyjamas at Harrods during a trip to London a few weeks before.

He came to sit on the edge of her bed. She could still faintly smell his expensive aftershave and feel the warmth of his body through the quilt.

'I'm afraid,' he said after a worrying pause, 'that it will have to wait until after the wedding. Even then . . .'

'What d'you mean?' Her hands became still.

'It's just that the wedding will have to be our last big expense for a while. I've been meaning to make an opportunity to speak to you about it but I've put it off, hoping that it might not be necessary.'

Desna's heart thumped dully in her chest. 'What do you mean, exactly, Roy?' The animation drained from her voice.

'Listen, Des. Don't think I begrudge a penny we've spent on the house so far. You've made a grand job of it. I thought we were riding the recession pretty well, and we are, all things considered, but one can't dodge it completely.'

'How serious is it?' Desna found it hard to get her lips round the words.

'I've been running over a few figures with Matheson,' Roy said. 'I usually let him get on with it, claw back what he can from the tax man and so on, but there's a limit. He's a good chap, and when he suggests that we shall have to go a bit steady, I'm inclined to believe him.'

Slowly Desna screwed the lid back on her fancy jar of hand cream and returned it to her bedside table as if renouncing such trivial luxuries.

'But what about the wedding?' she said, aghast.

'Your father's bequest is paying for the wedding,' he said, 'well, more or less. It was your decision to use it for that and that will go ahead as planned. I wouldn't want it otherwise. Besides, I've no intention of letting the world think we're skint!'

'But, Roy. Are we?'

'Of course we're bloody not! I just said we shall have to go easy.'

'We could cut down on the wedding arrangements?' she suggested.

'No! Bugger it!' He frowned and she saw that even to have appeared to economize over the wedding would represent a blow to his pride that Roy would never countenance. 'All I'm saying,' he said, 'is that we'll have to put any major work on the house on hold for a bit. Don't look so damned stunned! It's nothing I can't handle. You know me! So no need to get the wind up. There are always ways. Always.'

'But you'd tell me if there was anything badly wrong, wouldn't you?'

'Trust me. I'll find a new angle. In fact I may already have hit on one but I can't say anything until I'm sure it'll work, so don't ask me.'

He leaned over and pressed his lips to her forehead. 'You just concentrate on the wedding and leave the rest to me. It's not your problem.'

'But it is!' she said against his chest. The strong tangle of hair that sprouted in the V of his pyjamas chafed her cheek. 'It scares me.'

'And you can cut that out. Leave it to me,' he commanded. He lifted her chin and put his mouth on hers. 'Hmm. You taste nice. Like honey.' Then he reached over and turned off the light by her bed so that the room was full of shadows. He tugged off his pyjama jacket and then reached down to pull her nightdress over her head. Kneeling, he pressed her against the bedhead, his hand cupping her breast and fumbling with her nipple. She clasped his thighs, her head against his abdomen. His muscles were as hard as they'd ever been though his body was thicker, heavier. The covers slid to the floor and he manoeuvred her until she was laying across the bed.

Roy had always been quick to arousal and impatient with delay; middle age had not produced any noticeable changes or diminution of desire. Her groans, whimpers and inarticulate cries still provoked in him a violent response, like a temporary frenzy; on several occasions it had resulted in dark bruises on her pale skin. Until lately they had been well matched in sexual appetite; and until lately she had never seriously considered the outcome if they had not been. She had no doubt at all that Roy would have looked elsewhere. For all she knew he already did. It was not something she cared to think about.

His body covered hers; he raised himself on his arms and her legs enfolded him. His climax came swiftly, and with a fierce gasping groan and a last momentous thrust that nearly propelled her off the bed, then he collapsed at her side.

Desna lay, at first spreadeagled, her eyes closed, then curled up foetus-like against Roy's hard body. He radiated heat like a stove but almost immediately she reached for the quilt and covered herself. Instead of the usual expansive calm and the voluptuous burgeoning of every part of her, for which she was prepared to submit to the occasional incidental buffeting and mauling, she was experiencing an unaccustomed chill. His last thrust had hurt her inside. Her cry had not been one of ecstasy but of pain. All over her body she felt a profound sensation of malaise. This was the third time in recent weeks that she had failed to reach orgasm although she had been clever enough to fake it. Not to have done so would have meant harsh questioning from Roy. She'd been left sore, sleepless and with a vengeful sense of being used. For the first time since she'd been married she had a terrible sense of loneliness, as if she was an outcast from some magic circle.

'Be a love and bring us some sandwiches,' Gordon said. 'Tuna and mayonnaise for me and egg for Toby. Make sure you ask the man if the tuna's rod caught, mind. I'll watch the shop.' He rootled in his pocket for his wallet and extracted a five-pound note which he handed to Harriet. 'And get some for yourself while you're about it.'

Harriet shrugged her arms into her old navy jacket. 'Anything else?' she asked. 'Cream slice, doughnuts?'

'Don't tempt me, girl! But don't be long, lovey. This guy is coming to show me his etchings at one thirty.' He caught her expression. 'No really!' he said.

Harriet went out into the wind. There was a hint of rain in the air and fat clouds bunched up behind the tower of St Saviour's. She went down the steep, narrow slope between old half-timbered buildings: shops, offices and estate agents crammed incongruously into their ground-floor rooms. With the speed of habit she descended a flight of steps wedged tightly between high walls. Coming up from the other direction an old woman struggled with shopping bags, hanging on to the metal handrail while she stopped to take breath.

'Think I'd be used to 'un by now,' she said between puffs.

'I'll take your bags to the top if you like?' Harriet offered on impulse.

'No, my lover. Don't you worry. I can manage.'

Harriet didn't insist but went on her way. The old woman probably thought she'd make off with her shopping. Such things had been known to happen, even in Dartmouth.

The steps emerged on to a narrow street at a lower level and she headed for the newly opened sandwich bar. It was a tight squeeze inside, just enough room for the counter, the young man behind it in his green and white overalls, and a maximum of three customers at a time. Harriet gave her order and left with the sandwiches, bursting with filling, snapped into their triangular plastic boxes.

She was about to turn back when she stopped abruptly and swung round, careering into a man in an Aran sweater and yellow sailing boots. Confusedly she apologized, her eyes still fixed on what had first forced her attention. Next to the sandwich bar was a second-hand clothes shop; occasionally Harriet bought things there but from their cheap, everyday range. What the shop specialized in was period costume: Victorian nightgowns, pelisses and bonnets, Edwardian bustled dresses, flapper shifts and severe forties jackets as well as top hats, boaters and fifties cartwheels.

Tastefully draped over a stand behind the twelve small panes that made up the window was a dress like no other she'd ever seen, of a colour she could hardly describe. She took it to be a twenties style in silk georgette, though she wasn't very knowledgeable about such things. She was reminded of cobwebs, of smoke, and the oyster greys of a certain type of rainy sunset. It hung straight from shoulder to hem with a band of silver beaded embroidery at the hip, with more beads at the neck and hem. It was a translucent fall of fabric over a silk underslip; it would be like wearing a cloud or a drift of river mist. Beside it, on a dummy display head, was a helmet made of a network of the same silver beads that decorated the dress. A pair of grey silk pumps with silver buckles completed the outfit. It seemed to Harriet that the owner of the shop, knowing that she must pass, had arranged the window display on purpose.

She stood entranced. Never before had she been the slightest bit tempted by mere clothes. Their function as far as she was concerned was to preserve decency, to keep the rain off and the cold out. Even so, she was honest enough with herself to know that only certain types of garments were acceptable to her, so to say that she was not fussy about her clothes would not be true. Her taste was formed early, by her father. The more he pressed Desna to dress their daughter in pretty frocks, to do her hair up in ribbons and encourage her childish awareness of herself, the more Harriet resisted and opted for jeans, shorts and tee shirts. It was the only way she could find of resisting his absolute power over her.

All at once she saw herself in the dress, felt its silkiness on her skin as the drift of fabric, freed from the low waistband, brushed against her legs.

Clutching her plastic bag of sandwiches and almost without thinking she pushed open the door and went inside. A bell rang and a woman emerged from behind a curtain at the back of the shop, a fat pincushion fixed to her wrist.

'That frock in the window . . .' Harriet stammered.

'Ah, yes. The twenties dress. It's gorgeous, isn't it?'

'How much is it?'

The shopkeeper was about Nell's age. She wore black with an old-fashioned shawl pinned round her shoulders with a huge antique brooch. She went to the window and examined the price ticket that hung from the back of the dress.

'A hundred and eighty-five,' she said, looking at Harriet doubtfully. Obviously the girl was very taken with the dress. She remembered seeing her before, in the Yardarm Gallery where she had once bought a small aquatint of her shop.

'Do you think I could . . .?' Harriet's request petered out into embarrassment.

'Would you like me to get it out for you?' the woman asked.

'Oh yes, please. If it's not too much trouble.'

It *was* trouble since there were plenty of urgent repairs to be made in her workshop but the woman removed the dress and held it up at shoulder level, allowing the skirt to drift over her arm. 'It's beautiful, isn't it? It's the genuine article and in such good condition.'

Reaching out, Harriet felt the softness of the material and the texture of the beading where it was worked into geometric patterns. The grey was not a dead compromise colour but one of indescribable subtlety breaking like a wave over the woman's arm and on to her hand.

'You could try it on if you like,' the woman said, suddenly

feeling generous. Besides which she rather wanted to see the dress on such an excellent model, even if she was as poor as a church mouse. 'It's your size.'

The changing room was behind the curtain. Harriet removed her boots, coat, jersey, her short skirt and leggings and stood in her bra and knickers. The woman helped her slide the dress over her head and did up the small buttons at the back. The mirror was in the dark little shop and Harriet stepped in front of it, seeing a stranger who appeared to be cloaked in clouds, touched with a shimmer of silver, a dipping sash hanging almost to her feet which were bare. Without a word the woman fetched the headdress from the window and placed it on Harriet's head. An exotic and glamorous waif looked back at them. Even the shoes fitted.

'You'd probably have to do something with your hair,' the woman said. 'Though, perhaps not . . .' She wanted Harriet to have the dress more than she could admit. A forlorn hope. Harriet stood for several minutes, turning to examine the back in the mirror. It was perfect; but she could never have it.

Back in the minute changing room Harriet put her everyday clothes back on again. When she emerged she was apologetic. 'I'm so sorry to be a bother. But I'm afraid Mummy wouldn't like it.'

The woman was about to put the dress back in the window; immediately she revised her ideas about her customer.

'But *you* do?'

'I love it,' Harriet said, colouring. Then with vehemence: 'I absolutely love it.'

'What sort of occasion did you have in mind?' the woman asked.

'Quite formal, really. Well, actually, my wedding.'

The shopkeeper smiled quite suddenly. To Harriet she seemed more approachable all at once.

'But it would be perfect! I don't think you could possibly find anything that would look more lovely on you. I really do mean that!'

But Harriet shook her head. 'I'm awfully sorry but I'm afraid it wouldn't do.' She retrieved her bag of sandwiches. Embarrassed beyond belief, she rushed to open the street door, mumbling apologies.

'I shall be open until six o'clock in case you change your mind,' the woman called as Harriet stumbled out into the hard light of reality. In fact the shopkeeper usually closed at five thirty but so, she knew, did the Yardarm Gallery. Half an hour longer was neither here nor there with plenty of mending and pressing to be done.

Harriet flew along the street, past the sandwich bar and up the steps two at a time. She hoped Gordon hadn't noticed how long she'd been. But he said it didn't matter.

'The man with the etchings is late anyway,' he said. 'Let's go into the back office and eat our sandwiches there. I've put the kettle on for coffee. Toby's gone out to buy paints, he won't be long.'

They sat where they could keep an eye on the gallery. Harriet perched on a stool and Gordon in a swivel chair at his desk, the mugs of coffee steaming beside him.

'You look very smart today, Gordon,' Harriet said, tucking into her cheese and tomato sandwich. 'Is that a new suit?'

'Yes. Do you like it?'

'Nice colour. What sort of green would you call that?'

'The shop said olive but that sounds rather boring, doesn't it? Like a farmer's Barbour. I would prefer to call it myrtle or perhaps fir green.' He grinned. 'Or parsley green, or seaweed green . . .'

Harriet giggled. 'Or broccoli green or marrow green, or seasick green . . .!'

'Lovey! Steady on! I'm eating my sandwiches!'

'Anyway, it goes beautifully with your aubergine jersey. If you had a tan handkerchief and black outlines you'd look like a Braque still life.'

'You're getting frighteningly knowledgeable, sweetie,' Gordon said, stirring demerara into his coffee straight from the packet. 'But then I always believed you know a hawk from a handsaw. I must get you to look at this chap's etchings when . . .' he looked at his brightly coloured plastic watch '. . . *if* he turns up.'

'I'd like to. But I don't know much about it.'

'Don't give me all that meek guff. How many years have you been here now? Of course you know something about it!' He took a bite from his second sandwich. 'By the way, did something happen while you were out? You looked rather pink when you came in, or was it just the cold?'

'It was nothing really. I tried on a frock in that antique clothes shop.'

'My goodness, you're going it a bit, aren't you? Trying on frocks!'

She coloured. 'To get married in . . . I thought.'

Gordon stopped laughing. 'Come on then, tell. But I thought you were having it made by the wonderful little woman in Totnes?'

'I was. Well, I expect I am. Mummy and I went to see her and we've more or less decided . . .'

'But?' Gordon drank his coffee but without taking his eyes off her.

'There was this twenties frock in the window. I saw it when I was getting the sandwiches. I tried it on.'

'Did you, by heck! And it looked divine, I've no doubt.'

'It was just what I should like.'

'So where is it?'

Harriet shook her head. 'I didn't actually buy it! Of course I didn't!'

Gordon banged down his coffee mug. 'Well, why bloody not, for pity's sake? I'm sorry about the swearing, lovey, but sometimes you drive a chap to it! When Toby deigns to put in an appearance I'm going to frogmarch you down to All Our Yesterdays, or whatever it's called, and see this creation for myself.'

'You can't! You mustn't, Gordon!'

'Why not, for goodness' sake?'

'Listen, Gordon. You just can't imagine the row! Mummy wouldn't like it because she has her own ideas about the wedding dress and you must admit that she's got very good taste. But

Daddy! Daddy would literally freak out if he knew I was wearing a second-hand dress, particularly one like that. He'd call it dowdy and frumpy. He'd probably refuse to walk down the aisle with me!'

'Isn't this supposed to be *your* day?' Gordon said drily. 'And hasn't your old man heard of "something old" or "something borrowed"? I should think it would fit into one of those categories rather well.'

'Not for Daddy it wouldn't.'

'Need he know it's old?'

'He'd find out. He always has ways of finding out. You don't know Daddy. Besides the dress looks nineteen twentyish.'

Gordon had had enough to do with Harriet's father to know that he'd rather not know him any better. In the gallery Harriet was efficient, knowledgeable and deft, but he'd seen her exactly the opposite when she was anywhere near her father. Sometimes Gordon felt he wouldn't be responsible for his actions if he actually witnessed Roy Hindmarch in the act of putting his daughter down.

'Why don't you get Mo and your ma on your side?' he asked. 'Surely they can talk him round?'

'Daddy never listens to Mo. And when all's said and done, Mummy would always give in to him. I don't suppose she has ever gone against him, not for anything serious.'

'I thought your ma was a very strong lady. She certainly gives the impression of someone who knows her own mind.'

'She does, and she is strong. All the same, she would never defy Daddy. She uses her strength to boost him up.'

Gordon shook his head. 'So it really is goodbye nice frock, then?'

Harriet nodded with the appearance of briskness. 'Would you like some more coffee?'

'No, lovey. Too much coffee has a disastrous effect on my bladder, as you know.'

The subject of the frock was dropped and soon afterwards the young man with the etchings turned up. Gordon remained in the office to go through them while Harriet minded the gallery.

They had recently hung an exhibition of large, rather atmospheric abstracts which she liked because they suggested rocks and streams, caves, and misty swathes of woodland. So far, they hadn't sold many on account of their price. Instead, the first customer bought the framed watercolour of Dartmouth Castle, competent but unexciting, that had so displeased Mo.

In between customers Harriet allowed herself to think about the dress in the window as if she were sipping some wonderful aromatic wine, knowing she would never be permitted to finish the glass. The garment had scarcely been worn. She wondered who it had originally been made for. Could she even still be alive, eeking out her days and her memories in some old people's home? But she was probably dead. If there was some kind of afterworld, Harriet mused, would she perhaps be sad to see her beautiful dress hanging unwanted in the window of a second-hand clothes shop? It would probably be acquired for a museum or used in some TV costume drama. Unless Harriet herself bought it.

But she would never have the courage to face the colossal, unthinkable row that would ensue if she not only bought it but insisted on wearing it on her wedding day. She felt hot and sweaty at the very thought. It was just the kind of thing that was likely to precipitate one of Daddy's apparently irrational rages, except that Harriet believed that inside he was quite cool and in command. The thought of her father in a rage caused her hand to tremble and she had to throw away the label she had been making out in her careful script.

Her parents had made love last night. She'd heard Desna's cries from her own room, which was on the further side of the attractive gallery that ran round the entire first floor. Nevertheless, she had heard. Philip made jokes about his parents' sex life, which according to him was practically nonexistent, though he claimed that his father had occasional flings with other, unspecified women. But she found it hard to joke about her own parents in this respect. They obviously made love far more often than Philip's. When she was a child in the other, smaller house, not understanding her mother's cries at night, she had been deeply affected; she had scrutinized her mother's morning face for signs of distress and not finding them would bury her anxiety in even deeper perplexity. Occasionally she had seen bruising on Desna's pale skin, and her suspicions that her father held some fearful power over her mother seemed to be confirmed.

Even now, unlike Philip, she found it hard to reflect on her father's sexuality without a sense of distaste. It seemed to her gross and, what was more disturbing, inextricably part of his aggression. She'd seen him use the raw power in his dealings with other people, overriding them in conversation and probably in business deals too. In fact he often boasted of how he'd got the better of this or that client in the course of their negotiations. Her mother was the only other person he treated with apparent respect, at least in their daily lives, but this, Harriet was sure, was because Desna never seriously challenged him. Just as she herself did not. He was the powerful male, the paterfamilias, whose word was final.

But it seemed to her that she alone in the family had been singled out as the chief object of his disapproval and contempt. Even Rupert, who got into more scrapes than either of her parents ever guessed at, was on easy terms with their father. In fact his escapades, though vaguely worrying to Desna, appeared paradoxically to be looked on with something like approval by Roy. It confirmed him as a red-blooded male; whereas there was very little about herself that so far fitted into his notion of the stereotypical female. In childhood she hadn't cared for dolls and had had no winning ways. In awkward adolescence she had developed no taste for clothes, pop stars or make-up. Her one achievement in all her life that had stamped her as undeniably female was to get engaged to an attractive and approved young man. Roy thought in polarities with regard to sex. It was why he detested Gordon and Toby, the two nicest men she knew, after Philip.

Off and on throughout the afternoon, even when she was supposed to be concentrating on the young man's etchings, Harriet kept thinking about the dress. She heartily wished she had never seen it. It occurred to her that she might enlist Nell's help. She would be a powerful ally because nobody in the family queried Nell's good taste.

Later that afternoon, risking leaving the gallery to Toby for half an hour, Gordon was as good as his word and coerced Harriet into accompanying him to All Our Yesterdays so that he could see the frock for himself, though he failed utterly to persuade her to go in.

'It's really you, you know,' he said, peering through the window. 'You should let me see it on.'

'No!' Harriet looked ready to flee. 'No, I can't. The woman already thinks I'm a complete dipstick.'

'Please yourself,' Gordon said, 'but I think you're making a big mistake. I tell you what, why don't you get Nell to take a look at it? I'm sure she'd adore it.'

'I wondered about Nell.' Harriet thought for a moment. 'Ye-es. Perhaps I will.'

CHAPTER FOURTEEN

After she had rung Desna, Mo thrust a plastic bag containing her pyjamas and a toothbrush into one of the panniers of her bicycle. In the other she put a loaf and a jar of instant coffee wrapped up in a towel; you had to be ready for anything at Emmet's. 'I should be back this evening,' she told Persis. 'If I'm not, there's plenty of food in the fridge.'

'Goddammit, don't fuss. I'm perfectly used to being on my own.' Persis leaned against the door jamb, her eyes narrowed against the smoke that drifted up from her cigarette. 'In any case Nell might ask me to stay.' Persis' gruff voice broke and she coughed. It sounded like some rusty old engine turning over, Mo thought.

'I shouldn't think so. She has enough to do without that!'

Life at the cottage since Persis had arrived had been a series of skirmishes with points won by first one side and then the other. On the telephone Mo had protested to all three of her daughters about Persis' behaviour but secretly she quite enjoyed the way it kept her on her toes. All the same, it was a perfect nuisance that she hadn't been able to do any painting. Persis herself certainly never appeared to do any drawing.

'It's all in here,' she said tapping her bony forehead. It made a hollow thudding sound.

'I don't believe you. I've seen some of your drawings.'

'Window dressing,' Persis snapped.

Mo slid the fluorescent strip over her tracksuit top and rolled the tops of her woolly socks over the cuffs of her trousers to stop the wind rushing up inside. 'I'm off then. Your taxi should be here soon. You'll have to go to the top of the steps to meet him,

189

they don't like coming all the way down here.' As she went she turned back to Persis and said sternly, 'I hope you behave yourself at Nell's. I've kept my side of the bargain all these years and now I expect you to keep yours. It's far too late for cats to be let out of bags. Far too late.'

'The bargain you made was with that randy bloody husband of yours. I was practically a babe in arms.'

'You were fifteen.'

'I was too young to know my arse from a hole in the ground.'

'You were never young. In any case, we had no choice. We did what we had to do.' Mo glared at Persis, her hand resting on the handlebars of her bicycle. Above them gulls screamed at each other, bickering over some prize morsel. 'Is this why you're here?' she said. 'Is this what this sudden reappearance is all about? Because if it is, I can tell you this: if you dare tell Nell the truth after all this time, I'll hound you from now until the day I die. You'll never get another moment's peace. I've asked nothing from you, even when things were hard and you were rich enough to keep all of us without even noticing, so leave *us* in peace now. I'm warning you, Persis! I can be utterly ruthless when I'm provoked.'

'No need to go barking mad! I shan't say a fucking word if that's the way you want it.'

'And for God's sake behave yourself. Not everyone is as tolerant of your foul mouth as I am. Speaking of which, I don't know what you've got to be so bad-tempered about. Your life has always gone just as you wanted. You've absolutely sod-all to complain about.'

Persis gave a yelp of derision. 'In any case, can I help it if you've spawned a trio of gutless flatfish? Am I the only member of this poxy family who has any balls at all?'

Mo lifted up her bicycle and prepared to hump it up the steps towards the road. 'Nothing would surprise me about you!' she snapped.

Mo made her way through the haphazard hills around Totnes where numerous streams and small rivers skittered in steep wooded valleys before they joined the Dart. One of them ran past the end of Emmet's orchard. In the yard the dogs greeted her enthusiastically.

Emmet herself was in the kitchen pouring boiling water into a bucket of dog biscuits, pale as death and with a scruffy bandage on one hand.

Mo came through the door, stripping off her waterproof cycling gloves. 'And what in God's name are *you* doing? I thought you'd be in bed.'

'Hallo, Mo.' Emmet croaked. 'It's sweet of you to come but I can manage, really.'

'Pull the other one. You look awful!' Mo removed the rest of her cycling gear. 'Look, let me do that. I can't understand why you're not in bed.'

'Not possible. I had to tell Barney what to do, he's not absolutely used to it yet. And get Beth off. And see to Tom who says he has flu too.'

'Where is he?'

'In bed. I was just going up to take his temperature.'

'I can at least do that.' Mo waded through the dogs who milled round her legs in greeting and fetched the thermometer from the cupboard. 'Has he had any breakfast?'

'Yes. The usual.'

'Have you?'

Emmet shook her head and blenched. 'Don't mention food.'

'I'll go and see to Tom and then I'll come and sort you out, my girl.'

Tom was laying in bed with *Stig of the Dump* secreted under the duvet. He moaned tragically when he saw Mo; she popped the thermometer into his mouth. 'Hallo, old chap.'

'I've got a terrible backache,' he mumbled through the impediment, his eyes bright and watchful. His temperature was normal. Emmet shook the thermometer down. 'You'll live,' she said. 'Is the headache very bad?' She felt his pulse and that too was normal.

'Hmm. I've got flu. I feel crappy. Mum said I needn't go to school.'

'All right, darling. You stay there. I expect you'll feel better tomorrow.'

'I might not,' Tom said doubtfully.

'I'll bring you a drink later.' She attempted to tidy his bed but Tom, conscious of the incriminating book, resisted.

Back in the kitchen Emmet was handing the bucket of feed to a young man, thin as a hairpin, and reiterating instructions in a hoarse whisper.

'Right. You leave it all to me,' he said. 'I know the drill. I've cleaned them out and done the water. I could have done the food too.' He looked into the bucket and then across to the two women with a grin. 'No good keeping a dog and barking yourself, mate!'

'Thanks, Barney. You're a fast learner,' Emmet said. 'I did the chickens first thing. Now there's just the handfed birds left in here.'

'You've got a new client here, then?' he said, indicating a closed box containing a partridge with a broken wing. 'That's all you need!' He'd had his hair cut at the weekend and it now resembled a russet-coloured mat rather than the flue brush of last week. He wore his usual body warmer over a thick, paint-flecked jersey.

'By the way, Mo,' Emmet said, collapsing into the chair by the Rayburn, 'this is Barney. Barney, this is my mother, Mrs Joubert.'

He transferred the bucket to his left hand and wiped the other on his jeans before holding it out to Mo. 'Hi,' he said. 'How's it going?'

Mo shook hands stiffly. She wasn't at all sure about his cocky familiarity. Even now he was moving about the kitchen as if he owned it. He opened the door of the Rayburn to a sad glimmer.

'Look at that!' he said. 'The fire's nearly out. Thought it was a bit nippy in here. I'll get some wood in for you before I take this to the beasties.' He took the bucket and went out whistling an approximation of 'Nessun dorma'.

Mo watching him go, frowned. 'You stay there and I'll make you some tea,' she said to Emmet's drooping form. 'Then you should go to bed.'

Emmet put her good hand to her head. 'Oh, please. No tea! I might just manage a glass of water though.' She fumbled in her pocket for her painkillers but changed her mind. They would only make her sick. Mo fetched her a glass of water and pulled the kettle over on to the cooling hotplate. 'I'll make you a hot-water bottle.'

Emmet sipped the water. 'I'll have a hot-water bottle but I can't go to bed. I've got two fledglings that have to be fed hourly. And I have to set the partridge's wing after it's settled down a bit.' There followed a low-key argument as to whether or not Mo could feed the birds and cope with the other chores as well. Tom's distant voice could be heard calling out for Emmet. Mo went upstairs where Tom told her that he really wanted to see his mother and where was she?

'Your mother isn't well. You mustn't keep calling. I'll get you everything you need now, then you must pipe down, d'you understand?' she said firmly. Tom sulked.

In the kitchen Barney was packing logs into the Rayburn. Emmet was packing food into the orange gape of a small bird, the fine skin of her forehead puckered with the effort. There were two hectic spots of colour on her cheeks and she seemed to have shrunk into the makeshift knitting that had once been a jersey. Her feet in huge socks were stuffed into a pair of muddy lace-up boots.

His tasks finished for the time being, Barney left with a promise that he'd look in later.

'Please don't,' Emmet said huskily. 'I can't afford to pay you extra time.'

'Don't worry about it,' he said as he went. They heard the sound of his motorbike starting up and its snarling diminuendo down the lane.

'He seems a bit fresh,' Mo said severely. 'I hope he's all right. He looks the type to muscle in and take advantage.' She piled the breakfast things on to the draining board and commenced the washing up.

'Take advantage?' Emmet would have laughed if she'd felt better. She finished with one bird, put him in the cage and took out another. 'Like ravishing me on the log pile, you mean? In any case, I don't suppose I shall be able to keep him for long. Maurice says we can't afford him.'

'Maurice affords what he wants to afford, if you ask me. Look at all that high-tech equipment of his!'

'He needs that for his work,' Emmet said.

'This water's only lukewarm. By the way, what have you done to your hand?'

'I cut it on a tin. I'm supposed to get the dressing changed sometime. The water will be fine now that Barney's made up the fire.'

Emmet put the bird back in the cage and raced to the outside lavatory where she heaved over the pan for a few minutes, bringing up almost nothing. She had hardly eaten for twelve hours. She felt deathly tired and her mind spun like a mouse on a wheel as she thought of all that had to be done that day. Emmet adored her mother but housework was not really Mo's forte and she hadn't any idea of the routine with the animals. Added to which, she handled the children with old-fashioned severity that usually upset Tom, if not Beth.

Tom had read a few pages of *Stig of the Dump*. He'd read it twice already and on this occasion his attention constantly wandered, ever aware of the sound of voices downstairs. He heard his grandmother's brisk tones and his mother's unfamiliar croak. And he heard Barney. Barney would be showing off as usual, sucking up to his mother to show her how utterly brilliant he was. Tom hated Barney already. He was affronted that the Barney downstairs had the temerity to have the same name as the boy in *Stig of the Dump*. It almost spoiled the story for him. He was glad when he heard the motorbike noise fade away down the lane. Barney had offered to give him a ride on it but he'd refused; not because he didn't dearly want to ride on Barney's motorbike, but because it would give the interloper yet another excuse for showing off, proving his superiority.

Mo brought him a Coke at eleven but since then no one had come up to see how he was. He might be dying for all they knew; he might have meningitis for all they cared. He was sure his headache was worse. He called out. His sheets felt itchy and crumby. He thrust his legs out of the bed. His pyjamas were too short for him and had a design of Ninja Turtles on them which he now considered babyish and stupid. Fortunately they had faded in the wash. He padded to the top of the stairs and listened. The voices murmured on, unheeding. Furiously he stumped down the stairs, making as much noise as possible. He stood accusingly at the kitchen door. His mother was lazing around on a chair and Mo wasn't doing anything important at all; just wiping off the kitchen table.

'Didn't you hear me calling?' he asked plaintively. 'I'm thirsty and my headache's worse.'

Roy and Desna drove Rupert back from school in a grim mood. Usually Desna fetched him alone but a call from their son's housemaster had made their joint attendance appear to be a matter of importance. What he'd had to tell them had been very unwelcome news. Desna couldn't imagine how Rupert could have greeted them so casually considering what Mr Naylor had to report to them during the painful and embarrassing hour in his study.

'Rupert is by no means one of our more difficult chaps. By and large he's extremely easy-going,' Mr Naylor had said. 'But I'm afraid that is precisely the trouble. He's very bright, as I'm sure you know, but his academic record is, not to put too fine a point on it, abysmal. He's not even as keen on his sports as he used to be.'

'We were looking to the school to keep him up to scratch,' Roy said, glowering. 'Are you saying you've failed?'

'No, I'm not saying that,' Mr Naylor said evenly. 'But education these days is more of a reciprocal arrangement than it used to be.' He gave a short laugh. 'We've never relied on six of the best here even in the bad old days . . .'

'Never did me any harm!' Roy growled.

'We hope that given the right environment and enough encouragement and incentive, the boys will give of their best.

And I must say it usually works.'

The school had been Desna's choice for these very reasons. Since Roy had allowed her no alternative but to send Rupert away to school, he had at last agreed to one that had a reputation for being reasonably benign.

Up to now, Roy had been inclined to take a lenient view of Rupert's record, if not the school's, in the matter. In the interview he had mentioned that he had replaced his son's Mirror with a Laser on his sixteenth birthday as an incentive to work harder at school. What more could he do? Surely it was up to the school?

It was then that Naylor had brought up another little matter, reluctantly, he said. Rupert had been involved in a fracas in the town with one or two other lads from the school and had been brought back in a squad car. He did not mention that the boys had all been drunk for fear that the parents would accuse the school of negligence. Fortunately the police had been busy with a bomb scare that weekend or the young lads could easily have finished up in more serious trouble. Neither did he mention that certain quite large sums of money had gone missing at the school and, while there was no actual proof, all the circumstances indicated Rupert Hindmarch.

The long and the short of it was that Naylor wanted them to take Rupert away. Not, perhaps, immediately but certainly by the end of the following term. Naylor himself had been all for getting rid of the lad at once but in a heated staff meeting the English Department had prevailed; Rupert Hindmarch was playing the lead in *Henry V* early in the following term and the whole production depended on him.

'In the long run we think your son might just need a different kind of establishment altogether. A sixth-form college might give him a sense of being more responsible for his own progress. More adult, less of a schoolboy.' Naylor raised his brows, seeking agreement.

After that the interview had become quite awful. Desna reddened at the memory. Roy had lost his temper and accused the school of taking his money on false pretences. 'The very least you could have done was to give him a bit of a kick up the backside so that he could manage a few decent GCSEs. Now you're saying he'll probably have to retake in October . . . if that is, you are good enough to allow him to stay.' Roy paced round Naylor's study, red-faced and brimming with anger, so that when Naylor proffered some innocuous defence of the school, for a tense minute Desna was afraid Roy might knock him down.

'There's absolutely no malice in the lad,' Naylor said as calmly as he could in the circumstances, though he wasn't absolutely sure if he believed this. 'It's just a question of finding some way of motivating him . . .'

'Which you lot obviously can't.' Roy stood over Naylor menacingly. 'Right. I'm glad I know where we stand. If you can't manage the lad we'll find someone who can!'

Rupert had been sent for. Naylor had suggested that they were prepared to keep him until the end of the following term because a change now would jeopardize his examinations but Roy was too angry to listen.

In the car, Desna glanced at her husband's stony profile knowing that it wouldn't be long before he remembered that the school had been her choice. And it wouldn't take him long after that to come to the conclusion that he had been a complete bloody fool to take into account the opinion of a woman when it came to the education of his son.

Rupert himself slouched in the back of his father's BMW fantasizing that he was a world-class surfer, a surfing superstar, being driven by his chauffeur, car phone at the ready. Desna was his secretary, her fingers poised over a laptop, busy organizing his hectic worldwide schedule. Naturally he would have been driving himself (and not in a BMW), but imagination had to make some compromises. While he had been staying with Adam Young at Christmas, Adam had shown Rupert his four customized and mind-bogglingly expensive surfboards and spent the whole of the last term banging on about how much he was looking forward to getting in some serious surfing in Cornwall at Easter. He nattered on *ad nauseam* about the charge of a big wave, about getting barrelled, about checking out the sets and, above all, about the fabulous surf chicks. He played heavy metal groups called The Angels and Red Hot Chili Peppers and showed Rupert his tattoo. His parents were apparently quite laid back about Adam's latest craze, supplying the dosh when required, without asking a load of questions like his own parents most certainly would. He wished his old man was as generous as Adam's. He didn't count the new Laser; boats were for the middle-aged or for kids. Things would be more difficult now that the wimp Naylor had grassed him up and put his whole scheme at risk but he didn't doubt he could put down a routine on his old man, kiss arse and so on, so that he didn't give him too hard a time over it. One thing he absolutely wouldn't be able to put up with would be another term of bullshit from Adam Young. He had no doubt that once he'd had a chance to get a real crack at surfing himself he could hammer Young into the ground; he felt in his bones that it would be something he would excel at. And Young would have no chance with the chicks; he was shorter than Rupert, as well as being bandy and zit-encrusted.

The arrival back at Mount Huish was nothing like the usual high-spirited and relaxed occasion. Desna went indoors with scarcely a word.

Roy said grimly, 'We'll have to discuss this in my study after dinner.'

It would give him a chance to simmer down, Rupert thought as he began dragging his stuff out of the boot. He'd wait a few days after that and then start working on his father in earnest. He'd have to set himself up with all the gear before the end of the holiday. If his father jibbed, he'd just have to sell the Laser to get the dosh.

In the kitchen he found his mother on the phone to Emmet, asking how she was. It appeared she had some bug or other. He helped himself to a slab of homemade bread and cheese.

Without Roy present Desna allowed herself a gesture of love and welcome, laying her hand briefly on Rupert's cheek, smiling.

CHAPTER FIFTEEN

Nell covered the miles between Dartmouth and Totnes in record time. All the same she would be late opening the shop. It had been a strange and inconclusive morning beginning with an urgent and enigmatic telephone call from Harriet asking if they could possibly meet in Dartmouth at lunchtime. She agreed, though it was not terribly convenient. After that she'd had what she had hoped would be a businesslike and productive interview with Ben, her accountant, which turned out to be neither.

She'd sat opposite him in his small office over a baker's in the High Street; the smell of newly baked bread having ascended the stairs with her, now permeated the room.

'I've looked the Cornucopia books over as you asked,' Ben said, 'and they appear to be perfectly healthy.'

'So if they are, why are you looking so doubtful?'

Ben fixed his eyes on the page of figures in front of him, his head slightly bent. Nell noticed that his hair was receding more than she remembered though he was scarcely older than she.

'How soon were you thinking of making this move?' he asked.

'Well, as you know, I rent both the shop and the flat so I have no capital tied up there. It would just be a matter of giving notice and transferring my stock to Cornucopia.'

'And what about your capital? I see you've built up quite a tidy sum there. That little bequest from your father gave it a boost.'

'It's not attracting much interest where it is since I have to have access to it so it might as well be put into Cornucopia as well. I had originally planned to buy the flat and the shop premises but that's all changed now.'

Ben looked up. 'So where would you live?'

'With Daniel, of course.' She smiled. 'This time we want it all to be official. We're getting married, you see.'

Ben looked nonplussed. 'Really! Well, congratulations! Second time lucky, eh?'

'I think so, yes,' Nell said quietly. A glow of happiness had filled her to the brim since the moment that Daniel had suggested marriage. It was only two nights ago over another meal in another secluded restaurant that she had at last given him an absolutely firm answer. She had agreed to throw her lot in with his for a second time both as a marriage and a business partner; it had been on Daniel's insistence that her accountant saw his books.

'I want the whole thing to be on the right footing right from the start,' he'd said. His still unlined forehead gave him a look of youthful innocence, his mobile mouth so often smiled that his present gravity lent him, paradoxically, an almost comic expression.

'Are you absolutely sure you know what you're asking?' she said. 'You were never one for commitment, were you?'

'All changed,' he'd said simply. He'd twirled his credit card at the waiter and they'd left the restaurant. Outside he had executed a few deft dance steps while humming 'Happy Days are Here Again', making Nell laugh inordinately. It would have been naïve to imagine that everything would now be plain sailing. Of course not. Daniel had changed but he would always be Daniel, thank God: mercurial, impulsive, impatient and unpredictable, all reasons why she loved him but not qualities that made him easy to live with. In any case, she believed that she had enough caution, level-headedness and tenacity for them both.

'All the same,' Ben said – cautious Ben – 'I think it would be wiser not to sink all your capital into the new venture until you are quite certain how things are going.'

Nell frowned. 'What d'you mean, how things are going? Cornucopia isn't a new venture, you know.'

'Remember the saying about having all one's eggs in one basket.'

'As you can see,' she nodded at the books laid out before him, 'Cornucopia is doing very well. The export market to America and the continent is particularly thriving, it seems to me.'

'He takes rather a lot out of the business. He does love his classic cars, doesn't he?'

'If you're successful why not enjoy some of the rewards?' She stood up. 'Ben, I'll have to go. Anna said she could only spare an hour.' At the door she turned. 'By the way, Ben, I managed to pick up some Victorian garden urns . . . are you still interested?'

'Oh, right. Lovely. Yes, I definitely am. They're for my courtyard.'

'That's what I thought.'

'Thanks. I'll come up and take a look. Meanwhile, I'll keep these books for a day or two longer if you don't mind, Nell.' Ben rose to his feet and came round the side of the desk. 'Don't do anything hasty, will you? Keep me posted.'

Nell left, feeling Ben had rather taken the wind out of her sails. Her mind had been so full of a new picture of herself. Always she had detected in Desna the faintest air of patronage and authority towards her younger sisters. It was kindly meant, naturally, but on occasion she still found it intensely irritating. Living in a rented flat, even with a thriving business, could hardly be compared with Desna's grand lifestyle. Now she saw herself as having the best of both worlds, running a flourishing business, married to a successful man and living in her own house – if not the little Regency rectory, then somewhere quite as attractive. Perhaps that would at last put Desna and her on an equal footing.

But breaking the news of her coming liaison to the family would not be as easy as telling Ben; though even Ben was evidently not as pleased for her as she had expected.

Anna had scarcely handed Nell the keys of the till and gone on her way when the door opened and an extraordinary-looking woman marched in. Her almost pure white hair seemed to stand up round her head like a halo, she wore jeans and cowboy boots and a shirt buttoned to the neck under a leather jacket. She carried a canvas bag slung over one shoulder. Ignoring the contents of the shop she subjected Nell herself to a searching scrutiny. Nell knew at once who it was.

She held out her hand. 'You must be Persis,' she said smiling.

Persis ignored her hand and simply continued to stare at her in a manner that seemed purposely designed to inflict the maximum discomfiture. Nell, however, had enough experience of difficult customers not to feel too much disconcerted by this.

'You're not as tall as I expected,' Persis said. 'Though you have an uncanny resemblance to him, good-looking bastard that he was. I hope you don't take after him. That shit'd screw anything that moved.'

'If you're talking about my father, I never really knew him and in any case, he's dead, so what's the point?' Nell said sharply.

Persis pulled up a metal garden chair and plonked her bag on the matching table. She fished out her cigarettes.

Nell pointed to a discreet sign which asked customers to refrain from smoking. 'If you don't mind,' she said.

'If you don't mind,' Persis mimicked but she put the packet away. 'Anyway, this randy father of yours at least left you some of the old spondulicks so I suppose you think he wasn't such a bad fellow after all?'

'I would rather have had a father when we were kids. Not that Mo didn't do her best.'

'Mo is not a natural earth mother type,' Persis said, stretching out her booted feet. 'All the same, you stood a better chance with her than with me.'

Nell looked faintly puzzled. 'You never had kids, did you?'

Persis fished for her cigarettes again and had one lit before Nell could speak. 'One frigging fag won't hurt!' she said fiercely. 'Did I have kids? Well, no. Not in the nurturing sense.'

Nell translated this as meaning a possible miscarriage. She wondered if this preposterous exterior concealed some ancient havoc from a former rackety way of life or simply a preposterous interior.

'I never had kids either,' she said. 'It's too late now anyway.'

'What d'you mean, too late! You forget I know when you were born almost to the minute. If you *want* a litter of ankle biters for Christ's sake have them. Don't stand there and moan about it!'

'I wasn't moaning. I merely said—'

'I heard what you said.' Her aunt appeared to have lost interest in the conversation. Instead she was gazing round the shop as if noticing it for the first time.

'So you sell this crap for a living, do you?'

'Yes, I sell this crap for a living,' Nell replied venomously. 'It's perfectly frightful what some people have to do to earn a crust, isn't it?'

Persis threw back her head and roared with laughter. It reminded Nell of a horse neighing. At the same time she saw that her aunt must once have been quite attractive. And in a certain way, still was.

'And never inherited the divine afflatus from your mother?' Again that penetrating stare.

'Or apparently from my father. He taught at the art school Mo went to, didn't he? Though he went into advertising in the end.'

'He was always a whorer of one sort or another.'

'You knew him?'

'You could say that.' Persis gave an almost wolfish grin.

'Desna remembers him slightly but he left when I was still a baby. We occasionally got birthday cards from him, when he remembered. I wish sometimes I had known him.'

Her aunt got to her feet abruptly and picked up her bag. 'Don't waste any regrets on that prick. Just take the wampum and be grateful.' She began to poke around the shop, eyeing everything critically. 'Mo says you have a new man. I expect he's a son of a bitch like them all.'

'Daniel's all right!' Nell felt provoked into saying. 'As a matter of fact, I may even marry him.'

'Oh, sure, sure. Daniel, eh? By all means fuck the bastard but

203

for Christ's sake draw the line at marriage. And watch your back. Remember they'll all shit on you from a great height sooner or later.'

'You're angry because you made a mess of two marriages.'

Persis looked at Nell sideways. 'Is that what you think? Oh, well. Dream on, baby. Anger isn't always about men. There *are* other things, you know.'

'Please, Persis, don't tell anyone about this yet. I want to break the news to the family myself. They don't know about Daniel yet.' Nell cursed herself for so foolishly blurting out his name.

'If that's the way you want it, sure,' Persis said carelessly. Her easy reassurances quite failed to set Nell's fears to rest.

After Persis left Nell became unusually busy, for that time of year at least. There was hardly a moment to think about her aunt but when she did it was with the deepest misgiving. Persis now possessed the information that she was about to embark on marriage, and a marriage that would be considered by her family to be a disaster. She couldn't believe that Persis was to be trusted, yet she had put herself in a position where she was compelled to do so. Added to this she had a vague feeling that there had been some kind of subtext to their conversation that she had somehow missed.

At one o'clock she closed the shop and drove to Dartmouth to meet Harriet. Harriet had brought sandwiches and a Thermos of coffee, which they consumed sitting on a bench overlooking the harbour. Last time Nell had looked at this view it had been dark and she had been with Daniel. Now spring seemed to have come suddenly and activity on the river had increased. Yachts were being painted, the cruise boats had begun to convey the first of the trippers along the sinuous course of the Dart up as far as Totnes and back, and small boats and inflatables zipped from the quay to moorings in deep water. The tide surged in, carrying with it fragments of coloured seaweed; reflections of boats and the houses and trees of Kingswear rocked on the water surface in a patchwork of white, blue, pink and pale green slashed here and there with yellow and orange. The winter smells of dank water and the faint odour of rotting fish had been replaced by that of fresh paint and the sharp tang of salt.

But Harriet was too much on edge to linger. She hurried Nell away on their mysterious mission, stopping abruptly at All Our Yesterdays. Inside the shop she commanded Nell to wait while she dived behind a curtain with the owner of the shop. When she emerged she was wearing a dress the colour of wood ash with a little beaded helmet like dew on spider webs. Nell gazed at her niece. It wasn't that the dress wrought any fundamental change, it was just that it dramatized something in Harriet that, almost, Nell wished did not exist. That amount of vulnerability could only bring the child pain, couldn't it? Yet it dramatized her beauty too and that was surely a good thing?

'What do you think,' Harriet said shyly. 'Gordon saw it in the window. It was his idea to have it put back until you saw it on.'

'Your wedding dress, of course.'

Harriet nodded. 'You don't think it's too *OTT*?'

Nell shook her head. 'No, I don't. You look wonderful in it. Wonderful.' A thought struck her. 'Has Desna seen it?'

Harriet shook her head vigorously. 'No. I thought I'd ask you first. I wouldn't want to fuss Mummy with it if you thought it was awful.'

Nell inspected the dress carefully, taking the fabric in her hand.

The woman who owned the shop chipped in eagerly. 'I don't think you'll find anything wrong . . . and it's already been expertly cleaned.'

Nell could see that there was indeed nothing wrong . . . with the dress. But she knew instinctively that Desna would not approve. Des had already gone on to her at some length about the little dressmaker in Totnes and the perfectly gorgeous fabric and design they'd hit upon. And it was nothing like this.

'I think it's perfect,' she said. 'You look fabulous in it.'

'You think I should have it? You think it would be all right?'

The eagerness in Harriet's expression touched her.

'Yes, I do. It's perfect. But what about the other dress, the one Desna was telling me about?'

Harriet looked aghast suddenly. How could she have forgotten about it? Then she said, 'It's not absolutely definite yet.'

'Then I think you should make up your mind quite quickly, darling. It is your wedding, after all. If you want me to, I'll speak to Desna about it. Say how nice it looks on you and so on.'

Harriet fiddled with the sash. 'It's not only Mummy,' she said in a low voice. 'There's Daddy.'

'He won't take much interest, surely?'

'He might not appear to on the surface but he'll want to know every single detail of everything to do with the wedding. And he won't like this dress. I can tell you that already.'

Nell was afraid she was right. 'Then you'll have to be firm with him. It's your frock, not his!' Even as she spoke Nell knew that she could never visualize Harriet standing up to Roy, not even on so personal an issue as the dress she wore. Just because it was his daughter's own choice would be enough for him to put his foot down; and this dress in particular would practically guarantee a violent reaction. It made Harriet look just too waif-like and unusual. He would never stomach it.

'It's up to you, Harry,' she said without much hope. 'I adore the dress. You obviously love it too. If you love it enough so that you can't visualize wearing anything else, buy it. And argue later. For what it's worth, I'll back you up if you want to make a fight of it.'

At the mention of a fight Harriet visibly quailed. Then she hurried into the back of the shop, took the dress off as quickly as the fragile material allowed and scrambled back into her everyday clothes. With a gabbled excuse to the, by now, exasperated shop owner she abruptly dragged Nell out onto the street. To Nell's dismay she saw that Harriet's eyes were brimming. She gave up any hope of getting back to Totnes before two and suggested they went for coffee somewhere.

When they were settled in a cosy inglenook next to a blazing fire Nell stirred her coffee thoughtfully. 'It's important to fight for some things, you know, Harry. Things that really matter.'

Harriet's eyes had stopped brimming and she had recovered her equilibrium. She gave a short laugh. 'Frocks don't matter really, do they? What's important when it comes right down to it is that I'm marrying Philip.'

'Of course. I quite agree. You love Philip. I'm not saying that a frock is important in itself but standing up to your father – and even to Desna – might be. It's easy sometimes to convince ourselves that we don't really want things if the achieving of them would mean that we have to exert ourselves and do things that frighten us.'

Nell thought for a moment that Harriet was about to cry again. 'I expect you think I'm a complete wimp,' the girl said.

'No, I don't. Your father can be quite overpowering when he chooses and defying him won't be much fun. All the same, I don't see what he can do if you've made up your mind.' She laid a hand on Harriet's. 'Courage, old thing! I'd go for it if I were you. I'm sure Philip would be very proud of you.'

Something about the last thing Nell said appeared to do the trick. Harriet gulped down her coffee and waited impatiently now for Nell to finish hers. Then she propelled Nell back to All Our Yesterdays and, fumbling, she wrote out a cheque while the astonished woman enfolded the dress in tissue paper and placed it carefully in a flat box. She packed the headdress and the shoes separately. They were now both pushed for time and Nell made her way quickly to the car park, feeling joyful about Harriet's new-found courage but also bemused and suffering from indigestion.

Harriet hurried back to the gallery stupefied by what she had done.

When Nell finally arrived back at Alfresco a customer was already waiting outside, peering through the window, a hand cupped round his eyes.

'Sorry I'm late,' she said breathlessly, as she unlocked the door. 'Oh, hallo Hugh!'

'Hallo, Nell. I was in Totnes and thought I'd look in.'

She took off her coat. So much had happened since she'd last seen him that she had almost forgotten her afternoon at Chapel Abbey and her irritation at what she saw as his unnecessary mystification over the existence of an ex-wife and a child; what was the little girl's name? Paula, Laura?

'How's Laura?' she said, remembering.

'She is very well.' He sloped round the shop, hands in the pockets of his ancient leather coat. He paused at a Portland stone column with an interesting patination. 'This is nice. I have a use for this. How much are you asking?'

Nell told him. She shut her bag in a drawer under the counter. 'You're not interested, are you? I thought you liked to discover bargains of your own.'

'I think this is a bargain. Are you sure about the price?'

'It's about as much as I can expect to get as things are.'

'I'll take it.' Hugh reached into his breast pocket and took out a cheque book. He leaned on the counter, hair flopping, signed the cheque, tore it out and handed it to her with his cheque card. 'There you are,' he said.

She looked at him as if he'd gone mad. 'Hugh, why did you do that?'

'I like it. I saw it from the window. It will make a perfect base for a stone bust that's been knocking round the place for years. If you hadn't come when you did I was contemplating a little smash and grab.'

She picked up the cheque, suspecting that this highly extravagant gesture was an indication that he still fancied her. All the same it was a great deal of money to fork out for an infatuation. 'Well, if you're sure about this. But I think I should give you trade discount.'

'I'm not trade. I'm bona fide retail so stick it in the till and shut up!'

She smiled and though she was quite unconscious of it, the sight increased his heart rate almost unbearably. Even more so when she bent to fill in the cheque card details and he noticed the way her dark hair had been cut urchin-style, revealing the graceful shape of her neck and a tantalizing part of her ear.

'Would you like it delivered?' she asked.

'Only if you do it personally.'

She saw she had fallen into a trap. If he chose to spend vast sums of money on a whim, that was his business. There was no need for her to feel a sense of obligation towards him.

'I shan't have time to do that. I'll get Stan to do it . . .' Then she saw he was laughing.

'No need to be so defensive,' he said. 'I know when I'm being given the brush-off.' Restlessly, he began to roam round, inspecting first a lead wall fountain, then the stone putto with the bunch of grapes as if trying to make up his mind about something. Then he sat on the chair that Persis had occupied earlier that day and said, 'I'm sure you've realized that I like you, Nell. I think it will be far less embarrassing in the long run if I tell you that straight away. I always have liked you . . . very much as a matter of fact. But then you were already hitched up with Dan Thorne and it looked like there was no hope for me.' He glanced outside, trying to judge whether two window shoppers were about to come in. They didn't. He went on. 'That's when I married Helen, which turned out to be a colossal mistake and unfair on Helen. We both knew quite quickly that we were almost completely incompatible but by then Helen was pregnant so we decided, rightly or wrongly, to at least make an attempt to make the marriage work.'

Nell said quietly, 'There's no need to tell me all this, Hugh.'

'But there is. I'm sorry to be a bore. I just want you to hear the facts and then I'll shut up. Helen pushed off to America with someone else when Laura was six but they found that a young kid was cramping their style so, to my great joy Laura came to me. I think I was a bit of a recluse after that, just Laura and me at Chapel Abbey. I concentrated on her and the business for a long time before I discovered that you and Thorne had split up . . .'

'That was ages ago.'

'I only found out recently. Timing is apparently not my forte.' He gave a short laugh and got to his feet. 'In any case, I obviously hadn't a hope at any time. You're sure to have found someone else.'

Hugh's unburdening had been intensely embarrassing. Nell found herself fiddling unnecessarily with a pile of papers that lay on the counter. It seemed neither the time nor the place for confidences of this nature, since she all the time expected an interruption. The one sure way she could get rid of him was to tell him the truth.

'Hugh, you know I like you, I've always thought you a very nice person and I'm sorry your marriage didn't work out . . . but I have to tell you that there is someone else. Daniel has come back and this time we plan to get married.' She gave a brief nervous laugh. Telling Hugh was like a dress rehearsal for when she at last broke the news to the family. What was more, the look of shocked surprise on his face was precisely the look she feared she would receive from them.

'Nell, I'd no idea!' he said at last. 'Are you absolutely sure about this?'

'Of course I'm sure.' His incredulity was highly irritating, insulting even. 'I know people like to think of Daniel as a complete shit, but they're wrong, quite wrong. And I'm not a complete fool either. I'm going into this with my eyes wide open, believe me!' She spoke more heatedly than she intended; but he was the third person today who had taken it upon themselves to give her the gypsy's warning and she was getting more than a little fed up with it. It made her more determined than ever to prove them wrong.

Hugh looked stunned. He felt almost incapable of speech. Then: 'Please, Nell. Please, for God's sake, don't rush into this. I know you're telling me to mind my own bloody business but give yourself time . . .'

'Look, Hugh, I'm sure your judgement over eighteenth-century spoons and classic columns is immaculate,' she allowed herself a small smile, 'but not when it comes to marriage. Then you're just as fallible as the rest of us.'

He opened his mouth to say more, to plead with her to wait but at that moment a customer came into the shop. All he could do was to take his classic column and leave.

CHAPTER SIXTEEN

Desna fetched a raised asparagus and egg pie from the freezer, and packed it in a box with a couple of cartons of soup and some fruit and set off for Drake's Farm in her small Fiat.

As she drove into the yard a young man on a motorbike roared out, giving her a familiar wave as he went. The dogs, who had been seeing him off, greeted her.

'I suppose that was Barney,' she said as she went into the kitchen, almost falling over several cats and a hen who were sitting companionably on the mat. 'Shoo!' she said, evicting them.

'I'm in here,' Emmet croaked from the scullery. Desna popped her head round the door and was confronted by the usual collection of insanitary cages and their occupants. Emmet was on her knees loading dirty clothes into the washing machine.

'Darling, what *are* you doing?' Desna took an apron and some rubber gloves from her bag and put them on. 'Now go and sit down and let me do that.'

'Hallo, Desna. You're an angel to come but I could have managed, really.' All the same Emmet went into the kitchen and collapsed into the battered old armchair without too much protest. In the last two days she was getting used to being ordered about, first by Barney, then by Mo, now Desna.

Desna began to sort the washing into whites and coloureds.

'Don't bother about that,' Emmet said tiredly. 'I never do.'

'No wonder everything the Darby family wears seems to be such an odd grey colour. Listen, when I've done this I'll take you to the surgery to have your dressing changed. And you must see the doctor while we're about it. You look awful.'

211

'Thanks,' Emmet said drily. 'Des, there's a problem. We shall have to take Tom with us. He hasn't been to school for the last two days.'

'Then you should have got the nurse to call here. What's the matter with Tom?'

'He says he has flu too. Actually I don't think there's anything wrong with him but I haven't the energy to fight over it.'

Desna turned on the washing machine and came back into the kitchen. 'What's the phone number of the surgery?'

'It's written on the side of the dresser.'

Desna made an appointment for later that morning for both Emmet and Tom, then she went upstairs.

Tom was putting the finishing touches to his Stealth Bomber. He looked up when Desna came in. 'Hallo,' he said.

She kissed him on top of his head. 'Hallo, Tom darling. I hear you have the flu.' She sat on the bed.

'No one cares if I *died* up here,' he said. 'Last night they nearly forgot to give me my supper.'

'Now, Tom, we all have to go to the doctor's this morning.' She picked up scattered garments from the floor. 'I've made an appointment for you too so get dressed as quick as you can, there's a good boy.'

'I don't want to go to the doctor's.'

'I'm afraid we all have to go. Even if you weren't ill you couldn't stay here by yourself, you know. In any case the doctor may have to give you some antibiotic. Have you any clean underpants?'

Tom shook his head. 'No . . . why can't I stay here? I shall be all right by myself.'

'Are you saying you're not ill after all?'

'I *am* ill but I don't want to go.'

Desna looked at her watch. In the end it took her ten minutes to urge Tom out of bed and into his clothes. It used up most of her reserves of patience.

She had been in a state of shock since yesterday's unpleasant interview with Mr Naylor. She couldn't believe in the ultimatum they'd been given. It seemed terribly unfair since some boys of his age were far worse than Rupert. At least there had been no absolute expulsion, it had all been tactfully handled; suggestions made, alternatives quoted. She had expected more of an outburst from Roy when they reached home and it was true that he was extremely angry at first; but after Rupert had been closeted with his father for an hour after dinner – her presence was not requested – they had both emerged in a better mood. They seemed to have struck some kind of bargain. So far Roy had not told her what it was.

Tom slouched rebelliously downstairs and sat in the back of Desna's car, kicking at the seat with his scuffed trainers until Desna snapped at him to stop it. She was aware of a puzzled glance from Emmet.

'I'm sorry, Emmet,' she said, feeling she should apologize though she didn't know why. The car was almost new. Roy had given it to her for her birthday. 'We had a bit of a session with Rupert yesterday. The school say he hasn't been working, though he must have done *something* right since he's playing the lead in *Henry V* next term. They even suggested we sent him to the local sixth-form college.'

Emmet gave a croaking laugh. 'I can't imagine Rupert among the hoi polloi. But I *can* imagine him playing *Henry V*. Good for him.'

'It would save us some money if we took him away, I suppose.'

'I never thought I'd live to hear that the Hindmarches are short of money!'

'Of course we're not. Not in that sense, but Roy says we shall have to be careful. Everyone has to be careful nowadays. You never know what might happen.'

'What about the wedding?'

'I'm insisting on paying for that with Father's bequest.' Desna glanced at Emmet who was slumped in the passenger seat. 'What a pity he wasn't your father too, you could do with a nice little legacy.' Desna stopped the car at the junction and edged out into the road that led to the village.

'Hmm. Maurice is talking about an economy drive too. He doesn't want me to employ Barney to help with the animals, even though I can pay him with what I get from my writing.'

'Well, I don't think this is a very opportune moment to get rid of Barney. All the same, perhaps when you're better you should have another think about all these extra little mouths you have to feed.' She glanced in the mirror at Tom. 'The animals, I mean.'

'I don't like Barney,' Tom piped up from behind them. Since Desna had stopped his kicking he had been whistling tunelessly between his teeth. 'Just because he has a motorbike he thinks he's great. *I* think we should get rid of him too.'

Desna drove into the surgery car park. They got out of the car.

Emmet held her son firmly by the shoulder with her good hand. 'Listen, Tom. Don't you breathe a word to Barney about this. We need him just now.'

Tom muttered under his breath as she propelled him through the surgery door.

An hour later, after a detour to the nearest chemist for more antibiotics, they returned to Drake's Farm with Emmet's dressing renewed. Tom was declared fit, which only exacerbated his bad mood. On the kitchen doorstep was an anonymously donated closed cardboard box containing an injured rook.

'I think it's dead,' Desna opined hopefully. Tom for once agreed with her.

Emmet, forgetful for the moment of how lousy she felt herself, put the box on the kitchen table and took the bird out, cradling it against her clean white bandage and blowing on its feathers to ascertain the extent of its injuries.

'No,' she said in a pleased voice, 'it's in shock. It looks as if it's just a broken leg, though you can never be absolutely sure. It's been shot. Tom, hand me the bottle with the dropper. I'll just give it some antibiotic and have another look at the leg later.'

Tom sighed and handed his mother the bottle. Desna watched her sister. She would, most probably, forget to take her own antibiotic so intent was she on battling for the life of one ugly-looking and ungrateful bird. It seemed to have come round and was attacking the dropper with its fearsome beak. She remembered Emmet as a child bawling and inconsolable after the death of a pet rabbit; but an Emmet who was just as capable of sticking out her small chin and fighting like a hell-cat when she came upon some boys tormenting a hedgehog.

All the same, Desna was also aware of Tom's silent withdrawal upstairs.

'I don't know how you can bear to handle it,' Desna said. 'Look what it's done to your jeans.'

'A little shit never hurt anyone.' Emmet put the bird back into its box and wiped her trousers with a piece of kitchen towel.

'I think that saying should be carved in stone over your door.' Desna took out the asparagus and egg pie which she had left in Emmet's fridge. 'Pie all right for you or would you prefer soup?'

'I'm sorry.' Emmet sat in the chair, feeling wiped out all of a sudden. 'I love your pies but I might not even be able to manage soup. Tom will, though.'

Desna put the pie into the Rayburn oven. 'About Tom,' she said judiciously. 'He doesn't seem very happy. He always used to be such a contented little boy.' She put more logs into the Rayburn and dusted off her hands.

'Tom's all right. Just growing up, that's all . . .' Emmet broke off in a sudden paroxysm of coughing.

'You should be in bed. I can do everything down here.'

'You won't be able to do the animals and once I go to bed I shan't be able to get up again.' Emmet's voice was muffled by a wad of tissue. 'Oh dear, I think I'm going to be sick.' She rushed out of the door in the direction of the outside lavatory. When she came back she looked very pale. Desna sat her in the chair and felt her forehead. 'I'll make you a drink, you mustn't get dehydrated. What would you like?'

'Just water, thanks.'

'Is Barney coming back this evening?'

'I've asked him to, yes.'

'He knows what to do?'

'Yes.'

'Thank God for that. Listen, Emmet, I want you to ask him to come in every morning and evening until you're better. I insist on it and I insist on paying him.'

'No, no. You can't do that,' Emmet said wearily. But she hadn't the energy to resist. She relapsed into a state of utter weakness, slumped in the chair. Desna covered her up with a duvet and put her rubber gloves back on to tackle the kitchen. She began by banishing all the cats and dogs and then made an onslaught on the littered worktops.

'Didn't Mo do *any* cleaning yesterday?' she said, half to herself.

'Sort of,' Emmet rasped, 'but cleaning isn't quite her thing. She did get the children to bed in record time, though.'

'Right, that's all I can do for the moment,' Desna said at last. 'Now I think I should go up and see Tom.' Perhaps she could find out if there was anything in particular that he was anxious about. All the same, she felt ill equipped to deal with the problems of nine-year-old males. Rupert was away at school by the time he was nine. She had always felt cheated of the important stages in her son's development. He'd presumably found others in which to confide unless, that was, he had learned not to confide at all, which was what she suspected. He certainly never talked to her about anything important.

Rupert stayed in bed until eleven o'clock, after which he got up and went down to the kitchen, naked except for his short towelling dressing gown. Carol was there, cleaning the floor, so he helped himself to a bowl of Coco Pops and took it back to his bedroom. While he ate he listened to The Angels at top volume. Then he had a shower, lingering to examine his physique in the full-length mirror. There were no large mirrors at school. He'd put on some muscle; his pecs were quite respectable and at least he wasn't bandy like Adam or gross like Chisholm. He scrutinized his dick thoughtfully, wondering if he was right in thinking that it had grown lately. It was about average for his year but was it average generally speaking? One thing he knew: it was bigger than Adam's pathetic plonker.

He put on jeans and a sweatshirt under sailing waterproofs and padded down the path between the rhododendrons to the boathouse. It was in the process of being painted. After what his father had said last night he was surprised that the dosh could be found for such inessentials.

He opened the doors of the boathouse and jumped into the inflatable. The Laser, which had been his pride and joy on his last birthday, he scarcely glanced at. He started the outboard of the inflatable after one or two attempts and pushed its blunt nose out into the river, swung it round in an arc and headed downstream for Dartmouth.

The wind gusted into his face and whipped his hair about; the sense of freedom and wellbeing released some of his frustration at being cooped up in school for a term. It wasn't too warm but it seemed to him a great day. The tide was about to turn, so going back would be much quicker. Green was beginning to appear on the massed trees to left and right, the water gave back a million sparkling reflections as he approached the entrance to Noss Creek. Then he was level with Hindmarch Marine where there were signs of activity. He spotted his father and Philip, both in old jeans and navy guernseys, chatting to a tall chap with slicked-back hair. Rupert cruised by, not stopping. He wanted to keep out of his father's way as much as possible this Easter, keep a low profile. Last night had been pit city until he managed to talk the old man round.

His father had been standing in front of the fireplace in his study waiting for him, his thumbs hooked into his pockets. Rupert perched himself on the corner of the desk.

'Now you listen,' Roy had begun. 'I've been on the blower to Naylor and we've come to an understanding. He says you can see out the academic year where you are and sit your GCSEs providing I can guarantee, A, that you buckle down to it and B, that you bloody well behave yourself. Right?'

Rupert nodded. He wanted to say, 'Yeah, yeah, yeah,' to demonstrate his total boredom with this idea but he desisted. No point in winding his dad up more than he already was.

'So from the very first day of term it's nose to the bloody grindstone for you, d'you hear? Bugger it, I was already grafting damn hard when I was your age – and it was the making of me . . .'

Rupert suppressed a yawn. 'Yes, sir. You told me.'

'Right. Well, the agreement is that at the first sign of slacking, Naylor will have carte blanche to sling you out. Then you'll have to study for your exams in the local comprehensive . . . if they'll take you.'

Rupert quailed. 'You mean, with all the spotty oiks!' He refused to believe that his father would act on such a dire threat. He had a curious feeling he might not last five minutes with the 'spotty oiks'.

'And you can take that supercilious look off your face. I mean what I say. Perhaps a spell in the kind of school I went to would do you a power of good.'

Rupert grinned disarmingly. Then, with the appearance of utmost gravity, rearranged himself into a less casual pose. 'Look, Dad, I don't know what happened last term. I guess I sort of freaked out. I'm sorry about it and I don't blame you for being hacked off. But you and Naylor needn't worry, I've already decided to get my arse into gear from now on. I know I can do it. It's just a matter of boning up on the syllabus and dashing it all down while it's still red-hot. Perhaps it's just as well if I cram at the last minute, my long-term memory's crap anyway.'

Roy grunted doubtfully. 'What I then want to know is if you intend to keep it up, get your exams and go for A levels. Because, if you don't I'd sooner know now and save myself the trouble of looking for somewhere else to send you, and a great deal of money. I suppose we're still no nearer to knowing what you intend doing after you leave school altogether?'

Rupert thought that telling his father he fully intended to be discovered as a potential surfing superstar by the end of the summer, with offers coming in from all round the globe for sponsoring and promotions, would not be a smart move. Besides, if he was going to get started at all he needed to keep the old man sweet.

'Not exactly, no, sir. But I really do promise to give these GCSEs my best shot.'

Roy scrutinized his son narrowly. 'I'm glad it's beginning to dawn on you that nothing's for nothing in this world. I'd hoped you'd come into the business one day along with Philip but that's up to you. As for where you go after next term that will depend on your results . . .' Roy hitched up his trousers, a gesture that seemed to indicate the interview was at an end. Rupert lingered at the door.

'What is it now?'

Rupert came back into the room and sat in Roy's leather armchair, leaning forward confidingly.

'Dad, I was wondering if I could have an advance on my allowance. There's some gear I have to get.'

'What sort of gear?'

'These guys from school asked me to go surfing with them in Cornwall next week. You know, check out the sets, but I said no.'

'That's all right. You can't surf. Check out the sets?'

'They were going to give me a start but I said that you probably couldn't afford the gear. Surfboard and so on.'

'Can't afford a bloody surfboard!'

'That's what *they* said.'

'Well, if it'll keep you out of mischief, you can go ahead but only if I have your solemn promise that you bloody well stop farting about at school and get down to it!'

Rupert grinned. 'I promise on my honour to stop farting about and get down to it.' He got up. 'Thanks, Dad. You're the biz.' He knew his father had no idea what a decent surfing board cost, let alone the wetties and rash vests. Never mind, by the time he found out it would be too late. It wasn't enough, but he had very carefully saved the money he'd liberated from Chisholm's locker. Chisholm shouldn't have put it there in the first place, it was against school rules, but the stupid prick was always boasting that his old man was stinking with it. He deserved to lose it.

Work was in progress on some of the moored craft. Spring cleaning – the start of the season. The time was when Rupert would have wasted no time in getting his own boat out into the river, even getting it up on the slipway and scraping, painting, mending and polishing with all the rest. Now it all seemed like one big yawn, something he had left behind, though he hadn't said as much to his father last night. He had led him to think that sailing was still number one and that surfing was just a minor interest; in fact sailing now seemed pathetically tame. Definitely not for him – not now.

Approaching Dartmouth he cut back the engine and allowed the Zodiac to nose its way through buoys and mooring lines until he reached the pontoon where he tied up. He shinned up the metal ladder on to the quay and made his way towards the main shopping streets.

On his way to his destination he caught sight of a long silk scarf in the window of a boutique. It was part of a display of spring outfits and was in just the kind of colours his sister went in for; blacks and neutrals with a dash of bright blue. Not that she thought much about clothes, not as much as he did, in fact, but she liked scarves to tie up her hair with. Besides, in spite of being about to get hitched she had struck him as looking a bit down last night. She probably wanted cheering up. He fingered Chisholm's cash in his pocket. If his dad was about to shell out for the surfboard he could probably spare the odd tenner for a present for Harry. He went boldly in to ask the price. Female establishments held no terrors for him and as he expected, in no time the young woman behind the counter was hurrying to remove the scarf from the window.

'It's twenty-eight ninety-nine,' she said apologetically.

'Whoops!' he said. He hesitated, his head on one side.

'Could you wait there, sir? I might be able to get a reduction.' She disappeared into the back of the shop. When she came back she was smiling. 'Mrs Rogers says she could let it go for twenty-four,' she said.

Rupert smiled, giving the young woman the benefit of his beautiful even teeth and the tantalizing little crevices at the corners of his mouth. 'That's more like it. Could you giftwrap it for me?' He would still have plenty of money left over for his other expenses that morning.

After that he went to the Yardarm Gallery where Harriet was in the act of removing a painting from the wall so that a client could have a closer look at it.

'Would you mind if it remained on display until the exhibition finishes?' she asked when the client reached for her credit card. Rupert watched as Harriet negotiated the sale and sent the customer away, delighted with her purchase. He could never reconcile this Harriet with the one he saw at home. He gave her a kiss on the cheek, his mouth open to savour his sister's delicious skin. He wished though that she wouldn't always pull away when he touched her. For Christ's sake, he didn't mean anything by it, she was his sister after all. He just liked touching women and there was fat chance of it at school.

'I've brought you a present,' he said, thrusting the parcel into her hands.

'Rupert! What a surprise.' As Harriet fumbled with the wrapping Gordon wandered in from the back office.

'Hallo there, Rupert. How's things?'

'Great,' Rupert said. Harriet glanced at him. So he'd got round his father in the end. The scarf tumbled out of its paper.

'Nice!' Gordon exclaimed. 'Clever old Rupert.'

'It's . . . gorgeous,' Harriet said. 'Rupert, this must have been terribly expensive.'

'Don't worry about it,' Rupert said expansively.

Harriet kissed her brother, more circumspectly than he'd kissed her. 'That was very sweet of you, Rupert.'

'You like it?'

'Of course I do. It's perfect and I love the colours.'

'That's all right then. Look, I have a few things to do. Shall we meet for lunch?'

Harriet looked questioningly at Gordon. 'Do you need me at lunchtime?'

'Darling, we always need you, but just this once we'll just have to manage, won't we?'

Harriet laughed. Rupert strolled around for a few minutes looking at the displays, then he left, searching for a particular square, one he couldn't remember hearing of until recently. It turned out to be more of a courtyard than a square. He found the poky entrance to the establishment he sought, glanced round, then ducked his head and went inside. The interior was cramped, in a leather chair a client was already seated, his arm bared to receive a picture of a mermaid. While he waited Rupert picked a more modest sun design from the crowded display on the wall.

'I don't see why your relations have to be so involved with one another,' Daniel said. 'I hardly ever see mine.' He was sprawled on Nell's sofa, a can of lager in his hand, his red braces visible under a black waistcoat. He gave the impression that clothes were of no interest to him while at the same time managing to look trendy, with a hint of the arty. It was different when she had first known him, when he had been always slightly scruffy.

Nell, with her back to him, checked her reflection in the mirror, running her fingers through her short hair which was all that was necessary to tidy it. They had just made love. It had been even better than before, now that they were becoming used to each other again.

'It seems natural, that's all, since we live near to one another,' she said turning round. 'Besides, I like my sisters. And my mother.'

'I got away from my family as soon as I could.' Daniel stretched and yawned, nearly spilling his drink. 'My mother in particular. Boozy old bat.'

'I thought your mother was rather sweet.' Nell picked up her drink and sat next to Daniel on the sofa. 'Is she still alive?'

'Old soaks never die. She's in a home.'

'Do you go to see her?'

Daniel finished his lager and put the empty can on the floor at his feet. 'Look, don't let's talk about my ma, if you don't mind.' He let his arm fall across her shoulders. 'Let's talk about us. Has your accountant chap had time to cast his eye over the books?'

'Yes.' Nell sipped her drink. 'He's a cautious old so-and-so though. He doesn't want me to put all my capital into Cornucopia.'

'Oh well, it's his job to be cagey. All the same, you won't see too much return on your capital unless you put it all into Cornucopia. And it might limit the kind of expansion we could go in for.'

'I explained about that.'

'After all, it's not as though you were making a fortune where you are. And we *are* going to get hitched. Did you tell him that? Or don't you feel absolutely committed to the idea yet?' He leaned forward to look into her face.

'You know I do, Daniel.'

'Cornucopia will be as much yours as mine when we've actually tied the knot, you know. This time I want us to be one hundred per cent united and take all our decisions together. For better or worse and all that.' He grinned. 'Not like before when we never acted as a real partnership.'

Nell looked at his eager face, his dark hair still rumpled from bed, his eyes bright with enthusiasm. Her emotions, her heart and even her quick intelligence were already willing hostages to his beguiling charm; she could not have escaped now even if she'd wanted to. It had been the state of being that had made their previous abrupt separation such a catastrophic shock, why it had taken her so long to recover, if she ever had. It was slowly dawning on her that the four-year hiatus had been due merely to their immaturity, just a hiccup in a relationship that had been foreordained from the very beginning. A sort of amazed happiness filled her that he was now even keener on marriage than she was. Marriage as an institution had never meant that much to her, or to him for that matter. It must be a sign of his newly developed sense of responsibility.

'For better or worse,' she repeated, half joking.

'So when are we going to sort this lot out then?'

'My lease is due for renewal in June but I expect I can sublet if I have to.'

'We don't want to wait until June. At least *I* don't want to wait until June.' He leaned back against the sofa and put his hands behind his head. 'How's this for a scenario? You give notice on the shop and flat more or less straight away, transfer your stock and capital to Cornucopia by the end of the month, April that is, then we finally get hitched on the twenty-first. I thought it might be nice and corny to have an Easter wedding but I suppose that's too short notice.'

'*Much* too short.'

'You don't want a big affair, do you? I thought a registry office.'

'Yes, of course. I shall have enough of big weddings this year as it is.'

'How come?'

'Desna's daughter, Harriet, is getting married in July. You remember Harriet?'

'I thought she was just a kid!'

'Time passes, Daniel.'

'Who's she marrying? Anyone I know?'

'The Emmerson boy. You remember the Emmersons?'

'Vaguely. Lawyer chap, wasn't he?'

'The son works for Roy.'

'Hmm. Cosy. Nice spot of nepotism never did anyone any harm. But to get back to us, what d'you think?'

'I think it's all rather quick.'

'Why wait?'

'I shall have to buy new clothes.'

'You know you always look fantastic. You have the best dress sense of anyone I know.'

She wanted to be with Daniel, married or not, more than anything she had ever wanted before, but a remnant of common sense told her that time should be allowed for the financial arrangements, if nothing else, to be conducted in a proper businesslike manner. Besides, she would need a space to bring the family round to accepting the idea of her and Daniel being back together again. Every time she thought about telling them her skin prickled with apprehension; and every time she remembered that Persis might so easily betray her before she had a chance to talk to them, her blood felt cold in her veins.

Not that her marriage was conditional on their approval, but not to have Daniel welcomed into the bosom of the family would be both awkward and very upsetting. She wished more than anything that she had been better able to disguise her past pain and hurt from her mother and sisters in order that their opinion of Daniel would not now have hardened into intractable opposition. Now she would have to undo all that, assume some of the blame for the past, plead mutual misunderstanding. At least the Easter get-together at Mount Huish would give her the opportunity she needed.

'When are you taking me to see The Old Rectory?' she asked. 'Since I shall be living there before long I really think I should take a look at it quite soon.'

'There doesn't seem to have been time,' he said. 'I was going to suggest it tomorrow evening but you've told me you're rushing off to see Emmet.'

'I have to. Emmet's ill.'

'Can't her old man manage?'

'They're separated. Sort of.'

'Well, are they or aren't they?'

'It's difficult to say.'

Daniel shook his head, baffled. 'In any case, you might not like The Old Rectory.'

'Not like it! You're joking!'

'I've been thinking I should live nearer the business, as a matter of fact. I had actually begun to look at one or two properties in the vicinity of Cornucopia.'

'Well, I hope we shall be able to decide something like that together. Don't you dare offer for anything unless I see it first!'

He grinned. 'Darling! Would I?' He reached for her and burrowed his head into her neck, pulling her on to his lap. Her body responded instantly; it was as if her flesh were melting.

Morgan came into the room on quiet feet and sat in front of them fixing Daniel with an amber stare.

'That animal is trying to put me off,' Daniel complained.

'I think that's the idea.'

'Well, I've got news for him,' Daniel said, his mouth against her throat. 'He hasn't a hope. Let's go to bed again.'

The car with the Bonne Bouche logo was already parked on the drive when Desna got back. The appointment had been for three thirty and it was now three forty. She hated being unpunctual but even with the best will in the world, coping with the domestic arrangements at Drake's Farm was an inexact science to say the very least. She felt flustered, an unusual sensation for her.

'Mrs Turnbull, I'm so sorry!' she said as they emerged from their respective vehicles. 'Have you been waiting long?'

'Two minutes, that's all,' Mrs Turnbull lied soothingly. 'I've used the time to check up on what we have already agreed.' She smiled. 'Please call me Stevie, won't you?'

'Well, come in, Stevie. Let's have some tea and relax.' They went into the kitchen together. To see her pristine working environment was a joy to Desna after the chaos of her sister's kitchen. Carol had done the floor, the worktops and the cookers. Everything shone.

She made tea and led the way into the sitting room. Thankfully the house was empty; Rupert must still be out. On the sofa Stevie took a small laptop computer out of her briefcase as well as a sheaf of brochures and catalogues.

'Before I forget, I wondered if you'd had any more thoughts about the parking,' she said. 'Only we shall have to be prepared for several of our vans as well as the guests' cars.'

'Roy and I have discussed that. He suggested we use the paddock at the back of the house. A neighbouring farmer has some sheep on it at the moment but that's no problem.'

'Good. We'll have a look at it afterwards. Now, I've brought some suggestions for decorating the marquee. I thought, since the colour theme is this rather subtle pink and pale grey, that you might consider something like this . . .'

It seemed to Desna that Stevie Turnbull was a most unlikely-looking person to be running a catering outfit. Before they had actually met, Desna had conjured up the image of a plump, homely woman or alternatively, a smart well-dressed business female, briskly efficient. Stevie Turnbull fitted into neither category. She was tall and rangy and looked as if she should be out exercising the Labradors in the grounds of some country estate. Nevertheless, she came highly recommended, appeared to know her job and understood perfectly that Desna was looking for something upmarket and different from the usual type of reception. Which she made no bones about warning her client would necessarily be more expensive.

They covered every aspect of the event from wedding cars to favours for the female guests. Stevie noted everything down on her laptop computer, estimating prices, making suggestions, warning of possible problems. By the time they had finished everything was decided.

'Now all you have to do is to make the cake and leave the rest to us,' Stevie said with a smile. She hooked her floppy fairish-grey hair behind her ears and gathered up her brochures. For some reason Desna wanted to delay her.

'Have another cup of tea,' she offered, rising.

'Actually, I'd love one. All that talking has made me thirsty.'

Desna made fresh tea and renewed their cups.

'Have you always done this job?' she asked.

'Goodness, no! I got into it quite by chance. An old school chum was running a catering business in a small way, then she found herself being asked to organize other aspects of the arrangements, like cars and videos and it began to grow. I was newly divorced and looking for something to do and she took me on on a part-time basis. Now I work full time plus!' Stevie sipped her tea and looked sombre. 'As a matter of fact, Sonia was diagnosed a few months ago as having multiple sclerosis. It's very sad, but sooner or later she's going to have to give up. Her husband wants her to quit at once.'

'I'm sorry. That will make things difficult for you, won't it?'

Stevie nodded. 'I'm afraid so. It's been an awful blow.' Then she smiled. 'We're so well organized that at the moment it's not too bad . . .' She glanced at her watch. 'Now, I think I should just have a look at the size of your paddock before I go, just to make sure it can cope with the overflow on the big day.'

Mo had taken the opportunity of Persis' temporary absence to set up her easel and continue with the work that had been interrupted by her sister's arrival. She squinted critically at her unfinished painting, knowing at gut level that the natural impetus that had carried her along so far had been lost. She liked to complete a painting at one sitting, working at top speed, but the break had put the kibosh on all that. She might get back to it or she might not; perhaps when Persis had departed . . .

She flipped through her sketchbook and came across the drawing she'd made of Harriet eating cheese on toast. She smiled to herself, remembering the occasion and the exact components of the image as it had appeared to her that evening.

She saw at once how she could translate it into paint. The yellow light from the table lamp behind the head; the hands poised in the foreground; the face in violet shadow; a streak of burnt orange from the scarf that tied up the hair; patches of tan, black and off-white, all that could be seen of the cat Polly Chrome asleep in the basket; a sweep of faded blue on one side, her old coat thrown over a chair.

Elsewhere in the world, artists were displaying dead animals, filling rooms with water or plaster, and peeing into sand moulds; but Mo was content to apply pigment to jute in the traditional way. Just after the war, when she had spent three years at art school, where she had met her first husband, discussion was rife over the relevance of easel painting. It was still going on to this day. Until they had sorted it out one way or another, she'd carry on, refining her style, exploring the medium and experimenting with colour.

She removed the unfinished canvas from the easel and stuck a fresh one in its place. She squeezed a worm of cobalt blue on to an old plate, dipped in her brush and began to delineate a series of almost abstract spaces on the canvas, frowning and pursing her lips as much over the shapes behind and around the figure as over the figure itself. All these spaces had a value that must be carefully weighed as to size and eventual colour and tone. The trick was to try to visualize in advance how intense, how colour-saturated, how translucent or opaque, even the type of brush stroke they were to be. Sometimes the painting came off completely, sometimes in part, sometimes it refused to gel at all.

Today, however, she felt that it might just work. Glancing out of the window as she painted, she caught sight of Persis crouching crablike on the mouldering deck of the *Prudence*, a camera clamped to her eye like a barnacle. She would be well occupied for some time. Quite suddenly she had lost the air of suppressed anger and frustration that had hung about her since she'd arrived and became obsessed by the various hulks up and down the river, declaring herself fascinated by their resemblance to split open ribcages. She had even persuaded a patient boatman to convey her about the river while she photographed them from every conceivable angle.

Mo smiled to herself as she later caught sight of Persis actually making a drawing of some apparently important detail, something she vowed she never did. Window dressing! Mo thought to herself. Oh, yes?

She realized how the time had passed when Persis strode through the door, stowing her camera away in her capacious bag, though there was no sign of the sketchpad.

'I suppose you want tea?' Mo said. 'Or are you still on the hard stuff?'

'You have such a quaint turn of phrase,' Persis said, turfing Rose Madder off the sofa and casting herself down on it instead. The cat sat at a distance and indignantly licked her flank where Persis had touched her. Persis stuck her feet up on the arm. 'I'll have both.'

'Put the kettle on then. I haven't finished yet. There are buns in the cake tin.'

Persis yawned and reached for her cigarettes. 'Buns! What next? Never mind, I can wait.'

Mo continued to paint in silence. Persis smoked. Then she said, 'How's that Frenchman's brat today?'

'I suppose you mean Emmet? She's not at all well; Desna was with her this morning. Nell's supposed to be going over this evening.'

'Ah, Nellie. Elea-nor.' She elongated the sound of the name. 'What a monicker!'

'You chose it!' Mo was goaded into saying.

'So I did. Poor kid. Now I'd just call her "brat".' She blew a perfect smoke ring into the air. Naming kids was to acknowledge their existence.

'I hope you said nothing to her about you-know-what.'

'You-know-what! Ha! Don't you trust me to keep my trap shut?'

'At a distance, maybe, but I don't like all this close contact. When are you going home, anyway? You said the renovations wouldn't take long. Surely you have work to do, commissions to get on with?'

'I got stumped. Stale, stymied. What you will. Needed a new direction.'

'That's not what you said when you first arrived. You said it was because you were having the studio enlarged.'

'That too.'

'So are you still stymied?' Mo lifted an area of surplus paint off the canvas with her thumb.

'I'll tell you later.' Persis continued to smoke in silence. She had not told Mo the whole truth about the so-called renovations to the studio. Mo painted on.

Then Persis said, 'I'm afraid Nellie is going soft in the head.'

'Why on earth do you say that?'

'She's going to shack up with this fella of hers.'

'I knew she had a new man. I didn't know they had plans to live together.'

'Not only live together! They're getting hitched apparently.'

Mo's brush stopped in mid-air. 'I think you're mistaken.'

'Please yourself. But that's what she told me. Some character called Daniel.'

Mo began to wipe her brush very carefully on the paint rag. 'Say that again.'

Persis twisted round to look at her sister. 'Guy called Daniel. Didn't you know about him?'

'You know perfectly well I didn't,' Mo said grimly. 'Anyway, you've got it all wrong. She *used* to live with a chap called Daniel. Years ago. Not now.'

'She appears anxious to repeat the experiment, stupid little cow.'

'She told *you* all this?'

Persis snorted with laughter. 'I take it that this will not be a popular move with her nearest and dearest. I don't think she actually wanted you to know. Oh, well! It can't be helped. You had to sooner or later.'

Agitated, Mo began to clear up her painting things, her mood completely shattered. 'I'm absolutely astonished she told you,' she said, upset to find herself trembling. 'If this is your idea of confidentiality, the sooner you go home the better!'

'If it's any comfort,' Persis said, puffing out another smoke ring, 'I don't believe she meant to tell me at all. It sort of slipped out.'

CHAPTER SEVENTEEN

Philip parked his old Land Rover under the chestnut trees that lined the churchyard of St Clement's in the Wood, Upper Ash.

'Right. Let's get it over with,' he said.

The evening sunshine slanted obliquely between the trunks of the trees and lay on the road in slabs of gold. The four-square church of St Clement's in the Wood, bathed in butter-yellow light, looked as if it had been cleft from one solid block of stone and put down against its backdrop of tall beech trees. The Reverend Gerald Peters greeted them from amongst the long grass and tilted gravestones where he crouched, gazing up at the squat tower.

'What on earth's he doing?' Harriet said as they pushed open the gate.

'Be with you in a moment,' the vicar called and lifted a camera to his eye. He clicked the shutter, changing the exposure several times for each shot. 'There we are,' he said, getting to his feet and approaching them, hand outstretched. 'Just keeping the records straight and checking up on the wear and tear.'

As well as the camera, he wore binoculars round his neck, both resting on his sturdy chest. He was short and stocky and although not more than forty-five, was already quite grey. In his eye the fire of enthusiasm burned. Harriet knew him slightly from rare family visits to St Clement's.

When they had shaken hands and Harriet had introduced Philip, Mr Peters immediately handed her the binoculars, urging an inspection of the west wall.

'See that?' he said. 'Cracks! Means there's some subsidence going on. Mind you, this part is fairly new, the vestry was added in the last century. Eventually we either demolish or shore up, d'you see? Do you know how old the church is?'

'Norman, isn't it?' Harriet suggested tentatively.

'Come with me and I'll show you something. I think you'll be interested.' He led them inside through the wire bird-doors in the porch until they found themselves standing at the base of the narrow turret that contained the staircase leading to the tower. 'See that?'

'Herringbone moulding?' Harriet supplied dutifully.

'Saxon. Possibly tenth or eleventh century. There was a Saxon church here originally, d'you see?' They stood by the door. 'Did you happen to notice the corbels outside?'

'Corbels?' Philip queried, wondering where all this was leading. He glanced at his watch surreptitiously.

'They're carved brackets. Come and see. I hope you're not too squeamish.' Outside he thrust the binoculars at Philip. 'It's just as well one can only make them out with the bins.'

Philip focused on the series of corbels under the eaves, one in particular. 'Holy shi— Goodness, that's a bit fruity, isn't it?' he said.

'Celtic influence. Sheela-na-gig,' the cleric said with a chuckle. 'I'm sure it doesn't shock you young people but it would some of our parishioners. Fortunately, it's rather high up. In those days they had a different approach to procreation. History. Fascinating!'

Philip hesitated and then handed the binoculars to Harriet with a joking comment.

She saw a bug-eyed female monster that spread apart its own genitals with its hands, an expression on its face that could only be described as a leer. 'I see what you mean,' she said, trying to appear blasé.

'So much for what one might call the profane. Let's have a look at the sacred.' Mr Peters trotted off inside again. They followed. Harriet whispered in Philip's ear: 'This isn't quite what I expected.'

'I suppose we'll get to the nitty-gritty sooner or later. Sooner, I hope.'

Inside they stood in the chancel while the vicar held forth about the fourteenth-century screen, pointed out the piscina which, with the canopy over it, had apparently been walled up in Cromwell's time and discovered again much later. There were also some remaining scraps of an early mural; a devil spearing a couple of unfortunate lovers. After that Mr Peters turned his attention to the windows, showing them what was left of the decorative fourteenth-century stained glass. At last he pointed out the fine wagon roof.

'The bosses are a delight. See that one! Noah and the ark,' the vicar looked grave suddenly. 'But as you see if you look closely, all is not well. Have a squint through the bins.'

They obediently did. 'Looks like you've got a bit of woodworm up there,' Philip said.

'I should say. It'll have to be chopped out, of course. But God knows when. We've only just finished paying for new flashing. Damned shame, but there it is. Heritage – the buzz work nowadays. But let's face it, nobody's ever going to build churches like this again. Nobody's going to build churches much at all! Where are the craftsmen in the modern world who could invent and execute work like this?'

Philip shrugged. He knew craftsmen; bloody good ones. But they built boats, not churches.

'Mind you,' the cleric went on, a glow in his eye, 'the church used to be dictatorial in the extreme with their masons and woodcarvers, parting them from their families and sending them wherever they pleased, sometimes for years, or until the work was completed. Did you know that? So you could say there was a down side. Makes it all the more important that their work doesn't go to waste, d'you see?' He looked at them with bright enquiry, like a robin. Harriet who had been wondering what this was all leading up to, now began to have an inkling.

'Right, then. You two young people will have other calls on your time so I won't keep you . . .' He hesitated as if remembering the purpose of their visit. He indicated some rush-seated chairs. 'Let's sit down and we'll have a chat about the marriage service, shall we? I take it you already realize that Christians believe marriage to be a holy state . . .'

They chose the 1928 marriage service, leaving out the word 'obey' and arranged about the banns. A very few minutes later the interview finished with a prayer and a jovial enquiry about whether they had discussed the music with Janet.

'Janet?'

'Our organist. And you must let us know if you'll be wanting the bellringers and the choir.'

'Thanks. I'm sure we will.'

'Off you go then. Give me a call later on so that we can arrange for a rehearsal. Any questions about anything else – well, you know where I am. Before you go, you better take one of these . . .' He trawled in his pocket and produced a couple of leaflets, leaving them with a cheery wave.

Harriet glanced at what had been thrust into her hand; they were not, as she expected, potted advice on the solemn oaths that they were about to undertake.

'And what,' Philip said, watching Mr Peters' stocky figure disappear into the dappled light of the lane that led to the vicarage, 'do you think that was all about?'

Harriet showed him the leaflets.

'"A History of the Parish and Church of St Clement's in the Wood, Upper Ash",' he read out loud. 'What's that in aid of?'

'I'm just beginning to understand. It's emotional blackmail. Daddy's not going to be very pleased, I'm afraid.'

Philip unlocked the door of the Land Rover. 'I don't know about Roy, but your mother's not going to be too pleased if we're late for dinner.' Desna had invited Philip back after the interview with the vicar. 'Come on, I don't know about you but all that history has made me hungry enough to eat a herd of wildebeest.'

Later that evening, after dinner, they escaped down to the boathouse. They sat on the decking, huddled in thick jerseys against the chill. Philip put his arm round Harriet, holding her close.

'So you think the vicar is going to touch the old man for a generous donation to the fabric fund, do you?'

'Don't you?' Harriet said, gazing into the silky blackness of the stealthily moving water.

'You could be right.' He pulled her even closer. 'I wish to God we didn't have to go through this bloody charade. I've half a mind to push off somewhere, just you and me, and stuff it all.'

'Me too. I wish we could.'

'Look, I've had an idea. How about you and me ducking out at Easter? We could take a long weekend off. Go to London, anywhere you like, just for a break from all this.'

'You mean, get married?'

'Well, no. I don't think we could manage that in a weekend.' He grinned in the darkness. 'Your mother would throw a wobbly. No. I meant get away for a few hours. Would you like that?'

'We couldn't do it at Easter. All the family's coming then: Mo, Emmet and Nell and everyone, remember?'

'Soon, though?'

Harriet listened to the soft soughing of the wind in the trees, interspersed by the trial hoots of an owl. She knew precisely what Philip's suggestion meant; that they should sleep together. The opportunities for sex had been few and far between and hedged about with difficulties. Philip shared a flat in Dartmouth with a young man called Andy, but even when Andy had helpfully agreed to spend a night or a weekend away, Harriet had demurred, found excuses. Philip himself spent a great deal of time away, delivering boats, staying over in ports from Holland to the Med, or even on the far side of the Atlantic. But this in itself was not an insurmountable obstacle; they were both aware that the fundamental problem was Harriet's reluctance.

Philip stroked her cheek with his thumb. When the silence became protracted he said, 'Harry, what are you afraid of? I've no intention of raping you, you know.'

'I know. I know.'

'What then?'

'I'm afraid it may change things. Change how I feel about you, I suppose. And change how you feel about me. And I'm afraid I may not be any good at it.'

'At sex, you mean? That's nothing. No one's good at it to start with.'

'I suppose there does have to be sex?' Unbidden into her mind came the grotesque image of the carving on the church. From the perspective of the present day it was some sort of joke, wasn't it? Certainly Philip and the vicar seemed to think so. Or did some lingering whiff of atavism remain in civilized exteriors. Was any man to be trusted? Even Philip?

'Were you planning on some sort of platonic setup then? Because if you were you've got the wrong chap.' In the darkness he turned her until he could see just a glimmer of light in her eyes. Gently he gathered her in his arms and pressed her down on to the decking. He began to kiss her, caressing her mouth and eyelids with his tongue. At last he said, 'Don't you feel anything at all when I do this?'

'Yes. I like it when you hold me.'

He pulled at her thick jersey and let his hand stray to her breasts. 'And this?' But he already had his answer. She turned away and struggled to sit up. The temptation to force her to submit was overpowering but in the end he broke away and sat apart from her. For the first time he began to fear that she would never agree to sex and experienced a hot burst of anger at her rejection of him. It had so happened that no girl had ever refused to sleep with him, but this was mostly due to his skill at reading the covert language of sexual exchange. The present situation was completely baffling and furthermore was undermining his belief in himself. Harriet was the first woman he had ever really loved, though love seemed too general a term for what he felt. He adored her, was obsessed by her exquisite beauty, every turn of her head fascinated him; sometimes when she looked at him he felt himself drowning in her gaze. She had a quality of mystery that he had never before encountered and it had totally beguiled him. All the same, to avoid the unimaginable embarrassment of having to put a stop to Desna's formidable accumulation of wedding arrangements, he was going to have to win Harriet over, and soon. It would tear him apart to be without Harriet for the rest of his life, he couldn't believe that he would ever again love anyone; but neither could he contemplate a marriage in which sex was to be had by seizure, not by mutual desire. It simply wasn't his scene.

'I'm sorry, Philip,' Harriet murmured, feeling hot tears prickling her eyes. 'It's not because I don't love you. I do. Really I do.'

'Most guys would think you had a funny way of showing it. Most guys would have given up altogether.' Philip was aware that he sounded harsh, surly, but he couldn't help himself. 'I sometimes wonder if you're ready for marriage at all.'

Harriet was silent, in an agony of fear that Philip was about to finish it altogether. How would she survive without Philip? He was the rock she clung to. Without him the random currents of life might sweep her away.

'Perhaps we *should* go away somewhere soon,' she said quietly. 'If we went right away from everything, just the two of us, I expect it would be all right.'

Philip relented, squeezing her hand in his. He leaned over and kissed her. 'That's a deal, then . . . and Harry, it will be all right. I promise you. You did go to see the doctor to fix up about going on the pill, didn't you?'

'Yes.'

At least that was something, Philip thought. If she was taking the pill, it showed that she hadn't ruled out sex altogether. The only reservation he still had was that the first weekend that he was not either delivering boats or otherwise required at the yard was the week after Easter. He hoped it wouldn't be too late.

Desna leaned against the stone balustrade and watched Harriet and Philip as they slowly ascended the path from the boathouse. It was dark but the path was lit sporadically by lights fixed to the trunks of trees and half hidden by the leaves of the rhododendrons. The two of them walked heads bent, engrossed. How fortunate she was to have such a beautiful and gentle daughter; and how fortunate too that Harriet had found a potential partner who could only be described as ideal. If Desna had planned it herself she couldn't have found anyone better for Harriet. Philip was hard-working, intelligent – intelligent enough anyway – and most important of all, could be relied on to be kind to Harriet. It worried her sometimes, this extreme sensitivity of her daughter's and she had feared in the past that this very combination of beauty and overt vulnerability would attract the worst kind of male. It was strange, but she had never visualized Harriet as a career girl, only as needing the protection of a good marriage. She would be practically holding her breath until Harriet was safely united with the ideally suitable Philip.

At least Harriet was beginning to take an interest in the wedding arrangements. She had agreed on the design and colour of the wedding dress, white silk with a shell-pink underskirt that would be subtly flattering to her delicate skin. And she had made a decision about the colour of the bridesmaids' dresses. Desna hadn't been keen on the grey herself but it would probably go down well with Faith and Tessa, who were both very modern young women, even if of totally different types. She wasn't sure about the Wakeham twins. Roy had absolutely insisted that they be asked; all the same, she believed that they would be keen enough to go along with whatever was chosen. Beth, with her nimbus of pale hair, would look adorable even in a bin liner.

Desna turned away. She didn't want Philip and Harriet to think she had been spying on them. The narrow path on which she stood led from the kitchen garden, winding among the trees at the edge of the lawn to a secluded viewpoint that overlooked the river. She sat on the bench that she herself had had placed there, pulling her jacket closer. The scent of the primroses and narcissi, which glimmered palely among the tree trunks, filled the air and assailed her nostrils. Below her she could just hear the rush and gurgle of the river, above her the tentative calls of owls.

She adored all the sounds and scents of Mount Huish at all times of the year. The beauty of the house and its setting filled her with a passionate love such as nothing else could, apart from her children. She thought guiltily of Roy who had made possible the realization of her dream, for Mount Huish had been more like a nightmare when they'd first moved in. She did not have to look far for the origin of her guilt. She not only no longer felt passionate about Roy, she wasn't sure if she really even liked him any more. This frightening discovery was the prime reason for her to be wandering about in the garden in the dark. It was unlikely that anyone would miss her, however; Rupert was upstairs in his room listening to loud music, Roy was in his study telephoning.

She realized that the conversation at dinner had been the final straw of a process that could have been going on for months. It explained a great many things: her failure to achieve anything like sexual satisfaction – her reluctance to make love at all, in fact – the falling asleep at odd times, her unaccustomed irritability. She had even occasionally detected feelings of envy when she compared herself with Nell and Emmet. Things must be pretty bad if she was becoming jealous of Emmet!

Dinner had started off as a pleasant family meal, made more convivial than usual by the constant stream of jokes and banter kept up by Philip and Rupert, especially Rupert who was in particularly good form. Philip regaled them with the story of their encounter with Gerald Peters and his obsession with ecclesiastical architecture.

Roy was amused. 'Got you off the hook, then? You young heathen.'

Philip tucked into his steak diane with enthusiasm. 'Yes, I wasn't sorry to miss out on the lecture about the holy state of matrimony and all that.' He glanced at Desna. 'Not that I don't think one has to take it seriously. I just don't like someone else telling me what I should be thinking. Duty and all that . . .'

Roy passed his plate so that Desna could help him to more glazed carrots. 'I'm inclined to agree with you there. Mind you, if you're having a church wedding, one has to go along with it to a certain extent.'

'Yes, sir. I do see that.'

'Marriage is a contract like anything else. It involves duties and obligations.'

'Duties?' Harriet queried before she could stop herself. Rupert snorted with amusement. Harriet flushed.

'What's wrong with duties?' Roy said loudly, though he was still in a good mood.

'I hadn't thought of marriage in those terms, that's all,' Harriet said, wishing she hadn't spoken.

'You're a dreamer, young woman,' Roy continued in his jovial mood. 'Duty is what it's all about when you get over the hearts and flowers bit. That's so, isn't it, Des? Duty and responsibility.'

Desna had her fork halfway to her mouth. She had so far kept out of the conversation but now she found herself staring fixedly at Roy as if he was a stranger. She muttered something but Roy was oblivious, in full and jovial flight as he often was when people other than the family were present. He went on to talk of marriage as if it were a business contract and it dawned on her for the first time that this was indeed how he saw it. Any failure to abide by its rules, whatever they were, was a dereliction.

So what she had considered to be a marriage all these years had been, to Roy, simply a bargain, a contract much like any other. All the while they thought alike, had the same goals, all had gone smoothly, carried forward by Roy's impressive will. There had been occasions, in particular about the bringing up of Harriet and Rupert, when she knew they had differed but it had been all too easy to bury her misgivings for the sake of a peaceful domestic exterior. Conflict of any kind did not fit in with Desna's vision of Mount Huish as a haven of tranquillity and beauty. Her creation had been so successful that it was the first thing visitors commented on when they saw it for the first time.

The conversation had flowed on without her. Roy had commented on Harriet's new scarf. He said that he hoped she was beginning to smarten herself up a bit.

'It was a present from Rupert,' Harriet said.

'Was it, indeed?' Roy looked at his son quizzically. He was glad to hear that he was thinking of someone beside himself for a change. He'd do. In spite of Rupert's failings, Roy saw a great deal of himself in his son, which accounted for his indulgence. 'You bought it in Dartmouth?'

'I saw it in a shop and thought it would just suit Harry.' Rupert passed up his plate for second helpings.

'Good,' Roy said. 'Pity you didn't get yourself a haircut while you were in town. If your hair gets much longer you'll have to buy a scarf for *yourself*.'

There was general laughter.

'I'm serious,' Roy went on. 'What do the school think about it?'

'They don't mind. I said I wanted it like this. It's to do with my interpretation of Henry V.' There had in fact been arguments with the English Department, who at first insisted that long hair wasn't historically accurate. Rupert had won the day; he was too good in the part to make it an issue. He tucked into a second steak. 'Ma, this is mega, mega good,' he said.

Desna smiled, fully aware of her son's talent for being charming, but she was too troubled to take any comfort from his words.

Now Desna made her way back to the house, driven by the chill of the evening. Her life was in a state of change. Soon both the children would be gone, leaving her alone with Roy. Even Roy himself was different lately. More than once in the last few weeks, she had detected in him a sense of what she could only describe as suppressed excitement. It had the effect of making him far more tolerant of Rupert's conduct than he might otherwise have been. It had also resulted in his being even more sexually demanding than usual. This for her, in her present turmoil of spirit, had been the most difficult thing of all. She would have to do something about her apathy and anxiety. She wondered if Nell's acupuncturist could help her.

The telephone was ringing as she let herself in through the conservatory door. It was Mo with some garbled story that Persis had apparently got hold of; quite obviously without a shred of truth to it.

'You yourself told me what Persis is like,' she said severely. 'I

243

naturally won't be able to judge for myself until I meet her.'

'I'm sorry she hasn't been to see you yet—'

'I would have come to you but you said she's been too busy apparently.' Too busy to see me but not too busy to see Nell, Desna thought.

'She has some bee in her bonnet about the old hulks on the river. She's been out photographing them.'

'Well, you can tell her that she's wrong about Nell. Daniel hurt Nell very badly indeed. She'd never take him back.'

'She loved him, Desna. It's not beyond the bounds of possibility—'

'Someone should ring her and ask,' Desna said. 'It's no good speculating. But I'm quite sure you're wrong.'

'I've chopped up enough wood to be going on with,' Barney said, dumping a load of logs next to the Rayburn and stacking them neatly. It wasn't all he'd accomplished that morning. Besides the cleaning out and feeding of the birds and animals, a slightly wonky pile of ironing stood on the table as testimony to his industry.

Emmet looked up from her task of setting yet another broken wing, a kestrel's this time. She'd banished the cats to the yard. Afterwards there were the other cages to be worked through, feeding, cleaning and checking injuries.

'Thanks, Barney,' she said croakily, dabbing her nose on the sleeve of her jersey. She was pale and there were dark circles under her eyes. Her bandaged hand, now protected by a rubber glove, held the kestrel firmly while she explored its wing for ominous pulverizing of the bone. It felt like a simple break, thank goodness.

'You don't look too clever. D'you think you'll be okay?'

'I can manage. You haven't left me anything to do except the cooking. Tom and Beth will have to be content with frozen veggie burgers again tonight.' She began to tape the wing. 'The rest is just feeding the monsters every so often.'

Barney picked up his cup of almost cold coffee and leaned against the rail of the Rayburn, sleeves pushed up to reveal his wiry arms with their dusting of red hair and freckles. 'I've had to cancel making a start on Mrs Draycott's rock garden today while I go and have a butcher's at some bedsits.'

'I thought you had one. Over the newsagents.'

'They want me out. Their son's coming out of the army.'

'Oh dear, Barney.'

'No sweat. I'll find something else. I can doss down anywhere.'

Emmet finished confining the damaged wing while the kestrel fixed her with a steely stare. Gently she replaced it in its box and closed the lid. For a moment she leaned back in her chair, overcome with weakness. 'Of course you could stay here if you like. As a temporary measure until you find something. As you know we've plenty of spare rooms, some of which are habitable.' With a great effort she reached into a cage and closed her hand over a baby pigeon, hideous in its scrawniness.

'That's an idea,' Barney said. He took his empty cup over to the sink and rinsed it out under the tap. 'The attic overlooking the garden's a nice big room. How much would you ask?'

'Goodness. I don't know.'

'I'm paying thirty at the Hicks'. With the use of bathroom and kitchen.'

'Well, it's there if you want it. If you don't find anything in the village.'

'Right. I'll bear that in mind. Thanks.' He dried his mug and put it on the dresser. He grinned. 'I'd be on the spot for morning and evening chores, wouldn't I?'

Emmet hadn't the heart to remind him that she couldn't afford to employ him on a daily basis indefinitely. On the other hand, rent for the room might go some way towards paying for his help. She banished the thought. She'd be well soon and not in need of much in the way of assistance; meanwhile she had to admit that it was a great relief to have Barney's reliable presence around the place. If he were here she might even be able to take the children out for days in the Easter holidays. Tom had been pestering to go tenpin bowling, an outing that Maurice had refused point-blank even to consider. Since he couldn't drive she supposed there was some justification for this. But not being able to drive was not his only, or even his prime objection.

'How far from here is the nearest tenpin bowling place?' she asked Barney.

'There's one near Exeter, I believe. Why?'

'Tom's crazy to go bowling.'

'Why don't you take the two kids there in the school holidays?'

'Our old banger can only manage a few miles at a time . . .'

'It's not that far. Anyway, I could fix the car up for you.'

'Do you know anything about it?'

'Enough, I expect.'

'Hmm.' Emmet was doubtful. 'We'll see. At the moment I can't visualize doing anything ever again. My head feels like shit.'

'You'll be fine in a day or so. I think bowling's a great idea. It would cheer Tom up. He's been a bit out of whack lately.'

'He doesn't like me being ill.'

'I don't suppose you're too keen on it either. Anything else you want before I go?'

Emmet shook her head. She put the pigeon back in its cage and closed the door. 'Perhaps you could put these cages back in the scullery so that I can let the cats in again.'

After Barney had complied, he put on his leather jacket, fixed on his motor-cycle helmet and opened the door. The cats streamed in.

'Good luck with the househunting,' Emmet said as he went.

Although Barney looked at several rooms to let, he drew a blank. In spite of his boast at being prepared to doss down anywhere, there were limits. One room was little more than a broom cupboard; one was made practically lethal with the reek of resinous adhesive from a furniture workshop underneath; in a third the landlady would not let him keep his motorbike anywhere on the premises.

'I don't like the motorbikes,' she said. 'Beastly, noisy, oily things.'

That evening he gave Emmet a humorous account of his failure to find anything suitable. 'I'll have another shot at it tomorrow,' he said philosophically.

Emmet crouched over the sink washing up the supper things. Tom and Lee were upstairs. Beth was watching television in the sitting room.

'Come on,' Barney said. 'Let me do that.' He took over at the sink and Emmet went back to her chair without protest.

'You can't waste any more working hours looking for somewhere to live,' Emmet said. 'There's a perfectly good room here going begging. And there's even a place under cover for you to keep your bike.'

'You sure about this?' Barney stacked the last of the dishes on the draining board.

'Of course I am.'

'Right then. I'll move my stuff over at the weekend, if that suits you. I could even give the room a going-over with white paint one evening.'

'Whatever you like,' Emmet agreed.

'There's one thing . . .' Barney began, with a grin.

'Yes?'

'There'll be gossip in the village. Me lodging up here with you.'

'Don't be ridiculous. I'm a married woman!'

'Well . . .'

'Come on, Barney. You can't be serious?'

'OK, then. If you don't mind I'm sure I don't. What about your old man?'

'What about him?'

'He might not like it.'

'Don't worry about that. Maurice will be pleased to think there's a little extra money coming in.'

As soon as the sound of Barney's motorbike had faded into the distance, Tom and Lee put in an appearance.

'Has he gone?' Tom asked.

'Has who gone?'

Tom and Lee exchanged glances. 'That man. Barney.'

'Yes. Barney's gone,' Emmet said. She was slumped in her chair, her hand to her throbbing temples, hoping that the antibiotics she had taken would at last begin to take effect before morning. She didn't even have the energy to make a comment on Tom's unreasonable aversion to someone who was currently keeping their fragile family barque afloat.

The house was silent. The others had long since gone to bed and presumably to sleep. Only Harriet was still awake.

Although she was in her pyjamas and dressing gown, she was seated at her desk finishing the drawing of the sheep's skull. It wasn't quite as accurate as she'd hoped but it seemed to her that it was stronger and more confident than usual. The whole thing was bolder and more three-dimensional. She was learning.

She held up a mirror to check for distortions and as she gazed the familiar shapes seemed to slew and metamorphose until they had rearranged themselves into a likeness of the carving she had seen on the church. Sheela-na-gig. The goddess of creation and destruction. Birth and death. The Celtic Kali. She felt herself trembling and let go the mirror abruptly. It clattered on to the desk, chipping a corner.

After a moment she dared to look at her drawing again. Her breath came back to her; the sheep's skull was still a sheep's skull, a symbol of death she had always previously taken for granted. A natural process, not grotesque and menacing. Sheep died. People died. She herself would one day die. This fact had never disturbed her unduly. So what was she afraid of? Surely not Philip? She loved Philip. But would Philip eventually subjugate her entirely as her father had her mother? Possess her, take away her free will, make her into a non-person swamped in another's identity. She loved Philip but would she have to submit to him as her mother did to her father? Would she merely exchange one control for another? All at once she found herself wishing more than anything that she could talk to her mother. But Desna would never understand; besides, she was so engrossed in the wedding arrangements that Harriet hadn't the courage to suggest that there might be problems.

Her mother had been very quiet at dinner. It occurred to

Harriet that the wedding arrangements wouldn't be making her look so troubled. There must be something else. She frowned as she bent over her work again.

CHAPTER EIGHTEEN

'Mummy, Mummy, wake up!' Beth's panic-stricken cries tore through Emmet's consciousness. All the chores completed for the time being, she had at last given in and gone upstairs to lie down. Perhaps because the antibiotics were at last taking effect, the feverish state that had paradoxically kept her restlessly on her feet, if totally dysfunctional, had broken and she had fallen into the first calm sleep for days.

'Mummy, Mummy!' Beth was shaking her now and her screams were piercing.

'Beth! Whatever . . .' Automatically Emmet put her feet on the floor, fumbling for her jeans and boots, bleary-eyed. She had stripped down to her tee shirt and pants before she had crept under the duvet to sleep. It was Saturday and Beth had been to play with Dinah's little girl, Rebecca, for the afternoon. Tom had stayed home to work on one of his model aeroplanes, Lee being otherwise occupied.

As Emmet pulled on her boots she heard Dinah coming up the stairs. Surely it wasn't five o'clock already! Dinah appeared at the doorway looking white and shocked.

'It's all right, Beth! It's all right!' she kept repeating, though it patently wasn't. 'Emmet, I think you'd better come.'

'Someone's let all the birds out,' Beth screeched. 'And they're all dead!'

'Dead? What's she talking about?' Emmet asked, her heart thumping unnaturally in her chest, as they all careered back down the stairs.

'Vandals. They've had a go at the aviaries.' Dinah held the sobbing Beth to her side.

251

The kitchen was a desolation of feathers, bird droppings and dead or dying birds. Although Emmet had trained the cats as far as possible not to chase the birds, the stimulation had been too much for them. Some of them had taken the opportunity to hook down any birds that were still fluttering, panic-stricken, against the windows. In the corner, one of them was chewing the head off the starling that Emmet had been feeding only that morning.

Emmet ran to the scullery to find all the cages wide open. Some remaining birds were floundering about the floor, others cowered in their cages. The injured crow had somehow managed to make its way to the top of a cage from where he was cawing hysterically. As soon as they had heard Beth's screams the dogs had begun to bark furiously.

It was a scene surpassing her worst nightmares, but somehow Emmet found herself acting with a coolness that she was very far from feeling. She ordered the dogs to stop their racket and, with Dinah's inexpert help, managed to capture the remaining birds and get them back into their cages. The two young rabbits were found cowering under the old armchair with the frightened kittens. Their foster mother was mewing in perturbation, too upset to join in the carnage.

It was only after they had restored some order that Dinah said quietly, 'It's outside too, I'm afraid.'

Emmet felt as if she had been punched in the stomach. Beth had cast herself into the armchair with Mogsy, who was too old and lazy to bother with the birds, and was crying noisily into her fur.

'Stay there, darling!' Emmet ordered. She went outside with Dinah, her heart sinking at what she might find.

It was bad. All the doors of the orchard aviaries were open, though some of the birds were still inside, especially the permanent residents whose incapacities made it impossible for them to flee. Others had flown though most were not yet ready. They might or might not survive. Fortunately the cats had found the pickings too good in the kitchen and had not yet discovered what lay outside; but the crows, those great opportunists, had taken advantage of the bonanza and their chicks fed well that day. The grey hen had retreated to the top of the log pile in a fluster of feathers, the mallard with the broken wing was nowhere to be seen. The owls had presumably been too sleepy to fly but they called restlessly from their perch on the topmost branch of the apple tree in their large aviary. It appeared that the vandals had made no attempt to kill or maim the birds but opening the cages and panicking the inmates had an equally disastrous effect. Emmet hurried to the outhouse where the injured hedgehogs were kept. All seemed to have vanished.

Emmet and Dinah did the rounds of the aviaries, closing the doors and collecting the small corpses as well as the barely surviving. They hardly spoke.

'How many do you think you've lost?' Dinah said, their grim task finished at last.

'About half,' Emmet said, more calmly than she felt. 'Dead or flown. Not to speak of the hedgehogs. I might be able to find them later. Some of them could have gone out anyway in the next warm spell . . .' Suddenly she stiffened. 'Tom,' she whispered. 'Where's Tom?'

Both women tore into the house, Emmet now very near to panic.

'Tom!' she shrieked, as soon as they arrived at the kitchen door. Beth began crying again, loudly.

They met Tom on the stairs. 'What's the matter?' he asked, ashen-faced.

Emmet hugged him. 'Thank God, darling! You're here. Are you all right? I thought . . . I thought . . .'

'What's happened?'

'Someone's been in while we were upstairs and let all the birds out. It's an awful mess. Are you sure you're all right? Did you hear anything?'

'No, I had my door shut.'

'I think we ought to ring the police,' Dinah said pragmatically, going over to the telephone.

'Of course,' Emmet said. Her panic had lessened but she still wasn't thinking coherently.

As Dinah made the call Emmet went to the cupboard to fetch the killing bottle and a biscuit tin. She retreated to the scullery and administered a merciful end to the dying birds they had collected. It wasn't until she had completed the hateful work that she found tears were dripping down her cheeks. She wiped them away impatiently. There was still so much to be done.

Dinah had put down the phone. 'They're sending a squad car as soon as they can.'

There was a moment's silence, except for Beth's continued whimpering.

'It's funny the dogs didn't bark,' Dinah said. 'Are you sure you didn't hear anything, Tom?'

Tom shook his head vehemently. 'No. Nothing.'

'How did they get in, d'you suppose?' Dinah said.

'I hardly ever lock the door when I'm in,' Emmet said. 'I'm afraid it would have been easy.'

The police car was there in fifteen minutes. They asked a great many questions and looked at all the cages and the heap of dead birds.

'None of these padlocks has been forced,' the sergeant said after an examination of the outside aviaries. 'Do you always keep them locked?'

'Always,' Emmet said firmly.

'Who else has keys?' The sergeant was a big man with a short black beard. His radio crackled intermittently.

'Only me. I usually have them on me but sometimes I hang them on a hook on the dresser . . .'

'Where were they today?'

Emmet hesitated. 'On the dresser.'

'So anyone could have walked in and taken them?' the policeman said severely.

'Not really. There's the dogs, you see . . .'

The sergeant exchanged glances with the WPC who was with him.

'Who else has access to the place who would be familiar with the dogs?'

'Besides myself and the children, only my husband. Oh, and

Dinah, of course,' she smiled wanly at Dinah. '. . . and then there's Barney.'

'Barney?'

'He helps me out occasionally. But this is ridiculous! Barney couldn't have had anything to do with it. He adores animals!'

Nevertheless, she was persuaded to give them Barney's address. 'But he won't be there after today,' she added.

'Do you know where he'll be after that?'

'Yes. Here.'

Emmet was aware of another exchange of looks between the sergeant and the WPC and realized which way the policeman's mind was working. She felt quite sick. What if she had made a quite profound error of judgement and Barney was not what he seemed?

They left at last, saying they might return. When the police car had disappeared out of the yard Dinah made tea, hot and strong, for everyone. They sat round the kitchen table without speaking; tears streaked Beth's cheeks, Tom was as white as ever. Emmet felt a deep and alarming depression. If the police were quite wrong to suspect Barney, as she believed they were, then whoever had done this thing could come back at any time. They would never be safe.

'It wouldn't have been difficult to pacify the dogs,' she said aloud. 'They're terribly soppy. Throw them a titbit and they're anybody's.'

Dinah looked doubtful. 'Of course there is one other person who knows the dogs and knows where the keys are kept,' she said at last.

Emmet put down her cup, frowning. 'Who?'

Dinah glanced at Tom. 'Why, Lee Arnold, of course.'

CHAPTER NINETEEN

Mount Huish glowed palely in its springtime setting of every kind of green, from the citrusy colours of the new beech and the bronzy-greens of the oaks from which some said the river derived its name, to the sombre darkness of the holm oaks. Now that it was Easter the Montana clematis was a cloud of pale pink beyond Desna's terrace and the wisteria was already displaying long tassels of amethyst buds.

The house itself was humming with activity. Carol was upstairs making up beds for Nell, Emmet and the children, who were to stay one night, and for Signor Bonicelli who was to stay two. Mo and Persis would come for the day on Easter Saturday and Easter Sunday; in that way, Mo believed she would be able to curtail her sister's opportunities for creating embarrassment. Philip's sister Tessa and Faith were coming on Sunday.

Roy and Philip were due back from the yard as soon as they could get away. Harriet was laying the long satinwood table for lunch, while in the kitchen Desna cooked, wearing a vast white apron, and a red and white scarf tied over her hair. Finished dishes were either already in the freezer or were being prepared for lunch, by which time everyone would have arrived. Rupert was in the kitchen with Desna, seizing the opportunity to make himself as amenable as possible. If any problems should arise about the two surfboards, wet suits and other gear he'd ordered, he might need his mother's support; she could always be relied upon to be on his side. Besides, as soon as the stuff came through, he'd want to be off to Cornwall where he had arranged to meet up with Adam and the other surfers.

'When's the tribe due?' he asked. He leaned against the dresser,

257

hands in pockets. Out of school uniform, now in jeans and black tee shirt, he appeared older. Desna was proud of his looks. He was already as tall as his father and had inherited the thick dark hair of both his parents, though his was inclined to curl.

Desna took a container of black olives out of the fridge. 'I hope, twelve thirty.'

Rupert leaned over and helped himself to an olive. 'Hmm,' he said appreciatively, popping it into his attractive mouth.

'Have a biscuit if you're hungry,' Desna scolded him. 'There are some in the tin, or make yourself a sandwich . . .'

'Mum!' he said, grinning. 'Don't fuss. You trying to fatten me up, or what?' He roamed around, lifting the lids of saucepans and sniffing. 'By the way, Mum, about the surfing, I was going to ask you—'

Harriet came in. Impossible to broach the topic that was uppermost in his mind with his sister in the offing. Harriet wasn't as green as she was cabbage-looking, she always knew when he was after something. Anyway, she was a fine one to criticize when you thought of how much the parents were about to lash out on her!

'Da da-de dah.' He whispered the wedding march mockingly. Harriet ignored him.

'Which table napkins do you want me to use?' she asked Desna.

'The white linen, darling,' Desna said, bending to check on the game pie in the oven. 'Did you lay the small cutlery for Beth?'

'Yes. Where is Signor Bonicelli to sit?'

When the seating was agreed upon, Harriet went back into the sitting room.

'Who's this Bonicelli dude?' Rupert asked. 'Why's he coming anyway?'

'You know your father often invites clients to Mount Huish, especially when they've spent a lot of money at the yard.'

'They don't usually *stay* here,' Rupert commented accurately.

Desna didn't answer. She was concentrating on the task of trailing caramelized sugar over a series of upside-down bowls.

'What *are* you doing?' Rupert wanted to know, looking over her shoulder.

'Darling, don't loom so or I'll never be ready,' Desna snapped. 'Go and see if Emmet and the children have arrived.'

Carol came in and asked if there was anything further she could do.

'We're all set now, I think,' Desna said. 'Is it still all right for tomorrow?'

She had asked Carol to interrupt her own holiday to help for an hour or so on Easter day.

'I'll be over about nine,' Carol said agreeably. Desna put a decoratively wrapped Easter egg into Carol's hands. 'For Davy,' she said.

Carol sped down the drive on her moped. She never minded doing the odd extra hours for Mrs Hindmarch, since she got paid handsome overtime for it. Mrs Hindmarch was not a mean employer and one always knew where one was with her, not like some. At the gate she met her employer's sister with her kids in the beat-up old Ford Escort she drove. Funny that one sister should be so rich and one apparently so poor.

Emmet stopped the car on the gravel at the back of Mount Huish. She pulled on the handbrake, which made a peculiar scrunching noise. She really would have to get the car serviced soon; Barney's tinkering had kept it on the road, but she doubted all the same that it would pass its approaching MOT.

Her hand was almost better, and the bandage had given way to a modest taped job. She got out and opened the rear door to help Beth with her seat belt. Tom managed his own but with the same withdrawn expression he'd worn ever since the vandals had struck. Beth had been terribly upset at the time but had seemed to get over it more quickly than poor Tom. Maybe it was also because, since she had not invited Lee Arnold to play since the disaster, Tom had been rather lonely. She had asked Tom to invite other friends to play but he said it wasn't the same.

The police had questioned Barney extensively but he had been working on Mrs Draycott's rock garden that afternoon.

'All the same, it doesn't clear me,' he told Emmet with devastating candour, 'because Mrs Draycott was out for part of the time. I could easily have biked over here and done it.'

'Except I don't believe for a minute you'd be capable of any such thing,' Emmet objected. She had seen him cradle hurt creatures in his unexpectedly sensitive hands.

'You're too trusting, Mrs Darby,' he said with a grin. 'Does that mean it's still all right if I move in?'

'Of course.'

The police may have had their suspicions but they were no further forward in positively identifying the culprit or culprits and Emmet suspected that they regarded the case as closed.

They entered Mount Huish via the back door and were greeted by Desna, Rupert and Harriet. There were hugs and kisses all round.

'How are you, darling?' Desna said, giving Emmet a fleeting appraisal. Her sister was noticeably thinner and there were faint dark smudges under her eyes. 'That was a horrible business, first the flu and then those beastly vandals.'

'We're all fine now,' Emmet said, thrusting a box of free-range eggs into Desna's hands. It was difficult to find anything to give Desna, she already had everything. 'Here you are. I stuck the shit and feathers on myself!' She grinned.

'Emmet, how gorgeous. Thank you. Brown ones too!'

'We've found most of the hedgehogs,' Beth piped up. 'Only not Houdini, he was there all the time. Mummy says the others can go free now, except the blind one and the one with only three legs . . .'

'Really, darling? Rupert, take the children through to the games room. I'm afraid there won't be time to swim before lunch.' Desna noticed the look of disappointment on their faces. 'But there'll be plenty of time later. You'll have all afternoon.'

They disappeared, shepherded by Rupert, and Desna turned back to Emmet who, she was glad to see was looking quite presentable in a roughly ironed but clean tartan shirt, probably bought at some car boot sale, a nearly new jersey and jeans mercifully free from bird droppings.

'Let's have a drink before the others come,' Desna suggested. 'What will you have?'

'Something decadent, please. Like gin and tonic, for instance,' Emmet said. Harriet filled glasses with homemade lemonade and went to find the children. Desna and Emmet sat on high stools sipping their drinks, surrounded by the appetizing smells of lunch cooking.

'Who's holding the fort today?' Desna asked.

'Barney.'

Desna glanced at her sister anxiously. 'Is that wise, do you think, after all that . . .'

'Barney's okay. I'm convinced of it,' Emmet said vehemently. 'If you want to know the truth, I think Lee did it, though there's no proof, of course. I've never been very happy about Tom associating with him but I feel sorry for the poor little toad, and Tom . . . well, Tom's besotted with him for some reason that's quite beyond me. Perhaps Lee lends him street cred or something.'

'The whole Arnold family is a bit rough, isn't it? Didn't you tell me once that the older boy's on remand?'

'I can't blame Lee for that. All the same, he does tend to strike one as a boy with a grudge. Not without reason, I'm bound to say. I think the child has had a pretty raw deal.'

'What do the police say?'

Emmet shrugged. 'I rather suspect they think as I do.' She finished her gin and tonic. 'That was really good. The last booze we had in the house was that gorgeous bottle of wine from that local vineyard you gave me for Christmas. Is Nell here yet?'

Desna was on her feet again, putting warm, homemade rolls into a cloth, then laying the cloth in a basket. 'Not yet.'

'And the new man. Is she bringing him?'

Desna frowned. 'No.'

'I hope that doesn't mean he's a dork.'

'Mo thinks it's Daniel,' Desna said.

'Never! What on earth makes Mo think that? Did Nell tell her?'

'No. It was something Persis said.'

'Judging by what I've heard of our famous aunt so far, I'd take that story with a lorryload of salt.'

'I tried to get it out of Nell the other day when she came to swim but she clammed up.'

'We must make a concerted effort to winkle it out of her this weekend. But I'm absolutely convinced it's not Daniel!' Emmet got to her feet. 'Can I do something?'

'It's all under control. You might help Harriet and me carry the food in as soon as everyone's assembled.' At that moment Harriet came quietly back into the kitchen.

'How are the wedding plans going?' Emmet enquired, hoping to bring her reserved niece into the conversation.

'We seem to be making progress at last,' Desna answered for her daughter. 'We've chosen the design for the wedding dress, haven't we, darling? And I'm finding the woman who's organizing the catering and the marquee is an absolute wonder. They do everything, the flowers, the video, the lot. It will save me so much time, I can't tell you!'

'Do they do everything *well*, that's the point?'

'Brilliantly, I'm told. She only employs the best, apparently.'

'Well, bully for her!' Emmet couldn't resist the tiniest dig. She glanced at Harriet, who was arranging a last-minute table decoration with shortened narcissi and hart's tongue fern. Harriet's face was rosy with embarrassment. Why did the poor girl look so . . . hunted was the word that sprung to mind?

'It sounds terribly exciting,' Emmet said to make up for her recent irony. 'What colours are you having?'

Desna needed no encouragement to expand on what was now her favourite topic. It had been the same, Emmet remembered, when Desna was doing up Mount Huish, just after she and Roy had bought it. Obsessive, almost as if the house were making up for some deficiency or some disappointment in Desna's personal life. Certain people hinted to Emmet that the reasons behind her own preoccupation with the welfare of animals were precisely the same. Naturally she didn't agree. She felt perfectly content with her life. Marriage had been a mistake but it had given her the children so she had never regretted it.

Harriet took her floral arrangement into the dining room. Desna glanced at Emmet, her colour higher than usual.

'Have you decided what you'll be wearing for the wedding?' she asked casually.

'Good heavens, no. Why, have you?'

'Not yet. I expect I shall go up to London for it. Want to come?'

'You're joking,' Emmet said with a spurt of laughter. 'I couldn't even afford the rail fare!'

'You know you'd be welcome to some of Alec's bequest if you're stuck,' Desna said, but without much hope. Emmet had even refused her offer to pay Barney for extra help.

'No thanks,' Emmet said briskly. 'I'll manage.'

Desna knew that she would never have the courage to broach the subject again. The best she could hope for was that Emmet would just wear something *ordinary*. She changed the subject, voicing her doubts about Harriet's choice of colour for the bridesmaids; then there were sounds of new arrivals and Desna hurried to remove her apron.

Roy, Philip and Signor Bonicelli arrived together. It was the first time Desna had actually met the Italian and she was impressed. He was a tall man, taller than Roy, and powerfully built. The two men together seemed to fill the spacious hall with their physical presence and the air of authority that surrounded them. Bonicelli bowed slightly over Desna's hand, insisting she call him Enrico. She saw him taking in every detail of the house and her own appearance at a glance. His dark hair, thinning over a high, intelligent forehead, was slicked back and worn rather long at the nape. She put him between forty-five and fifty. He was immaculately dressed in the Italian style.

'A charming house and, if I may say so, a charming hostess,' he said.

Roy introduced him to Harriet and Emmet and led the way into the sitting room. Desna stayed behind to greet Nell, who had just pulled up outside. The door of the van slammed and

Nell appeared. Desna saw at once that she looked different. Her sister was always well turned out but today there was an extra glow to her skin and her dark hair shone under a craftily twisted scarf. She took off her jacket as she came; underneath she had on an oversize shirt, a patterned waistcoat and her huge amber beads.

She looks twenty again, Desna thought enviously, while I feel staid and middle-aged. They hugged and went to join the others. Neither Desna nor Emmet failed to notice how avidly Enrico Bonicelli's eyes seemed to consume Nell.

'A hit,' Emmet murmured in Desna's ear.

But Nell had turned away and was making a point of seeking out Harriet.

'Have you told your mother about the frock yet?' she whispered.

Harriet shook her head. 'I was hoping to do it this weekend while you were here. Will you help me?'

'I'll do what I can, Harry—' she broke off. Isabel and Giles were arriving. Leaving Roy to introduce Bonicelli to his parents, Philip came across and swept Harriet off to the kitchen where he thrust a parcel into her hands. Inside the inexpert wrapping was a lavishly illustrated book on the work of Georgia O'Keefe. 'I knew you had some prints but I didn't think you had a book,' he said casually.

Harriet turned the pages. 'It's lovely, Philip. How clever of you to know I wanted one!' She kissed his cheek and he turned his mouth to hers.

'It's not my birthday,' she said.

'Do I have to wait for your birthday to give you things?' He held her at arm's length, looking at her. 'Later,' he said, 'I have something to tell you.'

'Tell me now.'

He put a finger to his lips, shaking his head. 'Uh-uh. All will be revealed.'

Mo and Persis arrived by taxi, which Desna had insisted on paying for since no one was free to fetch them. Mo brought her sister into the room where everyone was talking at once. Beth had deserted the games room where Rupert was teaching Tom to play snooker, for the more interesting territory of the grown-ups. She immediately attached herself to Signor Bonicelli, who declared himself charmed and enchanted, touching her spun-gold hair and calling her an angel. He stood, glass in hand in front of the fire. As a special dispensation to an honoured guest, Roy had temporarily surrendered his prerogative to occupy this favoured spot and was busy pouring drinks at the sideboard.

'Enrico, may I introduce my mother, Mo Joubert and my aunt, Persis Dane.' Desna who had only that minute met Persis for the first time was finding it difficult to take her eyes off such an extraordinary-looking woman. As Mo had warned, she had made no concessions to the occasion. She needed only a wide-brimmed hat on her frizz of whitish hair and a pair of chaps to be all set for riding the range.

Mo shook hands with Bonicelli but Persis just nodded, being too busy lighting up to spare a hand apparently. To his surprise, the Italian found his position in front of the fire had been usurped; the terrible woman, Persis, was all of a sudden, standing where he had stood, one booted foot on the fender and a cloud of smoke round her head. A glass of whisky had miraculously appeared in her hand. Someone said something along the lines of it being nice to be all together for Easter.

'It may be Easter but it's cold as buggery out there,' Persis remarked casually. Mo glanced at her severely. In a very short time she had at least learned that Persis never felt the cold.

Enrico knew better than anyone how to outmanoeuvre his rivals and enemies so it came as a complete surprise to find himself routed, and by a woman. He supposed she was a woman – more of a Medusa, he would have said. Perhaps he had been too busy appreciating the female beauty otherwise present to notice by what sleight of hand she'd ousted him.

He made use of the opportunity to seek out Nell, who was sitting on the sofa, looking like a Leonardo Madonna, with an arm round the child Beth, who was clinging to her affectionately. Bonicelli thought it made a charming picture, and said so. His compliment seemed to please the child more than the woman.

'Mummy had to put them to sleep.' Beth made room for the Italian next to her on the sofa and resumed the tale she had been relating. 'She put them in a box and they went to sleep. But she said they didn't feel anything. Mogsy was very good, though. She didn't eat any of them . . .'

Bonicelli smiled. His English was good but he was completely failing to grasp the gist of what the child was saying; he was no nearer to embarking on an intimate conversation with Roy Hindmarch's beautiful sister-in-law and was resigning himself to awaiting another chance when Isabel laid an elegant hand on his sleeve and asked him a question about the refit of his yacht. Naturally, he was aware that her body language was engaged in another kind of communication altogether but he was quite used to that. He took it as his due. And there was no harm in it.

Desna, who had gone back to the kitchen to lay out the food ready to be transferred to the dining room, announced that lunch was ready and sent Philip to call Rupert and Tom. Harriet shyly showed everyone to their places, managing to seat Persis between Philip and Mo where her mother hoped she could do least damage. When she had helped to carry in the last of the dishes, Harriet herself sat between Giles and Tom.

There was a choice of mushrooms flavoured with dill to start with, or soup, which was a delicate blending of celery and stilton. Then game pie, with kidney bean hotpot for the vegetarians, besides a wonderful selection of vegetable dishes.

'I expect you'd like the hotpot?' Harriet asked Tom, serving spoon poised.

'No, thank you. I'd like what you're having.'

Harriet glanced at Emmet, who looked surprised, then shrugged. Harriet passed Tom's plate to Desna for game pie.

'Don't give him too much,' Emmet said. 'He's not used to meat. He may not like it.'

'I will,' Tom replied firmly.

Roy filled the glasses. He was in ebullient mood, playing host with his usual confident mastery.

'This is very ripping. Top hole, I think you say?' Bonicelli's gaze took in the linen-shrouded table, the game pie with its golden crown of pastry, the perfectly presented vegetables, and the gleaming silver and glasses and was impressed. He hadn't expected anything like it outside London. And he was also considerably surprised to see a family gathering that he would have taken for granted in Italy but not in England. Except that such gatherings were, sadly, no longer at all usual in his own family.

Harriet attempted to engage Tom in conversation, trying out most of what she knew were his favourite topics. It made it easier to forget her own shyness. She was only too well aware that successfully negotiating the passing of the numerous vegetable dishes without mishap was no cause for complacency; her father could pick her up on anything, however small. Though he was less likely to do so when he was in company and in expansive mood, thank goodness. But Tom appeared preoccupied and gave her only monosyllabic answers.

Her father barked out one of his usual commands and she stumbled to her feet to help Signor Bonicelli and Giles to more vegetables. Giles had a good appetite; at least he did when he ate at Mount Huish.

Mo and Emmet exchanged glances. It had been some time since either had seen the relationship between Roy and Harriet in action; the fact that Harriet was doing what her father wanted in marrying his valued sidekick did not appear to have improved matters very much.

Philip asked Persis if she'd heard how the renovations on her studio were going.

Persis leaned back in her chair; she had eaten a little of the game pie filling and poked at some of the vegetables. She reached into her breast pocket for the ubiquitous Gitanes but stopped short of actually lighting one. Instead she tapped the packet impatiently on the table.

'If that bloody architect is to be believed, they've nearly finished. I hope to my specifications. If not, someone's nuts will be in the wringer, you can bet on that!'

Desna glanced involuntarily first at Enrico, on whom understanding was slowly dawning, and then at Isabel and

Giles, both of whom looked amused; finally at Tom and Beth. Rupert and Philip laughed, Rupert uproariously.

'Was the game pie all right for you,' Desna asked her aunt quickly, not sure if Enrico's expression conveyed mirth or shock, 'or would you like some of the vegetarian hotpot?'

'Don't fuss over me,' Persis said grandly. 'I can live on the sniff of an oil rag. Besides, I don't like messed-about food.'

Desna felt heat rush up her cheeks.

Mo gave a snort of derision. 'Listen, Persis. There's no need to broadcast to all and sundry that when it comes to food you have absolutely no discrimination whatever. Putting the best food in the county in front of you is casting pearls before swine. A bloody waste!'

Harriet glanced at her father who looked as if he was about to explode.

'I quite like nuts,' Beth said conversationally. 'Especially peanuts. So does Jack. Jack is a squirrel . . .' She stopped, then said severely, 'Why are you all red, Rupert? Why are you laughing? Jack could have got *killed*, you know.'

'I'm sure Desna has nothing to fear from the opinion of someone who, by their own admission, can live on the smell of an oil rag.' Isabel slipped the knife in and turned it deftly.

Persis shifted her ice-cold stare to Isabel, as if noticing her for the first time. 'Have we met?' she asked innocently.

'Of course you've met Isabel,' Mo said. 'I introduced you myself. Don't start your games here, Persis.'

Persis looked at Nell. 'Nell understands me, don't you, Nell?' she said with heavy emphasis.

Roy stood up, his face flushed. It was difficult to tell if the cause was emotional or vinous. 'Right now, if everyone's finished, Desna, perhaps we can have the dessert.' Mo had the impression that he had clicked his fingers but she could have been wrong.

'Enrico, let me refill your glass,' Roy said.

Fresh conversations were studiously begun by Mo, Emmet and Giles. Enrico glanced across the table at Nell and raised his glass a fraction in salute. Nell gave him an abstracted smile and turned away. She was too preoccupied with the logistics of damage limitation when she finally conveyed her news to the family.

Desna and Harriet saw to the dishes. An orange-flavoured caramel came in individual bowls, trapped in a net of sugar. Beth gazed at hers in wonder. She lifted the filigree topping and nibbled bits off the edge in ecstatic concentration. She had forgotten her mystification as to why Rupert thought peanuts were funny. She hoped that later she would have room for some of the treacle and ginger steamed pudding that her aunt had just put on the table.

Harriet noticed that even the mouth-watering desserts failed to stimulate Tom's appetite. In spite of his boast, he hadn't been able to finish the game pie. But she had other things to worry about. She caught Nell's eye at last; Nell smiled and nodded as if to confirm to Harriet the support she'd promised. It wasn't much comfort; almost she wished that the silver-frosted grey dress were still hanging in the shop and not after all in her wardrobe, swathed in a plastic dust cover.

After lunch Roy and Signor Bonicelli retired to Roy's study with coffee and brandy. Harriet and Philip stacked the dishwasher and tidied the kitchen. Rupert, still doing his utmost to be adult and amenable, took the children down to look at the river and later to swim in the pool under his promised supervision. Giles and Isabel dozed at one end of the spacious conservatory with the newspapers and their coffee cups at hand. Mo had taken Persis for a brisk walk along the path that wound through the trees by the river. Mo took a sketch book, Persis took a camera.

After Desna, Nell and Emmet had cleared the dining room, they drifted together into the conservatory towards the end furthest from where Isabel and Giles now indisputably slept. Desna had made more coffee and they chatted idly, catching up on family news. Except Nell, who now she had the perfect opportunity, found her nerve failing her. She looked out across the garden and wondered what it would be like to have this sort of view to look at every day.

Even shrouded in a fine mist of rain the garden looked wonderful; green and mysterious, with the trees as backdrop. Their new leaves were weighed down with moisture as were the narcissi at their feet. Nell hadn't seen the garden at The Old Rectory yet. But she would, soon.

'I love the way you and Nell did this place out,' Emmet said. 'I wish we could afford a conservatory at Drake's.'

'Couldn't you? When Maurice sells his next book?'

'Whenever *that* will be. This one's taking much longer, he won't say why. In any case, we have to mend the roof first. I found a pigeon in one of the attics the other day.' Not the one Barney had moved into fortunately. That one was still quite sound.

Desna smiled. 'Why should you care? You have pigeons in the kitchen, after all.'

'Not so many as I once had, unfortunately,' Emmet said sadly.

Desna looked grave. 'No.'

They both glanced at Nell who had remained silent during this exchange.

'Desna, you said you weren't keen on grey for the bridesmaids' dresses,' Nell said quickly, feeling something was expected of her.

'Not at all,' Desna shrugged. 'But there you are, Harriet seems quite set on it.'

'Grey can be quite stunning, if it's the right grey.' Nell thought of Jane Eyre and her pearl-grey silk.

'All the same!'

'Even for the bride's dress.'

'Oh, no! Anyway, we've chosen Harriet's dress.'

'You mean, *you* have.'

'Harriet chose it!' Desna's voice rose a fraction.

'Desna, Harriet has something to show you upstairs,' Nell said evenly. 'And please don't fly off the handle when she does. She asked me to speak to you about it first. For what it's worth I have to tell you that I approve, so don't be too hasty . . .'

Desna flushed, sensing conspiracy. 'What are you talking about?'

For an answer Nell went and fetched Harriet from the kitchen where she had been in earnest conversation with Philip. Harriet looked like a frightened rabbit but Nell pressed her arm and steered her into the conservatory.

After some hesitation Harriet took her mother upstairs. As their voices faded away Emmet glanced at Nell. 'What on earth was all that about?'

'Wedding dresses,' Nell said.

'Oh.' Emmet lost interest.

Nell felt vaguely guilty. She had press-ganged Harriet into facing a situation that filled her with trepidation while she herself had funked telling her two sisters about her resolve to marry Daniel Thorne.

Emmet hummed tunelessly as she retied the laces of the trainer that she had propped on her knee. 'We all thought you would have brought your new man here this weekend,' she said casually. 'What was the matter? Did you think he might freak out if he had to face the whole family in one go?'

There was a silence. Then Nell said, 'I've just dropped one bombshell. That's enough to be going on with.'

'What d'you mean – bombshell?'

'Oh, you might as well know. I'm getting married. Quite soon.'

Emmet felt her jaw drop. She sat forward in her chair, gazing at Nell dumbfounded. 'It's not true, is it, Nell? Not marriage?'

'Don't look quite so shocked, Emmet. People *do* get married, you know. Even me!'

Emmet glanced across at Giles and Isabel. Giles was quietly snoring. Isabel had her head back and her eyes closed. Emmet spoke in a low voice. 'Mo told me you were going out with Dan again. Put me out of my misery and tell me it isn't him?'

'Don't look like that!'

'It is, then.'

Nell nodded. 'But he's changed, Emmet! Don't judge him on how he used to be, for God's sake. He's matured, grown up. He loves me. I love him. We're getting married. Doesn't that fact alone convince you that he's not the same person he was four years ago?' She knew she was protesting too much. If even the tolerant Emmet was having difficulty swallowing this, what hope did she have with the rest of the family?

Emmet only shook her head. 'You mustn't, Nell. At least wait. Wait until you're sure.'

'I am sure,' Nell said, setting her jaw stubbornly. 'Quite sure.'

Roy and Signor Bonicelli sat opposite each other in dark leather chairs, a bottle of cognac between them on the desk, a haze of cigar smoke wreathing the room. They were in celebratory mood.

'You're doing the right thing, old chap,' Enrico said. He passed a beautifully manicured hand over his scalp, smoothing his already slick hair. At his cuff gold and diamonds glimmered. 'The Virgin Islands will open up a whole new market, in particular the American market. And such a perfect climate! Perfect for bareboat or full-crew chartering.' He smiled, displaying extremely white teeth. 'The sunshine will make all the difference. Not like here.' His gaze was directed out of the window at the view of saturated garden and grey sky. It was not, of course, the first time he had expressed these sentiments but before they had been in the line of persuasion, now everything was decided they simply confirmed what they had both accepted long since.

'Naturally, I haven't mentioned anything to Philip yet but I'd still like him to keep this end ticking over with repair work, just for the time being. But in due course I reckon he'll want to join us in BVI, especially if the business there is picking up . . .'

'Which it will be. I still don't know why you don't sell up in the UK completely. You'd release far more capital, that way.'

'I'm a cautious bugger at heart, Enrico.' Roy laid his cigar on the edge of a solid brass ashtray, allowing the ash to tumble off in a soft grey pile. 'Besides, as I've said before, the sale of Mount Huish should raise more capital than I'd immediately need.' This was true. The agreement was that Bonicelli was to supply the bulk of the capital and Roy the expertise and the responsibility for getting the enterprise off the ground initially. In fact Bonicelli could easily have supplied all the necessary funding but he firmly believed that a man who had sunk his own money in a scheme was likely to be more determined to make it work.

'You're right about the young man. I was watching him at luncheon. I can't see him being content with a small *fetta di torta* for long. Besides, you'll very soon need his help to run our end, depend upon it!'

Roy nodded thoughtfully. He had got over the rage prompted by Persis' remarks at lunchtime and was back to his original ebullience.

'My only regret, dear fellow, is over the delay. It seems a great pity that you are unable to act before July.' Bonicelli held his cigar an inch or two from his mouth while he spoke.

'You must understand, Enrico, that it's not going to be easy to break the news to Desna over the sale of the house; she's absolutely fixated on the place. And asking her to curtail the wedding arrangements or bring them forward will make things more difficult than they need be. I'm going to need her co-operation to get Mount Huish off my hands. Wives can use some pretty subtle ways of throwing a spanner in the works once they get upset, as you know yourself!'

'A spanner? Oh, I get it!' Enrico thought of his troublesome ex-wife and her constant demands and smiled a slow smile. Fortunately, information as to the precise size and extent of his assets had so far escaped the best efforts of her lawyers. He intended to keep it that way.

'It's a very beautiful house. You should have no difficulty at all to sell it. So beautiful a place but always rain, rain, rain, alas!' Bonicelli put his cigar between his lips and drew on it, considering. 'When will you tell Desna?' he asked.

'I will have to choose my moment. Probably after the weekend when everyone has gone and we are alone.'

'Ah. That is sensible.' He raised his glass. 'Well, old fellow, here's to partnership!'

They drank. Enrico looked at his new partner and congratulated himself on finding just the right man for his scheme. First, he knew boats, was an expert in his field, and was cognizant with every aspect of sailing; second, he was British

273

and respectable, which would make things a great deal easier besides lending a certain cachet to the enterprise they were embarking on; and third, he was willing to get himself out of the rut and move his business to the other side of the Atlantic. Which took courage. For there was a risk in such an upheaval, albeit a small one. Not such a risk, however, as staying where he was, the way things were going.

Roy helped the two of them to more of the expensive cognac. He felt well satisfied. His only regret was that, being a man of action, he wasn't able to put his resolve into immediate effect. Pussyfooting around to accommodate his wife's predictable reluctance to leave Mount Huish and the time it took to see this wedding business off the ground didn't suit him at all. All the same, it would probably take a month or two of coming and going to fix up the BVI end and, besides, if Desna had any sense she would jump at the chance of living in the sunshine rather than in the Devon rain. Not that she ever complained about it. She even seemed to like it.

There was one contingency to which Roy had already given some thought, although he had not imparted as much to Bonicelli. There was an outside chance that Desna might refuse the advantages of life in the BVI. He thought this highly unlikely, for what woman would not choose a greatly enhanced lifestyle in a wonderful climate? But if she did, then it would mean some heavy persuasion and if that ultimately failed, which he couldn't envisage, then the threat of a parting of the ways. Roy was all for sticking with marriage for as long as it worked – after all he had invested twenty-odd years of effort to mould Desna into the kind of wife that would do him credit and advance his career. He'd had one or two affairs, of course, but these had never threatened his marriage. Not for a moment.

But if Desna foolishly turned bolshie over it, then that would be her funeral. He was already committed to a change of direction. She would have to choose. Take it or leave it.

Desna sat on Harriet's bed while Harriet herself fumbled in her wardrobe and withdrew a large object shrouded in plastic.

Harriet's hands shook as she unsheathed the dress, and draped it over her arm. To her it looked as beautiful as ever, as if it had been woven from wood smoke and edged with dew.

There was a long puzzled silence but after what seemed to Harriet an eternity, her mother spoke. 'That's a very beautiful dress, darling.'

Harriet felt a cat's-paw of hope.

'But when were you thinking of wearing it?' Desna took the delicate fabric between her fingers.

'I saw it in this shop in Dartmouth. I thought . . . Nell thought too . . . that it was well, unusual . . .' Harriet knew she was gabbling. 'I mean, I know we've sort of chosen the wedding dress but Mrs Gillimore won't have started it yet, will she?'

Light dawned. 'You mean, a *wedding* dress!'

'I thought . . . yes.' Harriet held her breath.

There was another excruciating pause.

'I agree with you and Nell that it's quite lovely,' Desna began. 'I can see that it's been beautifully made . . . But, darling, you must see that it won't do.'

The fateful words dropped like lead weights. 'Why won't it?' Harriet managed to ask.

Desna spoke as kindly as she knew how. 'Darling, do try to be sensible. For a start, it's not a suitable colour. Not for a wedding. Surely you can see that? I'm still not sure about grey for the bridesmaids but I've gone along with it to please you. You must rely on my judgement a bit, you know.'

'But Nell said—'

'It's all very well for Nell. We all know that Nell has excellent taste but it does verge on the arty, which wouldn't be at all suitable in the circumstances. Added to which, of course, the frock is second-hand. No girl wants to be married in something that's second-hand. You don't, surely?'

'That friend of Nicola's wore her mother's wedding dress . . .'

'That was different. Besides, she had it made over. In the end it even looked quite fashionable. This is very nice but you must admit that it is a bit . . . how can I put it? . . . dowdy, you know.'

'Dowdy! Look, Mummy, why don't I just try it on? You'll see it doesn't look dowdy at all.'

'Very well, darling. Try it on.'

Harriet scrambled out of her clothes and slipped the dress over her head. Desna did up the buttons at the back. Then Harriet took the headdress out of its tissue paper and stood in front of her small mirror to fix it over her hair.

She turned round. What Desna saw was a wood nymph from some Victorian illustration, fey and elusive, as if a puff of the real world would blow her away. It was as if the dress had encompassed all the vulnerable traits that Desna had tried so hard to play down in her daughter, all the traits Roy was so contemptuous of, and distilled them together in that moment. And it was perfectly apparent that Harriet herself was quite unaware of the effect. Desna knew how Roy was hoping to present his daughter to the world: a young woman who was smart in every sense, but all woman: sophisticated yet feminine. Someone like Nicola Wakeham or Philip's sister Tessa who was expected to join them the next day. What Roy most emphatically would not want to take up the aisle on his arm was some creature from a fabulous world of the imagination, lovely to look at but far too insubstantial; odd and quite, quite impossible. Roy would have a fit if he ever saw the dress, which Desna vowed he never would.

Desna sighed. 'Yes, darling, I agree that it's stunning, but not for this. Not to get married in. Wear it to some fancy-dress party perhaps. It would be perfect for that.' Not that Harriet ever went to parties, fancy-dress or otherwise. But she might after she was married.

'Nell thought it was fine,' Harriet stammered, feeling as if she were literally shrinking inside the dress.

'I'm surprised she encouraged you, frankly. I don't think she should have. It's none of her business really, is it? And why Nell and not me?' The last comment came out as an accusation. She was angry with Nell for having helped put her in an awkward position. It was irresponsible of her.

Desna swallowed her irritation, got up from the bed and

kissed Harriet on the cheek. 'Cheer up, darling! No need to look so stricken. We all make mistakes. I know I made plenty when it came to clothes. I hope it wasn't too expensive.' She put a comforting arm round her daughter. 'Pop it back on the hanger now. I'm sure it will be lovely to wear for a party, you'll see. After all, you can still have the darker grey for the bridesmaids as you're absolutely set on it. I can see that it might look very well with the oyster pink we chose with Mrs Gillimore . . .'

Harriet stayed behind to put the dress back in the wardrobe. She was trembling and felt the sting of tears. She was more miserable than for a long time. All the same, it was only a dress after all; and she wasn't usually in the least concerned what she put on her back. Why had it all suddenly turned into something more important than just a wedding dress? She didn't care about the wedding itself, did she? All she wanted was to be with Philip.

The sun was breaking through some watery-looking clouds so she changed into old clothes. She and Philip had arranged to continue with the painting of the boathouse if the weather improved. Perhaps after time alone with Philip she could forget about the agonizing humiliations of the last half-hour.

Desna found Nell and Emmet still in the conservatory. A silvery light was infiltrating the trees outside and making patterns of light and shade on the lawn. Rupert appeared to have got bored with the role of nursemaid to the two children and had gone upstairs to play his loud music.

Emmet was recovering from the shock of Nell's announcement and the atmosphere between them had become so strained that Nell, unable to bear it, had gone to join the now fully awake Emmersons. When she saw Desna, Nell glanced across at her wondering what the verdict had been, but Desna deliberately looked away, her mouth in a hard line.

Beth padded in wearing her swimsuit but wrapped in a towel.

'Did you have a good swim?' Emmet asked her, using the towel to rub Beth's hair dry. The darkened tendrils lay on a neck as insubstantial-looking as a flower stalk. Emmet knew it belied the tough little character to whom it belonged.

'Yes, yes. Rupert taught me to dive.'

'Dive!'

'Well, a bit. From the steps. You see, you go like this . . .' She put her small brown hands together in front of her so they resembled a scallop. 'Then you push off with your legs, you see?'

'Very good,' Emmet said, smiling at Desna as she towelled Beth's back.

'Rupert can dive properly. He says he'll show me how to do that too. Next time, he said. Rupert has a tattoo . . . right here.' She twisted her head and placed one finger on her upper arm. 'Tom says he wants one . . .'

'Rupert has a tattoo?' Desna repeated.

'Yes. It's sweet. It's like a little sun with rays coming out all round. He says it's not quite healed up yet. He said it hardly hurt at all.' Beth shuddered. 'I wouldn't like it. Tom says he—'

'Where is Tom?' Emmet said.

'Getting changed in his room.'

'I don't believe it!' Desna said.

'He is,' Beth assured her.

'I mean about the tattoo.' Desna put her hand to her forehead as if to banish an annoying fly.

'I don't think Beth would have made it up,' Emmet said. She grinned. 'Boys! You never know what they're going to do next!'

'I don't think it's funny,' Desna said. 'I mean, a tattoo for God's sake!'

'He can always have it removed later,' Emmet comforted her.

Desna stood up abruptly. 'I'll go and see about tea.'

'Tea already!' Emmet said. 'Heavens!'

'It's nothing much. I made a simnel cake . . .' Desna escaped to the kitchen to take refuge in domesticity. Cooking and preparing food was like a balm; usually it had the power to calm her spirits. Persis being objectionably rude at lunchtime, Harriet buying unsuitable dresses, Nell encouraging her, now Rupert getting himself tattooed; it wasn't turning out to be the kind of family occasion she had envisaged. Mechanically she began to

278

lay out the blue and white tea cups.

Nell left the Emmersons and went in search of Harriet, but Harriet had already gone down to the boathouse with Philip.

Roy took Bonicelli on a guided tour of Mount Huish. The more he saw the more Bonicelli remarked on the probable financial outcome of its sale. He was unstinting in his praise of the house, its setting and the layout of the grounds; to him all things had their price, even beauty. Especially beauty. His wife had once been the most exquisite, the most glamorous, the most sought-after woman of her day. He had been the one who had triumphed over his rivals; now he was the one who had to pay.

Their perambulations took them to the boathouse where Harriet and Philip were applying the second undercoat of white paint.

'How goes it?' Roy asked, in jovial mood.

'We'll finish if the weather holds out.' Philip was again up the ladder; Harriet was working from the decking.

'Always the weather!' Enrico joked. 'You see, Roy, how your English weather interferes with business.'

The two painters worked in silence until Roy and Bonicelli had disappeared up the path once more.

'I'm not sure that I like that man,' Harriet said, dipping her brush into the can. 'I can't say why.'

'He's a bit of a smoothie but he's not bad. I think your ma quite likes him.'

'He looked at Nell a lot.'

'Did he? Well, Nell's good-looking and a sharp dresser. Just up his street.'

'Why is he staying so long? Daddy's clients usually only come for dinner or something.'

Philip came down the ladder and stood back, looking for bits he might have missed. 'To tell you the truth, I think they're cooking something up. Bonicelli was knocked out by the job we did on his Oyster. I think he has something else on the go he wants your dad's opinion about.'

'You don't know what?'

'Nope. But I think it's something big. I dare say we'll find out sooner or later.' Philip decided not to convey his faint anxiety about the Italian and his future father-in-law to Harriet; something was going on and he would give a lot to know what it was. Roy and Bonicelli spent frequent private sessions in the office at the yard to which he had not been invited. They were certainly not discussing the Oyster since that had been finished long since.

'Put down your brush,' he commanded.

'Why? We haven't finished yet.'

'I have something to tell you. Remember?'

Harriet glanced round almost in alarm. She finished her brushload and put it carefully into the turps, wiping her hands on a rag.

'Your dad said I could take all of next weekend off,' Philip said. With great self-restraint he stuck his hands in his pockets, deliberately not touching her. 'Andy has this chum in St Ives who has a cottage near the harbour and he's offering it to us for a couple of nights. I thought you'd like that – Cornwall, Barbara Hepworth, the Tate of the West and all that. What d'you say?'

The sense of doom which had that day begun with her mother's disapproval of her taste in wedding dresses, increased. But she had promised Philip that she would go away with him. And she would, although it might be the end of everything between them. At least then she'd know. The dreadful waiting would be over.

She nodded bleakly.

'You have been taking the pill, haven't you?'

'Yes.' It had given her headaches. The doctor said that if it did she would change it for another one, but she hadn't had time to go back.

'So it's all go, then?' Philip said, with mounting excitement. He reached out and pulled her to him. 'Don't look like that, Harry. Anyone would think I was some deadbeat schmuck, not the guy you intend to marry, for Christ's sake!' He grinned. 'Losing your virginity's no big deal, you know. It's part of growing up.'

* * *

Hugh Daish cast himself down next to his sister, who sat huddled behind a boulder the size of a double-decker bus. 'I think my pirating days are over,' he said breathlessly.

A fine drizzle had started five minutes before but neither of them had the heart to break up the children's game. Their excited cries echoed round the great pile of split and weathered granite stones that made up Hound Tor.

'I hope they're all right,' Stevie said. She had been christened Stephanie but was now generally known as Stevie. 'There's Theo right at the top. I daren't look.'

'They're a darned sight more sure-footed than I am. Like mountain goats,' Hugh replied. He looked at his watch. 'In any case, we'll have to go soon.'

'Good. I'm dying for a cup of tea. It's cold enough to do serious damage to brass monkeys. Even the sheep look shrammed. Easter, huh!'

'View's all right, though.'

Dartmoor heaved its great tan and purple flanks into a rolling succession of wildernesses culminating with mysterious granite outcrops. The landscape was dotted with surface stones and sheep; at a distance it wasn't always easy to tell the difference. Away to one side Haytor reared like a high and sinister fortress and behind it the Haldon Hills, half smothered in cloud, ranged down towards the sea. A steady, cold wind blew, drifting the sound of the baaing of the sheep towards them. A brave lark attempted a few descending notes overhead.

'Pirating apart, I thought you seemed a bit down,' Stevie said, tucking strands of hair back under her headscarf. 'Is the business going all right?'

'The business is fine. Two new titles out this week. The one on standing stones, and the other on the vernacular architecture of Devon.'

'That leaves the usual, I suppose,' Hugh's sister said knowingly. 'The trouble with you is that you're lonely.'

'Don't start that again. I made my mistake and lived to regret it, that's all.'

'It doesn't follow that you have to punish yourself – and Laura incidentally – for the rest of your life. Or did marriage to Helen turn you into an old cynic?'

'Not at all. If you must know, I've just discovered that the woman I always wanted in the first place has finally decided to get hitched up with an out-and-out shark. Tell me, Stevie, with all your mature good sense, how do you stop someone you love making a simply God-awful mistake?'

'You don't. Once you've done all you can to stop them it's just a matter of standing by ready to pick up the pieces later.'

'That sounds impossibly cool and sensible. What I really want to do is to rip off the devious bastard's trendy braces and strangle him with them!'

'If you think it would help . . .' Stevie smiled. 'But I take it the female in question, being of sound mind and mature judgement, is going into it with her eyes open?'

'No, she's not! Women have a total blind spot when it comes to Dan Thorne. I believe he mesmerizes them, like a snake with a rabbit. Not that I've seen a snake with a rabbit . . .'

'Surely not if they're intelligent,' sensible Stevie remarked.

'Don't you believe it! The women he attracts are usually highly intelligent – with one notable exception, Felicity whatshername . . .'

Stevie put a comforting leather-gloved hand on her brother's arm. 'Poor Hugh. Neither of us had much luck in love, did we? Never mind, I've got Theo and you have Laura. She's an absolute darling. And you never know, you might meet someone else tomorrow.'

Hugh shook his head, taking no comfort from the idea. Stevie seemed so much more resigned to her divorced state than he was.

'How's Sonia?' he asked.

Stevie looked grave. 'Not good. I don't know how long she can carry on. She gets frightfully tired.'

'And the business?' he said after a pause. 'Riding the recession?'

'You're joking. We're frantically busy. I should be doing a

final costing for a wedding as we speak. It's one of the biggest and most expensive we've ever done, complicated by the bride's mum wanting a very precise say in absolutely everything.'

'Sounds a bit tricky.'

'I admit it could be. But it just might be a turning point for the business. I think we were getting in a bit of a rut. She's given me all sorts of new ideas for some really classy food so it'll be a bit of a challenge, something quite outside the run-of-the-mill receptions we're usually asked for.'

'Expense no object, I take it?'

'Not so's you'd notice.'

'Think you can handle it?'

'I'm damned well going to try.' She stood up and banged her hands together to restore the circulation. 'Hugh, you should see the house! It's fabulous. Views over the Dart, boathouses, a vast conservatory, wonderful grounds, woodland walks, you name it! And about four times the size of Chapel Abbey.'

Hugh unfolded his long legs and stood up. He grinned.

'The trouble with you, Stevie, is that you're too easily impressed by large amounts of dosh.'

'I can't afford not to be. Besides, I like the woman. She knows what she wants. That always makes it easier.' She strode across the granite-littered turf calling. 'Laura! Theo! Where are you? Come on, we're going for a cream tea.'

Hugh joined his elder sister in the hunt among the rocks for their respective offspring. The Daish physique suited Hugh far better than it did Stevie; the rangy figure with large hands and feet did not become her half so well even though she did not, like her brother, compensate for her height with a slight stoop. They had both finished up making a greater success of their careers than they had of their marriages but whereas his occupation was to a great degree solitary and self-motivating, hers took her among people. Since she was a gregarious creature this suited her very well. However, she worried about Hugh; in her opinion he was a man who should be married.

The children appeared from an enormous vertical cleft in the rocks, their cheeks pink with cold and exercise.

'Is it tea time?'

'Did you see me right at the top?'

'Can we come here for a picnic in the summer?'

'The answer to all three is yes,' Stevie said.

'Did you know this place is an ancient monument?' Theo asked Laura. 'It says so on the map.'

'Of course I did. It's in one of Daddy's books.'

'Oh,' Theo said, disappointed at not being able to impress his cousin.

The children galloped ahead of the adults, now impatient to get back to Bovey Tracy and tea.

CHAPTER TWENTY

Harriet and Philip went straight from the church at Upper Ash after the service to meet Faith off the train at Totnes. Desna had eventually persuaded Roy and the Emmersons to attend the Easter morning service; she said it would be a courtesy to the Vicar. Harriet thought that Mr Peters would just think them insincere, but she went all the same.

Faith came down the platform towards them; black leggings, boots and a black tee shirt under a leather bomber jacket. Her brown hair was now shaved round her ears, the rest dyed raven black and worn in a fuzzy pile. She had on round, magenta-tinted specs and carried a canvas kitbag over one shoulder.

'Faith?' For a moment Harriet was not absolutely sure.

'Hi, Harry.' Faith put down her bag and hugged her old friend. She was shorter than Harriet, with a strong, wiry physique.

'You remember Philip?'

'We met once. Hi.'

'I'll take your bag,' Philip offered.

'No problem.' Faith humped up the bag herself and strode out of the station yard, following them to Philip's old Land Rover.

All at once Harriet felt acutely shy and was content to hand the conversation over to the others. Faith's changed appearance had thrown her. It gave her the impression that there was now an impassable barrier between them. And how would she ever be able to persuade her mother, let alone her father, that her friend would make a suitable bridesmaid? For this was the main purpose of Faith's visit. Her mother had made an arrangement for them to see Mrs Gillimore on Monday so that she could take Faith's measurements.

It would have to happen that they arrived back at Mount Huish just as Philip's sister was emerging from her Golf. Gusts of wind were tossing her dark blonde hair and snatching at her long silk scarf but she managed to look elegant just the same.

'Hi-i!' Tessa called. She had acquired a distinctive, fluting voice that Harriet supposed was the result of constantly being on the telephone. Harriet introduced her to Faith, whom she greeted in her usual friendly manner. Tessa was an extrovert.

'Where's your aunt?' Faith said in a gruff whisper, dumping her bag in the hall. Harriet wondered if she would have been able to lure her friend down to Mount Huish at all without the inducement of an introduction to Persis Dane.

'You'll meet her in a minute,' she said. 'We'd better take your bag upstairs first.' Her mother wouldn't like bits of luggage strewn around cluttering up the hall. 'Do you mind sharing my room? There's plenty of space.'

'No. It'll be great. Just like when I used to stay when we were doing our A levels. D'you remember?'

Harriet did remember. But they had more in common then. Now Faith belonged to another world. She even spoke differently; her well-modulated middle-class accent had given way to a flatter, all-purpose mode of speech. Harriet smiled to herself. She recollected that Faith's mother had once confessed that the principal reason for sending her daughter to a fee-paying school was to ensure that she spoke well.

'Like the way you've set this up,' Faith said, looking round Harriet's room. She chucked her bag on the bed Harriet had made up for her. 'Hey, the Georgia O'Keefe posters are great!'

'How's the degree course going?'

'Don't ask. I'm in the shit-house work-wise. My last assessment was dire.' She went on to speak of the course, the pressure as the date for the final degree show drew nearer, student relationships and student politics, her boyfriend and the inadequacies of the grant. To Harriet she was describing the life of an enclosed order. It only served to increase the distance that divided her from her friend.

Faith bounced on the bed. 'So what gross schmutter have you got in store for me, then?'

'I'll show you.' Harriet took a swatch of oyster-grey silk and a sheet of sketches out of a drawer.

'I'll show these to Tess later on. Tell me what you think first?'

'Colour's okay. It could be a trillion times worse.'

'Do you like the design? Is it too straight?'

Faith picked up a length of the fabric and held it across her chest. 'The straighter the better. Just don't give me puffy sleeves, that's all.'

Harriet giggled. Just at the moment nobody could have looked less like the traditional bridesmaid than Faith with her shorn hair, her bitten fingernails and her huge boots. She stuck them out in front of her. 'Is it all right if I wear these?' Faith asked.

'I'll let you know about the shoes. I expect they'll be the same colour as the dress.'

Faith fingered the shaved part of her head. 'I suppose you want me to grow my hair?'

Harriet grinned. 'Would you mind? It's not me, it's Mummy you see. You could shave it again afterwards, couldn't you?'

'Anything for my old friend. I hope you appreciate all the sacrifices I'm making on your behalf? When are we seeing this dressmaking person?'

'Tomorrow at ten.'

'You realize I shall have to go directly after? I can't leave Gunter alone for too long. He'll be after some bimbette if I stay away more than a day or two.'

Harriet stared. 'Surely not? I thought he loved you?'

Faith laughed. 'Sure he does. What has that got to do with it? You can't tell me that your gorgeous Philip doesn't do a bit of cruising from time to time?'

'I don't *think* he does,' Harriet said doubtfully.

'Don't believe it!' Faith lay back on the bed and folded her arms behind her head. 'Is he any good in bed?' she asked. 'Sorry, wrong question.' She giggled.

Harriet could never have brought herself to admit to her worldly-wise friend that she and Philip had not slept together – yet. Faith probably wouldn't have believed her anyway.

Faith sat up suddenly. 'I could murder a beer,' she said.

Tessa made her way to the sitting room and was soon in conversation with Roy, Signor Bonicelli, Nell and Philip. Emmet had escaped to the kitchen to talk to Desna and Mo about Nell's disturbing news. At no time had the forthcoming nuptials been announced with the usual excited congratulations; instead, word of it had circulated underground like Chinese whispers. Unlike Chinese whispers, however, the disagreeable truth had in no way altered in the telling. Now everyone knew that Nell was to marry Daniel Thorne but, as yet, few spoke openly of it.

'What can we do?' Desna moaned. She had temporarily forgotten Nell's interference over the wedding dress, now she was almost wringing her hands over the new situation. 'Do you think we should all get together, sit her down and tell her frankly that she's making a big mistake?'

'You know Nell. That would only make her more determined. Anyway, Nell said he'd improved,' Emmet said. 'Perhaps she's right. After all, none of us has seen him for years.'

'Nonsense!' Desna turned on the food processor and for a moment speech was impossible. When she switched off she said, 'You can't tell me that his kind miraculously turn into honest citizens!'

Mo sat at the kitchen table topping and tailing mangetout. 'I agree. Leopards and spots and so forth!'

'But have you actually heard anything bad about him in the last few years?' Emmet argued.

'I haven't heard anything of him at all,' Desna said. 'We don't move in the same circles, I'm thankful to say. Could you put those large dinner plates into the cool oven at the bottom, please, Emmet?'

Emmet leaped to her feet. 'Right. How many?'

'All of them. We're a bigger party today. Tessa and Faith are here.'

'Have you seen Faith yet?' Emmet asked, a secret smile on her lips as she loaded the plates into the oven.

Mo turned round and looked at her youngest daughter suspiciously. 'Why?'

'Not yet,' Desna said. 'Harriet will have taken her upstairs to freshen up. They'll be down in a minute.' She spooned the contents of the food processor bowl into a saucepan.

'Yes. I expect they will,' Emmet said.

Tom and Beth were in the conservatory. Early that morning Harriet had brought down all her old teddy bears, a toy lion and various other stuffed animals – as a child she had never asked for dolls – and lent them to Beth for the day. Beth now had them lined up on a sofa and was lecturing them in a monotonous whisper, occasionally changing their places or sitting one apart, apparently in disgrace.

Tom was kneeling on the floor with the pieces of a B-17 laid out in front of him.

Persis was in the conservatory too, her legs stretched out across the floor. With a Gitane stuck between her lips, she leafed idly through one of Desna's glossy magazines, looking bored out of her mind; a dangerous state for Persis to be in. Impatiently she tossed the magazine aside and for a few minutes she watched Tom meticulously laying out the pieces of his aircraft; then she went to sit cross-legged on the floor beside him.

'What is it?' she asked.

Tom looked round to see Persis' pale eyes boring through a haze of smoke. He wondered if she'd ever heard that you could get lung cancer from passive smoking.

'It's a B-17 Flying Fortress,' he said loftily.

'Bomber?'

'Uh-huh.'

Persis edged closer and picked up the leaflet containing the instructions. She perused it for about ten seconds and then tossed it away.

'Right. Let's start,' she said.

Tom stared at her. She had already picked up the components

of the fuselage. 'You do the wings,' she said.

Tom didn't like to disobey. He wasn't exactly scared of Persis but he was in awe of her.

'You like bombers?' Persis asked after a bit, frowning in concentration.

'Yeah.'

'They drop bombs, of course.'

'That's what they're for.' Very quietly Tom made a noise of falling bombs. 'Pow. Pow. Pow.'

'Smash up buildings, eh?'

'Sure. Sometimes.'

'Of course, they occasionally kill people and animals too, don't they?'

'You can't help killing things sometimes. You have to.'

'Yes, I suppose you do. When they're a threat or want to take things away from you.'

'Right.' Tom continued to whistle through his teeth as he worked. 'Pow. Pow,' he said softly.

'I suppose the thing to do then is to explain to everyone why you did it so they understand. Like the United Nations.'

'Yeah.'

'It gets things sorted out, doesn't it? Because otherwise they might even think someone else did it and that wouldn't be fair, would it?'

'No.'

'In any case, people don't always blame someone when they understand. When they have it explained.'

There was a pause. 'Sure,' Tom said. 'Sure.' From time to time as he worked, he glanced at Persis, a worried expression on his face.

'Persis, this is my friend Faith, from Bristol,' Harriet said. 'She's studying Fine Art.'

Persis had temporarily left Tom in order to recharge her glass from Roy's lavish supply. She regarded Faith through eyes narrowed against her own private smokescreen.

'Fine Art, eh?'

'Sculpture,' Faith elaborated hopefully.

There was a long pause during which Persis tossed two swallows of whisky down her throat.

'She was wondering if you might have any advice for her,' Harriet rushed in to fill the silence.

'Harry!' Faith admonished her testily.

'Sorry, I thought—'

'Words of wisdom, eh?'

'Well . . .'

'There's only one caveat one can offer female students of Fine Art, and it's this . . .'

Faith and Harriet waited while Persis exhaled a lungful of smoke.

'Beware of the sodding male lecturers. The received wisdom is that they're there to turn you into professional artists. I say balls! The sole reasons for your presence as far as they're concerned is to feed their egos and provide them with an inexhaustible supply of totty.'

Faith giggled. 'Is that really all the advice you ever give?'

'That's all you need.' Persis turned away and went back to helping Tom with his Flying Fortress.

Harriet and Faith looked at each other. Then Faith gave a great snort of laughter. 'I've got a quote anyway,' she said.

The dining table at Mount Huish just about accommodated the assembled party. With greater numbers Mo was less worried about the input her sister might have on the proceedings; in any case every family had to put up with the maverick element; not being it herself for once was a pleasant change. Roy would have to look elsewhere for his kicks. Up to now Persis had been keeping out of harm's way helping Tom to assemble his model aeroplane, though it was evident she had nonetheless found time to visit the drinks cabinet and refill her whisky glass several times.

There was bean and coriander *potage* to start with, or a small turbot steak in a cucumbery sauce, followed by a fragrant glazed ham and Desna's usual appetizing selection of vegetables. And as usual too everyone was full of praise, in particular Bonicelli, though he did not often prise his eyes away from Nell. Even Roy noticed the Italian's attention to his sister-in-law and began to think in terms of an alliance by marriage as well as a business partnership. It could well be a very profitable arrangement. Last night in bed Desna had told him about Nell's ridiculous plans to pick up with Thorne again, but he couldn't take this seriously. If Enrico was the man Roy thought him to be he wouldn't take long to sweep aside such lacklustre competition.

Faith ate hungrily, not speaking much, but remembering why she had always so much enjoyed her visits to Mount Huish. Her normal diet mostly consisted of coffee, things on toast and cans of beer. She also remembered the one drawback to Mount Huish. Harriet's old man seemed to be as much of a pain as ever. Overbearing bastard. She couldn't think why Harry hadn't buggered off long since. And she had lost all hope of having any sensible conversation with Harriet's famous great-aunt. She would have to be content with such words of wisdom as had already been forthcoming, unfortunately that advice was too late.

Roy sat at one end of the table and carved the ham. Desna sat at the other with Enrico beside her. According to Roy's instructions, Nell had been placed on the Italian's other side, much to Isabel's irritation, for she found herself at the furthest point from him, next to Roy. Persis had been hemmed in by Mo, Emmet and Philip, with Harriet opposite.

Desna tried subtly to grill Enrico about his business interests; she'd entertained some vague hope of discovering why Roy was giving the man such undivided attention recently. He was charming, friendly and talkative but she learned nothing. She was no match for his quick wits.

'And where is the Oyster now?' she asked him. Originally, Philip was to have delivered it but the plans had changed. Desna thought, deliberately.

'At Virgin Gorda just at present,' Enrico said, 'I go soon to do some cruising. I hoped Roy could get away for a few days and join me there. You too naturally. I guarantee that you would fall in love with the place just as I have done. I have some hopes that your charming sister could also join us.' He turned to Nell. 'I would look on it as an honour if you would be my guest, Nell.'

Nell shook her head, 'Thank you, Enrico, but I have a lot on just at the moment. I can't possibly leave the business.' She wondered if he had been told about Dan. If so, it hadn't appeared to put him off.

'And I have to turn it down too,' Desna said, smiling. 'With the wedding to organize . . .'

'Ah, the wedding.'

'You *will* be able to come, I hope?'

'Dear Desna, of course. I look forward to it with bated breath.'

At any other time the two sisters might have exchanged sly, amused glances but not today. Desna had not forgotten Nell's part in encouraging Harriet's preposterous ideas for a wedding dress. Nell was still angry that her forthcoming marriage to Daniel was being treated as if she'd declared herself as having some contagious and unmentionable disease.

Mo glanced across at Nell, noticing her daughter's smouldering expression and guessing the reason for it. Could she any longer think of Nell as her daughter? It had been so easy in the past, with Persis keeping her distance.

Today Nell's hair was swept back from her face with a scarf, revealing her high rounded forehead. A forehead so like that of Persis' that Mo wondered that the resemblance was not apparent to everyone. Nell lacked only the excessively square jaw and her eyes were a dark grey, not pale and penetrating. Persis had sworn that she had revealed nothing to Nell during her visit to Alfresco but Mo didn't trust her.

'Did Desna tell you that Rupert's gone and got himself a tattoo?' Emmet murmured in her ear. 'Something to do with surfing. The latest fad. Thank goodness Tom's still happy with model aeroplanes!'

'Desna's very upset but she's bearing up wonderfully,' Mo said, sounding amused.

'She doesn't seem her usual self,' Emmet speared a portion of roast fennel. 'I think she looks pretty uptight, don't you? Maybe she's not well.'

'Funny. She said the same about you.'

'Me! I have an excuse, having had the flu. And then there was all the trouble with the vandals . . . but Desna? Anyway, she would never tell us if anything was wrong. Not Des. She thinks she has to be perfect at all times.'

'Look who's talking!'

'You think I'm a perfectionist?' Emmet exclaimed.

'Not in the same way. Just bloody-minded. By the way, are you really having that young man as a lodger?'

'You mean Barney? Yes. Why?'

'What does Maurice think about that?'

'He won't mind. Anything to keep the Darby household afloat.'

'You realize he'll expect to sleep with you, I suppose?'

'Who?'

'Barney, of course.'

Emmet spluttered with laughter. She took a sip of wine. 'Barney! You must be joking!'

Mo shook her head pessimistically. She looked towards the other end of the table where Rupert was showing off to Tessa and Faith, laughing uproariously at something Faith had said. 'Poor Roy,' she said. 'His face when he clapped eyes on Harry's friend.'

Harriet observed the silent Tom beside her and the way that every now and again he would glance across the table at Persis. He seemed fascinated by her all of a sudden. Or was he frightened of her?

'Shall I top up your fruit juice, Tom?' she said. Tom shook his head even though he loved the exotic home-made concoction of banana, coconut and ruby oranges. He had too much on his mind.

Desna and Harriet collected the dishes. As Harriet bent over with a loaded tray a fork clattered on to the table.

'Harry, for God's sake!' Roy said brusquely. It was a source of constant irritation that Giles could produce a daughter like

Tessa while all he could manage was a tongue-tied booby. Tessa had conversed with him and Isabel in a sensible adult fashion all through the meal; even Faith had more to her, though he abhorred her appearance. She was lively at least, giggling at Rupert's tomfoolery. He watched her covertly. It was perfectly apparent to him that she had turned into what in his youth used to be called an easy lay, a scrubber, a tramp; Harriet, of course, was quite oblivious of it. So, strangely enough was Desna; but then both of them had led sheltered, pampered lives. For the first time during the years the girl had been visiting Mount Huish he was aware that he found her presence under his roof disturbing. He was both excited and faintly alarmed to discover that she was turning him on in a way that, for instance, the attractive Tessa could never have done.

The dessert was brought. Harriet was tense with the effort of ferrying dishes back and forth. She managed to help her mother pass the damson sorbet and lemon cheesecake without mishap though she couldn't have joined in the general chatter at the same time as her mother did. It made it almost worse to be conscious of conspiratorial grins of encouragement from Philip. Her hand shook as she put Tom's pudding in front of him, colliding with his as he reached out to take it from her. A moment later the remaining half-glass of Tom's fruit juice was spreading over the white linen cloth, creeping ever onwards amongst the spoons, forks and glasses.

'Can't you do anything right, Harry?' Roy barked. He had intended the remark to be a humorous observation, since they had guests, but his recent salacious thoughts towards Faith had disconcerted him and he unthinkingly lapsed into his usual mode.

Desna rose to her feet and said quietly, 'It's quite all right; the table's protected. I'll get a cloth.'

Harriet stood perfectly still, mesmerized by the peach-coloured tide. There was a moment's silence. Then Persis spoke, her resonant voice carrying the length of the table.

'Bleeding hell, Roy! No need to jump the bloody rails. What are you trying to do, for Christ's sake? I tell you, I wouldn't treat a sodding dog the way you treat your daughter.' Then as casually as if she hadn't uttered a word she reached into her pocket for her cigarettes, her eyes still boring into her adversary until she forced him to look away.

Roy said, through clenched teeth, 'You're drunk, woman.'

Desna came back into the ensuing silence with a cloth.

'Sorry, Desna, I'll skip the pud, if you don't mind,' Persis said, 'I seem to have lost my appetite.' She pushed back her chair and went off to smoke in the conservatory.

Harriet sat down, pale with shock and at that moment Tom's face crumpled and tears began to course down his cheeks which were red from the effort of trying to contain his emotions. He blamed himself entirely for the accident.

'Darling, whatever is the matter?' Emmet rose from her seat. She wanted to say that it wasn't entirely Tom's fault but she could see that it would hardly help matters. Tom made a move to leave his chair.

'Sit down!' Roy roared, furious in his humiliation and determined to restore control. He could hardly compel Persis to remain at the table but he could certainly insist that his nephew did. The fact that Enrico appeared amused rather than shocked didn't help; he wasn't to know that until quite recently the Italian had regarded such scenes of family strife almost as a matter of routine. In fact it gave Enrico a certain satisfaction that Roy was as incapable as he had been of exercising the sort of total control at home as he did in business.

Emmet ignored Roy. 'If you'll excuse us, Desna?' She and Tom left the table and the room. And left Roy determined that this would be the last family gathering he would endure until July and the wedding; after that there would be no more anyway.

Harriet felt reprieved. She ducked her head, not wanting to catch anyone's eye, sympathetic or otherwise, as she mopped up the surplus fruit juice and took the cloth back into the kitchen. By the time she returned Isabel and Giles had come to the rescue; the topic was now the perennial one of boats and sailing. Arrangements were being made for anyone interested to go down to the yard that afternoon to see one of the Whitbread

60s that was due to embark on the round-the-world trip in September. Roy, Enrico and the Emmersons were all talking animatedly about the prospect. When Harriet was fifteen her father had finally accepted the fact that to take her sailing was more trouble than it was worth, since she was always, without fail, seasick. She smiled across the table at the only person who was unlikely to sit in judgement on her. Beth was unmoved by the departure of her mother and brother and had finished her damson sorbet and started on a slice of cheesecake.

'Tom's always upset lately,' she confided to Harriet. 'I take no notice.'

'Why is he always upset?'

'Mummy says it's a phase,' Beth said grandly.

Faith glanced across the table at Harriet, catching her eye at last. Surreptitiously she raised one thumb and winked. Her visit to Mount Huish was turning out to be more interesting than she'd expected, though she was sorry poor old Harry had hit the shit again.

'. . . in the Hard Rock Café World Cup,' Rupert was saying in her ear.

'Eh?' she said. She had endured ten minutes of 'tailslides' and 'cutbacks' and instead was listening fascinated to the Emmersons and Roy talking sailing. It was another world.

'Why don't you come down to Newquay with me next week? I'm hoping to do some serious surfing.'

Faith grinned. 'You're joking. What's in it for me?'

Rupert floundered. If he was to win the best chicks, he thought ruefully, he'd better think of the right answer to this one pretty damned quick. He coloured as he intercepted a look between Faith and Tessa. They obviously considered him an immature git. It wouldn't be long, though, before they would have reason to change their ideas. Or perhaps they were the wrong sort of women anyway. The sort who never would regard watching him pulling a perfect barrel as the ultimate rush.

Faith turned her attention to the other conversation just in time to catch her friend's father watching her speculatively. So that was the way the wind was blowing, she thought. 'The nautical jargon must be catching,' she said aloud.

'What?' Rupert said.

Coffee was served in the sitting room. Carol had arrived during the meal and was already engaged in clearing up in the kitchen; Desna was not sorry that she had arranged for Carol to make and serve the coffee, for she was feeling absolutely exhausted. She had never, ever, endured such a difficult meal, and that included the time when one of Roy's clients – a man by the name of Rudge she had good reason to remember – had arrived well oiled and finished up abusing all the guests, and Roy most of all.

What had disturbed her most was Roy's reaction to the current situation. It was unlikely that anyone else had read the signs as accurately as she had done; she knew that beneath the front that Roy presented to the world was an underlying capacity for violence. Up to now, it had rarely surfaced. Early in their marriage he had disciplined her by a hundred distressing tactics, just short of physical violence, after she had shown a little too much independence or for having got some small domestic detail wrong, humiliating him, he said, in front of important clients. For years now she had been careful not to give him grounds for complaint. She had become very good at it. It had actually been a source of pride, she mused wonderingly.

'Leave it all to me, Mrs Hindmarch,' Carol said, glancing at her employer, who seemed uncharacteristically dithery. 'The coffee machine's on. I'll bring it in directly.'

'Sorry? Oh, yes. Of course. Thank you, Carol.'

Desna returned to the sitting room where everyone, except Emmet, Tom and Persis had assembled, strung out round the room in easy chairs.

For the first ten minutes Tom refused to do anything but lay face down on his bed. The guest room assigned to him was on the second floor, its dormer windows nestling high up among the sloping roofs of Mount Huish.

Emmet sat patiently on the bed beside him, waiting for the emotional storm to die down. She gazed out over the trees that screened the garden from the river. Extensive views of the Dart estuary would be how an estate agent would have described what she could see from the second floor. In the distance the tower of Totnes church was visible above the trees and some of the tors of Dartmoor.

Tom had lapsed into silence. She had already guessed that there was more to Tom's woe than a spilt drink and a barked reproof from Roy.

'You need not take everything your uncle says to heart, darling,' she said. 'That's just his manner. I don't suppose he meant to be so sharp.'

She didn't believe it for a moment. Roy liked to dominate. He was used to being in control and to not having his authority questioned. Over the years she'd seen her sister's free will collapse, progressively muffled by Roy's powerful personality. Nobody would have Desna down as a doormat, she appeared too competent, too apparently satisfied with her lot. All the same, Emmet thought, she'd had a particular role mapped out for her and she seemed satisfied with it. She had made her bed, or had it made for her, and she had been content to lie in it. A very comfortable bed, some women would say, which they would give anything to lie in themselves.

A loud sniff from Tom. 'It wasn't only Uncle Roy. It was Aunt Persis too.'

'You don't have to mind Persis! She's an artist. Artists are always a bit rude.'

'She said something . . .'

Emmet leaned closer. 'Darling, sit up. I can't hear you.'

'She said something,' Tom said louder. He still maintained his prone position however.

Emmet remembered that Tom and Persis had been together before lunch. 'When she was helping you with your model aircraft?'

'Yes.'

'What did she say?'

'Something about people taking the blame for something they hadn't done.'

'Did she mean you?' Emmet was puzzled.

'Yes. No. She was talking about Lee.'

Emmet frowned. 'Persis doesn't know Lee.'

'I know. But she found out something. I think she's a witch. Witches know things.'

'A witch! Come on, Tom, this is nearly the twenty-first century! And you're much too old to believe in witches,' said the pragmatic Emmet, struggling to understand. 'Besides, what is it you think she knows?'

Tom sat up abruptly, his face damp, red and boiling hot. He avoided his mother's eye.

'If I tell you you'll be terribly angry.'

'Listen, Tom. The last time I was "terribly angry" was when I found those kittens in a bag in the middle of the main road.'

It was the worst thing she could have said. 'That's what I mean!' Tom said, looking as if he was about to bawl again. He shook his head furiously. 'Anyway, it doesn't matter,' he said. 'It was nothing. I just had a tummy ache, that's all.'

'Oh, yes? Tom Darby upset and it's nothing! You never cried for nothing, Tom. Not ever. Not even when you were a baby. So . . .'

He glanced at his determined mother.

'So,' she said. 'I'm just going to sit here until you tell me, even if it takes until next week.

There was a lull in the conversation. Coffee had been brought in by Carol and some people were into second cups.

'Perhaps I can offer you a lift when we go down to see this wonderful Whitbread 60 this afternoon?' Bonicelli glanced at Nell enquiringly. It would be an admirable opportunity to get Hindmarch's beautiful sister-in-law alone, albeit for a very short time. All the same, he prided himself that a short time would be all he needed to initiate an affair.

Nell shook her head. 'I'm sorry. I have to get back by six,' she said.

'Oh, surely not!' There was a general chorus of protest.

Nell took a sip from the as yet untouched glass at her side.

The brandy didn't really make what she was going to say any easier but its effect might well deaden the impact of the expected response. 'Desna knew I wouldn't be able to stay,' she said raising her voice very slightly. 'Because tonight I will be having dinner with the man I intend to marry.' She paused. There was an embarrassed silence. 'I know that my marrying Daniel Thorne will not be a particularly popular move as far as this family is concerned but I think the very least you could do is to wish me well. You have all spent the last twenty-four hours trying very hard to sweep what you regard as an unfortunate fact under the carpet . . .' There were murmurs of dissent. 'Please don't deny it. All I ask of you is that you respect my choice and give me your blessing.' She fortified herself with a large gulp of brandy.

From the direction of the conservatory came the sound of a slow handclap. Persis was leaning on the door jamb.

'That's my girl!' she said. 'You tell the buggers.'

'Persis!' Mo cried warningly.

Roy spoke loudly enough to drown all comment.

'I don't think this is the time or place for this,' he growled. 'Nell knew bloody well how that particular announcement would go down with anyone in their right mind and she still chose to go ahead with it. Everyone knows the man's a bastard.' Roy looked round at Bonicelli and the Emmersons. 'I'm sorry about this but it has to be said.'

Emmet appeared at the door, sensing the atmosphere but not understanding its cause.

Roy turned his attention back to Nell and Persis, somehow managing to include Mo and Emmet in an all-encompassing condemnation. 'But I've had just about enough of my hospitality being rewarded by having the place turned into a bear garden! I won't have it, d'you hear. And anyone who doesn't want to stay here on my terms had better pack their traps and get the hell out!'

Persis threw back her head and let out a great bray of laughter. It reminded Mo of the complaints of donkeys tied up behind the taverna in Greece where she and Alec had spent their honeymoon. It also reminded her that it was time to leave.

CHAPTER TWENTY-ONE

It was not the ideal bolt hole but it was the only place Desna could be reasonably certain of being alone. There was a chill breeze blowing in from the west; it came across the river and agitated the swathes of narcissi growing under the trees.

She had done her utmost to smooth over the scenes of crisis that had all but wrecked her careful preparations for a happy family weekend; but it seemed that the others were determined to ruin it one way and another. All her experience as a hostess had proved unavailing in the face of the family at its worst.

She blew her nose, feeling tears at the back of her throat. Perhaps it was unrealistic of her to have such high expectations and to care so terribly when things went wrong. First Harriet clamming up and disappearing with Faith the moment lunch was cleared. Then the business with Tom; it was quite apparent that Emmet blamed Roy for shouting at the child, but she ought to have understood that Roy had slightly old-fashioned ideas when it came to children. All the same, Tom had been a very naughty boy – if he'd had some fatherly discipline from Maurice he would not have dared behave as he had. Emmet had practically been in tears when she'd told her.

'I can't take it in!' she'd said, her voice wobbling. 'After all these years of helping me look after the animals. I can't believe it! And I thought it was Lee all along . . .'

'Did he say why he did it?' They had been sitting in the kitchen apart from the others.

Emmet shook her head, not trusting herself to speak.

'Perhaps I should talk to him,' Desna said.

'No. I don't think that would do any good, thanks all the

303

same. He's says he's very sorry he did it now.' All the same. Emmet had detected a lingering resentment in her son.

'I should think so! Quite apart from anything else, he must have known how much it would upset you . . .'

'He used to be so fond of the animals,' Emmet wailed suddenly. 'I just can't understand it!'

No one was sorry that Tom had shut himself away in his room. Perhaps it was for the best while everyone thought what to do.

Then there was Nell – walking out after that disastrous announcement. To have come out with it like that had been most unwise since she must have known how they'd all react. Roy in particular had never made any secret of how he felt about Daniel. Now Desna felt her relationship with her sister to have been damaged. They got on so well together, being alike in so many ways, although Nell was usually described as being more volatile and emotional while she herself was thought to be steady and reliable. Good old Desna! All the same she wondered if these were not just convenient handles for other people rather than the truth. She wondered if there was after all so much difference between them as was supposed. Now Nell had left, deeply offended, followed not long afterwards by Persis and Mo. It was a pity about Mo but she was not sorry to see the back of Persis; in fact she put most of her troubles down to Persis' malevolent influence. She'd had no idea that her aunt was so uncouth, Mo should have warned her.

Just before she left Nell had apologized after a fashion. Putting on her jacket in the hall, alone with Desna, she'd said crisply. 'I'm sorry, Des. But you must see I can't stay. It would have been nice to think that the family could have approved my decision to marry Daniel but since no one can bring themselves to forgive and forget there's no more to be said. I've forgiven Daniel for what he did and I rather naïvely thought everyone else would too. But there you are . .' She opened the front door. 'Thanks for the lovely meal. At least there was nothing wrong with that.' Then she had gone.

The funny thing about it was that Enrico seemed not at all put off by Nell's outburst. He simply said how much he admired her and asked for her telephone number. Desna had had to dissuade Roy from giving it to Enrico though she had no doubt that the Italian was quite capable of discovering it for himself.

Desna blew her nose again and from her high perch watched the progress of a late pleasure boat chugging up the river, the sound of its Tannoy commentary coming to her faintly.

'. . . Mount Huish, built in the 1920s by a millionaire for his mistress. He was drowned off the Skerries rocks, after which the house was lived in by a famous playwright. During the war it was taken over by the Special Operations Executive and is presently owned by the Hindmarch family of Hindmarch Marine whose yard you may have noticed further down the river . . .'

The Hindmarch family! The Hindmarch family was in disarray, if only the speaker had known. Not for the first time recently she wished she had someone to talk to. This was something new; she had never been one for girlish confidences even when she, Nell and Emmet had been much younger. She thought of herself as being the elder sister to whom confidences were vouchsafed, not the one who confided. And she had never at any time communicated her most intimate thoughts to Roy. She found herself thinking of Stevie Turnbull and it struck her that Stevie was the kind of person to whom one could talk on equal terms. She looked the sort who would understand and who could be trusted.

The sound of the Tannoy came more faintly now. She looked at her watch. Time to begin the preparations for dinner. It was to be an easy meal, thank goodness, after having pulled all the stops out for lunch. Easier still now that some of their number had unexpectedly departed. All the same, her feet felt like lead as she made her way back to the house. For almost the first time in her life Desna Hindmarch was totally uninterested in the preparation of food.

'I told you years ago that you ought to stand up to your old man,' Faith said. 'I don't get it. You're over twenty-one now. Why don't you?'

She poked a floating branch viciously with a stick she'd found, trying to free it from its entanglement with the wooden piers that supported the decking. She and Harriet had escaped down to the boathouse to sit watching the river. Roy and Philip had taken Signor Bonicelli, Giles and Isabel down to Hindmarch Marine and Rupert was playing Red Hot Chilli Peppers in his room very loudly.

'Because I'd never win, that's why,' Harriet said. Her hands were folded into the sleeves of her thick jersey.

'Course you would if you put your mind to it. You have to know how to handle blokes whether it's your live-in lover or your old dad,' Faith advised her, in worldly-wise mode. 'They're all the same underneath.'

'Daddy's not in the least like Gunter. Daddy's tough. Even other businessmen are afraid of him.'

'You have an advantage over them. You're a woman. You have to remember that blokes have very iffy egos. You just have to be mega crafty. Decide what you want, go for it – and let him think it was his idea in the first place . . .'

'But that's dishonest!'

'Come on now! Get real, for Christ's sake!' Faith crowed. 'It's about time you learned that it's every woman for herself.'

Harriet shook her head. Faith had changed. She was a toughie now. Perhaps that's what you had to become to survive alone. Faith was to all intents and purposes alone these days, except for Gunter, and even he . . .

'Is that how you treat Gunter?'

'Him most of all,' Faith laughed, and gave a final heave to the branch, which spun away, carried by the olive-green water until the current took it, only to deposit it on a narrow, stony beach at the next bend.

'What about trust?' Harriet asked, thinking of Philip.

'Trust is fine as far as it goes but one must be realistic.'

Harriet wrapped her arms round her knees and stared at the smooth sweeps and dimpled eddies beneath their feet. It seemed to her that the river was not in fact a solid body of water at all but a tangled skein of separate currents interwoven beneath a surface that provided only a hint of all that secret turmoil.

'Handling your dad should be a breeze,' Faith assured her. 'But don't go in for head-to-heads because you'll probably lose. Make like the crab, see!' She scuttled her hand sideways, grinning. 'He won't know what's hit him until it's too late. He mightn't know he's been bullshitted at all if you're really cool.' Faith glanced at her friend without much confidence. She found it very difficult to visualize Harriet changing the habit of a lifetime and standing up to her father's bullying, however crablike she became. She couldn't see her using subterfuge and guile at all to get out from under. It was very depressing. She shook her head. 'You should have left home years ago,' she said. 'Now I suppose you'll wait until you and Philip do the dreaded deed.'

'What d'you mean, "the dreaded deed"?'

'Getting married, of course, you wally!'

'Oh, yes. I thought you meant . . . never mind.'

'Just make sure you don't make the same mistakes with Phil.'

'Philip's not like my father.'

'Listen, any man can get like your dad if you give him half a chance. It's a sort of Napoleon complex.'

Harriet got up abruptly. 'Look, I want to show you something.'

Upstairs in the bedroom Harriet showed Faith the grey and silver dress. She guessed that Faith would approve and she did.

'Wow, that's really cool. It must have set you back mega bucks. These things are highly collectable.'

'I didn't buy it for that. I wanted it as a wedding dress.' Abruptly she took it away from Faith and put it back in its wrapper. 'It's out of the question, of course . . .'

'Why? It'd be brilliant. I see now why you wanted grey silk for my frock . . .'

'Only a bit darker. But it won't do. Mummy says so and I see her point. Daddy would hate it. He'd say that people would think it terribly odd.'

'Nuts! Nothing's considered odd these days. You want to chill out, my girl, and do your thing.'

'Anyway, it's only a dress. I don't want to fight with my father over a dress.'

Emmet had found a peacock feather in the yard. 'What's a peacock feather doing here?' she said, turning it over.

'Funny that. I thought I heard one screeching the other morning,' Barney said. 'It must have moved on.'

'They say peacock feathers are unlucky, don't they?' she said tonelessly, examining the iridescent eye pattern. 'Or at least a bad omen.'

'Gordon Bennett! You don't think I believe that load of crap?' Barney said. He was busy with pliers and a roll of wire, mending weak places in one of the aviaries. He worked with shirt sleeves pushed up to the elbow, his forearms all tendon, freckled skin and a fine dusting of red hair. The day was not particularly warm but he wore frayed denim shorts. He didn't seem to feel the cold.

'You're a pragmatist,' she said.

'I don't know what that is when it's at home but I'm sure you don't believe it either,' he said, clipping off an end of wire with wire cutters.

'Me? No, not really. But since that business with the birds . . . since Tom . . .' She hesitated, glaring at the feather. She was not particularly proud of the way she'd handled Tom when he'd finally confessed to stampeding the creatures under her care. She had even come close to striking him.

'How could you!' she'd shrieked like a banshee. 'How could you! I thought you loved the animals. How could you have been so cruel; just as bad as the people who put kittens in the road to get run over!'

Tom had retreated into monosyllabic sulks, his face red from crying. All he would say was, 'I *told* you you'd be angry!' At last goaded by her accusations, he'd burst out, 'I didn't mean to be cruel to them. I just thought they made you work too hard. It was their fault you were ill. If you didn't have to work so hard you wouldn't have cut your hand and that . . .'

'But I don't mind the work, Tom. Can't you understand that?'

Perhaps he had but it did not radically change the situation, except that Tom was now genuinely appalled at the results of his actions.

'Barney, you have younger brothers and sisters . . . what do you think I did wrong?' The words came out with difficulty.

Barney glanced at her. 'Search me,' he said, unhelpfully. 'Nothing probably. Kids seem to expect more than we did.'

'We're not that old.'

'Things change quick. They like a lot of attention these days. My mum had five. We used to muddle along as best we could.'

'You mean I didn't give Tom enough attention?'

Barney laid down his pliers and stood back, searching along the fencing for more broken links.

'Reckon he was jealous of the beasties,' he said, snipping off another length of wire.

'Jealous of the animals! You must be joking.'

'I reckon.'

'I suppose you could be right. But he's always cared for the birds and animals as much as I do.'

'Kids grow up.' Barney deftly wove the new wire into the fence. 'And I'll tell you something else for nothing.'

'Yes?'

'He's jealous of me an' all.'

'Surely not?'

'I reckon so. If I'm to stay on here we better get that sorted pronto, don't you think?'

'What d'you suggest? If you're right, that is.'

'I'm thinking I could take the two of them somewhere that'd be different for them . . . You said something about tenpin bowling, didn't you?'

'We're completely stuck until the car passes its MOT. Which I can't afford to pay for at the moment.'

'I already worked it out. I can borrow this mate of mine's motor. He keeps it in good nick. What d'you reckon?'

'It sounds like a good idea, Barney. Could you ask your friend, d'you think?'

'Sure. I'll see him tonight.' Barney clipped the wire and began

309

to collect the remains of the roll and his tools.

'It doesn't seem much of a punishment for what Tom did.'

'This is something separate. I reckon he's had his punishment. Anyway, it doesn't strike me that you're much of a one for that,' he said, looking at her at last. 'What I think is that it's time for mending a few fences before any more fly the coop, if you get my drift.'

'I hope it's not as serious as that.'

'Just a manner of speaking.' He loaded his tools into the pannier of his motor cycle and handed Emmet the roll of wire.

'Will you come with us?' she asked.

'Natch. I wouldn't mind another go at bowling. And there's one good thing.'

'What's that?'

'I wouldn't charge for my time.'

'Oh, thanks,' Emmet said drily.

'I'm off to my mum's now. I told her I'd fix up these cupboards she bought at the car boot sale. I'll be back later this evening.' He put on his helmet – incongruous and top-heavy-looking with shorts – swung one leg over the bike and started the motor.

'Right, I'm off,' he shouted over the noise. 'Like that Lawrence of Olivier chap.'

'Who?'

'You know. The bloke in that film. Peter O'Toole. You remember?'

'Oh, yes,' Emmet said, smiling for the first time. 'Yes, I remember. Just be careful you don't finish up in a ditch like he did, that's all.'

Barney roared out of the gate and she turned back into the kitchen to prepare the mash for the chickens. They had joked about the possibility of Barney finishing up in a ditch but in reality the idea of it disturbed her. In a very short time he had become an indispensable part of life at Drake's Farm.

CHAPTER TWENTY-TWO

Although it was Easter Monday Cornucopia was open. The exterior was much as Nell remembered it, though now some attempt had been made to clear the surrounding clutter of old metals tanks and piles of wooden pallets left over from the building's factory days. All the same, the potholes and the weeds remained.

'You should get all this landscaped and put in some hard standing for cars,' she said.

'You see why the place needs you?' Daniel said as he parked the Jag. 'You always put your finger on what's needed at once. I've got so used to it as it is, I don't see it any longer.'

'It better be the first thing I pay for! I can't stand it like this!' Nell said laughing.

They went inside. The lower floor was full to overflowing with architectural salvage: doors, panelling, pews, gates, newel posts and balusters, and even one or two huge stained-glass windows. The floor above held furniture of traditional design made in the workshop from reclaimed pine: dressers, tables, chairs and cupboards. The air was heavy with the smell of wax polish. In another of the vast rooms old furniture awaited its turn to be renovated. The workshop, as ever, was presided over by Arthur, who had been with Cornucopia since the beginning. He greeted Nell without commenting on her sudden reappearance; his usual morose self, she noticed with amusement.

A young employee had called Daniel away to the telephone. Arthur fed a piece of timber into the band saw, its screaming making conversation impossible. He switched the machine off and removed the timber.

311

'I'm glad you're still here, Arthur. I don't suppose Cornucopia could do without you.'

'Might 'ave to,' was his only comment.

'You're not thinking of leaving, are you?'

'*I'm* not thinking of leaving. But we'll 'ave to see, won't we?' he said darkly.

Nell questioned him again but he wouldn't be drawn. Arthur had always been a pessimist, however, and one to keep himself to himself. She would have to ask Daniel about him; he was too good a craftsman to lose.

Daniel came back and, at his most expansive, showed her round, introducing her to the half-dozen or so sales staff. They were all new since her time, mostly fresh-faced and eager, very polite. The older ones who had been there longer, in particular a capable-looking woman called Moira, were also polite but Nell was increasingly aware of one or two odd, sidelong looks. Since Daniel was introducing her as his future wife and partner in the firm she could understand their curiosity, even apprehension. It was only natural.

'You're not thinking of giving Arthur the sack, are you?' she asked when they were back in the car and turning out of the yard.

'Good heavens, no. What gave you that idea?' Daniel said laughing. 'Couldn't do without Arthur . . . but don't tell him I said so.'

'That's what I thought. He seems to be of the opinion that he might have to leave.'

'You know Arthur! Sure to be something behind it. He probably wants a raise. That's usually his way of broaching the subject, if you remember.'

Nell dismissed Arthur from her thoughts. They were on their way to The Old Rectory, Dutcombe, which she was to see for the first time. She was immediately impressed.

'You never said it was a cottage *orné*!' she said. 'It's an absolute gem! I love it.'

In fact it could have, and occasionally had, appeared on calenders to advertise the charms of West Country life.

Whitewashed, thatched, with arched Gothic windows and a porch with barley sugar twist timber supports, it sat snugly behind a small front garden like a gingerbread house. Perhaps for this reason it had long since been sold off by the church who had supplied their incumbent with something more sensible instead.

At the rear was a larger garden with lawns, herbaceous borders and a single impressive cedar. According to local opinion the gardens had been let go during its present occupancy. Major Blunt had always kept them in exceptional order and had even opened them to the public on Sundays during the summer. The trouble was that in the two years that Mr Thorne had lived there, nobody had had a chance to exchange more than a couple of words with him, let alone remind him of his duty as a village resident. He was far too elusive.

A pile of unanswered mail awaited them on the mat.

'Bills, bills!' Daniel complained cheerfully, sweeping it all up and chucking it on the oak gate-leg table in the hall – for himself he always preferred the real thing rather than what was made up in his own workshops. 'Now, what d'you think?'

Nell looked about her. The floor was tiled in black and terracotta, the ceiling was rich with decorative plaster work. An arched doorway led into what had once been the parlour where three long windows allowed a view of the neglected garden the neighbours so much deplored. There was more good furniture including a George III longcase clock and a French rosewood vitrine. In the days when they had lived together none of their furniture was ever regarded as permanent; Daniel had always sold it on if he found a buyer who offered him a good price.

'It's charming,' Nell said. 'And I see you do a good line in antique dust as well!' She drew her finger along the surface of a table.

'Can't get the staff, you know,' Daniel said good-humouredly. 'And Flick never was much good at the domestic arts.' He grinned. 'A drink I *can* manage, though. Beer suit you?'

'Have you any tea?'

'Certainly. Indian, China, Earl Grey?'

313

'Whatever you have. Earl Grey.'

They went through into the kitchen. 'Not as imaginative as yours, I'm afraid,' Daniel said, plugging in the electric kettle. 'I haven't had time to redecorate.'

'I can see that.'

The kitchen was painted in what had possibly once been cream, the colour favoured by Major Blunt, which had now deteriorated to a dirty ochre. Apart from some modern appliances recently jammed into it at random, everything had the look of complying to the basic needs of its previous owner. While Daniel rummaged round in cupboards for teabags, Nell attempted to visualize the room as it might be.

'No Earl Grey, I'm afraid.'

'That's all right. Anything.'

The kettle boiled and they took mugs of tea into the sitting room. Daniel turned on the gas fire, another legacy of the Blunt era.

'I must say I'm sorry your family gave you such a hard time,' Daniel said, casting himself into a Victorian chaise longue. 'Evidently they have a pretty low opinion of me. The perfect shit, eh? How come, d'you think? After all, I never really knew any of them that well. We broke up, of course, but that happens to almost everyone these days . . .'

'I told you, Daniel, it took some getting over, your leaving, and I wasn't very clever at hiding it from them. Naturally, I regret not being more self-contained at the time, but there you are!'

'Poor Nellie! What a bastard I was! I can't blame your sisters and your ma . . . Mo.' Daniel had never felt comfortable with the pet name.

'Actually, Roy was by far the most objectionable and he's only my brother-in-law.'

'I can't say I ever liked that man.'

'The feeling was obviously mutual. If Roy had his way I'd be well on the way to marrying his friend Signor Bonicelli by now.' Nell drank her tea which tasted slightly musty.

'Who the hell's he?'

314

'Some Italian Roy's very thick with at the moment. Rich, apparently. He rang me this morning.'

'Who did?'

'The Italian. Wanted to take me out.'

'I hope you told him to piss off,' Daniel said indignantly.

'On the contrary. He's flying me to Paris on Friday for a dirty weekend.'

'He's not! You're not going!' Daniel caught sight of Nell's suspiciously serious expression and grinned. 'Rotten woman. You had me going there for a moment.'

'The bit about him ringing me was true.' Nell smiled at last. 'And he did want to take me out so don't get too complacent! *And* I had one other unexpected champion in the weekend.'

'I'm glad to hear it. Who?'

'My famous aunt.'

'Bully for her.'

'I can't quite figure out her attitude towards me.' Nell said. 'I would have called it proprietorial, if I didn't know better. It annoys Mo no end. At one point I even thought . . .'

'Thought what?'

'Several things she said to me when she came to the shop and then this weekend made me think . . .'

'Come on, Nell!'

'That she regarded me as hers – her child, I mean. That *she* was my mother, not Mo.'

'Wishful thinking, probably.'

'But she didn't seem particularly interested in Desna or Emmet.'

'Took a fancy to you, I expect,' Daniel said, putting his mug of tea down almost untried. 'As who wouldn't? You better watch out!'

'I must say I did wonder.'

Daniel held out his hand to her. 'Come here, Nellie, love. I hope all this family disapproval won't make you change your mind about us.'

She went to him and he held her against him, pressing his face into her neck. 'God, I missed you!'

'I was only away two days.'

'Two days too long,' he murmured into her ear. 'I was bored to death; I even took out a video, would you believe?'

'I would have liked you to come to Mount Huish with me, but it would have been too soon. I want to do everything properly this time.'

'Of course, darling. So do I. I wouldn't have gone with you anyway. You I love. Families I can do without.' He kissed the pit of her neck and held her buttocks hard against him. They were as firm as he remembered them.

The familiar longing spread through her body, as if she had been given an injection of some sensation-enhancing drug. Each smallest cell vibrated with pure joy and expectation and by the time they reached the bedroom her limbs felt heavy with an exquisite languor. Her body accommodated to his, holding it until for one heart-stopping moment they seemed to be literally one flesh.

They slept – side by side yet still entangled as if they were lifeless bodies hurled down and lying as they fell. Much later she stirred, waking to an unfamiliar reality, her eyes taking in the surroundings she'd scarcely noticed two hours before. Some daylight still lingered in the room, dimly illuminating the William Morris wallpaper of peacock feather design – not the correct period for the house, she thought fastidiously, but harmonious. One or two dark portraits decorated the walls and richer coloured patches suggested there had been others. There was a mahogany washstand tiled with a design of irises and the bare floorboards were partly covered with rugs but otherwise the only furniture was the magnificent half-tester bed on which they were lying.

She turned and the movement woke Daniel. Their eyes locked mesmerically for a long time, then he reached out for her again.

That night, lost in a reality where only she and Daniel existed, Nell forgot about the opinions of her family; and if she had remembered, they would have had no significance.

Daniel was slow to wake the following morning. Nell herself was in no hurry. She had arranged for Anna to do the morning at Alfresco and she would take over at lunchtime. She took her dressing gown from her overnight bag and pulled it on. Leaving Daniel to doze, she went downstairs to make some coffee for herself. She wandered from kitchen to sitting room to drawing room and back to the hall, her hands clamped round the mug, sipping coffee as she went. Yesterday they had gone to bed before she'd had a proper chance to see the house that was to be her future home. She was already brimming with ideas to enhance it. It was sure to be a listed building so it would have to be done with the utmost care.

She paused at the gate-leg table in the hall, now strewn with Daniel's unanswered mail. Automatically she gathered it up into a tidy pile. There were the usual gas and electricity bills, besides an inordinate number of communications from the Inland Revenue, and Customs and Excise. Daniel really was the limit! He had always been dilatory about his tax and VAT returns, and had normally left that side of things to her. She supposed she'd again take care of all that once she came back to Cornucopia.

Everything was set up for the closing down of her own business. She had given notice to the landlord that she would be quitting the shop and flat at the end of the month; a collection of large boxes was already filling up with personal belongings that were not immediately needed. In the coming week much of the stock from the shop would be on its way to Cornucopia, the furniture from the flat would be dispatched to The Old Rectory. Her savings would naturally be available for any further investment in Cornucopia that they deemed advantageous; landscaping the entrance for a start. Her new life would be about to begin. She turned over a letter with the logo of a local estate agent stamped on it and remembered that Daniel had mentioned that he had been thinking of selling The Old Rectory. She hoped he'd cancelled the arrangement because she already loved the house. Besides, now would not be a terribly good time to sell; he would be bound to lose money on it. Better wait until the market picked up, if it was absolutely imperative for them to be closer to the business.

Daniel came bouncing down the stairs, hesitating when he saw her standing by the table. Then he clutched her round the waist humming 'Dancing in the Dark'.

'Daniel! You're spilling the coffee!'

'Good morning to you too,' he said, kissing her.

Making more coffee in the kitchen she said, 'Your accounting is as bad as your housekeeping. Haven't you done anything about your tax affairs since Simon left?'

Daniel looked at her sharply over his coffee mug. 'Why? What makes you say that?'

'All that unopened mail on the hall table, that's what. You really are the end, Daniel. I suppose you're waiting for *me* to sort it all out!'

'Darling, I thought you'd never ask!' he said laughing. His face creased into the disposition of furrows and planes that lent him such an infectious charm, so that both men and women, on first meeting him, would immediately agree on his open and easy-going nature.

'So. How are we going to spend this morning snatched from our busy schedule?' he said lightly.

'I thought we might go and get someone to give us a price for landscaping the front of Cornucopia and laying down a decent parking area.'

Daniel groaned. 'Nellie, you're a slave-driver! I thought you were going to suggest going somewhere nice for a drink.'

'We could do that too,' she said.

Adam Young and an older friend by the name of Matt called for Rupert in Matt's Volkswagen Beetle. Rupert's brand-new surfboards were strapped to the roof rack with the others and they left for Fistral Bay in Cornwall. They would be staying at the Youngs' holiday cottage in Newquay. It was fortunate that Roy was already down at the yard with Bonicelli and the Emmersons so was not present to comment on the bumperless and apparently silencer-less car with its lurid turquoise livery. Desna herself was doubtful about the enterprise but fearful of seeming an over-protective mother. Besides, Mrs Young was staying at the cottage and Matt appeared to be a sensible young man in spite of his bleached and tangled locks and a sweatshirt with 'Surfers Against Sewage' emblazoned across it. In any case, Rupert was absolutely determined to go.

No sooner had the VW roared away from the front door than Tessa arrived in her car into which Desna, Harriet and Faith all piled in order to keep their date with Mrs Gillimore.

On the way to Totnes Tessa made conversation, regaling them with an account of a recent party at her tennis club.

Faith kept sliding significant, amused glances in Harriet's direction and waggling her eyebrows like Groucho Marx. Harriet was terribly afraid that Tessa would eventually sense the mockery behind Faith's exclamations of 'Wow!' and 'No shit?', which would be a pity because Tessa was only coping with a social situation the way she knew best, a way that Harriet couldn't possibly hope to emulate.

At Mrs Gillimore's, however, Faith and Tessa were in agreement. They both approved the grey silk and the fashionably simple cut. There was very little space to spare in Mrs Gillimore's room by the time the five women, a tailor's dummy, a large cutting table and several bolts of fabric were all crowded into it. There was no problem with Tessa's fitting – she already looked the part – but Mrs Gillimore had grave reservations about Faith. She had persuaded the presumptive bridesmaid out of her boots for the fitting but there was another problem.

'Um. I wonder . . .' she said. 'The hair, you know.'

Faith grinned and ran her hand over her shaved temples. 'No sweat,' she said generously, 'I've promised Harry I'd grow it just for the occasion.'

Desna let out a silent sigh of relief. The hair had been troubling her.

'There will be two more bridesmaids,' she told Mrs Gillimore. 'But Harriet and I thought it would be a good idea to get Faith and Tessa's opinion first. I'm sure the Wakeham twins will be happy to fall in with whatever we choose.' The Wakeham twins had been highly delighted to be asked.

'Now the wedding dress itself,' Mrs Gillimore said at last. 'Are you both agreed on the shape and the fabric? Because I think we should go ahead quite soon.'

319

Desna and Faith both looked at Harriet expectantly. Harriet looked at the floor, wishing she had never shown Faith the grey frock. She could summon up all her courage and insist, now, on her own choice but that would mean that she would have to play out the ensuing scene in front of both Faith and Tessa. Tessa had never been anything other than friendly, in fact she'd made huge efforts to get to know Harriet, but Harriet was convinced that her future sister-in-law would thoroughly despise the real Harriet and so had invariably scuttled back into her shell. But the thought of exposing herself to her mother's disapproval, besides Tessa's amusement, was more terrifying than incurring Faith's contempt and she found herself nodding, agreeing on the silk of palest ivory to be backed with pink. Faith could hardly have more contempt for her than she had for herself.

'Good. That's settled at least,' Desna said, so relieved that she had an answer of any sort that she was prepared to overlook Harriet's momentary hesitation. 'I know you'll love it when it's made up.' She turned to Tess and Faith for support. 'Don't you agree?'

'She'll look absolutely super,' Tessa said wholeheartedly.

'Yeah. Great.' Faith directed a fierce gaze towards Harriet, mouthing the words, 'Now, you fool!' at her; but Harriet looked away.

Desna and Tessa both began an intense conversation with Mrs Gillimore about shoes and headdresses while Faith growled in Harriet's ear. 'Why don't you say something?'

'I can't.'

'You'll look more of a wally than we will in that lot.'

'Please don't, Faith,' Harriet whispered desperately.

'So you'll get the twins to telephone for their fittings, will you?' Mrs Gillimore said finally. 'And Mrs Darby can bring her little girl along in June for hers?'

'Isn't that a bit late?' Desna immediately looked anxious.

Mrs Gillimore smiled. 'I learnt my lesson early on that one, by making the dresses of two ten-year-old bridesmaids three months before the wedding! I had to work all night to let them out with only hours to spare!'

'Oh, yes. Of course,' Desna said.

From Mrs Gillimore's they drove to the station to see Faith off on her train. Desna and Tessa waited in the car.

As the great yellow nose of the Intercity came round the curve of the track Faith gave Harriet an unexpectedly affectionate hug. 'All the best, Harry, love,' she said. 'I think your Philip's great. You'll have forgotten all about the bloody frock by August and I'm sure you'll get all your probs sorted once you get out from under.'

'It was lovely to see you. You will come down again soon, won't you?'

'Sure. I have to anyway, had you forgotten? For the fitting.'

'Yes, of course.' Doors opened and slammed.

'Though you didn't warn me there would be such a plethora of bloody bridesmaids. I thought it was going to be just the three of us.'

'So did I,' Harriet said despondently.

At the window, her kitbag on her shoulder, Faith closed one eye and held her thumb up in salute as the train moved off.

'Stay cool,' she called.

CHAPTER TWENTY-THREE

It was slack water at Papermill Quay, leaving the mud furrowed with a pattern of small streams and runnels; the gaunt ribs of *Prudence* jutted from it starkly. If it had been a normal kind of day Desna would have been amused to see that each rib was topped by a gull.

But it was not a normal day and Desna was too upset to notice. She didn't even acknowledge Mo's next-door neighbour, Delphi Wild, who was sitting on her doorstep suckling her baby and smoking an odd-smelling cigarette.

It was only when Desna was inside the cottage that she remembered that, of course, Persis would be present. Especially this early in the morning.

Her aunt was packing some items into a canvas shoulder bag. Mo was setting up her easel and laying out her paints.

Desna hesitated, unable to hold back an exclamation of disappointment.

Persis made a sound that was between a laugh and a cough. With her cigarette between her lips she said, 'Don't mind me. I'm just about to make myself scarce. My fisherman friend is due any minute; I'll wait for him on the quay.'

Mo said, 'What a lovely surprise. You don't usually visit this early in the morning. Have some coffee.' She tactfully didn't mention that Desna rarely visited her anyway, but preferred to entertain her mother at Mount Huish than slum it in Papermill Cottage.

'I'm afraid I've come at a bad time,' Desna said, already wishing she hadn't rushed off so precipitately.

'I'm off,' Persis said, looking at Desna through narrowed eyes that seemed to penetrate her innermost thoughts, so that Desna was relieved when her aunt went outside to talk to the woman next door while she waited for her fisherman.

'Sit down,' Mo called from the kitchen where she was already clattering cups and kettles.

Desna sat down and Polly Chrome came to sit on her lap.

'Push her off if you don't want her,' Mo said, returning with two mugs of coffee. 'She's moulting.'

Desna lifted the cat on to the chair next to her. Her navy wool skirt was liberally sprinkled with cat hair but today she hardly cared. There were worse things than cat hairs.

Mo looked at her daughter searchingly, noticing that the hand that accepted the coffee trembled and was not adorned with the usual beautiful ruby and gold ring; and the nail polish was slightly chipped on several fingers. More significantly still, Desna's face was blotched and puffy. This was all so unusual that Mo burst out immediately with, 'Darling, what's the matter? What's happened? Is it about Persis being so rude?' Perhaps Roy had got at Desna since the weekend over the social shortcomings of her relatives.

For a minute Desna drank, or pretended to drink, her coffee without speaking. Her expression was unsteady and her mouth trembled as much as her hand. Surely she couldn't be about to cry? Mo thought. Not Desna.

'Roy wants to sell Mount Huish!' Desna burst out at last in something like a wail.

'Sell! Sell Mount Huish? Desna, what on earth's happened? Has Roy gone bankrupt?'

Desna shook her head wildly. 'No, of course not! Quite the reverse. He wants to transfer the business to Tortola in the British Virgin Islands!'

'Where?' Mo couldn't exactly place the British Virgin Islands. Were they near the Bahamas perhaps? Or the Pacific? That was it. No, those were the Friendly Islands.

'The BVI. In the Caribbean.'

Mo was silent. For a moment she'd assumed that Desna had discovered Roy in some petty infidelity but when she came to think about it she realized that Desna's reaction to that would have been far more pragmatic. Desna was a realist. This was different.

'You better tell me about it,' Mo said.

It had happened the previous evening when Desna and Roy were alone together.

'Desna, we have to talk,' Roy said, handing her an unexpected brandy to accompany the coffee she'd brought into the sitting room on a tray.

The sun was tilting in through the windows, decorating the walls with patterns of honey-coloured shadows. Outside it striped the lawn with emerald and violet. Desna relaxed in one of the ample armchairs, flicking minute specks of dust off the dark blue Liberty print cover with a fingernail. She would have to have all the covers cleaned before the wedding. For a moment she closed her eyes.

'Are you listening, Desna?' Roy said sharply.

'Yes. Talk, you said. About the wedding arrangements, you mean?' She forced herself back to full attention. 'They all seem to be well in hand now, thank goodness. Stevie Turnbull is wonderfully efficient.'

'No, it's not about the wedding!'

Something in Roy's tone at last alerted her and she turned to look at him. He was standing by the fireplace, one foot in casual leather slip-on on the fender. Her heart felt as if it had been momentarily squeezed in a vice: now perhaps was the time he'd chosen to lecture her on her family's misdemeanours; or, since they were quite alone, he might even be going to mention her performance in bed. Perhaps he'd noticed how less than enthusiastic she'd been recently.

She put down her coffee cup. 'What is it, Roy?'

He took his cigar out of his mouth. 'As you know I've been having a good deal to do with Enrico just lately,' he said. 'The purpose I had in inviting him to Mount Huish over Easter, as you must have guessed, was not entirely for the pleasure of his company.'

325

She waited with a profound feeling of apprehension.

'I want you to listen carefully to this,' Roy went on, 'I've been giving the future of Hindmarch Marine a good deal of thought – what with the recession and this new Department of Transport code of practice. Frankly I didn't see where the business was going. We'd be ticking over, just about, but as you're well aware, that's not the Roy Hindmarch way. That firm going into liquidation was bad luck for them but bloody lucky for me, as I got that Oyster at a rock-bottom price . . .'

'Roy, I don't see—'

'Listen, Desna!' Roy snapped.

He went on: 'Another piece of good fortune was Enrico coming along just when he did, liking the Oyster and being prepared to spend a mint on the refit. I needn't repeat how impressed he was with our workmanship and efficiency. Impressed enough apparently to offer me a tremendous business opportunity I might never have been able even to contemplate on my own . . .' He waited, as if for her comment, but she'd been barked at once and was in no mood to repeat the experience.

'To cut a long story and a whole raft of negotiations short,' he said, as if she couldn't possibly have understood such detail, 'I shall be cutting down our activities here in Devon—'

'Cutting down! I thought you said—'

He held up a hand like a traffic policeman, though incongruously one with a cigar between his fingers, 'Wait! Enrico and I will be embarking on an entirely new enterprise in the British Virgin Islands. Chartering, brokerage and, of course, repair as we do here, but naturally on a far bigger scale and for a far more lucrative market, since it will be very much a year-round activity.'

'But how can you run a business abroad if you're here in Devon?' Desna said. 'Or does Enrico intend to run it for you?'

'Enrico is first and foremost a man of business, and a damned good one, otherwise I wouldn't dream of throwing in my lot with him. But you were right in thinking he has not much knowledge of boats, per se. No, the intention is to run down the Kingswear side of things, Philip is quite capable of attending to that while Enrico and I build up the BVI end. Then, later, Philip can join us there and be part of the new team . . .'

'You mean, *live* in the British Virgin Islands?' Desna felt her hands sweating with anxiety.

'Naturally, I could hardly, as you so rightly said, run it from here.'

'You mean you would be spending all your time there, with me here?'

'No, of course not!' Roy said with some asperity. He hoped Desna wasn't going to be obtuse over this. He had left breaking the news to her until Easter was over and the wedding arrangements well under way, but he couldn't delay it any longer.

'No. We would live in Tortola, naturally. In for a penny, in for a pound.'

'But what about Mount Huish?' Desna said, the words struggling out of her mouth as if reluctant to be expressed.

'We sell. It goes without saying that we couldn't afford to keep two places on the go . . . not at first anyway. Perhaps later—'

'Sell Mount Huish?'

'Don't look like that, Des. One can't make omelettes without cracking a few eggs and we shall need the capital, at least to start with. Enrico's supplying most of it but we can't expect not to make *some* input.'

'But couldn't you sell the business here if you're going to run it down anyway?'

'Look, I have absolute faith that the new venture will be a huge success but only a fool would leave himself without some kind of foothold in the UK. Initially, anyway. And we shall need time to build up the Tortola business. We're buying out a firm who have been running bareboat holiday chartering – Beneteaus mostly – but we want to expand into the luxury market, supplying crews and so on. With the Yanks so close I don't see how we can lose.' He stopped speaking and picked up his brandy glass, wedging it between his fingers and the cigar.

With an effort Desna forced her mind away from the only

thing he'd said that she had really been able to grasp: the selling of Mount Huish. 'But, Roy, what do you know of Enrico? How can you be sure that he's to be trusted? It's our whole life we're laying on the line. I get the impression that for him it may only be a sideline.'

'Come on now, Des! Do you take me for a complete fool? You don't suppose I haven't gone into this with a fine-tooth comb, do you? Why else do you think I employed those London lawyers and accountants instead of old Giles and Matheson's lot. They looked at the projections as well as into Enrico's soundness and found nothing to worry about at all, especially since he's providing the lion's share of the investment in the scheme.'

'But sell Mount Huish!' Desna felt a terrible coldness gripping her. She had always thought Roy felt as strongly about the place as she did. Now here he was relegating it to the past without a qualm.

'It'll be quite a wrench, I realize that,' he said calmly. 'But I believe that once you've seen Tortola you'll wonder why we didn't get the hell out years ago. Think about it! Sun, swimming in wonderful warm water – I know you love swimming – a better lifestyle altogether. Most women would give their eyeteeth for the chance.' Her shocked expression irritated him and he raised his voice. 'I've been getting thoroughly pissed off by the petty restrictions and red tape when one's trying one's best to run a business in this bloody country and, if you must know, pretty fed up by the rut we seemed to have got ourselves into. If Enrico hadn't come along at the time he did . . .' He paused in what had become a tirade, self-induced aggravation lending it an increased vehemence, especially as he became aware of Desna's shock and scepticism. With an effort he took a grip on himself. He went across to her and sat on the arm of her chair. Women always needed a bit of soft soaping when it came to change, being creatures of habit and strong attachments. He stroked her arm.

'Just let me show you something, will you?' He left her sitting, still shocked, in her chair while he went to his study, returning with a fat, glossy brochure. 'Take a look at that,' he said throwing it into her lap, and resumed his seat on the arm of her chair while she leafed through the brightly coloured pages: azure seas, white beaches, palm trees, long drinks on wide balconies, exotic flowers, red suns slipping down into dark blue horizons. Paradise.

'See what I mean?' he said. 'Don't tell me you couldn't do with some of that?' It was unfortunate from his point of view that this evening the sun continued to create dappled patterns on the creamy yellow walls of the room in which they sat. Outside a blackbird sang. He wished it would shut up and he wished it was raining.

'Roy, we can have holidays. We've always been able to get to the sun whenever we want.'

'Listen, you think Mount Huish is a nice house. I've seen spreads out there that would knock your eyes out.' He tapped the brochure. 'I'll take you out there soon . . . then you can see for yourself. Besides, have you ever thought what Mount Huish would fetch these days?'

Coming out of her shocked stupor at last she realized she was being hustled in the way Roy hustled his business colleagues and opponents. It struck a profound core of anger inside her. She stood up, emptying the glossy brochure on to the floor.

'I don't want to think of it,' she cried, pacing the floor. 'And I deeply resent the way this has all been wrapped up before I've even been given a choice. What you've done is unforgivable! You've committed us both to a completely new life without so much as a hint that anything was in the air. Oh, yes. You thrashed out every detail with Enrico, naturally!' Unaccustomed sarcasm embittered the words. 'But to me, to your wife, not a word! I suppose you've even discussed it with Philip!'

Roy was staring at her in astonishment. Desna had scarcely ever raised her voice to him and then only as a short-lived outburst. She was being an unreasonable and ungrateful bitch considering he had her best interests at heart. Serve him bloody right for spoiling her all these years.

'So this is all the thanks I get for trying to do better for you,' he said, dark with anger. 'And if you must know, I have *not* yet discussed it with Philip—'

'Or anybody it most directly affects,' she cried. 'How d'you know Philip will agree to it either?' Desna was at the fireplace where Roy had stood earlier, toying frenziedly with a small silver-framed photograph of Rupert that stood there.

'Of course Philip will agree to it. He knows which side his bread's buttered. I imagine he'll be a damned sight more grateful than you!' Roy himself now began to pace impatiently, his temper barely under control. 'And you wonder why I didn't discuss the scheme with you earlier! I'm bloody glad I didn't if this is a sample of the way you'd have carried on. If I consulted you every time I made a business decision we'd still be running a do-it-yourself repair yard like we did in the beginning. In which case we would never have had Mount Huish anyway!'

Desna looked at the photograph she still held in her hands. 'And what about Rupert?' she said, her voice unsteady. 'And Harriet? Is she to come to the Virgin Islands too? What on earth would *Harriet* do there?'

'Rupert will go to the new school. They'll push him through his A levels or I'll want to know the reason why! Then he can join the firm if he knows what's good for him.'

Desna shook her head repeatedly and felt tears on her cheeks. 'I can't believe this is happening. To suddenly find that I've lost control of my entire life. And Harriet and Philip's future all wrapped up for them! Everything decided for us,' she cried bitterly. 'And none of us with any say whatever!'

Roy stopped pacing abruptly and approached her. '*I* can't believe it either, if you must know!' he said harshly. 'A bloody nest of vipers is what I've got. Ungrateful bitch!' For a moment Desna had the impression that he was going to strike her. But he simply stood over her threateningly, which had always been enough to subdue her up until now. She flinched, but instead of hitting her he took her hand and ground the dead stump of his cigar in her palm.

'Thanks for your support in our new venture,' he said bitterly.

That the cigar was no longer alight did nothing to diminish the shock of his action; it had her standing by the fireplace motionless long after he'd left the room.

That night he raped her. At least that was what it felt like to Desna. As if to prove the futility of her opposition to anything he chose to do, he overcame her resistance, disregarded her body's unpreparedness and came into her roughly, not caring if he hurt her.

He knew that it was imperative that he demonstrate to her who had power and who, when it came right down to it, was without it. After all, it hadn't been he who had laid down the natural law that had given dominance to the male of the species. He thought that he had seen to it years ago that Desna understood that all the big decisions were his. Evidently he would be forced to show her all over again. Well, she wouldn't like it; neither, if it came to that would he, but it had to be done. Once she'd come to heel she'd realize it was all a storm in a teacup.

The story Desna told Mo was heavily edited but the gist of it was there. Mount Huish was to go. They and the business were to move half a world away.

Neither Mo nor Desna knew how long Persis had been standing at the door, arms folded across her chest. Mo glanced at her angrily. Persis shrugged. 'My nautical friend didn't turn up. Maybe he got the time of the tide wrong.'

'*You* got the time wrong more likely!' Mo said furiously.

Persis sat down on the sofa and put her boots on the arm. She lit a fresh cigarette from the stub of the last. She let out a smoky breath while both Mo and Desna stared at her speechlessly.

'It's not the house that's important,' Persis said staring at the ceiling. 'I must say that if it was me who had been so misguided as to marry the bastard in the first place, I'd be ecstatic with joy to see him disappearing over the horizon in his goddamned boat – but you won't be, of course. You're not the sort. You'll wring your hands but you'll let him sell the house all the same. Then you'll trot after him like the good, wee wifey you are . . . to the ends of the earth if necessary. I suppose one could say there is a certain nobility in that.'

Desna and Mo exchanged frantic glances. Then Desna placed

her mug of coffee carefully on the table and got up from her chair,

'Thanks for the coffee, Mo,' she said. Then she left.

She drove aimlessly round for an hour before she realized that she had somehow finished up outside Stevie Turnbull's house, the nerve centre of Bonne Bouche. For several minutes Desna sat in the car, numb, not knowing what to do next. Stevie would wonder why she was turning up without an appointment in the middle of a hectic morning. She was about to move off again when Stevie herself hailed her from the drive. Desna got out of the car.

'Hi there,' Stevie said cheerfully, her arms full of cardboard files. 'Come in. I'll just dispose of these then I'll make some coffee.' If she was surprised to see Desna she was disguising it well, Desna thought.

Stevie *had* been surprised to see Desna and she couldn't help but observe that her visitor did not look her usual composed, soignée self. Privately, she thought, The wedding's off! Mothers of brides had come to her before looking similarly fraught. A great pity, this was one wedding she had been looking forward to . . .

They sat in Stevie's sitting room, which appeared to be an overflow from the office, which itself lay behind the house in a single-storey extension.

'Sorry about the clutter,' Stevie said, sweeping a pile of papers from the table and laying down a tray of coffee. 'I'm afraid it's always like this, especially lately.' She paused to look at Desna. 'Is something the matter?'

'Oh . . . no.' Desna said. 'I just came to tell you that I'd sorted out that problem over the wedding stationery and that Harriet and Philip have chosen the music.'

'Good,' Stevie said encouragingly. So the wedding was still on. Not that the music had been any of her brief. 'What are they having?'

Desna glanced round the room distractedly. 'Oh, yes. Well, Philip wants the "Arrival of the Queen of Sheba", after the service, you know. Harriet wants Faure's *Pavane* at the beginning. I think that's a bit low-key myself but . . .' Her mouth trembled and she dived into her bag and produced a lace-edged handkerchief. She blew her nose. 'Oh dear,' she said brightly, 'I seem to have hay fever!'

'Desna,' Stevie said quietly, 'what's wrong?'

For a moment Desna's self-control held, then feeling the other woman's unspoken sympathy, it began to crumble.

'I've had a bit of a shock,' she said. To her dismay she felt her eyes filling with tears.

Stevie got up, rummaged in a drawer and produced a packet of tissues. She gave them to Desna.

'Tell me,' she said. 'If there's anything I can do . . .'

For a moment Desna couldn't speak. Eventually, in a rush, she said, 'We have to leave Mount Huish and I'm quite broken-hearted about it.'

'Oh, Desna! I'm sorry.' Money troubles, Stevie thought. Not unexpected these days. 'Are you saying you want to cut down on the wedding arrangements?'

'Oh, no. Nothing like that. A few weeks ago Roy was hinting that we should go easy on alterations to the house. I thought he meant the business was in serious trouble. Now I see that he was trying to soften me up for this new scheme of his. He wants us to move to the British Virgin Islands for good. Sell up the business here, eventually at least, and move us, Philip and Harriet over there. He plans to run a chartering business from Tortola in partnership with this Italian . . .'

Tears were running freely down her cheeks now, but somehow she didn't care.

Stevie went across and sat beside Desna, taking her hand. 'I'm so sorry about the house. I know you adore Mount Huish.'

'It's not only the house, much as I love it,' Desna said. In the hour that she'd been driving about the full import of Roy's scheme had finally hit her. She would leave behind not only Mo and her sisters but her friends, such friends as Roy had allowed her. Abroad she would be more dependent on Roy than ever, there would be no chance of meeting anyone who had not already been vetted by Roy. No one like Stevie, for instance. And she would leave behind her beloved Dart, the soft, embracing greenness of the Devon hills, the secret wooded valleys and the wild purple moor. Everything that meant home to her. She attempted to explain to Stevie.

'Does Roy know how you feel?' Stevie asked gently.

'Yes. Oh, yes,' Desna cried, pressing one of Stevie's tissues to her wet, burning cheeks. 'But it won't make the slightest difference. He says we have no option. It's for the business. Besides, it was all settled before he even told me.'

'I believe the Virgin Islands are extremely beautiful,' Stevie said. 'You might like it over there. Why don't you give it a try?'

On the desk the telephone buzzed suddenly. Stevie picked it up and murmured something into it before replacing the handset. She went back to Desna.

'We are supposed to be going over there in a week or two,' Desna said. 'He wants to show me how wonderful our life will be.'

'I think you should at least have a look,' Stevie said, attempting a balanced view against all her inclinations.

But Desna had known since the night before that there had been a fundamental shift in the situation. The wraps had been swept away from something ugly that had lain unacknowledged all her married life. The price of owning Mount Huish had been heavy; it had meant the giving up of her own freedom of choice in all but the most superficial aspects of her life, her domination by the will of another person. Worst of all it had required her silence over how her children were brought up, how they were treated, how educated. She had never admitted even to herself that this was the way things stood. Now the reward for her submission was being taken from her, what had she left? How could she express her self-disgust, even to someone as sympathetic as Stevie?

She looked at Stevie's capable hand as it lay on hers. Though the nails were clean and neatly filed, it was a hand that had seen more of the rough and tumble of life than she herself ever had.

'You see, Stevie,' she said, 'it calls everything into question now. I'm wondering if there ever was anything *but* the house all along.'

'You mean of your marriage? Surely that's not true?'

'No outsider can really understand a marriage, can they?' Desna said. 'There are things . . .' She stopped speaking and blew her nose.

'Listen,' Stevie said, 'I've been married too. And I've been through a pretty unpleasant divorce. I know there are things...' With her it hadn't been violence or other women but Mathew's paranoia. He had insisted that every last penny she spent was accounted for, his near hysteria if anything in the house was moved or changed in any way, his obsession with neatness and cleanliness . . .

'But were you ever,' Desna began, 'I mean, were you ever frightened of Mathew?'

'No, not frightened,' Stevie said, beginning to understand. She should have known; she'd met Roy Hindmarch, after all.

Desna got up suddenly and with false brightness said, 'Look, do forgive me. I didn't mean to burden you with all this. It was quite unpardonable of me, and when you're so busy too! I didn't even ask if you could spare the time. I mean it has nothing to do with the wedding arrangements, has it?' She gave a brittle laugh. 'I don't know why I came . . . it's just that my mother has my aunt staying with her just at present so it wasn't convenient to talk things over with her . . .'

Desna saw a hurt look in Stevie's eyes and stopped speaking.

'You came because there are some things one can't tell one's mother. And you came because you can trust me,' Stevie said gravely.

'Yes,' Desna said simply. 'I know that. I can't tell you how grateful I am that you listened so patiently.'

'Why don't you come again when I'm not so busy? What about tonight?'

'No. Not tonight. Roy will— Not tonight.'

'Tomorrow's Sunday. Why don't we meet for tea?'

'Yes. I think I could manage that. It depends on what Roy's doing. If he's doing extra time down at the yard I could be free.'

'He doesn't like you having friends?'

Desna flushed, unable to admit the truth. 'It's not that. He might have made a prior arrangement without telling me. He sometimes does. I'll ring you, shall I?'

'Yes, do, Desna. I mean that,' Stevie said.

CHAPTER TWENTY-FOUR

Harriet and Philip arrived in St Ives at lunchtime. The cottage that belonged to Andy's friend was minute, painted white and faded blue, and crammed with others round a square that was somewhat smaller than the sitting room at Mount Huish. Steps rose to the front door from amongst a miscellaneous collection of lobster pots, surfboards, oars and nets. Inside the cottage the outward facing windows looked across a jumble of slate roofs towards a sea incredibly blue even this early in the year and, in the distance, the Godrevy lighthouse.

The furnishing was basic. In one of the two tiny rooms there was a sturdy pine table, some rush-seated chairs and, squashed into one corner, a sink, cooker and worktop served for a kitchen. In the other room, taking up most of the available space was a double bed spread with a white, honeycomb-weave counterpane. On the bare boards beside it was a rag rug and a small chest of drawers. Someone had left a pot of red geraniums on the window sill. The bathroom and lavatory were reached through a plank door leading off the sitting room and down a flight of stairs enclosed by thick walls.

'It's beautiful!' Harriet couldn't help exclaiming, even in her nervous state.

Philip, standing behind her as they looked out on town and sea, put his arms round her and laid his chin on her shoulder.

'I'm glad you like it.'

She nodded.

'That's good,' he said. 'Now what about lunch? Let's just dump our stuff and find some nosh, shall we?' He felt her relax at once. What he really wanted to do was to rip off every last stitch of their clothes and fall on to the inviting white bed, which with any other girlfriend he'd ever had would have been precisely what they would have done. But with Harriet, if he was not to frighten her off the idea completely, he had to go easy.

'After that,' he said, 'I thought we might go round the Tate of the West. What d'you think?' He was not particularly interested in art himself but he knew it would please her.

'Great. I'd love that!'

In a pub they had fried eggs, bacon, chips and tomatoes, washed down with beer. Philip ate half Harriet's as well as his own. Then they made their way to the gleaming new art gallery wedged into its site between existing buildings, its panoramic main window overlooking the sea and the Patrick Heron stained glass dyeing the white interiors with red and blue.

'It's awesome, ain't it?' Philip said. 'I suppose everybody says the same thing but it really is like being on the bridge of a huge ship.'

'I expect that's why you like it.' She smiled at him and he congratulated himself for bringing her here. Her tenseness was easing.

She approved the spirit of the odd-shaped Alfred Wallises, painted on any piece of cardboard he had to hand. Philip liked their accurate nautical detail in spite of the strangeness of their perspective.

'He was a fisherman, you see,' Harriet explained. 'Though he didn't start to paint until he was nearly seventy.'

It wasn't all she explained to Philip. Later that afternoon they visited the Barbara Hepworth museum where her massive sculptures were interspersed with the exotic vegetation of the garden.

'How come you know all this?' Philip asked, intrigued by a completely new side of Harriet.

'All what?'

'About art. You've never had any training.'

'I read,' she said simply. 'And look. And Gordon tells me things. After seeing all this I've got lots of ideas for the Yardarm Gallery. I shall tell Gordon and Toby when I get back. I think we

338

should completely redecorate and rearrange it.'

'I hope they will be as enthusiastic as you are,' Philip said, squeezing her arm, still surprised by her ardour. He hoped it would spill over into other aspects of her life.

After that they wandered round the harbour and looked at the boats reclining on the mud at rakish angles since it was low water. Later Philip insisted on an expensive restaurant for dinner where he tried to encourage Harriet to eat and drink more than was usual for her. She had lost the look of animation she'd had while they'd been in the galleries; the tension had returned. Afterwards they walked back towards the harbour where, inside its protecting arms the boats were now riding in deep water. They watched reflections bob and shimmer; Philip put his arm round her shoulders and led her back to the cottage.

Indoors she went rigid as soon as he pulled her to him.

'Let's just take this slowly,' he said. He could no longer give her the option. He wanted her to understand that sooner or later this weekend he would make love to her. Sooner preferably.

He pulled her jersey off one shoulder and kissed her there, moving his mouth up to her neck. He kissed her ear, touching it with his tongue. Quickly he pulled her loose jersey off altogether, then her tee shirt. She stood passively, letting him.

'Let's go to the bedroom,' he said quietly and led her there. Methodically he removed the cover from the bed and turned back the duvet. He sat her on the bed and pressed her backwards on the pillows; unbuckling her belt, he eased off her jeans, then he dragged off his own clothes.

She had never seen him completely naked until this minute; she was shocked by the size of his half-erect penis, its ugliness such a startling contrast to the rest of his beautiful body. And how could her body possibly accommodate it? She looked away to hide her dismay, but when he began to remove her bra and pants she didn't resist. She had promised him, hadn't she?

The uncanniness of her resignation was having an unfortunate effect on Philip. The excitement that had been driving him all evening was ebbing away. Why did she have to behave like someone condemned to be shot at dawn? All the same he was

339

deeply moved by the fragile beauty of her body. The translucent quality of her skin, which he had always loved on her temples and round her eyes, was even more affecting on her small breasts and flat stomach. And the flowing lines of her long thighs swept so smoothly over her hips and into her small waist, framing the dark triangle of her pubic hair.

'You're an absolute knockout,' he whispered, 'a cracker.' He kissed her breasts very gently. 'You're not really afraid of me, are you?' he said when she involuntarily put up an arm to prevent him.

'Of course not,' she said. But her expression belied her words.

'You have to help a bit, darling,' he said. 'Put your arms round my neck.' She laid them across his shoulders and he brought their bodies together. He felt the soft coldness of her breasts against the warmth of his chest and at last found himself aroused. He lay beside her, stroking her body. He put his mouth on her nipples and caressed them with his tongue and finally reached between her thighs and pressed them apart, feeling the hardness of her muscle working against him rather than the softness he sought. For once he minded about her love of cycling.

'Let me, Harry,' he said softly in her ear. He was becoming so seriously aroused that it was more and more difficult to have patience with her resistance. He saw it as wilful, as if she were defying him. For once he knew that there was no need to use a condom and the prospect excited him even more.

He used force to prise her legs apart eventually, holding them with his knee. She gave a cry. He began to explore every part of her, ever more urgently. When he was on top of her he was already past caring if she was ready for him. She never would be ready, he decided. He had to take the initiative.

As he entered her she cried out again. It wasn't a cry of relief or satisfaction women sometimes made. It was more like a wail of desperation or agony. But he hadn't hurt her, had he? And it was too late. He reached orgasm with incredible speed, months of frustration ebbing from him into her. Then he collapsed on the bed beside her.

* * *

340

Harriet waited until she was sure that Philip was asleep, then she crept stiffly out of bed and went downstairs to the bathroom. She tried to pee but nothing happened. Except for the evidence of Philip's orgasm she seemed to have dried up completely.

She took out soap and flannel from her sponge bag and filled the basin first with warm water and then with cold, bathing that part of herself that was so agonizingly sore. Then she had a shower, after which she wrapped herself in one of the Mount Huish monster towels and went into the kitchen to make herself tea. As she sat at the table cradling the mug between her hands, through the window she could see the intermittent blink of light from the Godrevy lighthouse ... She felt tears sliding down her cheeks.

So that was what it was all about, she thought. All the fuss. Why her mother cried out at night. Surely it didn't go on being that painful year after year? No, she knew from her reading and from friends that it didn't. Would the liberated Faith speak about it so enthusiastically if it did? But even so, it must be, it had to be, tremendously overrated. It was just a sinister conspiracy to force women to submit, which for all sorts of reasons even women themselves had a part in; because it was a means to have babies and babies were what most women wanted, apparently.

Some animals began to die after they'd mated or produced their young, she knew that. The female octopus or the salmon, for instance. And some insects only lived their brief lives to produce others of their kind.

She thought she'd heard it said that everything that exists was created during the first Big Bang; afterwards it was just a continual recycling of atoms so that the dust from which both she and Philip were made could once have come from supernovas at extreme ends of the universe; even the dust that went to make up different bits of *her* could have come from opposite ends of the universe for all she knew. Stardust. Now flesh. Her flesh; Philip's flesh. Suddenly she felt trapped in her body, condemned to suffer its functions, its pains and the effects of its eventual ageing.

She liked to think that her spirit, once free, might be somewhere else. Floating above the countryside, the sea or the river, watching over things, like a nature spirit. She didn't believe in God, she never had; but neither did she believe that death was the end of existence.

She moved restlessly in her chair. Only once had she been this uncomfortable and that was when she'd had cystitis at the age of sixteen. It had been so painful then that she'd cried. It was painful now. Perhaps she should pack her bag and leave because if Philip tried to touch her again she would scream in agony. How could Philip have wanted sex with her when all she'd experienced was pain? Had he not even noticed?

Of course it made no difference to the degree of her love for Philip. She would always love him. But now there was a difference in quality. She had been right to believe that it would change them but if she wanted to be with Philip always, she would have to put up with sex. That was all there was to it. She rubbed the salty tears away with a corner of the towel.

'Harry? He was standing at the door in his dressing gown, his legs and feet bare underneath it, his head just touching the architrave. She looked up.

'Are you all right?' he asked anxiously.

She nodded.

He padded across the floor and kneeled on the floor by her chair. He put his head in her lap. 'I'm afraid I hurt you,' he mumbled into the towel.

She put her hand on his thick blond hair.

'Yes, you did,' she said. 'But I don't suppose it could be helped.'

342

CHAPTER TWENTY-FIVE

On the way home the children chattered ceaselessly in the back of the borrowed car. Barney drove, Emmet sat beside him feeling an immense sense of relief to hear Tom back to his usual self. Even Lee so far forgot himself as to enthuse over this new experience. It had only been possible to take the time away from Drake's Farm because there had been a lull in the continuous stream of fledglings that usually inundated them at this time of year. Emmet had seized the opportunity. Dinah had agreed to take over the essential chores in exchange for their taking Rebecca with them on the outing.

They had begun the day with a picnic on Haytor, which everyone had enjoyed even though it wasn't exactly picnic weather. After that they'd gone on to the Superbowl, which it had been hard to drag even Beth and Rebecca away from, except with the promise of massive veggie burgers, chips and ice cream.

Barney glanced at Emmet. 'I think we can take it that they enjoyed themselves,' he said grinning.

'It was ace,' Tom said. 'Specially when I whacked all those pins down in one go.'

'I liked the picnic,' Beth said. 'Can we do it again soon?'

'I know it wasn't quite your sort of caper,' Barney said to Emmet.

'Well, no. But they obviously had such a good time.' Emmet leaned her head back. 'And, Barney, it was terribly good of you to organize it all and come along to help with everything, I'm so grateful.'

'No problem,' he said with a shrug. 'Later, in the summer, we could do a few trips to Dartmoor and the beach. They'd like that,' he went on enthusiastically.

'Not Maurice's idea of a great day out, I'm afraid.'

'Takes all sorts,' he said magnanimously.

'I hope nobody's left any stray creatures while we've been away,' she said, her mind already back at the farm.

'The notice we made with the phone number of the nearest RSPCA was big enough.'

It was late by the time they delivered Rebecca back to her parents. Barney turned the car into the yard and doused the lights. The dogs greeted them as if they'd been away for a month. Barney made coffee while Emmet coaxed the exhausted children into bed. Lee was staying the night. There had been a marked change in Tom during the last thirty-six hours; his expression was more open, less cagey than it had been for weeks, months. Emmet had seen him with his head thrown back, yelling with excitement over newly discovered skills. He had even accepted an ice cream from Barney.

Safely in bed the children slept almost immediately. Emmet went downstairs. Dinah, who had shut up the chickens for them, had told them there had been a phone call from Mo.

'It's too late to call back,' Emmet said. 'I'll ring her in the morning.'

She did her usual late patrol of the cages and aviaries. All the hedgehogs who were fit to fend for themselves had been let go, though there were one or two they'd never found after Tom had turfed them out into the world, even though Tom himself had gone hunting for them at night with a torch. The weather had been reasonably mild so the chances were that they had survived. The birds who had spent time in the final hacking-off cages had been allowed to fly. Others had taken their places.

After it had all come out Tom had been overtaken by remorse and had made a great effort to be helpful again. The results of his actions had frightened even him; he had somehow expected the creatures simply to vanish, not succumb horribly to the activities of the cats and the crows. This time Emmet was careful not actually to ask him to do anything; she didn't intend to make that mistake again. In any case it wasn't necessary now; with Barney's rent coming in she could afford his extra help on a regular basis. Besides that, he had taken over various household chores as a matter of course, only expecting payment for the work with the animals that they'd agreed on in advance. For the rest of the day he would be off on his bike engaged in the jobs he'd always done; gardening, painting and a variety of odd jobs. Even so, he'd embarked on a plan he'd made to do out every room at Drake's Farm in the evenings. He said he preferred to get on with something useful than sit around doing nothing. Emmet had always considered herself more energetic than most but Barney was a dynamo.

'I'm thinking I might make a start on Tom's bedroom as soon as he's back at school,' Barney said, handing Emmet a cup of coffee when her rounds were accomplished.

'That's next Monday,' Emmet said, casting herself down in the old armchair. 'Yes, his bedroom's bad. The wallpaper's coming off all round that damp patch.'

'Right. So it is. We'll have to sus that out.'

'It's been like it for ages.'

'I reckon there's a flashing gone round the chimney. I better get up there and take a look.'

'I think we have a ladder somewhere.'

'That old thing!' he crowed. 'Gordon Bennett! D'you want me to break my neck? I broke that thing up for firewood weeks ago.' He grinned. 'No. I'll pick up a ladder from that hire firm.'

He was leaning against the Rayburn rail, his arms folded across his chest, his coffee mug enfolded in one hand. Emmet smiled to herself. Anyone looking in on this little scene would have us down as an old married couple, she thought. Mo's prediction that he would expect to sleep with her had not come to pass. Either he still regarded her as his landlady and nothing more, or he didn't fancy her because of her advanced years, or it could be that he was gay. She rather doubted the latter because he spoke openly of old girlfriends. Unless that was just a blind. But why bother to keep the truth from someone he knew to be open-minded about such things?

'Penny for 'em?' he said.

'What?'

'You were looking thoughtful. You still happy for me to be here? No beefs nor nothing?'

'No, no. The arrangement suits me very well, Barney.'

'That's all right then, because I like being here. I'm used to being in a family, see. Mr Darby hasn't said nothing, has he?'

'Maurice? Oh, no.'

'I can't figure him out at all, him.'

'How's that?'

'Look, he's got what some'd kill for. A lovely, kind woman and two smashing kids. What more could a bloke want?'

'Some want a good deal more, Barney. Or at least maybe they don't actually want those things at all. We're not all alike.'

'He should've thought of that before he took a nice person like you out of circulation.'

Emmet spluttered with laughter. 'What if I said that the arrangement suits me too?'

Barney looked into his mug as if he sought the answer to such a strange suggestion there. 'I don't believe it does. Does it? I mean, what about love and that?'

'Luve . . .' Emmet mocked, dragging out the word to make it sound ridiculous.

Barney frowned.

'I have the children,' Emmet said relenting. 'And the animals.'

'But what about grown-up love . . . you know?' he said. To her surprise, he blushed.

'You mean sex?'

'That too. But mostly I mean love. Companionship, like.'

Emmet squinted at him. 'You're an unusual young man, d'you know that?'

'Am I?'

'I think so.'

There was a silence. Barney looked at his feet in their scruffy trainers.

'We've had a long day,' Emmet said, springing to her feet. 'I think we should turn in.' She took Barney's empty mug from him. He came to life.

'I'll lock up,' he said.

When Desna turned on her heel and left the cottage at Papermill Quay, Mo and Persis stood for a moment, like figures in a *tableau vivant*.

Then Mo threw down the empty mug she'd been holding. It smashed to smithereens on the floor, frightening both the cats.

'That's it! That's the last straw!' she shouted.' You can bloody well pack your traps and piss off. I've had it up to here with you!' She made a dramatic gesture with the side of her hand on her throat.

Persis continued to lie on the sofa as if nothing had happened. She blew a smoke ring into the air. 'It doesn't suit me to go just yet. There are things I have to do.'

'We'll see about that!' Mo grabbed up the canvas bag Persis had arrived with and stumped round the cottage collecting every one of her sister's belongings and stuffing them into it, making a great deal of noise in the process, banging doors and drawers and hurling things around. When she had finished she took the bag outside and chucked it on to the quay. It narrowly missed sliding over the side and into the mud. Delphi Wild looked on impassively from her doorstep.

Back in the cottage Mo stood over Persis, her hands on her hips. Persis ignored her.

'You always were a spoiled brat and the years haven't improved you, have they? Success seems to have made you worse, if anything. To think how everyone used to indulge you when we were kids. Even me! Mother and Father thought the sun shone out of your backside, as well you know! *You* never had to suffer for your so-called genius but everyone else bloody well did, you saw to that! You were never to be crossed, I was told, because you were special. *I* wasn't, of course, but then I was just your older sister and only marginally talented. I was to be responsible. Always look after Persis, I was told, and give her

347

everything she wants. Deny her nothing. Well, eventually you wanted my husband, didn't you?'

'Come off it, Mo!' Persis said impassively. 'I was only fifteen and your bloody husband raped me. We both know that.'

'Nonsense! I've never seen any woman more determined to have a man. He was glamorous, good-looking and talented and you wanted him. You couldn't wait to lose your virginity! You considered having him your entrée to the arty set.'

'Balls! Alec was just a second-rate lecturer at a second-rate art school. Yet he thought he was God. *You* thought he was God simply because you were a humble student, without too much talent at that, when you married the bastard. Though I'll never know how you persuaded him to do that. Marriage was not exactly his style, was it?'

Mo was practically jumping up and down with rage. 'Alec always said I could have gone far if I hadn't had an impossible adolescent sister to look after . . .'

'And an adolescent husband, let's face it!'

'I grant you, he was a womanizer. I don't deny it. But we might have got over that, who knows? But you having his baby put the kibosh on all that. *You* weren't going to look after the child. Oh no! Not you! By that time you were going to be a "famous artist", weren't you? I wasn't, naturally, and besides I had one child already so I might as well look after yours too!'

'You offered.'

'What else was I supposed to do? You were still at school, for Christ's sake!'

'He could have been gaoled for what he did.'

'You egged him on. He wouldn't have looked at you otherwise. He had plenty better-looking girls than you to choose from . . .'

'I told you he was a lecher,' Persis said calmly. 'I'm glad you admit it.'

Mo turned away and began to put on her cycling gear.

'I'm going to see Desna. With any luck I might be able to repair some of the damage you've done. I don't mind what you say to Roy but I won't have Desna upset. I know she looks hard-boiled, but she's not. Far from it! And she's under a great strain

348

lately. She doesn't need you sticking your bloody great oar in.'

'I told her the truth, that's all.'

'Truth! What's truth? And what makes you think you have a monopoly of it?' Mo strapped on her fluorescent strip and fixed her cycle clips. 'I'm going. When I get back I don't want to see your ugly mug anywhere around. I have my key. Slam the door behind you when you leave.'

Mo arrived at Mount Huish just before lunch. Desna was going through the motions of preparing a meal. Rupert was still in Cornwall, Mo supposed. And she'd heard that Harriet and Philip had gone down to stay in a cottage in St Ives, a fact that in the normal way, would have aroused her interest.

Desna looked up as Mo walked into the kitchen via the back door. Mo saw that her daughter's face was puffy and that her eyes were red, though she had evidently made some effort with foundation and lipstick. Mo kissed her and put her arm briefly round Desna's shoulders, giving her a sympathetic hug before she went and sat on one of the trendy kitchen chairs.

'Darling, I can't say how sorry I am about what happened earlier on. If it's any comfort, I've sent her packing. I should have done so before Easter, I see that now. She's behaved abominably.'

Desna shook her head. 'It's not your fault, Mo.'

'Where's Roy?'

'He's at the yard. He'll be back in a minute.' Desna seemed less distraught, more her usual contained self. She continued her task of arranging a salad decoratively in a bowl.

'Look, darling, I still can't believe Roy is prepared to throw all this up for some harebrained scheme that might not even succeed.'

'Roy says that if we stay we might have to sell the house anyway, with business the way it is. He thinks he can make a lot of money in the new location, especially with Enrico backing him.'

'I wouldn't trust that Italian further than I could throw him, would you?' Mo looked searchingly at Desna.

'I think Enrico's honest enough, for a businessman, that is. The thing is that he's very, very rich. If the enterprise failed he'd stand to lose a bit of money, perhaps, but I dare say he's already hedged himself well against possible loss. It's all right for Enrico. But it would ruin Roy. He just doesn't seem to realize that they're not in the same league. And he won't listen to me, of course. He thinks I know nothing.'

'Can anyone stop this madness?'

'No. As I said, it's practically a *fait accompli*. And who knows, it just might make him very rich too.'

Mo shook her head. 'But he's still intent on selling Mount Huish?'

'He says he needs the capital.'

'You're not going to let it go without a fight, are you?'

Desna finished the salad, covered it with clingfilm and put it in the fridge. She sat down opposite Mo.

'It could be that Persis was right,' she said, a frown creasing the smooth skin of her forehead, 'and that I've become too attached to the place. You see, I could have got my priorities wrong.'

Mo was aghast. 'So you're going to go on playing the dutiful wife, are you? You're going to let Mount Huish go, allow Roy to uproot not only yourself but Philip and Harriet too, and follow him across the sea to God knows where?'

'Women do that sort of thing all the time. I'm not unique.'

The front door slammed and Roy appeared in the doorway. He frowned when he saw his mother-in-law. He still hadn't forgiven her for bringing Persis at Easter, and he suspected Mo of encouraging Desna in her pathetic attempts to put a spanner in the works.

'If you've come to persuade Desna to defy me, I have to say you're too late, mother-in-law,' he said. 'I've just given the estate agent the go-ahead to print a nice, glossy brochure on Mount Huish. I think I made his day!'

Mo refused lunch. The thought of eating with Roy would have choked her. Instead she pedalled home to an empty cottage. Persis had gone, thank goodness. She went to the telephone and dialled Emmet's number. Dinah replied. Emmet and Barney had taken the children out for the day, she said. Emmet and Barney, Mo thought sourly. She had been right; that young man was becoming far too familiar. Then she rang Nell. There was no answer.

At that moment Persis was checking in at a hotel in Totnes, or rather a pub, since she had a rooted dislike of hotels, as such. She called at Nell's shop but found it closed. She tried the flat but Nell was evidently out. Then she went to the quay where she attempted to persuade a man in a boat to take her down the river. He refused. He said he had to paint his boat that day.

Persis stalked off muttering imprecations. She had a meal of sorts at the pub while she waited for Nell to return. Where was the damned girl? Bored, she ordered another whisky.

It was quite late that evening before Nell got back to the flat. Morgan greeted her reservedly, trying to make her feel guilty for her frequent and prolonged absences.

'Never mind, old chap,' she said. 'When we're living in The Old Rectory you won't know yourself. Four times the territory and no need to fight that terrible old grey tomcat for it either.'

Morgan let it be known that he was not impressed with promises.

The telephone rang as she finished scooping out Morgan's food.

It was Mo. 'Darling, how are you? I rang earlier.'

'I'm all right,' Nell said crisply. 'Not married yet, you'll be glad to know.'

'Oh, Nellie, don't! You can't really blame the family for being concerned, darling, after all you went through last time.'

'Yes, well. This is different.'

'I'm sure we all hope so, sweetie.'

'Did you want something in particular, Mo? Because I really am terribly tired. I'm sorry, but there's been so much to do.' As well as torrid nights spent making love, she thought.

'You probably won't be interested,' Mo said brusquely, 'but I just thought I'd let you know that Roy and Desna are selling up and going to live in the Virgin Islands. Desna told me this morning. She's very upset about it.'

'Going to live *where*?' Nell said, so astonished that she forgot Mo's dig about her not being interested.

'Tortola.' Mo furnished Nell with the bare facts of the case.

'She can't!' Nell said flatly.

'She's just as pig-headed in her own way as you are, Nell. You *will* marry Daniel and Desna *will* go to the Virgin Islands with Roy. There doesn't seem to be anything I can do about either eventuality.'

Nell replaced the handset and stood staring at the floor. If she had been certain that Desna loved Roy more than she loved Mount Huish she might have been happy for her, whatever the risks of the case. But as it was . . . As it was, she was convinced that Desna was already unhappy in her marriage for reasons that she, being Desna, would never divulge. At one time she had suspected Roy of knocking Desna about but had never, ever seen physical evidence of it. All the same, there were other variations of violence besides the physical, of which she believed Roy quite capable.

The sound of the doorbell cut through her thoughts abruptly.

'Shit!' she said to Morgan. 'Whoever can that be?' Morgan didn't know. He continued eating.

Persis was standing on the doorstep. Nell's heart sank.

'I was just going to bed,' she said. 'I don't wish to appear rude but I have a lot to do tomorrow.' Like moving most of the rest of her stock to Cornucopia.

'When I was your age I never went to bed before three in the morning,' Persis said. She waved vaguely. 'I'm staying over there so I thought I'd just pop in for a nightcap.'

'I'll get some coffee,' Nell said reluctantly, showing Persis into the sitting room. She would give her some coffee and get rid of her as soon as she decently could.

'I'd rather have Scotch.'

'There isn't any,' Nell said. 'It's coffee or nothing, I'm afraid.' She went into the kitchen to make it, returning with two steaming mugs. They sat facing each other on either side of the fireplace.

Persis reached into her pocket and withdrew her hip flask, from which she spiked her coffee. 'The pub with no beer,' she said inconsequentially.

'Have you left Papermill Cottage?' Nell asked.

'She slung me out.' Persis grinned wolfishly.

'I see.' Nell was not in the mood to encourage elaboration. She would hear the details soon enough.

'We had a row.'

'Of course you did.'

'Why of course?'

'You like rows, don't you? Besides Mo's not one to put up with rudeness indefinitely.'

'Ho, ho! So there's a spark there somewhere!' Persis' pale eyes gleamed. 'I'm glad to see it. You're going to need a spark of *something* before long.'

'Whatever can you mean?'

'Never mind. Don't you want to know what the row was about?'

'I can't honestly say I care.'

'It was about you.'

Nell glanced at Persis sharply.

'Ha! That's got your interest!'

'No. Not really. I'm sure you're both perfectly capable of rowing about absolutely anything.'

Persis paid great attention to lighting a cigarette without bothering to ask if Nell minded. Her hand shook slightly and Nell thought, She's pissed.

'Mo's never forgiven me because *her husband* seduced me. What d'you make of that?'

'My father seduced you?'

'Precisely. I bet Mo never told you that? There's something else I bet she never told you too.'

'I don't know that I want to hear all this. It was a very long time ago.'

'About thirty-seven years, give or take nine months. Has that any significance for you?'

'No. Why should it? Look, Persis, I really haven't got time—'

'I had the bastard's kid, didn't I?'

Nell stared at her, full of apprehension.

'I expect you're wondering what happened to it?'

'No. I don't want to know . . .'

Abruptly Persis leaped to her feet and dragged Nell up to stand beside her so that their reflections appeared side by side in the antique looking-glass.

'What d'you see?' Persis demanded.

Apprehension became cold presentiment. They were the same height, those two reflections. The same high forehead. The eyes were a different colour but the same shape. The same high cheekbones, the same set of the mouth . . .

'You never noticed, did you?' Persis rasped quietly. 'And no one else has put two and two together, have they? You know why? Because you're a peach and I'm an old bat . . .'

'It's not true,' Nell said flatly. 'Mo would have told me.'

'Not telling you was part of the bargain.'

'You're telling me now.'

'Circumstances change.'

'I still don't believe it. This is all part of your determination to wind Mo up.' Nell sank back into the chair and put her head in her hands. 'Look, it's much too late for games like this. I'm tired. I wish you'd go.'

Persis thrust the hip flask into her hands. 'Here, have a slug of this. I know it can't be terrific news to know your ma's a disreputable old hag.'

Nell shook her head. 'I don't believe it.'

Persis pulled up a chair and sat beside her. 'Look,' she said conspiratorially, 'I've always insisted to Mo that Alec raped me since I was only fifteen, but that's not strictly accurate. If it makes you feel any better about your origins I can tell you that I fancied your father like the very devil. He was a handsome hunk, though I would never admit as much to Mo. I might have been only fifteen but I'll tell you this – I had a damned good time conceiving you!'

Nell leaped to her feet, her anger boiling over and seeming to fill the room. 'You're despicable! I loathe you!' she said violently.

'I won't have you as my mother. As far as I'm concerned Mo's my mother and always has been . . . always will be! I wouldn't have you for a mother if you were the last bloody woman on earth!'

Persis stood up, watching Nell closely. Even consumed with anger as she was, Nell could have sworn she detected a look of hurt. But that couldn't be. Not Persis.

'Well, if that's how you feel, so be it,' Persis said, collecting up her flask and putting it in her shoulder bag. She ran a roughened hand through her wild, white hair. 'But since you are my sprog in spite of all, I want to give you something.' She trawled through her bag and brought out a keyring with a couple of keys attached to it. 'These belong to my villa on Sikinos. If it should turn out that you suddenly need a short holiday in the near future I suggest you take advantage of it. One never knows when a bolt hole will prove useful, or when one has to count one's losses and start all over again.'

'I'm not interested in your fucking villa.'

'Please yourself.' Persis dropped the keys on the mantelpiece. 'I'll leave those here. Just in case. And since I don't expect you to give me a daughterly valediction I'll find my own way out.'

Nell heard the front door close and for a few minutes she stood perfectly still. Her first instinct was to call Mo in order to hear her deny the whole story. But it was far too late. Mo would be in bed and asleep. Or so she convinced herself. After all, Mo might not deny it; she might admit that it was true. And Nell wasn't sure she could take that kind of truth. There was a slight sound by her feet. Huge amber eyes looked at her from a piebald face. Morgan had forgiven her for leaving him so long alone. She picked him up and held his furry body next to her cheek. 'You couldn't care less who your mother was, could you?' she said. 'I wish *I* didn't.'

It was fortunate Roy was busy for most of the day that Desna planned to meet Stevie, even though it was Sunday. Now that he was perfectly satisfied that their future was assured and his course of action cut and dried, Roy had become a dynamo, seething with energy. He was rarely off the telephone or away from the yard. Her opposition to his plans had been rice thrown at a charging bull – of no account; and he appeared to regard his act of rape as normal sexual activity. Neither of them had mentioned it since, though it had rarely been out of her mind. She could not forget her humiliation at his hands. Yet an observer might think their life went on precisely as before.

'I suppose you *are* going to let Philip in on this sooner or later?' she said, watching him butter his breakfast toast meticulously. She drank some of her black coffee, surreptitiously downing two painkillers with it. She had woken with a crashing headache but if Roy saw her taking tablets he would only subject her to the third degree. Was she ill? Why didn't she go to see the doctor again? What reason could someone as pampered as she was have to be getting headaches?

'If you must know, I'm planning to tell him tonight when he and Harriet come back from St Ives,' he said. 'That's quite soon enough.'

'Don't you think that he might be upset that his part in all this has been taken for granted?' Desna persisted. 'I can't speak for Philip but I believe that Giles and Isabel were hoping you might offer Philip a partnership when he marries Harriet.'

Roy spread marmalade on his toast and bit into it. He rattled the pages of the *Sunday Telegraph*. 'Did they now! I notice they didn't dare make the suggestion to me. Time enough for partnerships when I see how Philip handles the yard by himself without making a hash of it. A bit of responsibility sorts the men from the boys, I always say.'

There were quite a few things Roy 'always said', Desna realized suddenly. She also realized that Roy was already relegating their old friends Giles and Isabel to the past. They had always been his friends rather than hers but she would be sorry never to see them again. Giles was a bumbling sort of a man, old for his years, but his heart was in the right place. Isabel was superficial and she could be catty but she was a loyal friend once she had decided she was on your side.

It was a wonder that she herself hadn't been relegated to

Roy's past, Desna thought as she observed him frowning over some article in the paper. Over the years she had painstakingly built the edifice that was their marriage, pushing anything unpleasant to one side. At the very moment she thought she should be congratulated on its near perfection he had trampled on it, crushing it into the ground. It had been a mere house of cards after all.

Yet he was quite unconscious of what he had done. It suited him to have an obedient wife in tow; it was very unlikely that he would find anyone as well trained as she was and as good a hostess for his social aspirations. Or anyone who would put up with his bullying, she thought bitterly. And he knew that as well as she did. He needed her. She was part of his plan.

'I'm going to Nell's wedding,' she said suddenly.

'She hasn't had the nerve to ask you, has she? After what she did?'

'No. But I shall go all the same. I think Mo's going and I expect Emmet will.'

'More fools you.'

'Nell might be right. Daniel may have improved. I think we should give him the benefit of the doubt. Besides, I should hate to think of poor Nell alone on a day like that.'

'Nell's perfectly capable of looking after herself, if you ask me. Except that I think her a stupid bitch to give Enrico the cold shoulder. If she'd played her cards right she could have been a very rich woman.'

'Money isn't everything.'

'It's funny how people who don't have to work bloody hard for it always say "money isn't everything",' Roy said, his voice hard.

Desna didn't reply. An argument would counteract any good the painkillers might be doing. Instead she said, 'I'm going to see Mrs Turnbull this afternoon.'

'Does she work on Sundays?' Roy said, back to the *Telegraph* again.

'Frequently, I believe.'

'Right. That makes two of us.' Roy found it hard to believe

that anyone worked as hard as he did, especially a woman. He never considered women's careers to be serious work.

'I'll leave you some tea on a tray.'

'Don't bother. I'll probably be late.'

Later that afternoon Stevie welcomed Desna into her small sitting room. She had tidied it since Desna's last visit and put a glass vase containing a branch of apple blossom on the table.

'I didn't ask if you would have liked to go out somewhere,' she said, taking Desna's coat.

'Oh, no. This is lovely. So peaceful,' Desna said, sitting down.

'Peaceful!' Stevie laughed. 'It's usually the epicentre of the purest chaos. But today I've switched any calls over to the office answerphone, so we should be left in peace. I'll put the kettle on.'

Stevie produced two kinds of tea and some light, melt-in-the-mouth scones with jam and cream.

'Oh, dear! All the no-nos!'

Stevie looked puzzled.

'I have to be careful with my weight,' Desna explained.

'But you're beautifully slim.'

'See! It works!' Desna laughed. 'But today I'm going to gobble up every last crumb. It all looks absolutely delicious.'

'What a pity a fabulous cook like you has to be on a diet.' Stevie looked appalled. 'You mean you can't eat most of what you cook?'

'I get fat just looking at it, I'm afraid. I'm not like my sisters who can eat anything without putting on an inch.'

'But why deny yourself all that just to stay as thin as a hairpin?'

'Roy loathes fat women,' Desna said.

'I see,' Stevie said and there was a small silence. She glanced at her visitor as she poured the tea. Desna was not only slim but had a natural grace of movement. Today she was elegant in a polo-necked cashmere sweater and a casual jacket in some dark wool check worn with immaculate trousers. Hard work went to produce this kind of finished result, Stevie thought. Her own wardrobe was somewhat hit and miss though she naturally made an effort when she was visiting clients; she tucked a strand of her straight, brindled hair behind one ear.

'You seem a bit better,' she said, passing Desna her cup.

'Talking to you helped. I've since done a lot of thinking – and a lot of crying, I'm afraid.'

'Have you come to any conclusions?'

'I don't know. It's all been such a shock. Then there's Harriet. She doesn't know yet – neither does Philip. It's going to affect their futures as much as mine. I just don't know what to do . . .'

'About?'

'Everything. The move, my marriage, the children. This will sound absolutely unbelievable to you but, you see, I've never had to make an important decision in my life before. For years Roy has taken all that from me. Now I feel like a babe in arms. I'm not even sure I'm *able* to make a decision even . . . unless it's between having cutlets en croute or cassoulet.'

'You underestimate yourself, Desna.'

'He never expected me to do anything but be a perfect wife and at first he could be pretty unforgiving when I failed to get things just as he wanted them. I had to learn fast or put up with days of his ill-humour.'

Desna toyed with the handle of her cup. 'But I did learn and in the end I got very good at what I did. I think Roy became very proud of me, though he never said so. It's nothing to boast about. The thing was that I wanted to do it; I wanted to please Roy and I liked the idea of being known as Roy's superwife. Mount Huish was part of all that. It was my reward. Even from the first when it was a wreck, I loved it, you see. It made everything seem worth while . . .'

They both sipped their tea. Stevie handed Desna the plate of scones. Desna took one and split it thoughtfully, adding jam and cream.

'These are as light as a feather,' she said.

'You were saying,' Stevie prompted her.

'When I think of the prospect of it all being taken away,' Desna went on, 'decamping and starting all over again – well, it won't be the same. I don't think I can do it, Stevie. In the beginning, you see, I loved Roy. I admired him. He seemed so reliable, so down-to-earth. My own father was totally irresponsible, always after other women and finally leaving Mo in the lurch completely and . . . the only memorable thing he did for Nell and me was to die and leave us twenty thousand each.'

'And Emmet?'

'Emmet wasn't his child. Actually, she could have done with it more than either Nell or me . . . but that's how things invariably work out, isn't it? I've offered her some of mine but she won't take it.'

'No, I can imagine.' Stevie sipped her tea.

'Of course, Roy's no plaster saint when it comes to women but with him his career always came first. Then me, some way behind, then the children and Mount Huish. It's still the business first but now the other things have to be sacrificed to keep it going. He has a ruthless streak; sometimes it frightens me . . .'

'So he considers the move to be more or less an accomplished fact?'

'Oh, yes.'

'And you?'

Desna finished her scone. She shook her head. 'I don't know. All the possible choices frighten me so much that I feel like a headless chicken . . . running round in circles getting nowhere. I expect you think I'm a complete wimp.'

'Not at all. Whatever you decide to do will be a very big step,' Stevie said. 'Are you joint owners of Mount Huish?'

'Yes. But that doesn't help at all. If I opposed the sale Roy could make my life a misery. You've no idea. And besides, would I want to try to hang on to it under those circumstances? Maybe my awful aunt Persis hit the nail on the head when she suggested I had my priorities wrong.'

'Priorities?'

'That I should be looking to my marriage and not fussing over a house, however gorgeous and however much I loved it.'

Stevie picked up her cup but didn't drink. 'It was so much easier for me to come to a decision about my own marriage,' she said. 'Mathew was quite simply driving Theo and me mad. I was quite sure that if any of us was to finish up in the funny farm it would most likely be me . . . and Theo, poor little scrap.

'But it had been going on for years, hadn't it? What changed?'

Stevie replaced her cup in its saucer. Then she giggled. 'It was the socks,' she said at last.

'Socks?'

'I told you about Mathew's fetish for cleanliness. Well, part of it involved always having to wash his clothes separately, especially when Theo was a baby. It was a terrible strain and awfully extravagant on electricity and water. I even had to feed Theo separately because Mathew couldn't stand the mess he made. The day was just after Theo's third birthday. My brother, Hugh, had given Theo some very jolly red dungarees he'd brought back from Italy. I must have been terribly tired or something but I put them in the wash with everything else, and of course the colour ran. Dyed all my underwear and all the rest of Theo's stuff pink which didn't really matter but a pair of Mathew's tennis socks had got into our wash by accident – he was very keen on tennis at the time. He found them before I had a chance to bleach them out and you would have thought the sky had fallen!'

'Surely he didn't notice one pair of socks?'

'You're joking! He knew intimately and accounted for every smallest item of his clothing. It made no difference that I promised to buy another pair, he naturally asked how often I'd been putting his things in our wash, and said that he could never trust me again. I never did convince him. He went on and on for hours . . . Theo began to cry. So I knew I had to do something. You see it was perfectly clear that Mathew would never get any better because he wouldn't admit that he had a problem. He just thought it was everyone else being untrustworthy.'

'So you got a divorce?'

Stevie nodded. 'Then after a year or two Sonia asked me to help her out and I never looked back, as the saying goes.'

'Where's Theo this afternoon?'

'With my brother. The one who gave him the red dungarees.

It's funny to think that if Hugh hadn't seen them in a boutique in Italy I might not be divorced.' She laughed. 'Though I'm sure something else would have precipitated it sooner or later. Theo likes going to see Hugh and his daughter, Laura. Hugh quite often takes Theo off my hands when I'm rushed, bless him.' She replenished Desna's cup. 'Poor Hugh.'

'Why poor?'

'He's desperately in love with this woman who's just about to marry someone else.'

'I see what you mean. There seems to be an awful lot of heartache going on at the moment.'

'We all get our share sooner or later. I'm just so sorry that you have all this now when you were so excited about doing the wedding.'

'All the same, whatever happens, I'm determined to make sure this wedding's a masterpiece. Between us, I know we can do it. Who knows, it might even change Roy's mind about selling.'

'It'll be a tremendous feather in the cap of Bonne Bouche. I just wish I had your help and advice for every wedding I did. Poor Sonia is finding it so difficult to cope, though she's putting a brave face on it.'

'How long can she go on?'

Stevie shrugged. 'She's only flogging herself now because she doesn't want to let me down. If only we could find someone reliable to help . . .' She glanced across at Desna who was, with total lack of guilty feelings, spreading jam on her second scone. Desna caught her eye.

'You don't mean me?' she said, the scone halfway to her mouth.

'You have wonderful taste, you're a brilliant cook and great on menus, by the end of July you'll have experience – what more could we ask for?'

'But I'll be in the Virgin Islands!'

'So you will,' Stevie said expressionlessly. 'I'd forgotten.'

Desna looked at her friend suspiciously. She was about to say something when their attention was grabbed by the arrival of a

362

vehicle outside. Doors banged and there were voices and laughter.

'Hugh's brought Theo back. Good. You'll be able to meet him.'

Two children burst into the room, followed by Hugh. Desna saw a tall, slightly gangling man with a slight stoop. His resemblance to his sister was marked. The same nose, which could almost be described as beaky; the same floppy, fairish hair flecked with grey; the same eyes, crinkled at the corners.

The children were clamorous.

'Mummy, you should have seen this great, enormous boat on the rocks.'

'It was all rusty.'

'The sea was all washing around inside it.'

Hugh laughed and waited to be introduced.

'Desna, this is my brother, Hugh. Hugh, Desna Hindmarch.' They shook hands.

'You look as if you've had a good time,' Desna said.

'We walked for miles along the cliffs at Prawle Point,' he said. 'They should be exhausted but I'm afraid I'm the one who's completely knackered.'

'Ooh, scones,' Theo whooped. 'Can we have one? That cliff path was quite dangerous in places, you know . . .'

The little girl sat next to her father smiling shyly, her hands tucked under her narrow thighs, her hair escaping from her pigtail in wisps.

More tea and scones were fetched, even though Hugh assured them that they'd already had tea in Dartmouth. Everyone chatted. Desna looked on, her spirits leaden with the thought that she had to return to Roy and all the problems that awaited her at Mount Huish.

Harriet set off for the gallery earlier than usual. She perched herself on her bicycle saddle as if she was sitting on eggs; the soreness had not had a chance to wear off. She wondered if men ever got sore making love and, if they did, whether in that case they'd still be so keen on it.

Last night when they had arrived back from Cornwall, her father had immediately called Philip into his study. She thought at first that it was because Philip had slept with her before the wedding until she remembered that her parents had waved them off on Friday quite normally. Her father had that secret, tense look of suppressed excitement she'd seen on his face frequently in the past few weeks. The two men had been closeted together for an hour and Philip had left soon after with scarcely a word to her. He had looked uncharacteristically solemn as he kissed her. Then he drove away.

She asked her mother if she knew what it was about but Desna's manner was oddly distraught; almost Harriet could have sworn, as if she had been crying.

The difference in her mother had been the first thing she'd noticed.

'Your father has some big changes in mind for us all,' Desna said when they were left alone.

'What sort of changes?'

'He said Philip would tell you. He said I'd only distort the truth,' Desna said with a note of bitterness Harriet had never heard in her mother before.

'You said changes for us all. Does that mean Philip and me too?'

'Your father wants to move the business to the British Virgin Islands,' Desna said. 'That's all I can say. Philip will tell you the rest.'

Desna laid her head on the chair back and closed her eyes. 'I'm sorry, darling. Do you mind if we don't talk about it any more tonight? I have a very bad headache and I do find the subject very upsetting just now . . .'

Harriet went over to her mother at once, concern in her voice. 'Mummy! Can I get you a paracetamol or something?'

'No, darling. I already took some.'

'Does he mean to take you to the Virgin Islands as well?' Harriet kneeled by her mother's chair.

Desna nodded.

'And you don't want to go?'

'Darling, can we talk in the morning?'

'Of course.' Harriet bit her lip. All kinds of questions seethed in her mind. Desna laid a hand on hers.

'Did you have a nice weekend?' she asked, opening her eyes.

Harriet nodded and looked away, knowing that her mother had read her expression. Desna lifted a hand to Harriet's cheek.

'Don't worry, sweetie,' she said. 'It isn't always a great success at first.' Desna didn't know how she found the strength of mind not to pour out her own troubles to Harriet. How shocked she'd be to know the violence of which her own father was capable. The previous night Desna had attempted to move to the spare bedroom but not before Roy had trapped her and forced himself on her again. Her resistance only excited him more and he allowed her to sleep alone only after she endured an hour of it. It was almost as if it were part of his purpose to pressure her into making the decision she dreaded.

'It'll get better,' she said to Harriet. And it can get worse again, she almost added, feeling like a traitor to her own daughter. 'But Philip's a good man. He's kind and he loves you very much.' No, Philip was as different from Roy as chalk from cheese. He hadn't Roy's obsessive will to succeed at all costs. He hadn't Roy's intelligence either, but Harriet could eventually supply what was lacking there. In spite of what Roy said about his daughter, Desna was convinced she had a good head on her shoulders.

Harriet lay awake for a long time that night, brooding. What could her father be planning for Philip and herself, and why did it cause Philip to leave without confiding in her? And what had happened to her mother in the weekend to make her look as she did? Could it be just the news that her father planned to move the yard? At last she turned on the bedside light and pushed back the duvet. Then she set up a wonderfully twisted piece of driftwood she'd found by the boathouse and continued the drawing of it she had started a few days before.

She and Philip had made love once more while they had been at the cottage. All Saturday she had been too sore even to walk. Philip had been remorseful but he said that it wasn't unusual the first time, especially if the woman was a bit small. This caused her to wonder how many 'first times' he'd experienced. These days, she thought glumly, probably not very many. These days it was considered distinctly freaky to still be a virgin at twenty-one. Perhaps Philip had been telling her father, man to man, that he didn't want to marry her after all, she'd been such a disappointment. She could imagine Roy saying he perfectly understood because he'd known she was hopeless all along.

The gallery was even more of a sanctuary than usual. They were particularly busy, even though it was Monday, normally a quiet day. A new exhibition of painted reliefs was attracting interest; people who had been just passing by, seeing the carvings she'd put in the window, came in for a longer look.

Gordon was pleased with the way things were going. 'Pity you missed the private view on Friday,' he said. 'We sold four reliefs in the first half-hour.'

'You see how well you get on without me!' she teased.

'Don't you remember that you were the one who interviewed Josie in the first place? Toby and I were in London that day, had you forgotten?'

'Oh, yes, so you were.' They were on one of their periodic forays to the London galleries, hoping to interest one of them in Toby's work. Harriet had been alone in the Dartmouth gallery, waiting while the young woodcarver had laid out her work, anxious for Harriet's verdict, which when it came was enthusiastic. Here everyone treated her as an adult, capable of taking mature decisions as a matter of course.

'Which leads me to what I wanted to ask you,' Gordon said. 'Toby'll hold the fort at lunchtime. I'm taking you out for a nice, expensive nosh.'

Harriet stared at Gordon in consternation. What could he mean? Was he planning to give her the sack?

'Don't look like that, Harry!' Gordon said. 'It's nothing bad, I assure you. Quite the opposite I sincerely hope.'

All the same, after the events at home Harriet was in a mood to be anxious. She expected the worst.

Lunchtime came. 'I'm afraid we can't run to The Pig in Clover,'

Gordon said. 'But this is the next best thing.' He ushered her into a pub known for its good food. He found them a corner table and ordered a lager each. They perused the menu while they drank.

'I wish you'd tell me now what this is about,' Harriet said, 'because I shan't be able to eat a thing until I know the worst, which will be an awful waste.'

'Let's order first,' Gordon said. When that was done he drank some of his lager and then, placing his glass on the dark wood of the table said, 'How long have you been with us, Harry?'

'You know how long. Three years.'

'You've learned a lot, haven't you?'

'Well . . .'

'Let's just say you have. Now! Toby says he wants more time to paint. As you know the gallery's never been quite his thing. He has an artist's soul, you see, and he gets impatient with the nitty-gritty of running the place . . .'

Harriet smiled. In fact, Toby did very little, leaving most of the work to Gordon and Harriet. Even when he was engaged in what, ostensibly he liked doing best, displaying the work, he invariably wandered off and left it to Harriet.

'As you know, we're tremendously excited about this exhibition Toby's been offered by Lombards gallery in Camden Town.' When Harriet had heard about it she'd had difficulty concealing her astonishment. Even loyal Gordon had appeared not a little surprised. However, it had been Toby's drawings from the 'drunken spider' era that had interested the gallery rather than his more recent efforts with driftwood and gobs of thick paint. In Harriet's opinion almost all their exhibitors were better than Toby, yet few of them had ever been offered a London show.

Disguising these thoughts, Harriet nodded sympathetically.

'The thing is . . .' Gordon said. He drew back as their food arrived. 'Ah, sustenance for the inner man . . . or woman as the case may be. This looks good.'

The waiter arranged their plates, cutlery and table napkins.

'Tuck in,' Gordon said, picking up his fork, 'As I was saying, the thing is, I still need an active partner to help with the running and so I'm offering this highly prestigious but probably unlucrative position to you, Mrs Emmerson-to-be.'

'Me!' Harriet stared at him, knife and fork poised.

'Don't look so astonished. Who else?'

'But I don't know anything about business. And wouldn't I have to put money into it?'

'You know almost as much about the business side as I do. And no, you wouldn't have to put money into it unless you happened to have some handy. In any case, you'll be busy setting up house, so I don't imagine you will. But, we are making a very slight profit so naturally you'll come in for a share of that.'

'Gordon, I never thought—'

'No, I know you never thought, but I have to tell you that you've been an absolute godsend to the gallery. I'm always getting the most complimentary feedback about you. Who better to have as a partner? Now, come on, Harry, don't keep me in suspense, say you'll think about it?' His face clouded for a moment. 'I expect you'll want to get professional advice or discuss it with your father.'

'No!' Harriet said fiercely. 'I don't want to talk it over with Daddy! Though I expect I'll mention it to Philip.'

'Of course you can look at the books and so on but you see those on a regular basis anyway. You know all our wicked secrets! But maybe you ought to get an accountant to look into it so you know all the pitfalls as well as the perks.'

Harriet nodded thoughtfully.

'Does that mean you'll consider it?' Gordon said, his mouth full of seafood platter, his eyes bright.

'Yes, Gordon, I believe it does.' Her smile was like the sun coming out from behind a cloud. 'Thank you for asking me. I think I should love to be a partner in the Yardarm Gallery.'

Gordon leaned across the table and kissed her cheek. Harriet was the only woman besides his mother he kissed with real affection.

Back at the gallery Toby greeted them with a mug of coffee in one hand, red hair bristling, earrings glinting, his huge boots stained with paint. 'Well! What did she say?' he enquired eagerly.

'All things being equal, she said "yes", I'm delighted to report,' Gordon said.

Being asked to share the fortunes of the gallery had temporarily put out of Harriet's mind both her physical discomfort and the other fears that seemed to beset her on every side: the impending changes at home, her mother's obvious distress and, worst of all, whether Philip could possibly continue to love her after her dismal showing in the weekend.

Gordon looked at her, his head on one side. 'You're not worried about our offer are you, Harry?' he asked. 'Because there's no compulsion, you know.'

'Why can't I come?' Beth argued. 'I want to see Nell getting married.'

'It won't be as you imagine, all white frocks, churches and bridesmaids.' Emmet said, bending to peer in the mirror while she hoiked up her hair into a frizzy topknot and fixed an elastic round it. Numerous tendrils immediately escaped to curl delicately round her ears. 'It'll be in a registry office and Nell will just wear her ordinary clothes. Be content that you'll be going to a really super-duper one in a few weeks.'

Beth sat on Emmet's bed watching while her mother donned the skirt and jacket she'd discovered in a charity shop in Totnes. The jacket was dark red velvet and the skirt longish with a fringed hem. With it she wore strapped fabric shoes and black leggings. When she was ready Beth followed her downstairs in the hope her mother would change her mind. Barney was in the kitchen mending Tom's bedside light. Tom was watching him attentively, so that he could remember how it was done. The dogs greeted Emmet in her wedding persona, sensing that something unusual was up. The kittens, now impossibly active, were chasing around underfoot.

'All set?' Barney enquired. 'Wow! You look a million dollars.'

'Ha-ha,' Emmet mocked.

'You do!' And she saw his approval was quite genuine.

369

'I don't suppose I'll be long,' she said, picking up the car keys. 'There's no reception as far as I know. Nell doesn't even know we're coming.'

'Nice surprise for her,' Barney said.

'I hope so.' Emmet turned to the children. 'Be good. See you later.'

They waved her off and she turned the car out of the yard and headed for Newton Abbot. On the way she passed Maurice's wooden bungalow. He had written to her the day before to let her know that he would be away in London for a few days, seeing his agent. His agent was probably getting fed up at the non-arrival of the manuscript. She hoped the book would be finished soon because the royalties from the last were falling off and there were bills to be met. She had started another article herself but articles wouldn't keep the wolf from the door for long.

The registry office was in a pleasant Regency square surrounding the church of St Paul; mature limes and conifers offered a green shade as she parked the car. The registry office itself was a substantial neo-classical edifice; spring sunlight bounced off its fresh yellow walls and white freestone. At least Nell had a lovely day for it, the first really warm day that year.

Mo and Desna were already there, waiting on the pavement outside. Desna looked regal in a beautiful cream suit worn with a silk shirt and wide-brimmed hat of deepest violet. Mo had done her best with a knitted jacket and patterned loon pants.

'Any sign of the bride and groom?' Emmet said joining them.

'Not yet,' Desna said as another wedding party jostled past them, awash in bright pastel colours. A sweating man in his best suit, camcorder aloft, careered backwards towards them.

'Perhaps we should wait inside,' Desna said, stepping out of the man's path. As they moved towards the door of the office an E-type Jag swept round the square and stopped with a flourish in front of the building. As he emerged, adjusting a cuff, all three women recognized Daniel immediately.

'He hasn't changed his style anyway,' Mo said grudgingly.

'Or his looks. He always was a handsome devil. And a shameless exhibitionist. Just look at that car! It's never struck me before but he bears an uncanny resemblance to your father.'

'I wouldn't know about that. But I'm terribly afraid he's just the same old Daniel after all,' Desna said glumly.

A second man got out of the Jag, walking slightly behind Daniel, who bounced up the path towards them. His walk had lost none of the slight swagger they all remembered too well, though he was better dressed now. He had on an expensively casual suit worn with a collarless shirt in some dark, fashionable colour and buttoned to the neck. He held out his hand, smiling extravagantly.

'This is unexpected,' he said, 'but all the better for that.' He held Mo's hand longer than strictly necessary. 'Mo, how are you? So glad you came.'

Mo stiffened at the familiar use of her name and said something like, 'Hmph.'

Daniel introduced the second man as Jeffrey, who was to act as best man and witness. They had the impression that the two men didn't know each other particularly well. Desna had already begun to move into the building.

'That's right. You go to the waiting room,' he said. 'I believe it's quite comfortable. I'll wait for Nell out here.' He looked at his watch. 'We're next. It's at twelve.' He frowned. 'She's cutting it a bit fine.'

'In that case, you ran it a bit fine yourself,' Desna said, looking at her watch.

It was two minutes to twelve and the registrar's assistant came into the waiting room to ask if they were ready. Emmet went out to see if Nell had arrived. Daniel stood on the pavement with the man called Jeffrey, anxiously checking his watch.

'Hasn't Nell turned up yet?' Emmet said. 'The registrar wanted to know if you're ready. I better go in and tell them we're running a bit late.'

'Thanks, you're a friend.'

At ten past twelve Daniel was looking less jaunty; at quarter past the next wedding party turned up and the registrar suggested that if the bride hadn't arrived in five minutes that perhaps they should allow the second wedding to go ahead before them. Daniel went outside again and looked up and down. At twelve twenty he went to the payphone and rang Nell's number. He wished they'd stuck to his suggestion and left together from The Old Rectory but Nell had some superstitious reservations about the scheme. He wished now he'd insisted. He already felt a complete bloody idiot, and in front of Nell's supercilious relatives too. All he got from Nell's flat was a message on her answerphone saying that she would ring back later.

'It's all right,' he said. 'She must be on her way. I expect she's got held up in the traffic.'

'Is she driving herself?' Desna wanted to know.

'No, she's coming by taxi with Anna, who was to be the other witness. We're leaving in the Jag.'

'I expect the taxi people forgot,' Emmet said. 'At least she's on her way.'

Apologetically, the registrar suggested he go ahead with the second wedding. The new party streamed in and went upstairs to the room where the ceremony would take place.

At twenty to one Daniel rang Nell's number again but there was still no reply. Almost immediately the registrar's assistant called him into her office. After five minutes he came out again, looking dazed.

'They've had a phone call from Nell,' he said, shaking his head in deepest mystification. 'She asked them to tell me that the wedding's off. She's not coming. She didn't even want to speak to me!'

Mo, Desna and Emmet exchanged glances in which astonishment, perplexity and relief were equally mixed.

'Oh, Daniel!' Emmet said. 'I'm so sorry. I'm sure there must be a good explanation.'

'I'm sure there is,' Mo said darkly.

'I think we better all go home,' Desna said.

Jeffrey looked at his watch. 'Look, sorry and all that, but I've got a meeting at quarter past.'

'Right, you go on,' Daniel said. 'I'll be in touch. Thanks, mate.'

Emmet said to Daniel, 'Come on, I'll take you for a drink. You look shattered.'

CHAPTER TWENTY-SIX

The sun scattered shards and slashes of light through the woven bamboo canopy on to the faded blue metal of the table and the paving beneath it. Some of the light struck Nell's glass of retsina so that it seemed as if there were a small light bulb inside. It cast a cone of brightness on to the table beside it.

Nell put her feet up on the slatted wooden seat beside her. Her legs were already brown under her tailored shorts though she'd made no deliberate effort to sit in the sun. She'd spent more time on the plain white bed inside the villa, alternatively in agonizing tears or cursing herself for a gullible dupe.

Below her, silvery olive trees and the occasional dark lance of a cypress led the eye to the piece of lapis lazuli that was the sea. The scent of a dozen fragrant herbs charged the air, cicadas seemed to make the heat audible, like drying bark. In such a place she should have been at ease, consoled. It was such a waste. Sophia who visited the villa every day to clean was becoming anxious for what she called 'Kyria Dane's guest'. Each day she brought food but very little of it was eaten; each day Despinis Nell spent too much time shut in her bedroom.

Abruptly Nell pushed back the chair on which her feet had been resting and left the terrace. Inside she rummaged in her suitcase and pulled out a towel and the navy and red swimsuit she wore every week when she went swimming at Mount Huish. She had shoved it in amongst her clothes as an afterthought when she packed, never believing she would ever be in the mood to swim. Drown, yes. Quite possibly.

She left the villa, plunging down the hillside through the olive trunks, so ancient that they resembled piles of old cordage;

dry leaves crackled underfoot. The spring flowers were almost over, the ground was already becoming parched, the grass yellowing in the sun.

The beach was small and made of fine, silvery gravel. Cliffs reached into the sea on either side, holding the clear turquoise cup of the bay in a languorous embrace. There was no one on the beach, it being difficult to approach from any direction except from the villa.

Nell slipped off her shirt and shorts and was about to pull on her swimsuit when she thought better of it. There was no one to see except Sophia and she never stopped working long enough to look at the bay. A thousand tiny stones cushioned her feet as she stood where the miniature waves unfurled themselves on to the beach, then she dived naked into the water. It had scarcely more density than the air. She struck out for the middle of the bay where she lay suspended, seeing many feet below shoals of glittering fish over pale blue sand.

There was nothing and nobody to stop her from swimming far out to where the dark blue water of the Aegean was flecked with white. On and on she would swim until exhaustion set in and all her grief, all her anger resolved themselves. It wouldn't take long in the end. Once before, when Daniel had ended their relationship and put Flick in her place, she had also contemplated that option but some stubborn pride had kept her going. Now anger as well as grief fuelled her. She could almost hear Daniel speaking of her sad demise, eliciting sympathy, especially from women. A man deeply traumatized by the death of his girlfriend just before the wedding, the details discreetly glossed over. She could see it all.

It had taken Morgan and a completely fortuitous meeting to wake her from what now seemed like a state of trance that had lasted ever since Daniel had taken her out to dinner at The Pig in Clover.

On the morning of the wedding she'd been up early. Across her room, hanging outside the wardrobe, was the outfit she planned to wear, bought specially for the occasion. It was a long coat of natural linen, high at the neck, Nehru-style and a matching skirt, very elegant and understated, according to the woman in the shop. Unable to stay in bed wide awake, she got up and took a long time over the shower. Then she put on a sweater and an old pair of jeans, for there were last-minute chores to be done before she dressed for her wedding. Most of the furniture in the flat had been moved to The Old Rectory, some she had sold. Superstitiously, she'd hung on to the marriage-tree rug and the head of Aphrodite; they would follow with the last vanload of her belongings when she and Daniel came back from their honeymoon trip to Florence and Venice.

Sun streamed into the flat, claiming back all the spaces where chairs and tables had once stood; it also laid claim to the empty shop below, for most of its contents now formed a special display at Cornucopia. The only arrangement that had not yet been completed was the transfer of the bulk of her capital, lately augmented by her father's bequest, to the Cornucopia business account. She had already given Daniel four thousand to put the alterations to the front of Cornucopia in hand, and she was impatient to see the landscaping done by the time they returned from honeymoon. She and Ben had had some brisk words about her arrangements. Ben had told her how unwise they were.

'Listen, I trust Daniel implicitly,' she'd assured her suspicious accountant. 'Besides, when we're married we intend to share everything. For better or worse, Ben! That's what marriage is about – or had you forgotten.' This was a bit hard, she realized afterwards, since Ben's own marriage was a model of rectitude. All the same, as soon as she returned from honeymoon and the lease of the shop and flat was up, she would transfer her money without further reference to Ben. She and Daniel had plans for more big improvements at Cornucopia.

In the kitchen Morgan eyed her narrowly. He had not failed to note the open but fully packed suitcase in the bedroom and the gradual depletion of his home territory. Nell had made an arrangement with Anna to come in every day and feed Morgan while she was away. After she came back she would undertake the delicate operation of his removal, with the last of her belongings, to The Old Rectory.

'In just over a week you won't know yourself,' she said to him as she scraped extra helpings of cat food out of the tin on to his plate. 'It will be so much better than here. Think of all that wonderful garden.'

Morgan mewed; he still had no confidence in her extravagant promises. Nell looked in the cupboard, wondering if she'd laid in enough cat food for ten days. To be on the safe side she decided to buy four more tins. You never knew with Morgan; sometimes he was quite capable of getting through more than a tin a day.

Throwing on her jacket, she let herself out of the flat and made her way down to the supermarket, thinking that the day could not be more perfect. It had that quality of light that seemed to mark the end of winter and the final arrival of spring. Housemartins and swallows wheeled overhead, whistling, checking out the old nest sites.

In the supermarket she grabbed some tins and stashed them in her wire basket.

'Good Lord, Nell! I haven't seen you for ages. Weren't we going to meet for a drink, or something?' The voice was unmistakable.

'Winnie Vivash!' Nell said smiling. 'What are you doing in this neck of the woods?'

Winnie was, as ever, bedecked with one of her flamboyant outfits and hung around with beads and bracelets.

'I gits about, moy luvver,' she said, exaggerating her soft Devon dialect. 'Up for a sale of Honiton lace, actually. Let's make up for past omissions and go for a coffee.'

'Winnie, I'd love to but I haven't time,' Nell said, smiling. 'You won't believe it but I'm getting married in a couple of hours' time.'

Winnie's eyes opened wide. 'Nell! You old dark horse. Who is it, for God's sake?'

Nell felt abashed suddenly. It was always the same, whenever she mentioned Daniel's name.

She lifted her chin defiantly. 'Daniel Thorne,' she said.

Winnie's eyes remained wide but now her mouth dropped open too.

'Aren't you going to wish me luck?' Nell said.

'I should bloody well think I am, darling!' Winnie said at last, recovering. 'You're going to need it, aren't you?'

Any remaining smile disappeared from Nell's face.

'Look, I know you don't like Daniel but there's no need to make it quite so obvious,' she said stiffly.

'It's just that, although I'm your greatest fan,' Winnie said, 'I never had you down as a sacrificial lamb. Laying down your life for your friend and all that.'

'What can you mean?'

'You can't tell me that you don't know how much trouble he's in? Daniel and Cornucopia both.'

'That's malicious nonsense.'

Winnie grasped Nell's elbow, her fingers digging in painfully. 'Look, lovey. Let's go and get that drink. This needs serious discussion.'

'I haven't got time . . .'

'Yes, you have. If you're as ignorant of the real state of Daniel's affairs as you appear to be, you better bloody well listen to your Auntie Winnie for a change. Let's dump this stuff and go.'

In spite of Nell's protests, Winnie propelled her outside, abandoning their baskets. In the supermarket car park Sean waited patiently, leaning against his vehicle.

'Lovey, get lost for an hour, will you?' she advised him. 'Meet you back here later, eh?'

'Oh, right,' Sean agreed good-naturedly.

In a pub in Fore Street Winnie ordered two coffees. It was too early to order brandy, which she would have preferred. They sat in an alcove in the almost deserted bar.

'So what's all this about?' Nell said, glancing at her watch. 'You better make it quick.'

'It won't take long,' Winnie said grimly. 'Then you can tell me to piss off if you like. First, tell me if you're planning to give up Alfresco, because when I passed it just now I noticed it was practically empty.'

'Yes, I am as a matter of fact. Daniel and I intend to run Cornucopia together.'

'So that's his game, is it?' Winnie said. 'And you're putting all your working capital into Cornucopia, I take it?'

'Look, Winnie, you're a good friend but I don't really see why—

'So you *are* bailing him out?'

'What do you mean? Cornucopia is doing particularly well at the moment.'

'Is that what he told you?' Winnie twisted her ropes of beads together so violently that one of them broke and scattered itself over the floor. Nell bent as if to retrieve them.

'Never mind that now!' Winnie commanded her, grabbing her wrist. 'Just shut up and listen. A friend of mine has been working for Daniel's outfit for some time now on the sales side. Moira. You may have met her.'

'Ye-es. I think I did.'

'There are no flies on Moira. She's not the usual kind of nitwit he likes to employ. Now, I met her only last week and she tells me that Customs and Excise are going through the place like a dose of salts. At any moment they're due to start on his private assets, house, car, private bank account, et cetera. Not that these will help them much. I believe everything's mortgaged to the hilt already. She tells me that they've been after him for months over serious misdeclaration penalties but he keeps dodging interviews or being out when they arrive. He owes nearly a hundred thousand back VAT.'

'A hundred thousand!' Nell shook her head. 'No! Your friend's got it all wrong. I just don't believe it.' But a memory came back to Nell of the doormat at The Old Rectory thick with brown envelopes: red-lettered gas and electricity bills, unopened correspondence from Customs and Excise and a plethora of others; some of which she would have known, had she not been deliberately blinding herself, came from a debt reclamation agency. Added to which, the sum of one hundred thousand pounds resonated like some doom-laden bell in her mind. The process of assigning her accumulated assets in the way of stock from Alfresco to Cornucopia was already completed; on her return from honeymoon she would transfer the remainder of her money from various bank and building society accounts. Ben had reckoned that together they amounted to a little over one hundred and fifty thousand pounds, acquired as much from interior design commissions as from Alfresco.

That Daniel had known what she was worth almost down to the last penny came as no surprise. He used to boast that he could tell what a punter could run to just by looking at them. Yet he was rarely taken in by outward show. He said that it was a very useful gift in a salesman. She never dreamed that he would use it on her.

'It's not only Moira,' Winnie said. 'There's Arthur too. He's terribly worried. He thinks he might get laid off.'

Of course. Arthur and his dark hints. Nell remembered Moira's speculative glances too. Perhaps they all looked to her as the saviour of Cornucopia and their jobs, so it wouldn't have been in their interests to spill the beans.

'I shall have to ask Daniel about all this,' she said at last, her head reeling.

'Yes, darling, do that. I wish it wasn't too early to order you a stiff brandy. You look as if you could do with it. Come to think of it, I could do with one too.'

Instead Nell drank her coffee, staring stupidly at the graining on the table.

Winnie said, 'If I were you, lovey, I'd ask the questions first and marry him afterwards, *not* the other way about.'

'We've booked up a honeymoon and everything,' Nell said in a small shocked voice.

'Sod the honeymoon! We're talking "with all my worldly goods I thee endow" here. So he'll lose a few hundred more, what's the difference?'

'I paid for the tickets actually,' Nell said in an even smaller voice. 'You see it was easier for me to book it than for Daniel, Cornucopia being right out in the sticks.'

He'd made a joke about it over the phone. 'I'll write you a cheque when I see you, sweetie. The least a chap can do is to pay for his own blasted honeymoon!' But he'd forgotten about the cheque and so had she. In any case, there was no urgency. Or so it seemed.

'Oh Christ!' Winnie groaned. 'I give up!'

Nell spent the rest of the morning with Winnie. They had the brandy eventually; in fact they had more than one. Winnie had rung Anna to tell her not to bother to turn up for the wedding, then she had hurried to the car park to tell Sean to leave without her and pick her up later. By the time Nell felt brave enough to ring the registry office she was slightly drunk and had to make a particular effort to make sure there was no misunderstanding. She would not be putting in an appearance. The wedding was off. By this time she had recollected other hints and indications that all was not well with Daniel's financial affairs; the way he had insisted, oh-so-casually, on how much joint finances would benefit Cornucopia, how together they could expand the business, improve the premises, take on more staff. With hindsight it was only too obvious.

That evening, when she and Winnie eventually rolled up at the flat, she drank some black coffee and rang Daniel. He'd obviously been drinking too. Enough, she discovered, for her to catch him off guard. He admitted he owed VAT but said it had nothing whatever to do with his wanting to marry her. That was something quite separate, he said.

'And, Nellie, how could you do that to me?' he said. 'There was I in the sodding registry office looking like a complete wally. It'll take some persuading for them to fix it all up again.'

'Don't you understand, Daniel? There will be no wedding, ever.' When she had at last persuaded him that she meant what she said, he became abusive.

'If you think you're irresistible just as you are, you better think again, Nell. Women of your age need a few material assets before they can expect to compete with all the young crackers a bloke like me could have any day of the week,' he said, adding, 'It was you who insisted on marriage. I just went along with it for old time's sake.'

'I insisted!' Nell cried, outraged.

Now that he had given up hope of her money, the truth eeked

out. She had allowed Daniel Thorne to betray her for a second time and she couldn't forgive herself. Yet even now, while her mind and emotions seethed with anger, her unrepentant body yearned for him, mourned his absence, was ready to resume allegiance like the traitor it was.

So she had picked up the keys of the villa that belonged to Persis and rung her to say she would like to take her up on her offer after all. Amazingly Persis asked no questions but half an hour later had rung back to say that her flight was booked and paid for, that Sophia was expecting her and that she was to be on the appointed plane. With no energy left to argue, Nell did as she was told.

Nearly three weeks afterwards, as she swam in this limpid sea, she was fitter, browner and more physically relaxed; but her bitterness, anger and grief still almost had the power to overwhelm her on occasion. It would have been the easiest thing in the world to switch it inwards, as women invariably did, and put an end to her life. Or turn to that other favoured option, punish herself by taking on the next shit who offered himself.

She swam back towards the pale shallows with the neat crawl perfected at the Mount Huish pool. Suddenly she felt homesick for Desna, Mo and Emmet. Daniel had inadvertently let it drop that they had all turned up for her wedding-that-never-was and she had been immensely touched; particularly as Desna had worries of her own. It seemed hardly believable as Mo claimed, that Desna would be leaving Mount Huish. Nell had never even contemplated such an eventuality. She regretted now that she'd been so absorbed with her own selfish concerns that she had thought no more about what was happening to her sister. She wondered if Harriet had won her battle over the dress.

She stood up and walked naked to pick up her towel. The water flowed down over her flesh and spattered darkly on the powdery stones at her feet.

It's time I went home she thought, as she towelled her hair.

Nell had no idea what lay behind the simple facts as Mo had

related them. Desna and Mo had not returned straight away from the Newton Abbot registry office. In fact they had spent the greater part of the rest of the day trying to find Nell. She did not appear to be at her flat but a telephone call to Anna at last confirmed that she was with a woman called Winnie. Winnie had told Anna that Nell would probably be staying with her. According to Winnie it had finally dawned on Nell that Daniel Thorne was a two-timing shit who was only after her money to bail him out of some bother with his debts. All Desna, Emmet and Mo could do was to go home and wait until Nell ceased to be incommunicado. Later, a smug Persis had rung Mo to say that Nell was staying at her villa in Greece.

Desna had almost forgotten that Harriet still didn't know the details of what Roy had in store for them all. She was making beef olives in the kitchen when Harriet arrived back from work, a little later than usual.

'How did the wedding go?' Harriet asked almost at once.

'It didn't,' Desna said. When she had related the whole story, she added, 'I can't tell you how relieved we all are. Thank goodness she found out before it was too late.'

'Poor Nell. How is she?'

'I don't know. We just hope she's all right. I left a message on her answerphone asking her to ring but I don't suppose she will. At least she's with a friend. Someone called Winnie. I'll try her number again later.' Desna put the ingredients for the stuffing in the food mixer. When it had finished whirring she said, 'How did it go today?

Harriet smiled. 'Gordon offered me a partnership.'

'Did he indeed!' Desna stopped in the middle of spreading the stuffing on a slice of beef. 'That was nice of him, but I thought he and Toby—'

'Toby doesn't want to take an active part in running the gallery any more. Actually he never has been much good at it.'

'But what will it involve?' Desna resumed her task thoughtfully. 'I mean you don't know anything about business, do you, darling?

'I don't know what it will involve yet,' Harriet said, feeling a shutter come down between them. 'Not much more than what I do now, I expect.'

'I'm sure it will, sweetie. In any case, there's something you have to know about Daddy's plans for the future before you make any hard and fast decision.'

'He doesn't really mean to move the yard to the Virgin Islands, does he?' Harriet sat on a kitchen chair and watched her mother's clever fingers roll and tie the olive. 'You see, I didn't take it seriously when you told me that. And it wouldn't mean he'd give up the yard here surely? What about Philip?'

Roy had ordered Desna not to tell Harriet anything until he got back that evening with Philip, when they would all have dinner together. However, for once in her life Desna decided that in abusing her as he had, Roy had forfeited his right to her loyalty. She would disobey her husband and ensure that Harriet was at least forewarned.

She began on another beef olive. 'Daddy's plans will affect everybody,' she said. Then she went on to tell Harriet about the deal with Bonicelli, the move to the Virgin Islands, the running down of the UK yard, Philip's eventual transfer to the new outfit – if he continued to prove himself – and finally the selling of Mount Huish to provide Roy's share of the capital.

'Sell Mount Huish?' Harriet said softly. 'He can't. Mount Huish is your home!' Desna did not fail to notice that Harriet had said 'your' home.

'I expect I shall be able to make a home elsewhere given time,' Desna said brightly.

'But you love it here. I can't imagine you anywhere but here. At least, near the river. Here. In England.'

'Daddy says the Virgin Islands are very beautiful. He wants us to have a short holiday there quite soon.'

'So you're keen to move there too?' Harriet said incredulously.

'No, I'm not keen, but Daddy says the outlook for business here isn't very good, or at least not as good as it could be in Tortola.'

'Tortola?'

'In the Virgin Islands. He says there are a lot of opportunities for holiday chartering out there. The weather is so much better for sailing, you see.'

'I don't think Philip will want to go. He likes rough weather sailing. What will happen if he says he wants to stay in Kingswear?'

'Daddy can be very persuasive. He'll say there's much more money to be made there.' Desna laid the final beef olive in the dish and went to rinse her hands under the tap. 'What do you think, darling? Would you mind if Philip wanted to go?'

A bleak look passed over Harriet's face. 'Yes, I would. I think Philip would be better on his own even if the money wasn't as good. I don't want Daddy to make him a partner.'

'You don't want . . .?' Desna stopped drying her hands and stared at her daughter. 'You never said that before!'

Harriet looked at her feet in their black boots. 'Well, now you say that Daddy wants to move Hindmarch Marine, it seems like a good moment for Philip to branch out on his own.'

'Does Philip feel like this?' Desna began to dry her hands again, but slowly.

'I don't know. I don't know what he thinks about this new scheme yet. We haven't had a chance to discuss it.'

'I expect he wanted to think it over quietly,' Desna said diplomatically.

Over Desna's beef olives the subject wasn't mentioned. They made small talk. Harriet said nothing of the partnership she'd been offered; it seemed small beer beside what was discussed as soon as they had their coffee in the sitting room.

Roy stood in front of the fireplace, cigar lit. Since the imprint of one of his cigars had been burned into her hand and into her memory, Desna could not look at him without a feeling of nausea. Yet he appeared to have completely forgotten his acts of aggression.

'Now, Mr Philip,' he said jovially, 'I've given you a day to think it over and discuss it with your parents if need be, what d'you say?'

Philip looked at Harriet. 'Sir, I think before I tell you what I think we should let Harriet in on it.'

Roy turned his attention to Harriet as if noticing her for the first time. Evidently he thought her opinion scarcely worth considering.

Harriet felt grateful to her mother for telling her about the proposals in advance.

'Harriet already knows,' Desna said bluntly. 'I told her.'

'I though I told you . . .' Roy's mouth tightened in annoyance. 'All right, all right,' he said impatiently. 'But Harriet will go along with whatever Philip decides, it goes without saying, once they're married.' He puffed on his cigar complacently.

'What I meant was,' Philip said judiciously, 'was that I'd like a chance to talk it over privately with Harriet before I commit us both to some fairly radical changes.'

Roy looked mystified. Then he waved his cigar vaguely in the air. 'Right. Right. Go ahead.'

Philip got up and looked at Harriet. 'Let's go for a walk,' he said, holding out his hand. 'Will you excuse us?' he added politely. Philip's manners were excellent, Desna thought.

Light remained in the west, filtering through the trees, though the river itself and the air above it seemed bathed in green light. Two salmon boats moved downriver, their nets stowed inboard. The new white of the boathouse hung above the scene, ghostlike. Two egrets roosted, exotic rarities.

'Are you all right, Harry?' Philip asked as they stood on the decking of the boathouse looking into the dark water.

'Hmm.'

'This has been a bit of a double whammy, hasn't it? What with everything else . . .' He meant the weekend in St Ives.

'It's worse for Mummy. I can see she really doesn't want to go. She would hate to leave Mount Huish. You see, it's been a sort of life's work for her.'

'But she'll go. He hasn't given her much choice, has he?' Philip said. He began to pace the decking. 'To tell you the truth I'm a bit pissed off by the way your old man's handled this whole business. Like only asking me as a sort of afterthought

387

when he had it all wrapped up with Bonicelli. And that's another thing. I don't think I could work with that chap. He's too much of a smoothie for my liking.' He turned to face Harriet, her face like a dim moon in the half-darkness. 'What do you think about it? Do you want to live in the Virgin Islands?'

'Mummy says you could make more money there.'

'That's not what I asked.'

Harriet hesitated. 'I'd go if you wanted me to. But I'd rather stay here if it's all the same to you – if you still wanted me, that is.'

'Still want you? Why did you say that, for pete's sake?'

'Well, you know . . . I wasn't much good at the weekend, was I?'

'So that's what's bugging you!' He came close and held her arms by the elbows. 'Look, you'll be fine. You're just a bit small, that's all. It'll get better, I promise. It was probably my fault anyway.' He kissed her forehead chastely. 'It's just that I love you so much.'

There was a long silence. Then she said. 'If you don't agree to go to the Virgin Islands and help run the business out there, I don't suppose you could stay with Daddy's firm. He wants to close down the Kingswear end eventually.' She had to make Philip understand that if he'd ever had any unconscious or even conscious expectations of advancement from marrying the boss's daughter, he should be prepared to revise them.

'I've always rather fancied having my own outfit,' Philip said. 'But it never seemed even remotely possible.'

'I suppose one need not close down this end. You could keep it going with repairs and charters and so on. If you made it a smaller operation entirely; sold off some of the moorings, for instance, you might eventually be able to buy it from Daddy. I mean you wouldn't make a great heap of money, like Daddy wants to do, but it would be enough for us, wouldn't it?'

Philip turned to look at her, smiling in the dark. 'You know, Harry, I think there's quite an astute business brain ticking away somewhere under there!' He ran the fingers of both hands under her hair. 'If I did hang on in here, I might need that. I'm okay on the practical side but I'd need someone with some business nous around if I went it alone.'

'I didn't think I had a business head, although . . .'

'What?'

'Gordon offered me a partnership today. He seems to think I'm quite good.'

'Bully for him. Will you accept it?' Philip paused. 'I don't suppose you'd even have mentioned it if I'd said I was keen on going to Tortola, would you? You'd have kept quiet about it!'

Harriet chuckled. 'I don't know. Anyway, I haven't decided. There are things to be considered.'

'Things like the future of Hindmarch Marine and our place in it, for instance?'

'Something like that. And I'd have to get some professional advice. Did you know that as a partner in a firm you are liable for all debts, even if you only have a five-pee share? Not that I think the gallery's going to go bust.'

'You seem to have all kinds of odd information at your fingertips, don't you?' he said, moving his hands down to her waist, under her jersey. This time she didn't move away from him.

'I want us to stay here, Harry,' he said. 'I want to have a small yard of my own. I'm not an ambitious kind of bloke.' He rested his mouth against her hair. 'And the sex will be fine, you'll see.'

'Yes, I'm sure it will,' she said. Now she knew what to expect it would be easier to pretend she enjoyed sex. She had definitely come to the conclusion that there must have been some huge conspiracy amongst women since the dawn of time, to pretend that they liked the discomfort, humiliation and domination the procreative act forced upon them. If they were dependent on their men, or worse still, loved them, or if they wanted children, what else could they do? Even these days, she decided, only women who didn't love were wholly free. That was the trouble, she thought. It immediately made freedom appear to be some kind of vacuum after all.

Rupert's friends dropped him off at Mount Huish on their way home. After a brief struggle to disentangle his surfboard from the others on the roof of the VW, he saluted his surfing companions as they disappeared down the drive and then sauntered in through the front door, sand scrunching between his bare feet and the polished parquet. He bumped into Desna who was emerging from the kitchen carrying a huge vase of cream-coloured tulips.

'Whoops!' he said. 'Hi, Mum.'

'Darling!' Desna leaned over the flowers to kiss him. 'You look as if you've had a lovely time?'

He was tanned, his hair was even longer than before and bleached with the effects of sun and sea. He was wearing a dirty tee shirt, shades and a pair of disreputable long shorts.

'It was quite insane!' he said, from which she gathered that it had been enjoyable. He followed her into the sitting room where she put the flowers down on a table and turned to look at him smiling, while he rambled on excitedly about 'barrels' and 'getting stoked' and 'sets'. And characters called 'Grommet' or 'Brad' or 'Kurt' or 'Daz' or some other short and guttural handle. Desna had previously thought that waves were a fairly frequent occurrence on the north Cornish coast but apparently not, according to Rupert, since he'd had to wait all afternoon for one. Adam Young he hardly mentioned even though he'd been staying with the Youngs. Desna made a mental note to ring Mrs Young to thank her for her hospitality. Outwardly she listened, making interested noises, the pleasure of seeing her son again shadowed by what hung over her, hung over the whole family, though Rupert as yet knew nothing of it.

'Darling, I think you'd better find a place other than the hall to keep your surfboard,' she said at last.

'Oh, right. I was just going to get the garage keys.'

'And I think it would be a good idea to shower and change,' she suggested.

He grunted. Coming down to earth wasn't so cool. He wanted to keep the sand and salt on his body for as long as possible since they were his last remaining contact with the only life he could possibly tolerate. He hadn't been discovered as a potential star as he had hoped – rather childishly, he now saw; but all the same, he knew he could be good given time and opportunity. And he asked a great many questions about what sort of money a top surfer could hope to make from sponsorship of one kind and another. The future looked great, though not the immediate future, of course. Salt-stained tenners rustled in his pocket; the holiday had supplied him with another kind of opportunity too.

When he'd scrunched off Desna got out the vacuum cleaner to dispose of the sand that had already got into more places than she would have believed possible in so short a time. It was good to see Rupert more enthused and alive than he'd been for months. Within the next few days though, he'd be gone and once again she felt she'd hardly seen him.

That evening Roy spoke to Rupert about the transfer of the business. Desna could not help noticing that he favoured Rupert, at sixteen, with a degree of consideration that he had denied Harriet. She saw that Harriet was aware of it too.

Rupert approved immediately. 'Sounds great!' he said. He thought at once of Apple Bay on Tortola that he had heard someone mention only that day as a wicked surfing beach. And the rum punch parties by moonlight and the year-round sun. 'Terrif!' It was also apparent that his father had been too busy to check his expenditure on surfboards. Thank Christ! he thought.

Harriet glanced at her brother's eager face. The tips of his lashes were bleached out and his eyes were slightly bloodshot from wind and salt – and booze, she imagined. Rupert was still no more than a big kid.

'But it's boarding school for you for at least another two years, my son,' Roy said, putting a forkful of apricot tart into his mouth.

'Yes, sir,' Rupert said, thinking that there were always the holidays and being able to boast to his less fortunate mates. 'Ma, could I have some more of that?' He passed his plate for more tart. Turning to his father he said, 'Sir, have you made any decisions about next year? I mean, if I can't stay where I am . . .?'

'Yes,' Roy said, munching his apricot tart. 'There's a place in Yorkshire that sounds very promising.'

'Yorkshire!' His father might as well have said Outer Mongolia.

'You'll go where you're sent. If I think it's suitable.'

'Have you tried anywhere nearer?' Rupert suggested desperately. 'Because all these places are crying out for sixth formers these days, there shouldn't be any great hassles. I was thinking of the cost of getting there . . .'

'That's not a problem,' Roy said with finality.

Rupert thought morosely that life was back to its frigging awful norm again quicker than he'd thought possible. The only relief from the generally heavy scene was his father's plan to move to Tortola.

'I've been working my head while I've been away,' he said, which wasn't quite the truth since he'd only that moment decided. 'I think I might like to join the firm after all.'

'This wouldn't have anything to do with it's new location, I take it?' Roy said with heavy irony.

Rupert grinned. 'Well, let's say it hasn't exactly put me off. But even before you told me I'd been kicking the idea around.'

'We'll see how prepared you are to kick around the idea of hard work,' Roy said, not without a trace of satisfaction. 'You don't imagine Hindmarch Marine happened by guess and by God, I suppose?'

'No, sir.'

Events of the following morning brought Roy's stratagems closer to completion. With an air of triumph he tossed a glossy brochure down on to the breakfast table.

'What d'you think of that, eh! I reckon they've done the place proud in the end. I'm bloody glad I turned down that pathetic photograph they originally proposed for the front.'

Desna picked up the estate agent's brochure. The cover was cut away to reveal a photograph of Mount Huish taken from the drive. 'I preferred the other one taken through the trees. It made it look mysterious,' she said, her heart sinking as she opened it.

'We don't want the place to look mysterious, dammit. We want it to look what it is. A bloody good investment.'

'Investment!' Desna said. Not that she wanted Mount Huish presented in any way whatever that would tempt anyone to buy it. She clung to the hope that with the market in its present depressed state, no one would. She turned the pages. All the features of all the rooms were meticulously listed. All the grounds described and photographed. It looked a highly desirable spread. The asking price astonished her; it was impossible to believe that the deposit they'd put on it all those years ago had been so difficult to raise. Now it would be considered peanuts.

'Let's have a squint?' Rupert said, holding out his hand over his Coco Pops. 'Cor, this looks the biz.'

'You're looking down in the mouth,' Roy said to Desna, pushing his cup towards her for more coffee. 'You're not still thinking we have any choice in the matter, I hope?'

'I don't know how you can bear the thought of other people living here,' she said, obediently filling his cup.

'That's negative thinking. What you've entirely failed to grasp up to now is what you'll be getting instead.'

'Why don't you take Ma out to the BVI and show her?' Rupert suggested helpfully, stuffing Coco Pops into his mouth while he turned the pages of the brochure.

'Don't worry, I fully intend to.' Roy presented the idea more as a threat than an inducement. 'And I don't think you need bother about who will live in the old place because it looks as if no one will. Live in it, I mean.'

Desna stared at him, her eyes wide.

'There's already an offer of sorts on the table,' he said exultantly, 'from a group interested in the property as a golf and country club.'

'I don't believe it!' It seemed to Desna that every day would bring fresh horrors. As if somewhere there was a list of punishments prepared for her to be got through one by one, blow by blow. That the fates, not content to see her bowed, needed to hammer home their advantage.

Mo was making another attempt to spend a morning painting. The last one had been seriously disrupted by Desna's appearance and the row with Persis. She had only twelve canvases and she'd promised Gordon twenty. Persis had departed. She was no longer in Totnes but installed in her renovated studio in Yorkshire and already giving her architect and builder hell, apparently. She said the studio was frightful and that she wouldn't be able to work in it.

Mo had not forgiven her sister for telling Nell about her true parentage; yet she'd known deep inside from the moment Persis had appeared on the scene, that she wouldn't be able to keep the knowledge to herself. All that it had succeeded in doing was to compound Nell's desolation and anger. As if it wasn't enough to have been let down by the man she loved, she had been let down by the woman she had looked on as her mother. The poor girl must be in shock to a terrible degree. Mo yearned to go to her, to explain how things had been; to be with her just in case she was tempted to do something final. Tears were in Mo's eye; the colours on the canvas appeared to run, dissolve in air. She threw down her brush. How the devil could she paint?

Persis had refused to say where her villa was. All she would impart was that it was on a Greek island. There were thousands of Greek islands, goddammit! Persis was acting as if she, Mo, was the enemy against whom Nell needed protection. The infernal cheek of the woman when it had been her fault right from the start!

Not that Alec hadn't played a major part too, in the beginning. Persis was twelve years younger than Mo and they had come from a household where Persis had been the undisputed ruler. Both parents had doted on their talented and hugely intelligent younger child. When first their mother had died and, soon after, their father too, Mo was left in *loco parentis*, compelled to bow to Persis' will, as they had.

Mo, at art school, had caught the roving eye of the assistant lecturer in painting, became pregnant by him and then married him. She was under no illusion that he had married her reluctantly, but even he could see that without parents to turn to and with a dependent younger sister, Mo would have been in a very difficult position. However, he had also not failed to observe that she had been left a substantial house not far from the college, so in the end he decided that the arrangement suited him very well. After all, there was no need to curtail his amorous adventures just because he was married. Not that he had any intention of seducing Mo's precocious but underage sister. Oh, no. That would be madness. Nevertheless, it had happened and the girl had got pregnant.

There was nothing else for Mo to do but to hush it up and take on the child as her own, as Desna's sister. It was agreed right from the start that the truth should never come out. From the moment Persis was eighteen they had lived separate lives. All Mo knew of her sister was that she'd later married a rich man, divorced, then remarried. She gathered the second marriage had lasted an even shorter time than the first. But what perverse instinct made Persis renege on her promise at this late stage was a mystery. Of course, Alec had left Mo in the end; initially with a woman who worked in advertising and who had lured him away from academe into her own sphere. He had finished with the woman but stayed in advertising. He had died leaving Desna and Nell, his only descendants, twenty thousand pounds each.

Mo frowned at her canvas. Abruptly she dragged it off the easel and hurled it across the room.

'Bugger it to hell!' she cried, 'And bugger Persis!'

CHAPTER TWENTY-SEVEN

Emmet was sitting on a disintegrating wooden bench in the shade of a very old chestnut tree, its bark twisted into a spiral round the trunk. The dogs were lying underneath the split and silvered table on which she worked; she was putting the finishing touches to an article she'd started weeks before. The sun warmed her bare feet through a break in the new leaves; above her, the tree offered up the white spires of its blossoms to a new generation of insect pollinators. Every now and again the scent of lilac drifted towards her from the other side of the garden.

Tom and Lee were sitting in the long grass down by the far hedge absorbed in the monotony of a pocket Gameboy that Barney had picked up in a car boot sale. Beth and Dinah's little girl Rebecca had set up a classroom on the lawn into which various toys and even some of the cats had been dragooned.

Now that the weather had improved so dramatically Barney was on the roof of the farmhouse mending the flashing. Emmet glanced up from time to time, nervous to see him padding about among the chimneys. She must remember to ask him if he had himself insured, since he was self-employed; being happy-go-lucky, it was not the kind of thing he would think of until it was too late.

The hum of insects, the contented clucking of chickens from the adjacent field, and the blackbird's sweet and piercing cadenza belting out from the ridge tile of one of the outbuildings made her feel almost too relaxed to concentrate. After a winter of mud, rain and cold this Spring Bank Holiday was like a benediction. But concentrate she must if she hoped to get the article typed that evening, for the one cloud on the horizon was the drying up of funds. Maurice's new book was still not finished. Perhaps it was just as well he spent more time in London with his agent these days; maybe she could spur him on to greater efforts.

Emmet went indoors to make tea for herself and Barney and to fill a large jug of homemade lemonade for the children. She put everything on a tray, plus a large slab of homemade fruit cake, took it out into the garden and laid it on the wobbly table. She called to Barney as he hammered away on the roof. The dogs bestirred themselves, scenting food. Earwig laid his head on Emmet's lap.

'Is this your lemonade?' Lee asked. His skinny arms poked out from his baggy tee shirt with some indecipherable logo printed on it. Both he and Tom wore back-to-front baseball caps that Barney had bought for them – in the ubiquitous car boot sale, it went without saying.

Emmet filled earthenware mugs for them. 'Yes,' she said. 'Is that a problem?'

'No. It's ace!' Lee said enthusiastically. Emmet looked at him in surprise. He had declared her lemonade sour at first. He must be acquiring the taste. The boys took their lemonade and cake away to their lair.

'Can we have some for our children?' Beth asked, pointing to the toys. The cats had wandered away. 'They're all thirsty.'

'You can get some of those plastic beakers from the kitchen and fill a jug from the outside tap if you like,' Emmet said. The two girls trotted off to fetch the jug and beakers.

Barney arrived, unhooked his tools from his belt and threw himself down on the warm grass. 'This is the life!' he said, looking up into the leafy canopy.

Emmet poured his tea and stirred two spoonfuls of sugar into it. He liked his tea sweet. She lectured him on his sweet tooth.

He grinned. 'I need it for the energy. I burn it up, see.'

And it really seemed as if he did. There wasn't a spare ounce of flesh on him. He was wearing his frayed denim shorts and the sun had scattered more freckles than ever on his spindly shanks. He rolled over on to his front, drank some of his tea and demolished a large chunk of cake.

'Will you finish the roof today?' Emmet asked.

'With a bit of luck. Good job I bought more flashing that I thought we'd need. I'll have to do the whole chimney in the end.'

'I'm afraid the house isn't in very good shape. Money's been so tight. We may even have to sell.' She would deeply regret having to sell. The apparent remoteness of Drake's Farm, with no other habitation in sight, had always been part of its appeal. She looked beyond the tangled hedge that marked its limits to the fields, and beyond the fields to the massed green of the woods that shrouded the hills. Cuckoos called all day from their ferny depths, and all night owls exchanged lugubrious greetings.

'Then you'd be daft,' Barney said. 'Plenty of things you could do instead. Bed and breakfast, fr'instance.'

Emmet laughed. 'Only for people who like ruins! Besides, visitors would upset the animals.'

'You could do the place up. But you may have to drop the animals.'

Emmet was silent. She drank her tea.

At last she said. 'I wouldn't want to give up the animals.'

'We could run it together, you an' me,' Barney suggested. 'It could be one of those places where animals are part of what's on offer. You know, ducks, rabbits, goats and that . . . We might even make cheese and sell free range eggs as well . . .'

'Here, hold on! You seem to be counting yourself in on all this!'

'You'd need me to fix it all up for you and help with the work. It's obvious.'

'What would be in it for you?'

'A share in the profits, natch.'

'What if there were no profits?'

'There would be.'

'In any case. It's impractical. You can't put injured wild animals on display.'

'I never said we would, did I?'

The dogs stirred. A voice calling distantly brought Barney's castles in the air crashing down. A woman appeared at the side gate.

'I'm sorry to bother you,' she said. 'I rang the bell but there was no answer . . .'

The dogs sauntered over to examine the newcomer. The middle-aged woman with two children in tow decided against opening the gate but stood holding a large cardboard box in her arms.

Emmet, in shorts and barefoot, went over to her. She knew as soon as she saw the box that there was to be a new addition to her charges.

'We were having a picnic by this wood,' the woman said anxiously. 'We found it all alone with no sign of its mother. We were told you take in abandoned animals.'

Emmet opened the box. Inside was a very young fox cub, its huge eyes looking up apprehensively from its dark russet face.

'You said you found it beside a wood?'

'Yes, yes. All alone.'

'I'll take it,' Emmet said. 'But I'm sorry to tell you that it wasn't abandoned at all. You see how healthy it looks? Its mother would have come back sooner or later to feed it.'

The woman looked frantic and a bit annoyed. 'Then we better take it back at once.' She turned to the children. 'You can remember where it was, can't you?'

One nodded. One shook its head. Emmet took the box out of the woman's arms.

'Sorry, it's too late, I'm afraid. The mother will know it's been interfered with. Never mind. I'll see what I can do.'

Barney strolled over and looked into the box. 'Hallo there, little fella.'

The woman and her two children left, squabbling over whose idea it had been to remove the fox cub.

'I'll settle it down and feed it,' Emmet said, 'but I'll have to ring the RSPCA to see if they have any more this age.'

'How's that?'

'It's better if they have the competition of others even if they're not related. It gives them more of a will to survive. Kept here on his own he'd probably finish up as a pet.'

'I see what you mean. D'you want me to give them a ring?'

'Thanks. I'll put him in the old hedgehog run for the moment.'

Desna rang just after Emmet watched the young woman from the RSPCA drive away with the fox cub. It seemed they had three others of the same age.

'Hallo, Desna. Is everything all right?' The news about Mount Huish and the proposed departure of Desna and Roy had been a shock for everyone. Emmet still couldn't quite believe that Roy intended to go through with it; she could not help thinking that there was bound to be some hitch that would make it impractical.

'*I'm* all right darling. I'm ringing about Nell.'

'Is she back?'

'Not yet. But I had a call from Winnie Vivash. You remember, Nell's friend? We seem to be getting to the bottom of why Nell backed out. Daniel owed an enormous amount of back VAT and Winnie believes he hoped Nell would pay it. Can you believe it?' Desna's voice sounded shocked.

'I'm afraid to say I can. Pity. I quite like Daniel.'

'Emmet! How can you say that? However, that's not the point. According to Winnie – goodness knows how *she* found out – Customs and Excise are just about to go through *all* Daniel's assets, which will include his house and everything in it. They are going there the day after tomorrow . . .'

'How on earth does she know that?'

'Don't ask me. But she's the sort of woman who has all sorts of contacts. She's in the antiques trade herself.'

'Why did she think you ought to know? What has it to do with us?'

'A great deal, unfortunately. Listen, Emmet, apparently the entire contents of Nell's flat are now over at Daniel's place. And the contents of the shop have all been moved to Cornucopia.'

'Nell had some valuable stuff.'

'Precisely. And what I'm afraid of is that Daniel will say it all belongs to him and persuade the VAT people to set it off against what he owes. There's nothing to prove that he doesn't own it after all.'

'Shit! Yes, I can see that he might think of something like that.

What can we do? It's very short notice.'

'Winnie's thought of that, bless her. She's made an arrangement with Daniel to fetch Nell's things tomorrow at two o'clock. I suppose he couldn't very well refuse.'

'Sounds like Winnie cares. I'm afraid poor Nell doesn't. She certainly didn't mention it on her postcard; in fact she scarcely mentioned anything. But we have to help Winnie. We can't leave her to deal with it on her own.'

'She has some man lined up who seems willing to help, but no van. I wondered if you and Barney . . .?'

'Of course. Barney has a friend with a Ford transit. Don't worry, we'll be there.'

'Barney seems to have a great many useful friends, doesn't he?'

'It's the alternative economy at work,' Emmet chuckled.

'The alternative what?'

'Never mind. See you there. Oh, I almost forgot. What's the address?'

Desna gave it to her.

Desna's Fiat and Barney's borrowed Ford Transit drew up outside The Old Rectory at five to two. Emmet had explained that it would be necessary to bring Tom and Beth since they were both still on half-term holiday.

'Can we help?' Beth asked.

'I'm sure you can. There are bound to be some small things to carry.' They all piled out of the van, meeting Desna at the gate. Just then a Discovery pulled up behind them and a colourful plump woman climbed out, followed by Hugh Daish.

'Hugh! What on earth are you doing here?' Desna exclaimed. The last time she'd seen him had been in Stevie's sitting room.

'I'm Winnie.' The plump woman came forward, hand outstretched. 'You seem to know Hugh already. Hugh's an old chum of mine. An old chum of Nell's too.'

'You never said you knew Nell!' Desna said, astonished.

Hugh laughed. 'I didn't realize you were Nell's sister,' he said. 'I wish I had.

'Well, perhaps we should get on with it,' Desna said, taking charge. 'I must say I'm not particularly looking forward to this. It would have been much less embarrassing to have left it to a carrier, but they wouldn't have known which things were Nell's.'

'I think perhaps Desna and I should go in alone to start with,' Hugh said.

'Don't let the man charm you into believing all the stuff's his after all,' Winnie said. 'He's quite capable of it.'

But her warning turned out to be superfluous. No one answered repeated knocking and ringing. There appeared to be no one in at The Old Rectory. After another half-hour's wait Hugh and Barney were getting restless.

'He's no intention of showing up,' Hugh said angrily.

Desna paced up and down. She looked back towards the village, for The Old Rectory was set slightly apart. There seemed to be no one about.

'What can we do? We can't leave Nell's stuff here!' she said, her hand to her mouth.

'We won't,' Barney said, speaking for the first time. He checked his belt for the tools which he invariably carried. 'Emmet, come with me. You kids stay with your auntie.' The two of them disappeared round the side of the building, leaving the others waiting at the front gate.

'What are you going to do?' Emmet asked apprehensively. Barney was squinting at a red alarm high up on the side wall. For a moment he hesitated at the padlocked door of an outhouse. The next moment the door was wide open and Barney was emerging with a ladder.

'Barney! You mustn't!' Emmet said, but she was giggling.

'It's all right. That type of alarm is rubbish. Wait here.' He laid the ladder against the wall, shinned up it, lifted the cover from the alarm with apparently no trouble and busied himself for a moment with a screwdriver and wirecutters, after which he replaced the cover, descended and put the ladder away again.

He grinned. 'My misspent youth,' he said. Then he used the screwdriver again on an arched window at the back of the house, levering it open.

'Just give me a bunk up,' he commanded.

'Get a move on then, for God's sake!' Emmet said as she bent her back for him.

The gap in the window was so small that Emmet was astonished when she saw Barney's skinny legs disappearing inside. The next moment his head appeared in the aperture.

'No problem,' he said. 'Let's hope the local neighbourhood watch are crap.'

'Barney, I don't think you should do this!' Emmet hissed.

'Watch me!' he said and vanished. The next minute he was opening the front door, its magnetic catches clicking back harmlessly, to the astonishment of the others who were waiting by the front gate while they discussed what to do next.

Desna looked round as if she expected a police car to roll up at any moment. 'We can't do this,' she said in anguish.

'Looks as if we are,' Hugh said, striding forward. 'Come on, Desna. You and Emmet will have to tell us what belongs to Nell and what doesn't. We wouldn't want to be accused of stealing!'

'Stealing! Oh, my God!' Desna said.

But Emmet was already inside, rolling up one of Nell's oriental rugs.

Barney and Hugh humped out all the large pieces of Nell's furniture, the others followed with smaller things. Tom and Beth, unaware of any irregularity, struggled out with items that were really too heavy for them. Now that the die was cast Desna shrugged off her initial consternation, closing her mind to the frightful possibility of the police arriving, hoping to get it over with as soon as possible as she busily identified those things that belonged to Nell.

To her amazement and relief the police did not arrive. Neither did Daniel. It was clear that he had never intended to. The work completed, Barney conscientiously closed the front door behind them and they journeyed back in convoy to Mount Huish, where their booty was to be stored. Emmet and the children travelled in Desna's car since both the Discovery and the Ford Transit were fully loaded.

A mile away from The Old Rectory Desna began to giggle

helplessly, tears squeezing out of her eyes.

'Steady on, Des! You'll have us off the road,' Emmet said grinning. 'I must say, though, that we made a cracking good team. We could make breaking and entering quite a lucrative little sideline.'

'We helped, didn't we?' Beth piped up from the back seat.

'Yeah, it was great!' Tom said, it having dawned on him at last that there was something vaguely irregular about what they had done. 'Just like the A Team!'

Desna was silent and Emmet glanced at her. It was a shock to see that her sister's recent tears of laughter had suddenly turned into tears in earnest. They were streaming down her cheeks, unchecked. Emmet touched Desna's arm.

'I'm so sorry about Mount Huish, Des. I wish there was something I could do.'

'Just pass me the tissues, will you, darling? They're under the dash.'

Desna dabbed at her cheeks. By the time they arrived back she had recovered her composure and handed round cups of tea and homemade cake as if nothing unusual had happened. The atmosphere turned into one of noisy celebration.

'Of course there is the contents of the shop too,' Winnie said slyly, sipping her tea, a huge piece of coffee cake in her hand. 'I was told that that's all over at Cornucopia if anyone's still in the mood.' But even the newly formed team of desperate criminals thought that might be biting off more than they could chew.

'I'm sure members of the staff at Cornucopia would know what had arrived from Alfresco,' Desna said. 'They can't all be dishonest.'

Hugh was in a curiously elated mood ever since Winnie had rung him with the news that Nell was not married after all, and enlisting his help. He was not prepared to let matters rest.

'I'll phone my solicitor as soon as I get back,' he said. 'Thorne's not going to get away with it. Not if I have anything to do with it.'

Desna looked at Hugh, then at Winnie, a question in her eyes. Winnie just smiled.

'Thank goodness that Daniel didn't get his hands on her money,' Desna said. 'She's worked so hard for it. I can't imagine what her accountant was thinking about.'

'There are such things as two sets of books,' Hugh said grimly. 'He probably only saw the authorized version.'

Emmet got up. 'Come on, my lot,' she said. 'Time to go.'

'Can't we stay and have a swim?' Tom pleaded.

'Not today. Chores to be done.'

'They would be very welcome,' Desna said.

'Thanks, Des,' Emmet said, kissing her. 'Another time, perhaps.' It seemed to her that Desna was in no state to deal with Tom and Beth. She had never seen her sister looking so brittle. 'Come on, Barney.'

'We were so grateful for your help back there, Barney,' Desna said. 'I won't enquire too closely about how you got into The Old Rectory but it worked out all right in the end, I'm glad to say.' Her attitude towards him had changed. Now that he had taken a risk for the sake of her sister she regarded him as a friend and ally rather than merely Emmet's lodger.

'How different she is from you and Nell,' Winnie said, as soon as the contingent from Drake's Farm had departed.

'She's our half-sister,' Desna said. 'Which might account for it. But she's always been something of a law unto herself.'

'Her fella's a nice bloke too. And their kids are a knockout. Fancy them joining in like that! To the manner born,' Winnie chuckled.

'Barney's not Emmet's "fella",' Desna said, amused at the mistake. 'He's a sort of handyman who happens to lodge with them.'

'You could have fooled me,' Winnie said. 'And there was me thinking how well suited they were.'

They too left soon after. Hugh took Desna's hand.

'I'll tell Stevie how I ran into you again under most unusual circumstances,' he said. 'She'll be highly intrigued.'

'I hope you won't tell her too much,' Desna said. 'I don't want too many people to know of my criminal tendencies.'

'*Our* criminal tendencies! We were all in on this one.'

* * *

Most of the wedding arrangements were complete. Desna was already sending out invitations and keeping a methodical check list of acceptances and refusals. There was no need for Stevie to come up to Mount Huish or for Desna to go to see Stevie, yet they continued to meet, snatching an odd hour here and there whenever they could. It wasn't easy. On one occasion Stevie employed an evening sitter for Theo but when Desna proposed leaving a meal for Roy to put in the microwave he had made such a fuss and had asked so many questions that she had never repeated the experiment.

Today they met at lunchtime. They sat in the corner of a pub situated halfway between Mount Huish and Stevie's house. The pub was large and sprawling with dark-stained beams, horse brasses, mock panelling and a reputation based on its carvery and lavish buffet. The two women, however, were content with drinks and sandwiches.

'You wouldn't believe the issue he made of just putting ready-prepared food in the oven,' Desna said. 'It's extraordinary when I come to think of it but in over twenty years I can't remember him ever getting a meal for himself, though I suppose I must have made some arrangements for him when I was in hospital having Harriet and Rupert.'

'Have you ever taken a lover?' Stevie said.

'A lover!' Desna exclaimed. 'The whole idea is inconceivable. He would have found out instantly. You can't imagine how jealous he is! He doesn't even like me having women friends unless they're the wives of his friends or business colleagues. You're the first person who isn't either of those things. I still correspond with a few old school friends who I arrange to meet when I'm up in London shopping, but otherwise you could say I'm like the princess in the tower.' She smiled wanly, shaking her head. 'I never thought of that till now. Was Mathew jealous?'

'I don't think it ever dawned on him,' Stevie said. She sipped her beer. 'Do you still love Roy, Desna?'

'I thought I did. At least until . . .' She couldn't bring herself to admit to another soul that Roy had raped her. The humiliation was so profound that she still had difficulty calling it rape even to herself. It was safer and less distressing to pretend that it was normal sex for which she had been unprepared. Her fault, in fact. She looked deep into her unaccustomed gin and tonic. 'Now I think I hate him!' she said, her voice low but with a bitter vehemence that startled them both. She fixed her eyes on Stevie. 'You'll probably think this is simply terrible but this morning at breakfast I looked at him and thought how much I'd like to kill him.'

'I'm sure that's not as unusual as you think. Thoughts like that, I mean.' Stevie put a hand on Desna's arm, briefly, as a gesture of comfort. 'What will you do? Will you fight for Mount Huish?'

'If I insist on us keeping the house it would mean that I would have to fight Roy. He would see it as me denying him the future he so desperately wants.' She took a tremulous drink.

'He would punish you?'

'Of *course* he'd punish me!'

'So you'll go to the Virgin Islands as planned?'

'I didn't say that.'

'Oh?' Stevie gazed at Desna quizzically.

'A few days ago you made a suggestion. Something about the possibility of me coming into the business?'

A light seemed to go on behind Stevie's eyes. Rather striking eyes, Desna thought. As were Hugh's. Grey with speckles.

'You're asking if I was serious?' Stevie said. 'Well, I can tell you. Yes, absolutely. If only you knew. I've been so worried about what will happen when Sonia's no longer able to cope— What already *is* happening. As it is, Dave, that's her husband, puts in a lot of evenings trying to help out but it can't go on like this much longer. That's how serious I was. Besides, I know already that we could work together. Are you saying—?'

'Stevie, I don't know. Let's just say I've been giving it a great deal of thought.'

'It would mean leaving Roy,' Stevie said quietly, 'if he's determined to go abroad.'

'Yes.' Desna stared at the noisy party at the bar on the other side of the room. 'But I just don't see myself ever having the courage to tell him. The trouble is that I really do believe in the marriage vows "for better or for worse". And Roy's given me so much. I certainly wouldn't have had two wonderful children or Mount Huish in the first place if I hadn't been married to Roy.'

'And he wouldn't have them if he hadn't been married to you! I hate to see you write off your own contribution as if it were worthless. Think what might have happened to Roy if he'd married a woman who couldn't have coped with all that!'

'He never would have,' Desna said stubbornly.

'Have you told Harriet what's in your mind?'

'Good heavens, no!'

'She'd probably be overjoyed to learn that her mother might be staying in England after all.'

'I couldn't be sure. I love Harriet but I still look on her as a child, you know. I wish I could say that we were close but I'm afraid it wouldn't be quite true. It's a hard thing to admit but I don't think I've ever really understood her.'

'I don't suppose any of us properly understand our nearest and dearest. I certainly never understood Mathew. Theo's a great deal more straightforward, thank heaven. At the moment anyway.'

'How is Theo?'

'Obsessed with maps, would you believe!'

'Maps?'

Stevie shrugged and laughed. 'Give him a Pathfinder Ordnance Survey and you've made his day.'

'And Hugh?'

Stevie grinned. 'High as a kite after that little adventure at The Old Rectory. I wish I'd been in on that myself.' Her expression changed. 'I've warned him about overoptimism but he's so relieved that Nell hasn't married Daniel that it's gone to his head. It hasn't quite registered yet that it doesn't necessarily mean she's going to fall into his arms instead.'

'Poor Hugh. If I had my way I'd have my wretched sister marrying him tomorrow.'

'Do you know yet when she's coming home?'

'According to her scrappy postcard, very late the day after tomorrow.'

'Perhaps we should send Hugh to meet her.'

'I'm afraid she'd never forgive us for interfering matchmakers!'

There was a pause in the conversation. The party at the bar noisily continued to celebrate the birthday of one of their number. Stevie pushed her plate and glass aside and leaned forward.

'You will let me know, won't you,' she said, 'as soon as you decide what you're going to do? But I think you should consider very carefully before you commit yourself to your marriage vows in a way that will condemn you to a life of misery. I've told you there would be a place for you in Bonne Bouche, but you don't have to go along with that either, if you don't think it's for you. It's your life. You have to decide what you really want to do.'

Desna twisted her hands together, her knuckles white. 'You're an independent woman, Stevie, so you've no idea how absolutely terrifying that is,' she said.

'Coffee?' the stewardess offered.

Nell nodded. 'Thank you.' Anything to stay awake. Heathrow would not be the end of her journey. She gazed out into a darkness that reflected only the ghostly images of herself and the stewardess passing and repassing behind her. Now it seemed that she had been away far longer than three weeks. Persis had insisted that she stay as long as she liked, just as she had insisted on loaning her the villa and paying for her flight. She had accepted, not particularly graciously, thinking that Persis owed her *that* at least. Not Aunt Persis: her mother. She had to keep reminding herself of that; for she had no longer any doubt that what Persis had told her was true.

Since she had, after all, decided that she had to go on with her life somehow, she supposed she would have to get a job and find somewhere to live. Both her sisters would offer to put her up, so would Mo, but she couldn't face any of them. No one would say, 'I told you so,' but she would never be able to bear their sympathetic looks while, privately, they all shook their heads and thought her a fool. Before she left, Winnie had offered her a bed for a few nights until she got fixed up. She would go to Winnie. Winnie understood the risks involved in love affairs better than any of Nell's well-meaning relatives.

Besides, she wasn't ready for Mo yet. She still blamed her for not being her mother. And for not telling her.

The engine note of the Boeing 767 changed and points of light appeared outside the window as they leaned down into the final approach.

Desna and Mo were waiting at the barrier. Nell nearly turned her head away when Mo kissed her. Desna grabbed her holdall.

'Come on, darling. You look exhausted. Let's get to the car and take you home.'

'Home?' Nell repeated dazedly. The truth was that she no longer had a home; or a business. The contents of the flat and shop were now at The Old Rectory or Cornucopia. Daniel had probably sold it all off by now as a punishment for leaving him at the registry office with egg on his face. Humiliation of that kind he would not easily forgive.

CHAPTER TWENTY-EIGHT

The ceiling fan turned lazily overhead, wafting warm air over Desna's face. The horizon neatly divided sapphire sky from a sea that varied in colour from citrine to peacock and cerulean. The other islands were smudges of lavender, the sails of distant yachts mere punctuation marks. To one side of the wide verandah of the estate house reared the peaks of Tortola covered in frangipani and groves of banana and mangoes. Goats roamed the lush paradise, geckos waited on the white walls for unwary insects. It was a land of idyll and legend: Blackbeard, Treasure Island and exotic natural wonders. A playground for the rich and famous.

That morning Desna had swum and snorkled in a blue bay while Roy and Enrico discussed business down at the marina. She had hovered in clear water watching scarlet, yellow and turquoise reef fish lazily cruise or dart in restless shoals. It would have been perfect but for the fact that she had to return to reality and the same besetting problems as before.

Roy and Enrico were speaking to her of customized Beneteaus, of luxury thirty-three metre Jongerts, all yachts in their new fleet; and how they would be equipped with the latest Global Position Systems, echo sounding, luxury staterooms fitted out with teak and mahogany plundered from the world's endangered rainforests. They spoke of sheltered anchorages, trade winds, chase boats, and repair and provisioning facilities; of making money.

They were drinking rum punches, both the men sprawled in cushioned steamer chairs, taking time off to subject her to concentrated, not-too-subtle, sales talk.

'Paradise, eh, Des!' Roy said, his strong legs spread wide, his drink winking in the afternoon sun. His complexion had taken on a deeper tan than usual. A handsome man, with his thick silver hair. 'It'll be like being on one long holiday.'

'Yes, it's quite fabulous,' Desna agreed. She watched a gecko catch a fly with a hardly detectable movement.

'Promised you she'd change her mind once she'd seen for herself,' Roy winked knowingly at Enrico. Enrico was wearing pristine white slacks and a blue and white striped casual shirt, gold on his wrist and finger.

'Such a pity that Philip and Harriet were not able to come too,' Enrico said. 'It would help them to make up their minds. I myself thought that they would be "over the moon" as you say it.'

'Don't worry,' Roy assured him. 'Philip's already familiar with the islands. He did some skippering in the Caribbean in his time. He won't need too much convincing in the end, depend upon it. I expect he thinks he needs a bit of time to butter up that unenterprising daughter of mine. Young love, eh!' he laughed. 'He'll soon learn that women don't respect a bloke who's forever deferring to her, who doesn't know his own mind.' He glanced at Desna triumphantly. Desna swirled her drink round in the tall glass, not meeting his eyes. In the corner by the wall a cockroach made a daring daytime sortie. It was one of many Desna had noticed in this otherwise luxurious house. She had a horror of cockroaches that almost amounted to panic; they reminded her of a house they'd lived in for a year when she was twelve. Nell and Emmet had appeared oblivious but the cockroaches had made a lasting impression on Desna.

'We'll take off for Spring Bay and The Baths tomorrow,' Roy promised her. 'You'll like that. Natural wonders and so on.' The Moody had been sailed to the BVI some weeks previously. Now it awaited them at the marina. 'After that we'll take a look at property. That should interest you, Des.'

'Of course. That will be lovely,' she said. Both men looked at her quizzically for a moment. Roy was so absorbed in his present stratagems that she knew he was unaware that her response

414

was less than whole-hearted. Not that he'd care anyway. Her opinion counted for very little at this stage. But she believed Enrico saw beneath the surface to her inner discontent, probably speculated on how far she would allow it to affect her actions. Enrico was far shrewder than Roy where women were concerned.

'Roy has told me of your sister's unfortunate experience with that small-time crook,' Enrico said. 'I was sorry to hear it.'

'Daniel isn't exactly a crook.' For some reason Desna felt obliged to defend Daniel. 'He misinformed her about his financial situation, that's all. I'm sure many men do that.' She directed a slow gaze at Enrico and he smiled, thinking that he might have underestimated her.

'All the same, I hope you will convey my regrets to her. Though I may do so myself when we return to the UK.'

'I think it's too soon,' Desna said quickly. 'It will take her some time to get over this.'

'Of course. What a pity she couldn't have come out here with you and Roy. I would have done my utmost to see that she forgot that bad egg, believe me.'

'Right,' Roy said, impatient with a subject which interested him hardly at all. 'Enrico, let's take a look-see at those proposals for provisioning the club-class boats. I think we could make some cuts there without it affecting the product.'

That night they dined on French cuisine in an expensive restaurant. At some of the best tables Desna saw one or two famous faces from the pages of *Hello!* magazine. She wished now that Nell had come after all. Or Stevie. Except that she couldn't visualize Stevie in such a setting.

She had successfully schooled herself over the years against the need to confide in another female; until now she had counted it a sign of weakness. Or had it been simply a rationalization of her need to avoid Roy's disapproval of her having any close friends at all?

She drank more than she was used to and became very slightly drunk. Roy put it down to her relaxing her usual abstemiousness because they were on holiday. The truth was that she had ceased to care. She no longer had any incentive to watch her weight; besides alcohol helped to blunt the impact of Roy's insistent sexual demands that would be sure to come later. In the rented estate house with its spacious open plan there was no escaping them. She yearned for Mount Huish, for the river's reassuring murmur and for moist green woods.

The dead sheep had somehow become entangled with the piers underneath the boathouse.

'It must have fallen into the river further up and drowned,' Harriet said, unlocking the boathouse. 'I'll fetch a boathook. Maybe we can give it a shove.'

Philip took the boathook from her and attempted to prise the corpse free. 'This is not how I envisaged spending our time,' he said, grunting with the effort. He was staying at Mount Huish while Roy and Desna were away. Harriet had taken a week off, she was supposed to be shopping for her going-away clothes. Faith would come in a day or two and then there would be final dress fittings for them both.

'It must have fallen in some time ago. It still has its fleece,' Harriet said. 'The ones in our fields have all been shorn.'

'Ugh.' Philip made a grimace of disgust. 'It's a bit gamy.'

The body was bloated, almost blue, its wool half worn away, its legs set stiffly at each corner. The crows had been at it, probably the seagulls too. The head was already almost a skull, the flesh round the mouth had disappeared to reveal yellow teeth. Harriet would like to have drawn it but she did not dare suggest it to Philip who was in too much of a hurry to send it on its way.

A ketch puttered downstream under power. A man and a woman in identical waterproofs and yachting caps saluted politely, apparently not noticing Philip's grisly task. Swallows zipped about overhead emitting a high-pitched whistling. The pair of egrets that now seemed quite at home, preened themselves on the top branches of an oak.

'Ah, that's got it,' Philip said. He pushed the dead sheep into the moving current and they watched it revolve slowly. 'Like Eeyore,' Harriet said. 'Poor old thing. But it was probably a better end than being driven for twenty hours in a lorry before snuffing it in some appalling Spanish slaughterhouse.'

'You're being a bit morbid, aren't you?' Philip said. 'Bloody hell. I can still smell it! Anyway, it's SEP now.'

'Eh?'

'Someone else's problem.' He sloshed the boathook about in the water, then stashed it back in the boathouse. He turned to her. 'Look, we've got an hour before I have to be back at the yard. Let's go to bed.'

'Now?'

'Why? Haven't you ever heard of love in the afternoon? Specially, a nice lazy, hot afternoon, and preferably unaccompanied by dead sheep.'

Harriet chuckled.

'That's better,' he said. 'I like to hear you laugh. You don't do it enough.'

'There isn't much to laugh at lately with this new scheme of Daddy's in the air. Mummy's terribly upset about it.'

They walked up the path to the house, their arms round each other. With her parents away, Harriet was visibly more relaxed.

'Perhaps she'll change her mind when she sees Tortola,' Philip said comfortingly.

'And will you? Change your mind about going over there with the firm, I mean?'

He shook his head. 'I've been thinking about this notion we have for going it alone. I talked it over with the old man last night and he was pretty keen. Surprisingly really. I thought he would have been all for me going to the BVI. He says he doesn't trust the Italian. Not because he's an Italian, mind you. I'll say this for the old man, he's pretty square but he hasn't the xenophobic tendencies of some I could name.'

'Would he help you financially, d'you think?'

'As much as he could, probably.'

'Do you think we could manage?'

Philip gave her waist a squeeze. 'You make me feel as if I could do anything, Harry.'

'I expect we shall have to rely on more than feelings,' Harriet said, frowning. 'We shall have to talk about ways and means.'

'Don't be so bloody practical!' He kissed her.

When later that afternoon, they lay on her bed, naked, warm air moved across their bodies, saturated with the scent of summer roses. The shadows of house martins flickered restlessly about the room. In the distance a hay baler clattered and droned.

She was getting used to seeing Philip's body. Getting used to its demands too, though she never admitted to him that she didn't enjoy what they did together. Her mother had been right, it did get better in that her body seemed to have accommodated itself to the strange invasion; though she had only once felt a flicker, a merest hint, of what sex was obviously supposed to feel like. But she had learned what was expected fast, and because it was Philip and because she loved him, she hid her real feelings and made an effort to please him.

He stroked the warm, inner plane of her thigh and searched out her more secret places. He coaxed her hand to similar explorations. One day perhaps she would overcome her reluctance and learn the kind of spontaneity he sought from her.

Roy and Desna returned. Harriet was distressed to see that her mother looked even more unhappy than before, although only apparently to her own attuned eye. Philip, Isabel, Giles and even Roy declared her to be on top form; tanned, relaxed and more stunning than ever, according to them.

Faith arrived, wresting time from the exigencies of her impending finals. Her fitting was duly completed, without Tessa this time.

'I hope you appreciate that growing my hair has ruined my street cred,' she complained as she emerged from a cocoon of grey silk.

'I'm sure you'll survive,' Harriet grinned. 'I'll help you shear it off the minute the wedding's over if you like.'

Then it was Harriet's turn. She stood rigidly while Mrs Gillimore tucked and pinned. Desna and Faith watched, Faith sitting astride a bentwood chair, her booted feet planted firmly each side, her arms across the back.

'Not bad,' she conceded. 'You look almost like a real bride.'

'What d'you mean, almost?' Mrs Gillimore laughed, not altogether pleased with the bridesmaid's running commentary; or her appearance if it came to that, in spite of the fact she'd grown her shorn hair, thank goodness. And were those magenta glasses strictly necessary?

'Well, you know. Like everyone else.'

'Could you raise your arm a bit, Harriet dear,' Mrs Gillimore said, kneeling on the floor. Harriet obediently raised her arm.

'No, I don't think Harriet could ever look like everyone else,' Mrs Gillimore opined, glancing at Desna with a smile as she pinned the fabric so that it rested precisely on Harriet's narrow hipbone. Desna said nothing. If Harriet looked like any other bride then all the enormous expense would have been wasted. But then Faith had liked to knock anything remotely tasteful. It was just her youthful compulsion to shock.

'You look Italian,' Faith assured Harriet.

'Is that good?'

'Oh sure. The Italians are mega sophisticated,' Faith said airily.

'It'll please Signor Bonicelli then.' Harriet smiled wanly.

'I think that's about it,' Mrs Gillimore said, leaning back on her heels. 'Turn round, would you, Harriet, dear. Then have a look in the long mirror.'

Harriet looked and saw, as Faith had remarked, a bride like any other. Like a very tasteful Barbie Doll. She felt ridiculous, as if she'd just stepped off a production line labelled 'Brides'.

Desna looked at her daughter and thought how beautiful, how ethereal she appeared, even without the headdress.

'Abfab, darling,' Faith said. 'The biz. But Harry is one of those people who would look great in a bin bag.'

The last remark caused Mrs Gillimore to button her mouth against a tart reply. Days and days of work had gone into creating this gown. She would be glad to see the back of this obstreperous bridesmaid.

'Well, I don't think there will be any necessity for Harriet to wear a bin bag on her wedding day,' Desna said with a slight smile. 'She'll just have to be content with this.'

Faith grinned at Desna and put an arm round her waist, giving her an almost painful squeeze. 'Harriet, you've got a great ma,' she said. Under her tan, Desna's colour became very slightly heightened.

'The twins and Tessa have made an arrangement to come in next week. Do you want to be here for their fitting?' Mrs Gillimore asked. Desna suddenly felt exhausted at the thought of coming in again.

'No, I'm happy to leave it to you,' she said. 'You know what's wanted.'

As Desna drove them back to Mount Huish Harriet told Faith about the proposed sale of Mount Huish.

'Sell Mount Huish!' Faith yelped. 'You can't sell Mount Huish, Mrs H. You can't!'

'Roy wants to move the business,' Desna said. Harriet filled Faith in on the rest of the story.

'It will mean we have to live there, I'm afraid,' Desna said impassively.

'Sounds OK. Nice place I should think,' Faith conceded. 'But why give up Mount Huish? I can't bear it, Harry. Mount Huish is part of my childhood too, you know! Besides, you love it, don't you, Mrs H.?'

Harriet shot Faith a warning glance but it became apparent that her mother's famous composure was taking over.

'Sometimes one has to accept change,' Desna said. 'We outgrow certain stages of our lives and have to go on to other things.'

They arrived home. Desna swept the Fiat round in a semicircle and parked in front of the house.

'I can't believe how philosophical your ma is about this here move,' Faith said, as Harriet showed her to the guest room Faith usually occupied. Having to share at Easter had been an exception owing to the number of guests.

'I don't believe she is, actually,' Harriet said. 'I believe she's terribly upset, yet she's not saying much at all. But you know Mummy; talking about feelings makes her uncomfortable.'

'You'll be with Philip, and Rupert will be away at school, perhaps she thinks Mount Huish will be too big for just the two of them.'

'I don't think so.' Harriet stood at the window. From here she could see a distant view of Totnes church and miles beyond it. Ugborough Beacon and Eastern Whitaburrow on the fringes of Dartmoor. All views that were part of her childhood too.

Below her on her secluded terrace at the side of the house, Desna had taken her tea to the stone bench and was sitting in the dappled shade. The extra planting had been a success; the Pink Perpetue had almost covered the balustrade and the wisteria had flowered for the first time that spring. Next year should be even better.

And then came one of the constant small shocks that hit her anew each time she remembered that next year she wouldn't be here. Someone else would be thinking of this luxuriant bower as theirs; or perhaps they would have ripped it all out and concreted it over. She drank her tea. Everything was changing, she thought. Even Mo hadn't been quite the same since Easter. Roy had been harsh with her for bringing Persis to the house but what else could she have done? Persis' visit had been a disaster all round and had thoroughly unsettled Mo. And poor Nell had been desperately depressed and uncommunicative since she had returned from Greece; even Mo had hardly seen her. And who could blame her for being depressed at allowing herself to be conned twice by the same man? Desna found herself blaming Nell just a little for being a fool over Daniel but when it came to making a sacrifice of oneself over a man, who could say that she was any better? Nell had found a bedsit in Totnes. She had told Desna that she still had money in the bank but Desna guessed that was more by accident than design. Her sister's rescued furniture was still stacked in a spare room upstairs. Every time Desna rang her suggesting they met Nell made some excuse.

A robin piped at her loudly from the lime-green leaves of the wisteria. He was probably warning her off what he regarded as his patch. He was right. He would still be here when she was long gone.

There were sounds from the kitchen and Harriet and Faith came through to the terrace.

'You look like a Rossetti painting, Mrs H.,' Faith said. *'Persephone in her Bower.* You want to watch some dark stranger doesn't come and carry you away in his chariot.'

Harriet glanced at Faith wondering if she realized the aptness of her words.

'Who's carrying who off?' Roy appeared behind Faith and Harriet, apparently in a good humour. He spread his arms wide and put a hand on each of the young women's shoulders. 'Hallo, Faith! Still wasting the tax payers' money making stacks of bricks?' He laughed jovially. He retained a dim folk memory of some scandal at the Tate over a sculptor and a pile of bricks.

Faith's eyes narrowed behind her glasses. She slipped deftly out from the restraining arm. 'Right. Still hacking on.'

'That's stupid, Daddy,' Harriet dared to say. 'You don't know what Faith does.'

'Only joking! Only joking! Roy said. 'Best not to mention what Faith gets up to, eh! I've heard about art colleges.' He laughed and took a cigar from his breast pocket. His complexion was higher than usual. Desna was afraid he had had slightly too much to drink. Entertaining the new clients, she suspected – a couple who had won the pools and were in the process of buying from Hindmarch Marine.

'I've put the kettle on again,' she said because she could see Faith's dark brows drawn together in a thunderous scowl. 'Let's go and make some tea. Faith, I made some chocolate brownies because I remembered you like them.'

'I wish my ma remembered things like that,' Faith said. 'But going home does my head in these days.'

Before dinner and during the meal Roy increased his intake of alcohol by a couple of whiskies and two glasses of wine. Afterwards he had a large brandy.

Since they had returned from the Virgin Islands Desna had slept in one of the spare rooms. The holiday on Tortola had been a nightmare because of the impossibility of escaping Roy's attentions. She had come to the conclusion that he had begun to enjoy taking her against her will, as if it was something she'd dreamed up to add spice to their sex life.

The spare room Desna had chosen was not far from the master bedroom but some distance from Harriet's room because she didn't intend Harriet to know of the new arrangement if she could help it. Faith slept in one of the guest rooms on the floor above. It was a hot night and Desna had pushed off all covering except a sheet. It was one o'clock and she still hovered on the verge of sleep when there was a knock on the door.

'Who is it?'

'It's Roy. Unlock the door.'

She sat up in bed. Sudden heat soaked her in sweat. 'No, Roy. Go back to bed.'

'If you don't open the door,' he said very quietly but still audible, 'I shall hammer on it until you do.'

'You'll wake the girls.'

'Precisely.'

The shame of that possibility was too bad to think about. All the same, he could be bluffing. She refused again and he began to carry out his threat. The noise was terrifying. She flew to the door and opened it. He barged in, pushing her towards the bed as he came.

'No!' she said, attempting to resist. 'I won't put up with it.'

'What about wifely duties?' he mocked, breathing heavily. 'Have you forgotten those?'

'I've paid that debt in full,' she said. She wrenched herself out of his grasp and reached for her dressing gown. 'I want no more of it.'

'What makes you think you have a choice?'

'Because it's rape. You can be had up for rape.'

'A lot of bloody feminist nonsense, that's what that is.' He reached for her again but she slid out of his grasp.

'If you go on like this,' she cried, 'I shall go to sleep in Harriet's room!' She was standing at the door now, clutching her dressing gown together at her breast.

423

'Come here, you bitch,' he said. For a moment they wrestled in an intense and degrading silence. What allowed her to escape was a small thing. He caught the back of one of his heels under the stretcher of a chair that stood, for mostly decorative purposes, by the door. He grunted in pain and for a moment let her go.

Desna flew out of the door and along the gallery, not to Harriet's room but to one of the other guest rooms. She shut the door quietly, leaning against it gasping for breath, hoping that he hadn't seen her and that he would suppose she was with Harriet. She doubted that he would go to Harriet's room, even in his present mood. She was trembling and her heart pounded against her ribs like a trapped animal. She couldn't believe what was happening to her. These things just didn't occur in the well-ordered lives of the kind of people she knew. They just didn't. Choking sobs burst from her throat as she crouched against the door. To muffle the sound she pulled her dressing gown over her head.

Roy sat on the chair, breathing heavily and rubbing his heel. His anger at Desna's successful rejection was like a volcano inside him. He desperately needed to punish her. He couldn't *not* win. He was not used to denial in anything. It was a compulsion so strong that it drove him, almost as if he himself was at its mercy. The adrenaline racing round his body felt as if it would have powered a rocket; it had to have an outlet. He was a strong man and sailing kept him fit; the pain in his heel did not detain him long. He had no clear thoughts as he left the room, but acted instinctively. He was sweating profusely, his brain spinning with rage and alcohol.

He padded along the gallery, his feet bare, wearing only the dressing gown he had pulled on earlier. He paused for a second at Harriet's door and, hearing nothing, plunged on along the gallery and up the stairs to the top floor. He stopped at the bedroom where Faith had slept when she came to stay ever since she was a child at school. If he'd known then that she would turn into a slut he would never have had her in the house. But since she *was* in the house . . .

He tried the door. It wasn't locked, which proved to him at

once what sort of girl she was. The room was in darkness, but as his eyes got used to it, the faintest of midsummer gloaming revealed the bed and Faith's humped figure. Now in an urgent hurry, he dragged off his dressing gown and knelt beside her, pulling at the sheet which appeared to be wound round her sleeping form.

'What in the Sam Hill?' Faith lunged over and switched on the bedside light. 'Mr Hindmarch! What's your game?'

'I thought we might have a bit of a romp together, you and I, now everyone else is asleep.' His breath was coming fast as he reached for her breasts. He could see now that she was wearing only a longish tee shirt with nothing underneath. When she had woken it had rucked up to her waist revealing her smooth, strong legs and her neat fanny. He smiled as she pulled it down in a provocative gesture. Saucy minx!

'Sorry, Mr H., but you've screwed up this one. I think you should piss off back to your wife.'

'Come on. Don't tell me that you don't put it about a bit. I know your sort. You might fool Harriet and Desna but you can't fool me.'

Faith was by now standing on the far side of the bed. He couldn't take much more of this delay. His erection was almost painful. He moved quickly for so large a man, taking her by surprise. He grabbed her and began to tug at her tee shirt at the same time trying to force her back on to the bed.

'Look, chill out, won't you?' Faith gasped. 'I don't want to get heavy but if you don't pack it in, I have to warn you, you'll be sorry.'

'I doubt that!' He pressed his hot face against her neck.

'You *will* be sorry!'

'You're a little goer, aren't you?' He held on to her.

'OK then,' Faith said, and she brought her knee up into his groin with all her considerable force.

He keeled over at once with a terrible moan of agony and slid to the floor clutching at himself. He thought he might have a heart attack at the pain of it.

Faith picked up her magenta-coloured spectacles from the

bedside table and put them on, tucking them behind her ears. With them on she could see properly at last. Mr Hindmarch looked even redder than before in their rose-tinted glow.

'Sorry about that,' she said matter-of-factly. 'But you did ask for it, didn't you, and I did warn you.'

'Bitch, cow, dirty scrubber,' he muttered disjointedly, his breath hissing between his lips.

'When you're ready,' she said, by way of reply, 'I think you'd better go.'

He stumbled across the room, bending over like Groucho Marx. He fumbled for the door handle and let himself out.

Faith locked the door after him, straightened the bedside rug, drank from her glass of water, removed her spectacles again and got into bed. She went back to sleep almost at once.

Below her, Desna got stiffly to her feet from her crouched position and lay on top of the bed. She heard faint sounds, the closing of their bedroom door and then silence. At last her heart stopped leaping in her breast and her breathing slowed to normal. At least he hadn't attempted to wake Harriet up.

For the very first time she was beginning to see things with twenty-twenty vision. In handing power over to another person unconditionally as she had, she saw that she had been an accomplice in the making of a tyrant. All the insignificant little capitulations she'd made over the years had all gone to construct a monster, handing him the status almost of a god. But it wasn't in the nature of tyrants to be content with almost total domination; they had to hound their subjects until they were absolutely sure that no trace of defiance whatever still existed.

'Are there any sandwiches left?' Laura's face shone damply, her pale hair stuck to her temples and cheeks.

'I think so,' Nell said, looking in the bag. 'Are you still hungry?'

'No. We want to throw them to the seagulls, Theo and me.'

'Theo and I,' Hugh said automatically.

'Oh, Hugh! Shut up!' Nell said, smiling as she fished out the box containing the remains of the picnic.

'Thanks.' Laura grabbed the box and ran towards the stern of the boat where Theo was waiting. The gulls glided lazily over the wake of the pleasure craft but with their eyes ever peeled for the possible titbit.

'Don't throw the box too,' Nell called.

It hadn't been such a bad day after all, she thought. That morning she couldn't have felt less like going anywhere, let alone a boat trip down the Dart and four hours on a beach. But the feeling of nausea that she'd woken to had worn off while at the same time the dreary walls of the bedsit closed in. There seemed no good reason to refuse Hugh's invitation for an innocuous day out chaperoned by two children.

A breeze had sprung up on the return journey; it tugged at her hair and blew Hugh's longish forelock over his face. She watched him laughing at the children's antics. She had even laughed herself once or twice that day.

Hugh zipped up the bag and pushed it back under the seat. He glanced at Nell. The tan she had acquired in Greece had already been wearing off but now there was a renewed pinkness across her cheekbones. It became her. Asking her to stand in for Stevie had been a ploy, though it was genuine enough. Stevie had a big wedding to attend to in Torquay. He hoped that the presence of the children would convince Nell that there would be no heavy emotional undertones, no ulterior motives on his part and after some persuasion, it had worked. He *had* ulterior motives, of course, but they were well buried. He was convinced that even the slightest hint that he still entertained some expectations of something more than friendship would send her scuttling back into her shell.

The boat ploughed up the river towards Totnes with its attendant skein of gulls. They had passed Hindmarch Marine and were now approaching that part of the river where high woods cascaded to the waterline. Above, in a pale azure sky streaked by high cirrus, two parent buzzards wheeled and mewed, followed by their two smaller progeny.

'There's my sister's house, up on the right. You can just see it through the trees,' Nell said. 'Mo's cottage is further up river.'

'Stevie says that Mount Huish is for sale.'

'Uh-huh. Poor Desna. It's a terrible blow. She adores the place.'

'I rather gathered that. I hope the sale turns out not to be necessary.'

'My family don't seem to be having what you might call successful lives lately, do they?'

'Winnie says you're still doing the interior design schemes.'

'I seem to be busier than ever,' she said with a certain amount of wonder. 'I suppose now I no longer have the shop I'm accepting more commissions.'

'I understand you were responsible for the Mount Huish interiors. I thought they were stunning.'

It was the closest he'd come to a personal remark. Nell looked at him thoughtfully. He sat with one arm hooked over the back of the varnished seat. He was wearing an open-necked Viyella shirt, and a venerable navy guernsey tied round his shoulders by the sleeves; although he had on a pair of fairly disreputable jeans she noticed that he still clung to his excellent quality brogues. She smiled to herself. She realized that she felt not only at ease, but happy. The black dogs of depression and despair were at bay for a few hours. It was hard for them to coexist with the solid presence of Hugh and the high spirits of the children.

She watched as Laura and Theo tossed scraps of sandwich to the gulls, testing how adept they were at catching in mid-air.

'I hope they don't throw *themselves* into the water,' Nell said.

Hugh shook his head. 'They've always been encouraged to take responsibility for themselves. As soon as it was practical, anyway,' he said.

'I'm sure I should be too protective . . .' Nell began. She stopped. Parenthood was a dangerous subject just now. 'I meant to tell you,' she added quickly, 'how grateful I am to you for getting my stuff back from Cornucopia. And from The Old Rectory. There was no need to have gone to all that trouble, you know. I was quite resigned to its loss. I don't know how you managed to persuade Daniel to part with it at all. I was so sure he'd hang on to it . . .' There! She'd mentioned his name! It must be for the first time.

'I think he did have some thoughts about keeping it at first.'

Hugh himself had paid a visit to Cornucopia with his solicitor. Fortunately Winnie's friend Moira, who was in any case working out her notice, had kept a detailed inventory of the stock that had arrived from Alfresco; Daniel had succumbed after a few token arguments. Hugh was almost sorry for him. Customs and Excise had caught up with him at last. His flashy car had gone, The Old Rectory was up for sale, staff at Cornucopia had been got rid of, Daniel himself was lucky to have escaped with just his gigantic debts. But Hugh had no doubt that Daniel Thorne would bounce back. His kind always did. There would be other females equally prepared to be charmed, courted and finally, betrayed. There ought to be a government health warning stamped on the bugger's forehead, Hugh thought vengefully. Not that it would help. In all probability it would make him more attractive still.

They were passing Mo's cottage. The Wild children were playing on the quay. There was no sign of Mo.

'I must go and see Mo,' Nell said suddenly. 'I'm afraid I've been very unjust.'

Hugh looked at Nell curiously. 'You! Unjust!'

'I've hardly spoken to her since I came back from Greece. I'm afraid she's dreadfully hurt.'

Without really meaning to, Nell found herself telling Hugh about Persis and the story of her own unconventional birth and upbringing. It came out disjointedly and imperfectly but complete enough for Hugh to understand.

'I haven't told anyone else yet,' she said.

'I take that as a privilege then.' Hugh's spirits lifted in something like exultation. 'I've never met either Mo or Persis but it seems to me that Mo acted as she thought best. As Persis had agreed to keep out of the way she probably thought it very unlikely that you'd ever meet. I personally think that children should be told things like that as soon as they're able to understand, but not everyone agrees of course. What will you do?'

'Go and see Mo. Soon.'

'Good. I think you should.'

Nell looked at Hugh quizzically. Yes, he was the sort of man who would approve of cards on tables. He was a highly moral being. Not like Daniel, whose motives were governed by expediency, living off the cuff as it were. She wondered what Hugh really thought of her now he knew what a fool she'd been. Weak? Stupid? Not worth bothering about? Yet he'd asked her out for the day, albeit in the company of two children. Was he just being kind or was it possible he still carried a torch for her?

The box empty, Theo and Laura raced back to the adults.

'Did you see those two fighting in the water over that piece of sandwich?' Theo said. 'They were trying to drown each other. Wow!'

'Our sandwiches are obviously a highly desirable commodity,' Hugh said grinning.

Theo fished out the Pathfinder map and began to trace their progress up the river as he had traced it coming down.

Laura cast herself down next to Nell and laid her head on Nell's shoulder. 'Phew! I'm knackered,' she said.

'Laura! Where did you hear that gem?' Hugh said.

'*You* said it the other day!' she accused him correctly.

'Did I? Then I'm equally at fault.'

'Anyway. All the kids at the stables say it.'

'Not a happy choice of words in that context, I'm afraid.'

'Why not?' Laura wanted to know.

While Hugh explained, as far as necessary, the origins and meanings of the word to Laura, she leaned her head unselfconsciously against Nell. Nell put her arm round her, feeling something deep inside her respond to the child's proximity. It was too early for actual, physical stirrings; it was more like a correspondence, a mutual exchange.

The pregnancy tester she'd bought at the chemists had produced a positive result. The doctor and the morning sickness had subsequently confirmed it. But there was no reason for her to be surprised that she was pregnant for hadn't she almost consciously engineered it? That was before she'd found out that the father of this new life inside her was not the man she believed him to be. She had taken a considerable risk, trusting, as she had, Daniel's assurances that there was no question of the dreaded virus. He himself believed her to be on the pill, which was true, in the beginning. Two warring emotions, elation and dismay, struggled for supremacy. Yes, tonight she would go and see Mo. There was a great deal to tell her.

'Did you know that this bit of the river is called The Gut?' Theo informed them.

'It's the right shape,' Hugh responded, but his attention was elsewhere. All that mattered to him at the moment was that his daughter was being held close by Nell as if it were the most natural thing in the world; and both of them seemingly unconscious of its wonderful, heart-stopping, breathtaking significance to him.

Nell drove over to Papermill Quay that evening. Mo was busy stretching a new canvas, angrily aware that, in her present mood, she might not be able to cover it by anything other than some fatuous daub.

'Nellie, darling!' she said almost in trepidation. She threw down the staple gun she'd been using. The summer sun and wind had tanned her already brown complexion to a leathery darkness against her pale sandy-grey hair with its fuzzy plait.

Nell put her arms round Mo without speaking and held her close for a whole minute. When she let her go there were tears in both women's eyes.

'I'm sorry,' Nell said.

'Sweetie, it doesn't matter. I was to blame as much as anyone. I should have known that Persis would never be able to keep the secret indefinitely. I should have told you years ago.'

'It was hateful of me to treat you like I did after you'd brought me up and never made me feel any different from the others.'

'You *were* no different from the others as far as I was concerned. I loved all of you equally.'

'I know, I know. And things were so difficult for you when we were small.'

'We managed.'

'I loved my childhood. I didn't even mind some of the funny houses we lived in.'

'No, you didn't. And Emmet always settled down as casually as some gypsy child.'

'It's funny, but Desna was the one who got upset by the constant moving. She absolutely hated some of the places we lived in.' Nell smiled. 'I expect that's why she did that catering course.'

There was a small silence. Mo collected a couple of chairs and put them outside the front door. Flocks of gulls and high-flying swallows filled the evening air. The tide was fully in, gently caressing the side of the quay and almost completely engulfing the black ribs of *Prudence*. The yachtsmen out on the river struggled to trim their sails to catch the faintest remaining zephyr but the surface of the water was disturbed only by the occasional fish snatching at a fly – a mirror reflecting sky, woods, the coloured sails and the waterside dwellings.

Mo fetched drinks and they sat, watching the scene.

'I suppose I better tell you my version,' Mo said. She did, but the facts were the same in everything but small detail. At least Persis had not tried to conceal the fact that she had thrown herself at Alec.

'But there was no excuse for him, whatever I say to Persis,' Mo said severely. 'There was no getting away from the fact that she was under age and that the very least he could have done was to ensure that she didn't conceive.' She smiled and patted Nell's arm. 'Even though the outcome was you!'

'My father sounds totally irresponsible.'

'When it came to women, yes he was. Completely. But there you are. In quite a lot of important ways, he was very like Daniel.'

'Do you think that was why I fell for Daniel?'

Mo shrugged. 'I'm not very up on all this Freudian stuff. I think most of it's humbug myself.'

Nell chuckled.

'Will you see Persis again?' Mo asked cautiously.

'I think I will. I know now that I rather hurt her feelings too. Because she's so truculent I was tempted to believe that she hadn't any feelings to hurt; but she made all the arrangements for me to go to the villa. She didn't want me to pay for anything. It was almost as if she knew Daniel would let me down.'

'Perhaps she saw the likeness to Alec as well.' Mo stretched out her legs in their baggy pants. Her feet in their worn sandals were dark brown, her long toes skinny and almost prehensile. 'You know, Persis drove me almost out of my head while she was here, but in fact she isn't as bad as she likes everyone to believe.' Mo grinned. 'Though I couldn't think of anything worse than to have to live with her all the time. You know that Desna has asked her to the wedding?'

'After what she did at Easter!' Nell exclaimed.

'She said she was grateful to Persis though I can't think what for. She behaved abominably to Desna when Desna came to tell me about Mount Huish being sold.'

'Does Desna know about Persis being my mother? Does anyone know?'

'No. I've told no one. Not without your permission. I'll leave it up to you.'

Nell leaned over and kissed Mo's leathery cheek. 'Bless you.' For a moment she turned to watch the antics of the crew of a yacht that had managed to run itself on to a sandbank. 'Mo. There's something I have to tell you.'

Mo glanced at Nell. She still thought of her as her daughter and always would.

'I'm pregnant,' Nell said.

Mo stared at her. 'Pregnant! Oh, my God!'

'Don't look like that. You see, I don't mind about it. In fact, I'm glad.'

'But how could it have happened!'

'The usual way, I imagine,' Nell smiled.

'But how could you have let yourself in for an accident like that? And how can you be so . . . so serene?'

Nell got up and walked to the edge of the quay, still holding her drink; mineral water with a splash of lemonade. No more alcohol for her, for the time being at least. This was one baby that was going to get the best possible start.

'It wasn't an accident,' she said. 'I wanted this baby.'

CHAPTER TWENTY-NINE

Harriet stood at her bedroom window and looked down to where she had once been able to see lawn. Now, except for a section near the terrace and another at the far end near the trees, it was almost all covered by an enormous marquee. Gay ribbons fluttered from it and great urns of pink and white roses bordered the canvas tunnel that had been constructed as a triumphal pathway from the door of the conservatory. But there would be no real need of it today. It wasn't going to rain. In fact, though it was early, the sun already struck warm on her bare arms.

She had woken before six. Sounds of activity and the heavy scent of roses were filling the air by seven. Collared doves indulged their repetitive brooding conversations, interrupted now and again by the hectic call of the woodpecker and the mewing of gulls. Beyond the trees and the river the countryside had sizzled in summer heat for a week. Fireweed bloomed on the verges of roads, the downy seeds of sow thistle and dandelion drifted on almost still air. Young house martins dived and swooped above dark woods and blond fields. Everyone said that they hoped the weather would hold.

Her mother had told Harriet how pleased she was with the efficiency of Stevie Turnbull's arrangements so far. Harriet liked Mrs Turnbull; she was friendly and unpatronizing and treated her like a grown-up.

As the wedding day approached, and with it the time for the changeover for Hindmarch Marine, her father had become more overbearing, more dictatorial and more grimly unyielding than ever. Harriet could hear him now shouting orders, calling to her mother. If she hadn't thought it impossible she would have said her father's behaviour had been brought on by anxiety over the enormous leap of faith he was about to take.

Downstairs in a little-used sitting room, the presents were loaded on to every available surface. Desna had been meticulous about making sure who had sent what. Harriet felt ill at ease just looking at them. Conspicuous consumption, the sort of life she'd always known, made her feel slightly sick these days. The only gift that she knew she wouldn't resent was Mo's painting, promised as soon as Mo had completed the varnishing process. Her mother was deeply embarrassed about the title: *Girl Eating Cheese on Toast*. Harriet smiled. Poor Mummy!

She turned back into the room. The wedding dress with its classic lines and palest pink lining, hung outside the wardrobe door in its transparent sheath. In a box on the dressing table a thick circlet of flowers sat in the middle of a frothy confection of veiling. In another box in the wardrobe were shoes that exactly matched the dress. She would be the traditional giftwrapped bride given away by a father who had never owned her.

The new flat in Dartmouth awaited the return from honeymoon. She and Philip had agreed on Scotland. They had spent several days redecorating the flat and arranging the new furniture and several nights making love on the new bed. The sex had become bearable. She had tried to conform to what Philip wanted, though Philip had seemed in a world of his own, like a man bewitched.

There was a knock on the door and Desna came in. She kissed Harriet.

'Happy wedding day, darling! I just came to see if you were up.'

She went across and patted the wedding dress as if checking that it was still there. 'Would you like your breakfast up here or will you come down?'

'I'll come down,' Harriet said. She might as well face her father's uncertain mood and Rupert's clumsy jokes now as later.

'Happy?' Desna said, smiling.

Harriet, feeling deeply embarrassed by the question, turned

and reached for her dressing gown. 'Of course I am, Mummy,' she said.

'What do you want me to do with all these bits and pieces?' Desna indicated the table full of skulls, fish skeletons, sloughed snakeskins, driftwood and pebbles. 'I don't suppose Philip will want them in the flat. They're a bit smelly, aren't they, darling?' It had been quite a while since she'd been into her daughter's bedroom and she had been considerably shocked by their grisly appearance and detectable odour.

'I don't know. I might throw them away,' Harriet said non-committally, heading for the shower.

Desna went downstairs, making an unspoken decision to dispose of the offensive objects as soon as Harriet had left. In this hot weather the smell could only get worse. She couldn't allow herself to be unduly disturbed by Harriet's peculiar, unbridelike attitude. Harriet had never been a demonstrative child anyway, but it was rather obvious that as the day of the wedding approached, Harriet had become even quieter than usual. Excitement, probably. For someone as shy as Harriet even a lovely occasion like this would be a bit of an ordeal. But later, she would be glad. The memory of Mount Huish looking its absolute best would be something she'd always treasure.

Stevie had been a gift. Desna wondered how she would have managed without her. If the wedding had been the only thing on her mind its organization would have been an unalloyed pleasure, like the meticulous weaving of a thousand strands into one gorgeous tapestry. As it was, overshadowed by darkness and violence and terrifying choices, she had found in Stevie the sort of support and comfort she had once thought she would never need.

Rupert was in the dining room, consuming coffee, Coco Pops and a large plate of bacon and eggs, supplied by Carol.

'Do you want me to give your tails a final press?' Desna said.

'No, no. All done,' Rupert said. 'Carol did it for me. Don't fuss, Ma.'

Rupert, as one of the ushers, was to wear a hired morning suit, as were all the other males. Rupert rather fancied himself in his; it made him look older and slightly rakish. At the moment he wore a black tee shirt and frayed shorts.

'Where's your father?'

'Interfering with the blokes putting the chairs in the marquee, I rather fancy. Although I don't mean "interfering with" in the colloquial sense. Rather' – Rupert's success as Henry V had predisposed him to flights of oratory.

'Darling, we haven't time for your jokes this morning,' Desna said, frowning and peering out of the window. 'I hope he doesn't upset them. Stevie has got it all in hand.'

'Well, you know Dad!' Rupert helped himself to more coffee. 'Where's the blushing bride?'

Desna turned to her son. 'Rupert, listen. You're not to make any more stupid and childish remarks about blushing brides!' she said with unusual severity. 'Even you must realize you've done it to death already!'

Rupert jokingly lifted his arms as if to fend off a blow. He looked sheepish all the same; his mother hardly ever told him off. He was quite aware of the fact that both his parents had been reserving judgement on him since Easter. Praise for his Henry V had done him some good but his GCSE results were still to come; in any case, the prize prick Naylor still had it in for him and had even had the bloody cheek to question him over some missing cash, making no secret of the fact that he wanted him out. Arrangements for him to board at the school in Yorkshire were already completed but that was weeks away. All that mattered was that his parents had agreed to his staying with the Youngs in their cottage in Newquay for most of the summer. Newquay meant Fistral Bay and Fistral Bay meant surfing. Added to that was the prospect of living in Tortola and perfecting his surfing style on Apple Beach. The remaining time that he would have to spend in school telescoped away into almost nothing from this perspective.

Harriet came into the room and he contented himself with a modest 'Hi'. Carol brought coffee and croissants for Harriet and butter arranged in artistic little whorls by Desna herself.

* * *

Nell woke up in her rented bedsit. The sun had negotiated roofs and chimneys and arrived in the room in triumph as a golden patch on the wall and the drab porridge-coloured carpet. It highlighted the suitcases and the plastic bags stacked in one corner, never unpacked; she hadn't been able to summon up the energy or the inclination. The room otherwise was neither dirty nor particularly untidy but compared to her old flat she considered it a tip. It reflected her mood precisely. She hadn't even pressed the outfit she planned to wear today; it was the one she had been going to wear to her own wedding, which had hung in the wardrobe ever since. No one had ever seen it so no one would guess its original purpose, thank heaven.

It occurred to her that the skirt might no longer accommodate her expanding waistline; nevertheless, hidden under the long linen coat some strategically placed safety pins would never show. She struggled out of bed. Safety pins! Not long ago the thought of such slovenliness would have appalled her.

At the foot of the bed Morgan continued to slumber. He spent a great deal of time asleep since the move to the bedsit because there wasn't much else to do. He even missed fighting the grey tom cat.

Nell no longer had to race to the bathroom to be sick every morning. In fact, for a week now she'd been feeling exceptionally well and it showed. Her hair was glossier, her eyes brighter, her skin glowed and not only with the tan she'd acquired during this spell of hot weather.

She had thrown herself into work. She'd been given two substantial commissions redesigning the interiors of a waterfront property in Dartmouth and a vegetarian restaurant in Totnes. She had spent other days out with Hugh and the children; once, to Nell's surprise, Desna had joined them. Neither Hugh nor his sister had remarked on it but they were not to know that Desna hardly ever did anything apart from with Roy.

Nell had resumed her weekly swims with Desna at Mount Huish. The first time she went she told Desna that she was pregnant; she could hardly not have done so in view of her tumescent figure, but Desna was neither as astonished nor as condemnatory as Nell anticipated. Instead she was exceptionally practical.

'Are you going to have it?' she asked first.

'Of course I'm going to have it,' Nell said angrily.

'I only asked!' Desna said. 'Because it won't be easy. What about your work? How will you manage?'

'Having the baby won't stop me accepting commissions,' Nell said airily.

'There could be difficulties. When the baby's ill or when it's running about.'

'I'll manage.' Nell's chin was set stubbornly in a gesture Desna was familiar with. Whether it was men or babies Nell would persevere against all odds.

'Where will you live?' Desna asked, wrapping her hair in a towel like a turban. 'You can't keep a baby in that pokey bedsit.'

'I suppose I shall have to find somewhere else,' Nell said vaguely.

'There's no question of it!' Desna lectured her. 'Look, I shall have time. Why don't I look round for something for you?'

'You'll be abroad . . . or did you forget?'

Desna looked away as if the reminder embarrassed her. 'I shall be free for a week or two after the wedding. I might even stay on until Mount Huish sells. To keep an eye on it, you know.'

'Have you a buyer yet?'

Desna's face became a mask. 'There's a consortium interested. They want to turn it into a golf and country club.'

'Oh, Desna, how perfectly awful!' Nell folded herself into the white towel. 'Des, I wish you weren't going. I shall miss you so.'

Desna who had been pouring tea into two bone china cups, paused and looked at Nell.

'Will you?'

'Of course I will, dumbo!' Nell accepted her cup of Earl Grey. 'We all will. Terribly!'

Desna leaned back in her canvas chair, adjusting the tray unnecessarily. 'I sometimes wondered, you know . . . I thought . . .' What she thought but couldn't put into words was that her mother and her sisters were secretly amused by her obsession with what was correct. That they laughed, albeit kindly, at her conventional mind. At her preoccupation with pleasing Roy at all costs.

'Wondered whether you had any importance apart from owning Mount Huish?' Nell supplied. 'Look, come off it, Des. We love you, you idiot.'

Desna smiled. 'I've got lovely sisters,' she said.

'And that's another thing,' Nell said. 'There's one other piece of news I have to tell you . . .' And she told her about Persis. Even that didn't shock Desna as it once would. She appeared to have become inured to lesser shocks while the greater ordeal loomed.

Emmet, of course, had received the news of the baby with enthusiasm as if it were the most natural thing in the world, but then Emmet would.

But most of the time these days Nell bent over the table in her cramped new quarters, working out schemes, comparing fabric swatches and paint samples and ringing suppliers. It kept her mind off other things.

She lay in the cheap plastic bath, which was a particularly revolting shade of sugary pink, soaking herself. No showers here. Then she stepped out and reached for the towel. Glancing down at her wet body she saw that her neat breasts were already expanding and her stomach made a distinct mound between her hip bones. She passed a hand over the mound and smiled; it was hard to believe that there was another human being curled up in there, that she was no longer alone.

She glanced round the shabby bathroom with its cracked black tiles, the terrible lino the colour of burnt porridge and the ghastly orange and yellow flowered curtains. How could she have not noticed them until now? Was this the kind of dump to which she intended to bring an impressionable young life? She would have to do something about where she was going to live without delay, she thought, in sudden panic. Desna was right. She could not possibly bring a baby here. She would start to look for another flat tomorrow. Today, Harriet's wedding day, she would do her duty by the family and make a pretence of enjoying herself. It would be far worse for Harriet. The poor child must be dreading being on show; her shyness would make it an agonizing public ordeal. It was Harriet who ought to be married in the registry office in Newton Abbot. Nell resolved to ring her later to give her a boost before the off.

Hugh and Winnie, whom Desna had insisted on inviting for reasons about which she was mysteriously vague, were to call for her just before two. The wedding was to be solemnized at the church of St Clement's in the Wood in Upper Ash, at two thirty.

'Barney, round up the children, could you?' Emmet called. 'It's time for their baths.' She continued popping mealworms into the open beaks of two late fledglings. Beside her stood buckets of corn, flaked maize and kitchen scraps for the resident and recovering birds: the ducks, swans and seagulls, and the two domestic geese, escapees who had arrived from nowhere and who now kept company with the swans. The mammal population in cages and outbuildings consisted of two hedgehogs injured on the road, a young badger Barney had found caught by the leg in a wire trap, the usual collection of rabbits and an emaciated, evil-smelling and completely bald dog they'd found tied up with a piece of string outside the kitchen window one morning. Barney called him Kojak.

'Why Kojak?' Beth had wanted to know.

'You're too young to know,' Barney said. But they had bathed Kojak every day and fed him up and at last a fine down of hair had appeared on his pink body.

Barney appeared at the kitchen door, buckets clanking. 'Right. That's the chickens done.' He took eggs out of one of the buckets and placed them carefully in a basket by the sink. 'The kids are down by the stream, building a dam.'

'Oh, shit. That'll mean they're absolutely filthy. Though I suppose it doesn't matter, since they're having a bath.'

'I'll fetch them.'

He went off in search of Tom and Beth. They would have to arrive early at Mount Huish so that Beth could be popped into her bridesmaid's dress on the spot. Then Emmet and Tom would make their way to the church. Emmet had been pleased and not a little surprised that Desna had made a point of asking Barney to the wedding. Barney said that since churches were not quite his scene, he'd stay back to look after the animals and join them later at the reception.

The last of the mealworms were duly inserted into the waiting beaks and the fledglings put back inside their cages; Emmet looked at her watch as she pushed the kettle over on to the hotplate. There would just be time for coffee while she supervised the children's baths and cleared up the inevitable mess before she put her own glad rags on.

The kettle boiled and she made two mugs of coffee. The children came in, followed by Barney. She handed Barney his coffee and took hers upstairs to drink while she ran the children's bath.

'Beth first and then you, Tom,' she commanded.

'Must we?' Tom said. 'It's the middle of the day.'

'Yes, you must. You can use Beth's water, she wasn't as dirty as you.'

Tom put a finger in his mouth. 'Aargh!' he protested in horror.

'You can add a bit more hot water but not too much.'

'The ducks loved our dam,' Beth said stripping off her tee shirt and knickers. 'They paddled about and turned upside down.'

'I expect you stirred up a few titbits,' Emmet said. She turned off the hot water and picked up the soap.

'I want to wash myself,' Beth pleaded.

'Only if you promise to give your ears and neck a good scrubbing.'

'Course I will.'

'Have your bath as soon as Beth gets out, Tom,' Emmet called as she passed Tom's door.

Tom was in his newly painted room bent over a Gameboy. Barney had put up shelves for his toys and books. The almost but not quite discarded soft toys were on the top shelf, the books

443

and games lower down. On the wall Barney had fixed pieces of soft board on which Tom had pinned posters of red Italian sports cars, Tornados and some of his own drawings. New hooks had been screwed into the ceiling to show off his Stealth Bombers, his Flying Fortresses and his MiG Fighters to their best advantage. Tom no longer regarded Barney as an intruder but as part of the Drake's Farm establishment, even, Emmet had been intrigued to observe, as a role model. Something the absent Maurice could never be. For better or worse, Tom now saw manhood in terms of a chap who could mend a roof, a fence, or the plumbing. Someone who could understand the construction of his more intricate model aeroplanes without reading the instructions and who could plaster a wall or feed a fledgling with equal dexterity. In short, Tom was now prepared to overlook Barney's intellectual and educational shortcomings and verbal gaffes; in fact he had taken over some of Barney's favourite phrases himself. He had even accepted a ride on Barney's motorbike.

Maurice had been horrified. He had obviously been hard put to it actually to press the keys that spelled out 'Beam me up, Scottie', 'Nice one' and 'On yer bike'. The words almost stuck in his word-processor. 'Where on earth did Tom learn such infelicities?' Maurice wanted to know. The day before he had taken the children out for an afternoon. Whole days out were getting rarer. In fact, Maurice was very rarely at the bungalow at all lately. Emmet had never answered his note.

When Tom was in the bath, Emmet tackled Beth's hair.

'Ouch, you're hurting. When am I putting on my bridesmaid's dress?'

'I told you, sweetie. When we get to Mount Huish. Or not at all unless you let me untangle this mop.'

Emmet won the battle of the tangles; now Beth's hair looked more than ever like the 'milky doishel' Lee had once called it. Emmet left her to dress herself in clean knickers and tee shirt and some baggy pants made from an exotically patterned floral curtain, Beth's favourite garment at the moment.

Emmet went downstairs. In her pocket she had a further,

more important communication from Maurice. It had arrived that morning but she hadn't had time to read it until this moment. As usual it was brief but was all the same the longest letter she'd had from him for some time.

Emmet, dearest,

It has for some time now been my attention to move from Drake's Farm and take up residence in London. A move away from the rustic, some would say bucolic, environment has long monopolized my attention to the detriment, I believe (and others have endorsed this view), of my literary career. My expectation is that, once I am settled, my current m/s will progress apace and with it, I anticipate, my fortunes. To offset the expenses I shall unavoidably incur in London, I suggest you let the bungalow. It should bring in a very fair income in holiday lets. Naturally, I will continue to support you and the children to the best of my ability. It has occurred to me that it might be advisable at this stage for us to seek a legal separation or divorce, in which case the selling of Drake's Farm would seem to be the next logical step. Please let me have your thoughts on this proposal, soonest.

Yours affectionately, Maurice.

She stood in the middle of the kitchen, her empty coffee mug in her hand, thinking. A note at the bottom gave his future address. It looked familiar, then she realized it was that of his agent. His agent was a woman and it crossed her mind that Maurice might be starting an affair with her. Perhaps this was why he was asking for a divorce all of a sudden.

'What's up?' Barney wanted to know.

She passed the letter to him. 'Read it,' she said.

Barney struggled through Maurice's prose. At last he looked up. 'What's his game, d'you reckon?'

'I think he wants to tie off a few loose ends. He likes things tidy.'

'Has he ever asked for a divorce before?' Barney took her mug and put it in the sink with his own.

'Never.'

'You don't seem upset.' Barney ran hot water into the bowl and began to wash up, almost automatically.

'I suppose I'm not. We've grown so far apart. I didn't realize.'

'So what will you do?'

'Agree, I expect. If that's what he wants.'

'What do *you* want?' Barney asked, turning around.

'Me? Oh, I shan't mind. He can have his divorce.'

Barney began to dry up and put away the used crockery. 'Would you ever marry again?' he asked casually.

Emmet laughed and patted Earwig, who had come to lean against her. 'Oh, Lord, no. I couldn't be bothered with all that again.'

'No,' Barney said quietly. 'No. I suppose not.'

There was the sound of water gurgling in the pipes and Emmet turned abruptly and went upstairs in time to see Tom charging along the passage wrapped in a frayed towel and leaving a trail of wet footprints.

Emmet went into the bathroom to pick up the soaking flannels and mop the worst of the water from the floor.

Mo had decided to draw a veil over past differences and invite Persis to stay two nights at Papermill Cottage. But Persis, without any particular animosity, had opted for the pub in Totnes she'd used before. To be nearer Nell, Mo supposed. Belatedly, the woman appeared to have woken up to her responsibilities.

Mo got up early as usual. The light mornings made it almost obligatory, otherwise the sense of wasted time worried at her like a nagging tooth. She still had too much to do before she was ready to snuff it.

Finished canvases were stacked all round the room, some still drying out. Since Persis had left and, more particularly, since Nell and she had made their peace, Mo had worked like a demon and the fruits of her labours pleased her. She would be ready with the requisite number of paintings as soon as Harriet came back from honeymoon. The exhibition had been fixed for

September. The painting of which she was most proud was the portrait of Harriet eating cheese on toast, which was her wedding present. Desna had queried the title, she said it sounded undignified and although she didn't mention it, she had obviously been disappointed that Harriet's face had been largely in shadow. Mo grinned to herself as she picked up the canvas and examined it with a fresh eye. *The Girl with Fish* was good but this was better. Whatever Desna thought, the brushwork in that gentle violet shadow was more expressive than a thousand laboured details. The soft blur of the eye and a small warm highlight summed up Harriet's character perfectly. The streak of burnt orange and the patches of black and cream which represented Harry's scarf and Polly Chrome's sleeping form, linked the composition and tied it up as snug as snug. She was inordinately pleased with it.

Mo took a chair and her breakfast coffee outside on to the quay. The cats joined her, Polly Chrome to stare fixedly over the side of the quay wall. The tide was out leaving only the narrow channel of the leat to snake its way across the mud towards the main channel of the river. The mud kept the busy traffic on the Dart at bay for an hour or two leaving Papermill Cottages in splendid isolation. Mo surveyed the tranquil scene, relishing the opportunity.

Rose Madder sprung up on to her lap and curled herself into a ball. Mo stroked her and sighed with contentment. How good it was to be alone! The noisy Wilds had vanished a week previously; folded their tents and stolen away, she knew not where. Neither did the landlord apparently, who was not pleased because they owed rent. Delphi hadn't even said goodbye, which hurt Mo rather. She had made an effort to befriend the girl, had even supplied her with milk, bread and potatoes on several occasions when the children had nothing to eat. Delphi had never been particularly effusive in her gratitude but then that wasn't her style. Mo might even miss their noise in time but for the moment she was able to have the quay to herself.

Desna was sending a car for her at two. Meanwhile she would watch the darting swallows and the quicksilver glintings of distant water, listen to the leat gurgling down its secret valley and wait for the stove to heat her bath water.

It was not that there weren't clouds on the horizon. She had a deep and unbudging conviction that Roy and Desna were doing the wrong thing. Desna's troubled expression lately was evidence enough. Desna was all too clearly profoundly upset at the thought of selling Mount Huish and sailing off into the blue. Desna had never been one to confide in her mother but one didn't need to be a mind reader to guess what she thought of the whole business. Mo thought it was a madcap scheme and had said so, only to find herself on the receiving end of Roy's displeasure.

'Mother-in-law, stop interfering,' he'd said rudely. 'You know bugger all about it so stop sticking your oar in!' His face was as red as a turkey cock. He was even quicker than usual to anger these days.

Mo was not to be intimidated like Desna and Harriet. 'You're burning your boats, you silly man. Can't you see that? Who knows if this Italian is above board, anyway?'

'Do you really think I haven't looked into all that!' Roy seethed. 'Why is it you women think you can have your say in everything – even things you know nothing whatever about? What gets me is that you think you can stay under my roof and still presume to say what the hell you please!'

'I'm not staying under your roof. Desna just asked me in for a drink.'

Roy had stormed out of the room leaving Mo more convinced than ever that Roy himself was worried that he had bitten off more than he could chew.

Desna looked shattered. 'Please, Mo,' she begged, 'don't provoke Roy. He has so many things to worry about at the moment and I don't want him in a bad mood for the wedding.'

Now Mo tipped Rose Madder off her lap and went to check the progress of the water; not quite hot enough. Time for another cup of coffee.

She wasn't too worried about Nell any longer. It seemed to her that Nell would survive. The pregnancy had given her a new lease of life, softening the blow of Daniel's betrayal, giving her something else, someone else, to think about and a reason to work hard at her design commissions. Only time would tell if this second inoculation against the charms of Daniel Thorne would take.

Harriet was a different matter. She would marry her knight in shining armour who would rescue her from the dragon – her father – but then what? Philip would never turn into another Roy but would he allow the fragile chrysalis of Harriet's maturity to grow wings or would he bite them off as soon as they emerged? From the best of intentions, naturally. Mo stirred her coffee. She was getting her metaphors mixed. Knights in armour, dragons, butterflies. What next?

Harried nibbled at the croissant and drank the coffee that Carol had brought in for her. She wasn't hungry. Rupert read snippets from *The Times* and the *Daily Mail* by way of proving to his mother that he was going to behave himself and not upset Harry.

'It says here,' he said, to take Harriet's mind off things, 'that this chap had sixteen wives in different parts of the country.' He pushed his empty plate across the table in the vague direction of the kitchen without taking his eyes from the newspaper. 'Imagine supporting that lot!'

'What?' Harriet said.

'This chap with sixteen wives. Fancy supporting that lot.'

'I expect they supported him,' Harriet said crisply.

Roy appeared in the doorway. 'Rupert! Aren't you dressed yet? Get your skates on, for God's sake and give a hand!'

Desna came into the room. 'There's nothing to do, darling. It's all under control. Stevie's arrived; she'll see to everything. All we have to do is get dressed. Carol and I will lay out a light lunch for everyone in the dining room later.'

Roy glared at Desna for a moment as if one of the chairs had addressed him. Then, as if remembering that the day was supposed to be a happy occasion, he put a bearlike arm round her shoulder, giving her a squeeze.

'Harriet, darling,' Desna said resting a hand on her daughter's arm, 'if you've finished, I think you should go upstairs and start to get ready and I'll come up later to help you.'

Harriet escaped to her room. Desna looked after her retreating figure and sighed. She had hoped Harriet would have her hair done professionally; a style with tiny ringlets at the side would have looked enchanting under the headdress. But nothing could persuade her. On the extremely rare occasions when Harriet did decide to dig her heels in, it was useless. Her glossy reddish brown hair would be straight as a die, as usual. All the same, she had to admit that Harriet unadorned with fancy ringlets would still be an achingly beautiful bride. It had been the same over make-up, but then she thought that Harriet could probably get away with it.

In her bedroom Harriet sat on her bed feeling numb at the thought of what she would have to endure today before she and Philip were alone. Even sex held out fewer torments than the prospect of nearly twelve hours of being on public display. At least she'd have Philip by her side constantly; he was now quite good at fending off attention when she had made one of her gaffes.

She had been upset at first when Faith had accepted an invitation to stay with the Emmersons; Tessa had apparently convinced her that it would be better for the two of them to dress together and Faith, inconceivably, had agreed. Besides, she'd said that Desna would have enough to do without bothering about guests. Now Harriet was relieved. Having Faith's satirical eye upon her when she smothered herself in pink-tinged silk and an explosion of white veiling would be too humiliating. She felt a hot flush creep over her body at the very thought.

The wedding dress hung on the outside of the wardrobe, ready to put on. Harriet moved it aside and opened the door. Inside the grey dress hung, still in its wrapping, the headdress on the shelf above, the grey silk pumps beneath it. If only she had the courage.

'No hitches, thank goodness,' Stevie said. She and Desna stood at the entrance to the marquee watching a dozen helpers put the finishing touches to the tables, white cloths on each with a small vase of palest pink roses, each table surrounded by six gold-painted chairs. Every pillar was swathed in muslin and decorated with flowers, the canvas walls of the marquee were disguised with ruched muslin, the floor boarded and covered with sisal carpet except for the area designed for dancing. A quartet would provide a background of classical music for the reception itself, a small band had been hired later for dancing.

'It looks perfect. I'm absolutely delighted,' Desna said. Then in a lower voice, 'I don't think I could have accomplished anything like it myself . . . as things are. But when I took it on I'd no idea Roy was about to drop his bombshell. You've been a tower of strength, Stevie, you really have.'

'This is one occasion when I shall be sorry to see the wedding over,' Stevie said. She turned to smile at Desna. She was wearing a sensible navy suit with a cream blouse, one of the outfits she kept for 'her' weddings; smart but not too smart. 'You will keep in touch, won't you? And don't forget what we talked about.' She was already steeling herself for the inevitable moment, the anti-climax, when the high emotional mood of the occasion had worn off and all the impulsive confidences and promises were forgotten, to be swept up with the confetti and broken glasses. The rich could afford these ephemeral indulgences. They meant nothing.

'Of course I won't forget!' Desna said almost fiercely.

Roy came to stand next to them. At last he seemed satisfied with what he saw, Stevie thought. Desna actually seemed to relax when he put an arm round her shoulders. In a couple of weeks they would both forget that Stevie Turnbull existed. Start again. Pick up the pieces. Well, at least she was used to it.

'You've done a very good job on the marquee, Mrs Turnbull,' Roy said. 'Now about the grub . . .?'

'The refrigerator vans have just arrived,' Stevie said, back to her professional self. 'Don't worry, Mr Hindmarch, we shall be ready by the time you get back from the church.' As well as the commodious vans, their sides inscribed with the Bonne Bouche logo, the Mount Huish kitchen had been turned over to the catering team and was now a no-go area. But the cake that Desna had made herself stood in pride of place on the kitchen table awaiting its moment of glory.

Desna laid her hand briefly on Stevie's arm. 'Thank you, Stevie. We'll go and have lunch, then we'll get changed. I know I can safely leave everything to you.'

Emmet and the children arrived and joined the rest of the family for lunch. Afterwards Emmet sat in the conservatory while Tom and Beth finished their glasses of lemonade.

'Can I put my frock on now?' Beth wanted to know.

'Have your drink first,' Emmet said, 'because after you're dressed there'll be no drinks whatever until we get back from the church.'

'Why?' Beth said automatically, but she was staring round-eyed through the window at the decorated marquee.

'Can I get you anything else?' Carol asked.

'You're an angel, no.' Emmet collapsed into an armchair. 'Christ, it's like an oven already. What have you done with Davy today?'

'His father's looking after him,' Carol smiled.

'And how's the sociology course going?'

'Slowly, I'm afraid.' Mrs Darby was nice, Carol thought. She remembered things about you, treated you like a person. Not that Mrs Hindmarch didn't, but Mrs Hindmarch could be aloof. She looked at her employer's sister. Along with Mrs Hindmarch's mother, Mrs Darby could always be relied on to look slightly bizarre. Today she had on a overdress of what looked like badly knitted yellow string over two layers of blue muslin with an uneven hem. She was fanning herself with a yellow linen hat decorated with real cornflowers. Her hair was scraped up on top as usual but fastened with an orange ribbon instead of the usual elastic band. Carol slipped out as Roy came in.

Roy stopped abruptly when he saw Emmet.

'Hi, Roy. How's everything going? The marquee looks wonderful.'

'Splendidly, thank you, Emmet.' He eyed her suspiciously,

trying to ascertain in his mind whether she had chosen what to wear specifically to annoy him or because she didn't know any better. He decided, she being Emmet, it was the latter. In view of the importance of the occasion he decided also to take the bull by the horns.

'You know you could have asked Desna or Nell for help with your gear,' he said. 'In any case, I'm sure Des has something she could lend you for the day.' He had helped himself to his first whisky of the morning and stood rocking slightly in the doorway as he watched the caterers pass in and out of the marquee.

'I beg your pardon?' Emmet said. 'Beth, mind that lemonade. I think you better sit still until you've finished it.'

Beth obediently sat on the edge of a chair, its size dwarfing her. She had one eye on Roy of whom she was in awe.

'I said I'm sure Des wouldn't mind lending you a suit or dress. She's bound to have something suitable.'

'That's what I thought you said,' Emmet remarked, looking puzzled. She turned to her son. 'Tom, Beth and I are going upstairs to put Beth into her dress. Why don't you go and find Rupert?'

'Right. No sweat,' Tom said. Rupert arrived and Tom stared at his morning-suited cousin in astonishment. 'What sort of suit's that?' he said in a strangled voice but Rupert just grinned and ruffled Tom's hair.

Emmet glanced at Roy as she ushered Beth out of the room. 'I'm sure you don't mean to be offensive,' she said, 'so I'll just forget I heard that. Come on, Beth.'

Roy stared after her, frowning. Sometimes, he thought, women were like another species altogether.

Desna, wearing a suit of slubbed silk the colour of crushed blackberries, walked round her daughter, tweaking and smoothing. Harriet stood as rigid as a marble column, the separate, squared-off train a pool of ivory on the floor behind her. Her hair hung straight as a curtain, hitched away from her face by two clips.

Desna stepped back. 'Darling, you look absolutely lovely.

Come to the glass and look. There now. Aren't you glad we chose this design?'

Harriet looked in the mirror and saw what she expected. A dressed-up doll.

'Yes, Mummy. It's lovely.'

Desna kissed her. 'I know you don't believe it when people say you're beautiful, but it's true, you know.'

'That's more to do with you and Daddy than with me. It's my genes. I can't help how I look.' Harried smiled to soften the words. Shyly she put an arm round her mother's shoulders and kissed her. 'Thank you for all you've done,' she said quietly. 'Especially now when everything's so . . . so . . .'

Desna examined Harriet's face. 'You are happy about this, aren't you? I mean, you don't have any doubts about getting married?'

Harriet shook her head. 'No. I love Philip. I want to marry him.'

'You're absolutely sure. Because now's the time to say if you don't.'

For a moment Harriet tried to imagine what it would be like to call the whole thing off. She failed utterly. 'I'm just nervous about today, that's all.'

Desna put her arms round Harriet and held her close. She often longed to do this but something in her daughter's manner always kept her at arm's length. Surely a wedding was a good enough excuse. She felt her eyes filling. 'Good luck, darling. I know Philip will be a lovely, kind husband. I can't think of anyone I'd rather you married. He adores you and he's such a gentle sort of man, you know. And that's terribly important . . .' She drew away. What she had said was already too revealing.

Harriet was suddenly aware of the quality of her mother's pain and held her as if her role was that of the comforter instead of the other way about. She sensed some profound anguish for which even the leaving of Mount Huish could hardly account.

'I mustn't get salt stains on your gorgeous new dress,' Desna said brightly, stepping away. 'Sweetie, I think I just heard Tessa and Faith arriving. I better go. Do you want me to help you with

454

your headdress or will you get Tessa to do it?'

'Tess can you do it . . . or Faith,' Harriet couldn't help adding mischievously.

'Goodbye, my darling. Good luck.'

'Thank you, Mummy. It's all perfectly, perfectly wonderful. The marquee looks great. Much better than that hotel where Nicola Wakeham had her reception.'

Desna put her finger to her lips. 'Shh,' she said smiling. 'I think the Wakeham twins have arrived.'

'It's true all the same.'

A knock on the door and noisy chattering heralded Tessa and Faith in their pearly grey silk, followed almost at once by Beth. The Wakeham twins hovered in the passage outside, peering round the door to get their first glimpse of the bride. Desna greeted them, then left to do some last-minute checking downstairs. Emmet had put Beth into Tessa's care and had left with Tom for the church. Beth could hardly contain her excitement but she was struck dumb with amazement when she saw Harriet dressed up like a princess. It was like something out of a story. All this could hardly compare with the boring rehearsals in the church.

Tessa and the Wakeham twins exclaimed over the wedding dress.

'Darling, it's so much nicer than Nicola Wakeham's believe me,' Tessa hissed in Harriet's ear. 'Hers was a mess.'

Harriet stared at Faith. 'Faith! I hardly recognized you!' she said.

'Don't! I feel a right wally already.'

'Why?' Tessa said. 'I think the design's really trendy. Not bridesmaidy a bit.'

'Yes, it is!' Beth protested, her face outraged under her golden aureole of hair.

'Yes, poppet. Of course it is,' Tessa said, bending down to placate Beth. 'And you look great.'

'I suppose it's not so bad,' Faith said. With her shorn bits grown and without her enormous boots she was mortified to see that she looked very much like everybody else.

Tessa helped Harriet to arrange her headdress. She brushed her hair so that it hung neatly down her back.

'You're not planning on changing your mind, then?' Faith whispered with a significant glance towards the wardrobe.

Tessa and Beth were at the door. 'Come on, Faith,' Beth said in a panic. 'Or we'll be late.' The Wakeham twins had already gone downstairs.

'Change my mind?' Harriet whispered back. 'No, of course not. I can't anyway, it's too late.'

'Faith, are you coming?' Tessa called from the stairs.

'I'll ask the man to drive round a bit to hold things up.' Faith kissed Harriet.

'I can't. I can't!' Harriet cried.

'You can do anything you like today. Look, I'm off. I'll see what I can do.'

Desna appeared at the door for a last look at Harriet. 'Perfect,' she said. 'Good luck, darling.' She kissed her again with an air of almost wistful regret. Then she left.

Just as Nell had finished dressing the doorbell rang. Surely it was too early for Hugh and Winnie? The three of them were to travel to the wedding in Hugh's Volvo. Without her shoes she went to answer it. Daniel stood on the doorstep.

'Nell, don't shut the door on me,' he pleaded, but he was already inside. He was the very last person she had expected to see and she was taken by surprise. 'Please. Just hear me out. There are still things we have to discuss, unfinished business.'

'I don't think so, Daniel.' She held the door open. 'Please leave.'

'It's about the money.'

'Oh?'

'Could we discuss it upstairs?' They stood at the foot of the narrow, sordid stairs that led to her tiny flat.

'No, I'm afraid not.'

'If you insist then.' He pushed the door shut behind him. 'You see, my solicitor tells me that I'd be within my rights to keep that four thousand you gave me indefinitely to pay for the damage your chaps did when they broke into the Old Rectory.' He looked at her with a hurt expression. 'There was no need for that, you know. I was disappointed in you, Nell. I would have been within my rights to call the police.'

'Rights, Daniel? Rights?' Puzzlement in her voice. 'I don't know what you're talking about. As far as I know you supervised the removal of my furniture yourself.'

'I wasn't even present.'

'Daniel, I know nothing about it at all, but I suspect you're lying as usual. As you know I've been abroad.' She felt weak at the knees suddenly confined in the narrow passage with Daniel a foot away. ·

'I find it hard to believe you knew nothing of it.'

'Look, Daniel,' Nell felt heat rush to her cheeks, 'I don't want to end our relationship with some bloody sordid wrangle over money. You have the four thousand I gave you towards making a car park in the front of Cornucopia, and I paid for the honeymoon as I expect you remember. So shall we just forget the whole thing? I guess that's what this is all about. That you want to keep the four thousand? I am right, aren't I? Well, keep it then and give it to the VAT man. I don't care!'

'I'm sure you were able to get a refund for the tickets, that's why I didn't send you the money.'

'Stop banging on about money, Daniel!' she cried. 'If you couldn't have come here to finish things with some kind of dignity it would have been better not to come at all. How did you know where I was living anyway?'

'Never mind. What I wanted to say was that after that affair at The Old Rectory I'd rather that you confirmed in writing that the four thousand was a gift . . .'

'Get out!' she cried holding the door wide open. 'Get out!' She grabbed his arm and pushed. He stepped out on to the path outside.

'There's no need for this, Nellie!' he said. 'All I wanted was a reasonable and businesslike discussion, just to get things straight. You know we could still put all this behind us and make a go of it!' He dashed a hand through his dark curls. 'After all, we only fell out about money. In every other way we were great together, weren't we?' His eyes were reminding her of the ways in which they had been great together.

'We fell out, as you put it, because you cheated and lied,' she said. 'I'm afraid that's just the way you are, Daniel. It's second nature to you. You don't even know when you're doing it.'

'Look, hold on, Nellie. If it was only the money—' She closed the door.

If Daniel had deliberately tried he couldn't have given her love for him a more effective *coup de grâce*. She stood for a moment with her eyes closed, waiting for the thundering of her heart to quieten. Somehow, there were no tears left. She had already cried them all. Jolted into action by a sense of time wasted, she rushed upstairs and found herself washing her hands obsessively, rubbing soap into every pore. Then she fumbled clumsily for the phone, banishing Daniel from her mind. Like Scarlett O'Hara, she would think about him later. Or not at all if she could. She dialled the Mount Huish number. She had intended all along to ring her niece and was overwhelmed with guilt at allowing the events in her own life to blot out her promises to back Harriet up. Now she was probably too late.

Harriet was alone, fortunately. Carol put Nell through. Desna and the bridesmaids had gone downstairs.

'Harry, this is Nell. I just rang to wish you good luck, darling.'

'Thank you, Nell,' Harriet said politely.

'Have we a moment to talk?'

'Yes, it's not time to leave yet.'

'No, of course not. I'm only just leaving myself. I just wanted to say I was sorry.'

'What for, Nell?'

'I'm afraid I've been a woman of straw. I never backed you up over the dress. Things became so difficult . . . I think I lost my credibility after my outburst.'

'But you *did* back me up!'

'Not as much as I should have done. Anyway, I just thought I'd ring and tell you. I'm sure you'll look quite perfect in the dress Desna chose. I'm looking forward to seeing it in half an hour. You could never look anything other than gorgeous, love.'

'Thank you, Nell.'

'I better not keep you. I think I can hear Hugh's car outside. Bye, darling. Good luck!'

Nell hurried down the stairs and Hugh opened the car door for her, it being impossible to stop for more than a minute in such narrow streets.

Hugh allowed himself one keen, indulgent glance before he closed the door after Nell. His spirits rose and he drove only half listening to Winnie's outrageous gossip. One glance had told him that Nell was looking better, her skin had a bloom to it and her eyes a sparkle. She had even put on some weight. For a moment his eyes met hers in the driving mirror and they smiled in affectionate complicity at Winnie's expense.

'What's Laura doing today?' Nell asked.

'She's at the stables, where else?' he laughed.

'I went through a horsy stage once, believe it or not,' Winnie said. 'But I outgrew it, literally. They couldn't find a creature wide enough for my enormous bottom!' She chuckled. She had abandoned her usual flamboyant flounces for an emerald suit with a wide matching hat and a peacock-patterned blouse. 'Christ Almighty, tis 'ot! Much more of this and you'm 'ave to scoop I up off the floor with a spoon.'

The church looked idyllic in its verdant setting. Already cars were lined up along the road under the chestnut trees, sunlight penetrating the leafy canopy and glinting on metal. A stream of pink, blue, cream and lavender interspersed with sombre blacks and greys emerged from the cars and flowed up the church path.

Hugh helped Winnie and Nell from the Volvo. He had a mad desire to drag Nell into the church and compel the vicar to marry them instead, but he took a grip on himself and played his traditional escorting part like all the rest. Ever since he had discovered that Nell had thought better of marrying Daniel Thorne he had become almost obsessed with the notion of protecting her from harm of any description. For this reason being apart from her was a most refined variety of torture; he kept imagining the possibility of Thorne turning up on her doorstep and inveigling her back into his clutches, spiriting her away so that once more Hugh missed his opportunity and lost her. He couldn't force Nell to love him, and he certainly couldn't compete with the undeniable charm of the Thornes of this world, but at least he could give it his very best shot. If his luck held, she might even have gone off charm.

They went inside the flower-filled church. A grinning Rupert showed them to their seats on the bride's side. The organ played softly, competing with the hum of whispered conversations; the scent of hundreds of roses vied with that of Diorissimo and Joy. The ushers moved up and down the aisles showing guests to their places. Mo and Persis created quite a stir. Persis was wearing a long black dress, her bare, bony feet visible below it in thongy sandals. Over it she had thrown a black, fringed cape, on her head was a wide, black sombrero. She looked like a rather flamboyant extra from *The Magnificent Seven*. By comparison Mo was restrained. She was even browner and more leathery than usual; her grey plait, still wispy despite all her efforts, hung down over a slightly crumpled dark blue caftan, embroidered with gold, which she wore with her loon pants. She had found what she thought of as some rather jolly patterned pumps in a charity shop. Rupert sat them next to Enrico Bonicelli. Tall, sleek and immaculately dressed, his longish hair slicked neatly back, Bonicelli himself had been a subject of comment as he walked up the aisle. Persis subjected him to a detailed scrutiny as if she was seeing him for the first time.

Philip arrived with Andy, who was acting as best man, both immaculate in their morning suits with white carnations.

'Not planning to change your mind, are you?' Andy whispered, observing the large turn-out.

'Not for a moment,' Philip said firmly. Even the fact that he was slightly hung over from yesterday's stag party did not cause him to waver.

The church filled; some even had to stand in the side aisles.

* * *

Harriet was alone in her room. The rest of the family had left for the church. Only her father remained. He waited for her downstairs, topping up his whisky glass, she imagined.

Nell's words still rang in her head. She'd said, 'I'm sure you'll look quite perfect in the dress Desna chose.' Could she have said it as a challenge or had it just slipped out like that because she truly thought of it as Desna's dress? Not Harriet's choice but her mother's. She stood in front of the long glass, her bouquet in her hand. The bouquet was made from white roses that had pink deep down among the petals, some white lilies, jasmin and gypsophila. The woman in the mirror looked like a dummy in a shop window. Abruptly Harriet turned away from the hateful image, went to the wardrobe and flung open the door.

Downstairs Roy saw Desna and the bridesmaids off. There was one car left; the long black limo that was to take Harriet and himself to the church. He looked at his watch. There was just time for a quick snifter before they were due to leave; plenty of time as it happened. Everything was going like clockwork so far. He tossed back his whisky. After five minutes he called up the stairs.

'Harry, are you ready? It's nearly time to go.'

A faint answer. 'I'm just coming.'

After another five minutes he called again, irritation in his voice. This time he went upstairs and banged on his daughter's door.

'It's all right, Daddy. I shan't be long. My headdress needs pinning.'

Roy sighed and went back to the sitting room. Better not have another whisky. He called again after another five minutes. Now it really was time to go. He stood halfway up the stairs.

'Harry!' he bawled. 'Get a move on. What in God's name are you doing in there?'

In the hall he looked at his watch impatiently. There was a slight sound on the stairs and he looked up. Harriet came down to him as silent as a ghost, wearing a twenties-style dress of some gossamery material, a contraption of silver beads like a

461

helmet on her head. She held the bouquet that he'd seen sent up half an hour before. He was speechless.

Then: 'What the bloody hell d'you think you're wearing?' he roared, rocked to the core by what he momentarily thought was an hallucination. He was perfectly well aware of what his daughter *should* be wearing; Desna had showed him both the fabric and the design. He had approved. Of course he knew what a wedding dress should look like. And this wasn't it.

'I'm ready,' Harriet said softly, feeling the fabric lightly brush her legs as she stepped down into the hall.

'What in God's name d'you think you're doing? That's not the dress Mrs Gillimore made. D'you take me for a fool?' He looked at his watch. 'Get moving and take that thing off and get your wedding dress on.' He banged his hands together. 'Right now! I'll call Carol to come and help you.'

'This *is* my wedding dress. I've changed my mind. At least I haven't changed my mind. I wanted to wear this all along.'

'Have you gone completely insane? Get into the proper gear or I'm damned if I won't put you in it myself! Do you want to ruin your mother's day, for Christ's sake, turning up looking like some hippie tramp?' He stood over her. He had never struck her before, but then she had never seriously defied him before. Besides, his towering willpower had always been sufficient to nip insurrection in the bud.

Roy could almost feel his blood pressure rising. The little bitch! She was subtly using the time and the occasion, knowing all too well that she could force the issue. She was clever, he gave her that! It crossed his mind to call her bluff, to frogmarch her upstairs and force her back into the correct gear, but he didn't see how he could do it without a terrific scuffle that would in all probability wreck both the damned frocks and send Harriet into hysterics. Besides there was a certain light in his daughter's eye that he had never seen there before. Shaken, he realized that his docile, biddable daughter was prepared to fight him tooth and nail.

He was aware that the driver was standing in the doorway, apparently to remind them of the time.

'I'm giving you one last chance,' he said to Harriet in a low tone.

Harriet's mouth was unsteady and she was trembling, but she stood her ground. 'I get married in this or I don't get married at all,' she said. She braced herself. She felt sure her father was going to strike her.

'I think we should be on our way, sir,' the driver said. He couldn't quite make out what the fuss was about, the girl looked a million dollars to him. A bit unusual but that was her prerogative as the bride.

Roy hesitated, looked at his watch. The public disgrace of arriving either extremely late or not at all was too awful to contemplate. Harriet had won. 'You damned, blackmailing little bitch. I'll never forgive you for this. Neither will your mother. And you can tell Philip that neither of you will be wanted in Tortola, you can be sure of that.'

With set mouth and a face almost purple with barely controlled rage, Roy propelled Harriet out of the front door. The driver, as he helped her in, gave her a conspiratorial grin that was meant to make up for her father's ill grace. 'Don't worry, miss,' he whispered. 'You'll wow them, I'm telling you!'

Roy sat glowering in the corner as the car pulled smoothly away. The best he could hope for was that since everybody knew about Harriet's disinterest in decent clobber, they wouldn't be expecting much anyway. All the same, the thought of turning up at the church with *this* on his arm was a humiliation almost as great as the night that slut of a so-called friend of Harriet's had kneed him in the balls. He had been afraid at first that she'd done some permanent damage but he hadn't dared go to the doctor. It was probably that damned scrubber that had put Harriet up to this act of defiance. He felt heat rush to his face; it hadn't occurred to him before that she might have told Harriet about his visit to her room and that this was Harriet's way of getting back at him.

He sat as far away from his daughter as possible and maintained a stony silence, his only consolation that he would soon be on the far side of the Atlantic where the repercussions of this débâcle wouldn't reach. He hoped that Philip wouldn't take one look at Harriet in these weeds and run a mile.

Faith successfully delayed the bridesmaids' car by insisting she urgently needed a pee. She had persuaded the driver to stop at a pub, much to the annoyance of Desna and Tessa and the panic-stricken Beth. The Wakeham twins were pop-eyed in astonishment. In the end they arrived just a few well-timed minutes before the bride.

When Faith saw Harriet emerge from the limo she gave a short, explosive cheer. The other bridesmaids looked on in astonishment.

'That's my girl! You look absolutely great,' she hissed in Harriet's ear.

Harriet was still stunned by her own audacity. 'It was awful,' she whispered, pale with shock.

'So what? You did it. Bully for you!' Faith said as she lined herself up behind Harriet.

Desna had already made her way into the church. Roy forced his expression into something resembling that of a proud father as Gerald Peters greeted them at the door. The first chords of Fauré's *Pavane* stole through the church. God, even the music's weird, Roy thought.

He was aware that a soft buzz of whispered comment followed them like a sigh up the aisle and could have died of mortification on the spot. His rage towards Harriet for shaming him so publicly and comprehensively made it hard for him to bear the feel of her hand on his arm. He never would have thought she had the spunk.

Philip turned his head. He hardly noticed what Harriet was wearing, he only knew that she looked more stunning than ever, that he loved her desperately and that he wished the whole thing was over and they were alone.

Desna was sitting at the front of the church, shattered by Harriet's appearance and the dark rage on Roy's face that was almost palpable; to her at least.

The service began:

'I, Philip Nicholas take you, Harriet, to be my wife, to have and to hold from this day forward . . .'

Then. 'I, Harriet, take you, Philip Nicholas . . .'

The register was signed and the triumphal 'Arrival of the Queen of Sheba' echoed through the ancient church. Giles took Desna's arm.

'Philip's a lucky bugger,' he said, almost wistfully. 'I always thought Harriet was an absolute corker! Like her outfit. Trust you to come up with something unusual.' His words were almost lost as the church bells began their celebratory clangour.

And suddenly Desna saw that Harriet had been right and she had been wrong. The dove-grey dress suited her daughter's character in a way that the formal white could never have done. There was no getting away from it, she looked superb. Why hadn't she seen it before? It had been the same over some of the schemes for the house Nell had worked out for her; she hadn't understood the possibilities until it had been pointed out to her. Added to that, Harriet looked a different person entirely to the nervous girl she had taken leave of in the bedroom. There was an altogether new expression on her face. Her heart thudded uncomfortably as she realized that there had evidently been a battle royal between Harriet and Roy. To Desna, it was almost inconceivable, but incontrovertible all the same, that Harriet had won. Outside, Nell came up and kissed her.

'Des, that was a beautiful service. And I really think you and Harriet made the right decision about the dress after all. I'm sorry I interfered . . .'

'Don't be!' Desna found herself saying. 'You were absolutely right about it. Look, they want me for the photograph.'

Mo came up and put her arm round Nell. 'Persis is here somewhere,' she said. 'How do you feel about meeting her?'

'I don't mind. I'm ready for it. You know that things will always be the same between you and me; nothing can change that. I've decided that I can only think of Persis as a special sort of aunt.'

Mo grinned. 'She's special all right.'

Mo was dragged in for one of the photographs. Nell smiled as she watched the combined efforts of Roy and the photographer to put Mo where her unconventional appearance would have least impact. Emmet came up with Tom in tow. The likeness between Emmet and Mo struck Nell forcibly and not only because of their odd taste in clothes. She saw how Emmet's wiry prettiness would become Mo's leathery indestructibility.

'Doesn't Harry look a dream?' Emmet said. 'Like a wood nymph. Desna's a dark horse. She led me to believe she was going to wear just the usual kind of thing.'

Hugh found Nell again and at the same moment, so did Persis.

'I got your letter,' Persis said. 'From which I gathered Greece came up to snuff? I hope Sophia looked after you well?' Her pale eyes glittered under the huge, black sombrero.

'The villa was fine,' Nell said. 'I stayed nearly a month after all. And Sophia was most attentive. Thank you. Really! Thank you.'

'So what now? Since you've given that tricky bastard his marching orders?'

'I shall find somewhere to live and carry on with my usual commissions.'

Persis frowned and grunted. 'Well, you know where to come if you need some dosh. Might as well use your old ma for something.' She sounded almost proud, Nell thought.

'I think Harriet and Philip are on their way,' Hugh said. 'Ms Dane, may I offer you a lift?'

'That's very civil of you,' Persis said gruffly.

So Nell, Hugh, Winnie and Persis went together to Mount Huish.

Harriet and Philip shook hand after hand, their smiles becoming gradually fixed. Gordon and Toby's turn came. Gordon soberly dressed, his pigtail tied with a bootlace, Toby resplendent in a cream suit and a crimson striped shirt. They both kissed Harriet and gave her brotherly hugs.

'You did it! Brave girl!' Gordon whispered in Harriet's ear.

'You mean . . . got married??' she smiled.

'Well yes, that too. But the dress. Looks a dream.'

Roy was standing a yard or two away. He glared at the owners of the Yardarm Gallery but when their turn came, he pretended not to see their outstretched hands. He was already thinking that there were far too many weirdos around for his liking including some rustic oaf Emmet was trailing around with and whom she introduced as Barney.

'Barney who?' Roy said.

'Just Barney,' Emmet said. To Roy's astonishment Desna leaned forward and kissed the extraordinary yokel with his too large suit and his hairy tie.

'Nice to see you again, Barney,' Desna said.

Barney winked. 'Pulled any more B and E jobs lately, Mrs H.?' he said.

'What was he saying?'

'Nothing. One of Emmet's jokes, that's all.'

Emmet, Tom and Barney passed through into the marquee where they were offered drinks. 'Stroll on!' Barney said. 'Would you look at all this!'

'Pretty, ain't it?' Emmet said, taking in the muslin-swathed and flower-decked interior.

'Icky, icky,' Tom said, but not too loudly. He had just caught sight of the food.

'I thought you said Harriet was shy and had no self-confidence,' Barney said. 'It looked to me like she had scads of it.'

'Yes. That's what I was thinking,' Emmet agreed.

Beth was suddenly beside them, literally jumping with excitement. 'Mummy! Did you see me? Was I all right?'

Emmet picked her up round the waist and hugged her. 'Darling, you were splendiferous. You didn't put a foot wrong. *Now* you can have a drink!'

'Quick, quick! I'm absolutely *dehydrated*.'

'Dehydrated?'

'That's what Faith said. Isn't it right?'

'Yes. Perfectly.'

* * *

467

Harriet continued to shake hands and smile. She was aware of her father just feet away, playing his part as father of the bride as if the ugly scene between them had never happened. As nobody had anything but compliments for her outfit she noticed the twitching muscle at the side of his mouth gradually relax. It was an extremely odd and disorientating experience to know that she was no longer frightened of him; or at least no longer paralysed by the fear of displeasing him that had dominated her life until now. He had almost diminished to the point where she could look on him as an ordinary human being rather than a huge and terrifying god figure. She had defied him and survived. It wasn't about the dress after all, she realized as she mechanically shook hands with Mr and Mrs Wakeham. It was about growing up, finding resources inside herself that she hadn't known she possessed. Perhaps she would never throw off her fear of her father entirely but feeling Philip's sturdy presence beside her, she thought, It doesn't matter any more.

The vicar looked about him at the lavish display and frowned. The Hindmarch donation to the fabric fund was not as generous as he'd hoped. He'd heard before that Roy Hindmarch was a hard man of business. The rumours were not wrong.

Everyone was now drifting into the marquee and checking their places on the seating plan. It was all going very smoothly. Desna looked under the brim of her flattering blackberry-coloured hat to where Stevie stood inconspicuously at the side. Their eyes met and Desna smiled an acknowledgement as she made her way with Roy and the Emmersons to the long table arranged along one side of the marquee. She looked round, ever watchful that things were going according to plan. The house and the marquee looked gorgeous, the latter a bower of roses, just as she had envisaged. The scent was a balm to her troubled spirits. When this was over life would return to a harsh reality that she could hardly bear to dwell on; but for now she would enjoy what she and Stevie had taken months to plan. Meanwhile the food was served: a chilled cucumber and yoghurt soup, sea trout in aspic, spicy lamb and new potatoes glossy with butter and drifted with mint, a vegetarian gratin of vegetables followed by orange and strawberry mousse and raspberries dusted with sugar and served with mountains of clotted cream.

Everyone thought, privately, that Roy's speech was uncharacteristically low-key. Philip was not one for words; his speech was brief. Beth was astonished and excited when a toast was drunk to her, as one of the bridesmaids.

'Can't I drink it too?' she said.

'No, of course you can't, you airhead,' Tom remarked, tucking into more raspberries and cream.

Hugh leaned towards Nell. 'This is the sort of thing I avoid as a rule, but I have to confess that I'm having a rather sensational time,' he said.

'I'm sure Desna thinks it's more successful than the last wedding she went to,' Nell said with a deadpan expression.

For answer Hugh touched her arm briefly. He would like to have told her how heartily relieved he was that *that* wedding had not taken place, but he said nothing. In spite of Nell's dry comment he was by no means sure of her coolness on the subject.

Nell read his thoughts. 'You're a good friend, Hugh. I want you to know how much I appreciate what you did to get my stock back from Cornucopia.' She didn't mention the money Daniel still owed her. Nobody knew anything about that, thank goodness. And she herself just wanted to forget it.

Hugh's spirits rose and then plummeted again when she added, 'You and Winnie have been far nicer to me than I deserve.' She looked across the table to where Winnie was keeping Toby entertained with tall tales.

'Not nicer than you deserve,' Hugh said. 'Look, I'd like to take you out for a late dinner tonight. When this is all over, I mean.'

'What about Laura?'

'She's staying overnight with Andrea.'

'How is Andrea?'

'Well, I think. Why do you ask?'

'She had a miscarriage, didn't she?' Nell said.

'Yes, she did. You remembered!' Hugh said. 'She lost the baby, I'm afraid.'

Nell stopped eating all of a sudden. 'I'm sorry. Poor woman.'

There was a pause. Hugh waited, not wanting to put his question a second time.

'I think there's to be dancing here . . .' Nell said.

'Do you want to stay?'

Nell turned her glass round by the stem. She was drinking apple juice like Beth and Tom, Hugh noticed. 'No. Not really. I think I shall have had enough by then.'

'So?' Hugh tried not to let his eagerness show.

'Yes, thank you, Hugh. I'd like that. I think there's some sort of private family get-together later, but after that . . .'

'I'll reserve a table at The Pig in Clover.'

'Oh, no!' Nell said quickly. 'Not there. Do you mind?'

Barney was enjoying himself. Emmet felt oddly proud of him. Of course she hadn't missed Roy's hostile glares as well as a few raised eyebrows among the guests. The Wakehams seemed to think that he was one of the men left over from putting up the marquee, but Barney had no consciousness whatever of status, his or anyone else's, real or imaginary. He talked to everybody.

'This is wicked,' he said later to Desna. 'The kids are having a great time. You did a cracker of a job on this one. Everyone thinks so. I was speaking to this chap Peverill and he said it's the best thrash he's been to in years.'

Desna smiled to herself. Peverill was a dignified and patrician old man; and a member of the minor aristocracy.

'He wants me to give him a hand rebuilding an old wall,' Barney went on.

Desna hoped that Barney hadn't been touting for business but since the gentleman in question looked over and gave them both a friendly wave she supposed it was all right. Barney and Emmet found themselves talking to Bonicelli. After some initial difficulty, Enrico understood what Barney did for a living.

'Then you should come to Tortola with Roy,' he said. 'Our firm will pay good workmen well.'

* * *

Tom had become bored with the proceedings and since some of the younger guests had started a mini party round the pool, he took the opportunity to strip off his uncomfortable best clothes and practise his lengths.

Charging up to Barney he thrust his wretched, hot jacket at him. 'Can you hold this? I'm going to swim.'

'Oi! What did you last slave die of?' Barney called after him but Tom had gone.

Beth was in the marquee hopping about to the music provided by the band, finding an endless supply of males of all ages to accompany her. She was in seventh heaven.

Persis was sitting by the boathouse, her feet propped on the bottom rail of the balustrade with the perennial Gitane and glass in her hand. Beside her stood a deeply puzzled Philip whom she had practically press-ganged into following her to this secluded spot.

'What's this all about?' Philip said. He remained standing, leaning against the railings. He didn't anticipate being away from the proceedings, or from Harriet, for long.

'I don't approve of this sort of thing.' Persis waved her cigarette vaguely in the direction of the marquee. 'Push the boat out today, decree nisi tomorrow. Believe me, I know. I was married twice. Big mistake.' She picked a tiny scrap of tobacco off her lip. 'Especially the first, even though he did come across with a handsome alimony. So he should have!'

'You're a professional cynic. But that's nothing new. What did you want to see me about and why drag me all the way down here?'

'I wanted to talk to you privately,' she said. 'Somewhere where Enrico's spies can't hear us.'

'Spies! What on earth are you talking about?' Philip gave a short, explosive laugh.

'One never knows with that mother-fucker.' She blew a smoke ring and watched it drift away over the slowly moving water. On the far bank the electric-blue flash of a kingfisher flickered.

'Come on, now! Bonicelli?'

'Let me ask you something? Have you made up your mind about joining Roy and Bonicelli's outfit in BVI?'

'Not absolutely. I'd rather run a business here, if you must know. Solo. My own boss. But I may not have much of a choice. What Roy wants me to do is to wrap it all up here and then go over.'

'Why don't you buy him out? Then you could do what you bloody well wanted.'

Philip laughed. 'A chance would be a fine thing.'

'How much would he want for this end of the business?'

Philip told her. 'Mind you, that's just a rough estimate.'

'That much, eh? Still, you could sell off parts of it and keep going on repairs. Get together a decent team of craftsmen. You could use that bloke Emmet's knocking around with. He's got potential. Plenty of energy. Could be ambitious.'

'I don't want to go to Tortola. But what have you got against it? Tell me. I'm interested.'

'I told you! Because of that bugger Bonicelli, that's why. Listen, I lived in Verona for a while, knew his wife. His ex-wife now. Never met him, mind you. Not until I saw him at Easter. But I did know a crowd of his mates. Not good news. Bloody dodgy, as a matter of fact, and I've since heard one or two things that'd make your hair stand on end.'

'Like what, for instance?'

'The way he acquired the marina in Tortola for next to nothing, for instance.' She shook her head. 'I wouldn't care to be mixed up with that. Besides, those kinds of tactics have the habit of making some folks wild as a cut snake. And Roy doesn't need any more enemies, I tell you. And there are other things . . ' She went on to list a number of Bonicelli's activities that made Philip sweat under his formal suit.

'You sure about this?'

'Didn't realize it was the same bloke at Easter, to tell you the truth,' Persis went on. 'Didn't quite catch his name. But I've twigged it now and I know I wouldn't touch him with a frigging mile-long barge pole. Nice wife, though,' she added inconsequentially. 'Ex-wife, rather.'

'Have you told Roy?' Philip said.

Persis made a sarcastic crowing sound that ended in a cough. 'Jesus wept! You're joking, aren't you? Roy listen to me? Of course he wouldn't. Desna might but all she'd do would be to worry herself sick and not say anything. But you should take some notice if you know what's good for you. For the sake of that young Harriet if nothing else.' She pulled herself to her feet and flicked her cigarette end into the water. A dark fish rose slowly to investigate and then sank down again into the green depths. 'Besides, unlike most of the sons-of-bitches that make up your sex, I think you're probably all right.'

'Well, thanks!' Philip turned to face her. 'I hope you're right about this, because if I do anything about it I have to know you're on the level.'

'Am I standing here wearing this black hat? Are you standing there wearing a monkey suit? Of course I'm bloody on the level!' They moved off the decking and began to walk back up the path together.

'The thing is,' Persis said, 'I'd be prepared to back you if you wanted the dosh. Nell refused it, she's being very stiff upper lip and English about everything. She wants to be completely self-reliant, she says.' Persis frowned fiercely. She had needed Nell to accept her offer. 'Anyway, between you and me, she'll probably marry that guy with the stoop before long. Better than that other shit, anyway. Women like Nell ought to be married . . . Odd that . . .'

'Why odd?'

'Never mind. You'll be told sooner or later I've no doubt. Anyway, that's neither here nor there. You better concentrate your mind on my offer. Let me know before I leave this evening.'

Philip jerked his head up. 'As soon as that! I won't even have time to discuss it with Harry!'

'Make time. I know what she'll say anyway. You don't think *she* wants to go swanning off to the ends of the earth, do you? She wants to become a partner in that gallery she works in.'

'How did you know that?'

'I was speaking to the owner, what's his name?'

'Gordon.'

Persis stopped and fished into her pocket for her Gitanes. 'So what do *you* think of my offer?'

Philip was already clutching at the hope Persis had given him, while cagily wondering if she could be relied on. 'I'll let you know when I've spoken to Harriet.' Philip waited while Persis lit up. 'If what you say is true I think someone should warn Roy and Desna.'

Persis shrugged. 'Please yourself. Not that he'll listen to anyone, I can tell you that for nothing.'

'He's a very stubborn man when he has his heart set on something.'

They separated and Philip went eagerly in search of Harriet.

The sun blazed down, guests sat on the lawn in the green shade of the trees, or around tables in the marquee, talking. The more energetic danced. Members of the family circulated. Stevie's team had discreetly cleared the tables and left a buffet of snacks and drinks. An air of high summer languor caused guests who had originally planned to leave early, to stay on and enjoy what most now knew would probably be their last chance to savour the pleasures of Mount Huish. Rumours were rife. It was to be a golf club, a nursing home, a health hydro. No one knew for sure. Few were aware of the stir of extra activity that was galvanizing the family.

Giles, Isabel and Philip were talking to Desna at the side of the house in Desna's private garden, drinks in their hands as if this were just an extension of the party. Except that the door into the house was shut. Harriet was perched on the stone balustrade among the roses, listening. She and Philip had already decided on their course of action, even if Persis' allegations proved to be unfounded. It had been what Harriet had wanted all along.

Isabel was sceptical. She had always liked Enrico. 'After your aunt's performance at Easter,' she said dismissively, 'I wouldn't put much credence in anything she said. It seems to me she'd do anything to stir up trouble.'

'I don't agree,' Giles argued. 'I wouldn't have her down as a liar. Outspoken to a degree, yes. And bloody rude.' He lowered his voice. 'I've been a mite distrustful of Bonicelli from the start, but that was only a feeling, you know. Personally I wouldn't think it worth the risk. What if she's right?'

'It seems to me that Enrico's absolutely genuine,' Isabel said. 'I like him.'

'I know you do,' Giles said drily. 'But I'm afraid that doesn't necessarily mean he's on the level.' He looked towards Desna who was staring out across the kitchen garden as if mesmerized. 'You're very quiet, Des. What do you think?'

'I'm wondering who is going to tell Roy what we've heard. He won't believe *me*. He'll just say I'm a woman and couldn't know anything about it. He'll say it's feminine tittle-tattle.'

Philip and Giles exchanged looks. Giles said, 'Philip and I will collar him. Get him to his study on some pretext. Where's Bonicelli?'

'The last time I saw him he'd gone in search of Nell,' Isabel said, a lingering tone of regret in her voice.

'Could you try to get hold of Roy soon?' Desna said urgently. 'Only he's planning to make some announcement about it this evening when we all get together. I don't want him to make a fool of himself in front of everyone if it can be helped.'

Giles shook his head. 'I wish he'd let me in on it from the beginning. I could have put some enquiries in hand but he always insisted, kindly I have to say, that I wasn't up to it. I wouldn't know enough about international law. All the same I think that firm he went to in London were just after the fee. I don't believe their researches were any better than I could have carried out myself.'

'I think we better prepare ourselves for the possibility that it's already too late,' Desna said. 'He doesn't tell me much but I think you'll find that he's already committed.'

'I do hope not. All the same Philip and I . . .'

The door from the kitchen opened and Roy stood there, a drink and a cigar in one hand. 'What's this then?' he said jovially. 'A mothers' meeting?'

Giles went across to him and leaning an arm on the door jamb spoke urgently to him for a moment.

'What the hell for?' Roy objected, but he finally allowed himself to be propelled into the house and into his study by Giles and Philip.

'I think it's a fuss about nothing,' Isabel said, sipping her gin and tonic. 'All the same . . . I wouldn't want Philip to get involved in anything questionable.' She looked at Desna almost accusingly. 'You say you don't *know* if he's signed anything yet?'

'No.'

'How strange. Giles lets me in on everything. Absolutely everything.' Both Desna and Harriet knew that this was not quite the case but they said nothing. Desna looked across to Harriet. She had removed the beadwork helmet and clipped her hair back with two silver clips. 'You're not saying anything, darling. What do you think?'

Harriet got up and moved closer with an air of faint astonishment; this was the first time in her life that her mother had sought her opinion on anything important. 'I think that Daddy won't listen,' she said. 'And, Mummy, if he insists on going ahead in spite of everything I think you should think about you. Do you truly want to go with Daddy? Philip and I have more or less decided what we'd like to do. If we can.'

'And what's that?' Isabel was looking at Harriet in surprise. She had heard of marriage changing people but she never heard of it working as fast as this.

'We thought we'd tell everyone when we're all together this evening.'

Desna put her hand to her head. 'Oh dear!' she said. 'He's not family, of course, but I've asked Enrico and other close friends to join us later. Close friends!'

'That's all right,' Isabel said. 'He need not actually be *told* that you don't trust him.'

Bonicelli, who had been waiting his chance, caught Nell alone at last. He offered her a glass of wine which he had fetched with this in mind.

'Nell,' he said in mock surprise, offering her the wine, 'I hoped I might have a chance to speak to you.'

'Did you, Enrico?' She accepted the wine but didn't drink.

'Naturally I was very upset that you had been so let down by that blackguard. It's very hard when love goes wrong, when one is betrayed. I know exactly how it feels, believe me.'

'Do you, Enrico?'

'Of course. You may have heard that we Italian men are ardent lovers. We feel it very deeply when we are disappointed in love.' He looked at her, desire in his hard eyes. 'So when I heard that you were not after all to be married, though I was sorry for you, for myself I was rejoicing.'

'Were you?'

'It means, meant, that maybe there is still a chance . . .'

'I don't think so, Enrico.'

'It's early. You should give yourself the opportunity for finding out what a real lover is. Someone who can give you all you deserve instead of, forgive me, swindling you.' He gave her a look that had worked on women many times before.

'Thank you for asking, Enrico,' Nell said sweetly. 'But I don't feel like getting involved with anyone else at the moment. I'm sure you understand.'

Bonicelli gave the smallest of bows. 'Absolutely. I felt just the same for many days after a disappointing affair. I assure you, the last thing on my mind is to cause you any distress whatever. But if after a few days, weeks, I may be permitted to telephone . . .?'

'I don't think so,' Nell repeated. 'You would only be wasting your time, Enrico.'

'To waste time in that way would be a privilege,' Bonicelli said gravely, persuaded that Nell was as good as his. The rest was only a matter of time and a phone call.

'I would much rather you didn't,' Nell said, less sweetly. . Catching sight of Emmet, she signalled for rescue with her eyes.

Emmet joined them. She was fanning herself with a menu card. 'I'd give anything to join the children in the pool,' she said. 'What a pity we can't.'

Bonicelli looked less than pleased. Emmet was a pretty woman but with no style at all. In fact, it was hard to believe she was Nell's sister.

'That's absolute bullshit!' Roy said, turning on Giles and Philip almost violently.

'We thought you might say that.'

'Evidence. That's what I want. Who the hell told you, anyway?'

The other two looked at each other. Then Philip said quietly, 'Persis told me.'

Roy roared with laughter. 'Oh my God! What will the silly old hag think of next?'

'I believe her,' Philip said.

'More fool you! D'you think for one minute I didn't go into the man's credentials with a fine-tooth comb before I agreed to consider the scheme? You must think I'm losing my bloody marbles.'

Giles spoke in his lawyerish manner. 'There are plenty of ways of disguising the real state of affairs, especially if you're as rich as Bonicelli is reputed to be. Nobody seems to know how he got his money, do they? When I spoke to him at Easter he was extraordinarily vague.'

'So would I be if some complete stranger started asking me bloody impertinent questions! Come to that, how does anyone get their money? I'm perfectly willing to bet that there isn't a millionaire living who hasn't cut a few corners in his time. It goes with the territory.'

'I don't believe from what Philip tells me that we're talking minor infringements of the law here. I think it may well be more serious than that. Neither of us wants you to make a mistake that might prove costly, or even dangerous. We think it's best to be on the safe side, and get an independent firm of corporate lawyers to go through it again.'

Roy took a moment to light another cigar. He offered one to each of them but they shook their heads. 'Do you know what I think?' he said. 'I think you're a couple of bloody old women, if you must know. I'm particularly disappointed in you, Philip. I should have thought you'd have wanted the best for my daughter since you've married her. But I take it I was mistaken in you. That you're not interested in becoming a rich man or in making Harriet a rich man's wife?'

Philip shook his head. 'I'm sorry. No. I don't want to be an executive, I want to work with boats.'

'Right. That's your funeral then. But don't come running to me when I'm a successful man and you're on the rocks because it'll be too late. Rupert's keen to come out and join the firm as soon as he leaves school so I shall probably make him a partner instead. Funny how things work out! I thought at one time that you were the go-getter and that Rupert was the loser. But blood will out in the end, as they say!'

Giles went towards the door. 'Well, we've said our say. We felt it our duty to pass on what we'd heard, whether or not it's correct. Let's say no more about it. We don't want to fall out on such an otherwise happy occasion.'

'Right. No need to fall out as you say,' Roy said, recovering his humour. 'I think Philip's making a bloody big mistake, but there you are. In any case, the time to have issued warnings, even if they were justified, is long past. Everything is signed sealed and, almost, delivered. So you're too late, Giles old chap.' He thumped Giles on the back. 'You want to get out of the rut yourself, Giles. Not go round lecturing enterprising folk like some fucking old biddy!'

The family gathering took place in the sitting room just before Harriet and Philip left to catch their train. Even Tom and Beth were rounded up for the occasion. Barney, Hugh, Winnie, Tessa, Faith and the Wakehams hovered on the periphery. Bonicelli who saw himself as an honorary family member positioned himself next to Nell.

With Harriet beside him Philip cleared his throat to attract attention before he thanked Roy and Desna once more for what he called a 'mega successful bash'.

'Harry and I would just like to tell everyone what our plans are, if you can bear it,' he said with a grin. 'We both appreciate all Roy and Desna have done for us *and* Roy's generous offer to join him in Tortola, but after a lot of thought we have nevertheless decided to stick around in Kingswear.' He spoke directly to Roy. 'Sir, I'd like to carry on at the yard as you suggested . . . then we shall have to see. Gordon and Toby have generously offered a partnership to Harriet which she has decided to accept.'

'Bully for her,' Faith interjected with a grin.

'So one way and another,' Philip went on, 'you could say that we shall both be gainfully employed, for the immediate future anyway.' He looked round the room, aware of all eyes on him, certain of them speculative of what lay behind his words. Roy was red in the face and frowning. Philip made no mention of Persis' offer, he merely glanced at her with a conspiratorial grin. All the acknowledgement she gave was a fractional lifting of her glass. Philip turned to Harriet. 'I think Harry has something to tell you too.'

'Harriet had never in her life addressed a room full of people. A few days ago, a few hours ago, even, she would have positively refused such a terrifying undertaking but, though she was nervous and after some initial stumbling, she spoke up clearly, encouraged by Gordon and Toby who stood against the wall on the far side of the room. 'I'd like to thank Gordon and Toby for offering me the partnership in the Yardarm Gallery. I'm very pleased to tell you that the first show we shall be putting on under the slight change of management will be an exhibition of the paintings of that highly original painter, Mo Joubert, my grandmother.' She finished in a rush and sat down.

There was an outburst of clapping. Mo just grinned and shook her head as if to disclaim the compliment.

Harriet bounced up again and said breathlessly, 'And I should like to thank both my parents for a lovely, lovely wedding. I didn't think I would enjoy it, but I have.' She turned to Roy and Desna. 'Thank you.'

There was more clapping. Philip kissed her, then Desna.

Just as everyone was beginning to chatter and to replenish their glasses Roy assumed his usual place by the fireplace and raised his voice above the racket. 'Now I think it's my turn.' He glared round the room to make sure everyone was listening. All were, except Tom and Beth who were pushing each other. Roy continued, 'This celebration, as you all know, has been not only to mark the wedding of Philip and Harriet but is also by way of being a farewell party. A party in which Des and I say goodbye to Mount Huish and all our friends and family. By next month we shall be lounging in the sun while the rest of you will be huddled under umbrellas and looking out your thermals . . .'

There were one or two laughs. Enrico showed his white teeth and held up his cigar.

Roy went on. 'Naturally we shall be sorry to say goodbye to you all, sorry to leave Mount Huish and also sorry that Philip doesn't feel he can join us in the BVI. I hope that instead Rupert will eventually get his bloody act together and come and lend a hand . . .' He waited for the laughs which came from Bonicelli and the Wakehams rather than the immediate family, except Rupert, who laughed too loudly because he'd paid a great many visits to the bar. 'Once we've got ourselves established, however, you will all be very welcome to spend your holidays with us as often as you like . . . special terms to our friends for all crewed or bareboat chartering, naturally.' Faint laughter. 'Desna and I wish you as much success in your lives as we expect in ours. I'd like you to raise your glasses to all our futures . . .'

Desna felt the colour draining from her cheeks. For support and to control the very visible trembling of her hands, she grasped the back of a chair. She thought she was going to faint. She heard herself say, 'No!' and felt rather than saw, glances exchanged.

'Are you all right, Mummy?' Harriet was by her side, her hand on her arm.

Now was the time to tell Roy, everyone, that she would not be going to Tortola; that she would be staying here in Devon, but she seemed unable to get her mouth round the words. In any case, the moment passed. The toast was drunk and conversation had returned to normal. People were already drifting from the room.

'What's the matter?' Roy stood over her. Philip offered her a drink of water. Giles and Isabel looked concerned.

'Sit down, Mummy,' Harriet said. Desna obeyed. She had no option; her legs were refusing to support her.

'Give her air,' Giles said.

'It's all right. I'm not going to faint.'

'What's the matter with you?' Roy asked again, too loudly.

Desna looked at him, white-faced. 'I'm not coming with you, Roy,' she said clearly.

'Not coming? Not coming where?'

'To Tortola. I'm staying here in Devon.'

'You've had too much champagne, my girl. You're not used to it,' Roy blustered.

But Isabel was intrigued. 'Not go to Tortola? Do you mean that, Desna?'

'Of course she bloody doesn't!' Roy's face had anger banked up in it like thunderclouds.

'Yes, I do. You might as well all know. I'm going to help Stevie Turnbull run Bonne Bouche.'

'This is a load of damn nonsense!'

'No, Roy.'

'Are you sure, Mummy?' Harriet said breathlessly, hardly daring to believe.

Desna closed her eyes as if to shut out the ring of faces. Then, opening them again, looked at Roy steadily. 'Absolutely sure.'

Harriet was conscious of Bonicelli standing behind Giles, listening, taking in the situation. Roy became aware of him at the same moment.

'This is a lot of damnfool nonsense,' he repeated, turning to the Italian. 'Disregard it. There's been a lot of booze around today and Des is no drinker. She'll be bloody embarrassed by this little scene tomorrow.' He looked at the others. 'So don't any of you dare to tease her about this little *faux pas* or we shall fall out!' He finished on what he hoped was a humorous note, keeping his temper in check. 'Just be a little lenient to the mother of the bride, she's been working damned hard to make all this a success.'

Desna's voice was very clear. 'I'm not drunk. I shall be as sure tomorrow as I am today. I'm sorry, Roy. I had to tell you now, before it went any further. I wanted to tell you before but you wouldn't listen . . .'

'In my country,' Bonicelli said portentously, 'a wife considers it her duty to stand by her husband.' What his own wife had done he counted as an unfortunate aberration.

'And bloody right at that!' Roy snarled. There was a sudden brittle clatter of breaking glass. No one knew if he'd dropped his glass on the marble hearth by accident or deliberately thrown it. It sounded faintly shocking and transferred all eyes to him.

Kit and Helen Wakeham stood at the door watching with bated breath the first detectable rift they had ever witnessed in the wonderful edifice of the Hindmarch marriage.

Giles intervened. 'Look, Roy old chap, I think these things are better discussed in private. But I think it would be as well to take on board that Des means what she says.'

'Who told you to interfere, you damned old woman,' Roy said, thrusting his face forward aggressively. 'Just because you never made anything of yourself doesn't give you the right to dictate to those of us with a bit of spunk . . .'

'That's unforgivable!' Isabel exclaimed, forgetting she had once been attracted to Roy and thought something very similar about her husband.

'Shut up, you interfering bitch!' Roy shouted at her, his consumption of whisky during that day now beginning to tell.

Giles lashed out at Roy in a show of gallantry. But he was not normally a violent man, or any longer very fit, and the blow was totally ineffective. Roy's answering punch was that of a man who was both. It laid Giles out.

'Oh my God!' Isabel screamed, kneeling by her supine husband. 'Someone get a doctor!'

'I think Sally Bright might still be here,' Harriet said, while Desna looked on appalled at what she now blamed herself for instigating.

'I'll fetch her,' Harriet said and dashed from the room. Desna and Philip struggled with the intricacies of Giles' formal clothes, someone offered a large white handkerchief to hold against

Giles' bloodied nose. Bonicelli stood by the window. This was nothing compared to some weddings, indeed even funerals, he'd attended.

After the punch Roy stood over Giles for a moment or two as if he would have hit him again. Rupert and Philip pulled him away but he thrust at them violently and hurled himself out of the room. He had no idea where to go that was unlikely still to have a number of guests innocently to waylay him. There was no possibility of getting his car out of the garage since the yard at the back of the house was full of caterers' vans and the house itself held no corner where he would be likely to be left alone.

He stormed out through the back of the house and made for the narrow, little-used path that ended up eventually at the boathouse. He would take the inflatable down to the yard and let them all go to the devil!

On the path just before he arrived at the boathouse, he met Faith. She was sitting on a rustic wooden bench, smoking a roll-up. Immediately he recollected what had happened when they'd been alone together once before. Who knew if she was not responsible for the whole fucking mess? If she'd spilled the beans not only to Harriet but to Desna too, it would explain everything. She owed him, by Christ! His anger overflowed like lava.

'I'm surprised you came back here at all after what you did,' he said, wiping sweat from his streaming face. 'Only a slut would know that trick.'

Faith looked about her. There was no one else around.

'If you were thinking of having another go, Mr H.,' she said, 'I wouldn't if I were you. I can let out a holler that can be heard from here to the Lizard.'

'You won't have a chance,' he said, 'this time.'

He lunged at her, but she moved off the bench, side-stepping him. The amount he had drunk was beginning to tell; besides which, he was wearing unaccustomed new leather shoes which skidded on the dry leaves underfoot; he staggered, then lost his footing. He landed up against the trunk of a tree. For a moment he was winded. He tried to rise, then realized he had sprained his wrist in the fall. Or broken it. He looked at his hand and saw Giles' blood on it for the first time.

'Oh God!' he groaned.

There was a rustle of silk and Faith was kneeling beside him, fumbling for her hanky.

'Come on, Mr H. Let me have a look.' She wiped the blood away, thinking that it belonged to Roy, puzzled that there was no visible wound.

'Look,' she said. 'I don't think you should go in for this stunt. Why don't you knock it off? I mean, you must've been a real hunk once. I reckon I could have quite fancied you . . .'

Roy's anger seemed to have evaporated all of a sudden. His hand was painful. He felt ridiculous slumped against the tree with this girl fussing over him. He'd forgotten what had been on his mind when he'd fallen. Brushing aside her help impatiently, he struggled to his feet.

'You think I'm old, I suppose,' he said, fumbling with his tie, his waistcoat and his shirt, which were all awry. Why was it that every encounter with this bitch left him injured in some way?

She looked at him mystified. What did he mean? He *was* old.

'No. It's not that,' she said kindly. 'I expect that it's because you're not my type. You see, I'm a sucker for wimpish men.'

Roy made a sound of disgust. He sat on the rustic bench, his head bowed.

'I suppose you couldn't wait to tell my wife and daughter what happened between us last time,' he said bitterly. 'It would explain a lot.'

'What d'you take me for? Shooting my mouth off would have hurt them far more than it would have hurt you, believe me. No, you'll have to look nearer home for an explanation of what's gone wrong, Mr H.' Faith fished in her little bag and dragged out a battered box. She withdrew the makings of another roll-up, offering the box to Roy. He shook his head in disgust.

'I wish you wouldn't call me Mr H.,' he said.

She shrugged. 'So why're you skulking down here?' she asked him. 'I thought you were talking up a storm, trying to persuade your wife to buzz off to where-was-it?'

'I had a disagreement with Giles.'

'Giles?' Faith lit the scrap of paper and tobacco that constituted her cigarette. 'So what's with you?' she said. 'Why didn't you discuss the whole business with Desna before? Look what you've let yourself in for! I mean, like, it's pretty embarrassing, right?'

'It's Desna who should be embarrassed.'

Faith eyed Roy through the tiny smokescreen. 'Is that a fact?' she said.

Harriet and Philip stood at the front door wearing shorts, tee shirts and backpacks. Two further holdalls lay at their feet. Desna had once had visions of what Harriet would choose as a going-away outfit but as far as she could see, her daughter's most notable extra purchase had been a couple of filmy shifts to wear over her shorts. Andy stood by his car waiting to drive them to the station and all the remaining guests crowded round to wave them off. Faith ran up at the last minute, panting, but of Roy there was no sign. Rupert had been sent to find him but he had been unsuccessful. After attention from Sally Bright, Giles had recovered sufficiently to join them. Isabel held his arm tenderly, making him feel uncharacteristically heroic.

'I don't think we can wait for Roy any longer,' Philip said, looking at his watch. 'We shall have to go.' He kissed Desna and Isabel, then the other female members of the family.

At that moment Roy strolled up from inside the house.

'Already for the send-off?' he said heartily, as if nothing had happened. For a moment every member of the family gawped at him in astonishment. The guests who had not witnessed the scene inside the house chaffed him for nearly missing his daughter's departure and the moment was glossed over. The more observant noticed a coolness in the attitude of the departing couple when Roy stepped up to kiss Harriet and shake hands with Philip; but for its being such a public occasion, both Harriet and Philip would have dispensed with such a performance altogether.

Philip shook hands with his father, holding his arm. 'And for God's sake don't go taking a swipe at anyone else!' he said in a low voice that only his parents heard.

Giles grinned modestly, smiling at Isabel.

Harriet hugged Desna. 'I'll ring you from Scotland, Mummy,' she said quietly. 'Why don't you stay with Mo tonight? I think it would be better.' She meant safer.

'Stevie's asked me to stay with her,' Desna said. 'And I think I will.'

Harriet looked surprised for a moment. 'Good, I'm glad,' she said.

Philip and Harriet got into the car and Andy drove them off in a shower of confetti.

Philip took Harriet's hand and squeezed it. For two weeks they would be away from the whole lot of them. He would have her all to himself while they toured Scotland in a hired car.

Barney sat in the driving seat of the old Escort; Tom and Beth, now that they had been coaxed away from the delights of Mount Huish, were impatient to be gone. Rupert made faces at them through the window. Emmet hesitated before she got into the car.

'Are you sure you'll be all right, Des? Only you know you're very welcome to come with us.'

'I shall be perfectly all right with Stevie. And I shall want to wait until her people have finished here tonight. Besides, I have Rupert.' She put an arm round her tall son. Desna had the impression that she was simply going through the motions of normal behaviour; she was still numb with the shock of what she had done.

'Mo's staying on for a bit anyway.'

'Yes.'

Emmet put her arms round Desna and held her close. 'I can't tell you how glad I am you're not going,' she said. 'You won't allow Roy to change your mind, will you? I don't trust him after what he did today.'

'We shall have to talk about it, of course.'

'Then make sure someone else is there, Des. If he's been at the whisky he might even take a slug at you.' Emmet spoke earnestly, as if the possibility of Roy making a physical attack on Desna was almost inconceivable. If only she knew, Desna thought. If only anybody knew what lay behind Roy's conviviality. Today they had seen just the tip of a very considerable iceberg.

'Rupert, look after your mother,' Emmet said severely. To Desna she said, 'I'll ring you, sweetie. And thanks for a great day. We all had a wonderful time.' She got into the car and leaned out the window as Barney started the engine. It made a noise like an outboard. 'We thought you were heroic back there,' she called.

As they disappeared down the drive, Rupert put an arm round Desna's shoulders. 'Ma, I wish you would change your mind and come to Tortola with Dad and me. I know he went a bit ape back there but he'll be eating shit about it tomorrow when he sobers up.'

Desna felt a bleak sense of loss; the culmination of a process that had begun when they'd left Rupert standing on the steps of his first boarding school. You didn't own your children, you were simply loaned them for a few years. If you were lucky, she thought, something of value remained. But Rupert's words had already made it abundantly clear where his allegiance lay.

Back at Drake's Farm they all changed into their comfortable old clothes. There were chores to be attended to. Beth was reluctant to allow Emmet to peel her out of her silken finery but Emmet insisted.

'It'll take me forever to get the stains out as it is. Look at this! Apple juice, raspberries, grass!'

Beth gave in. 'But I will be able to wear it to Rebecca's birthday party, won't I?'

'Of course.'

The cats were already winding themselves round Beth's ankles, mewing for attention. 'All right, my darlings,' she said in a piping sing-song. 'Come with me.' She arranged the feeding bowls in a row on the worktop and fetched the cat food from the fridge, spooning an equal share in each. Mogsy, taking advantage of her privileged position, jumped up and began her meal before Beth had finished dishing it out.

'Mogsy!' she exclaimed in mock horror. Mogsy went on eating.

Barney was busy with the birds. Emmet and Tom went to feed the young badger. Afterwards, Tom, accompanied by the new dog, Kojak, who had developed a slavish devotion to the boy, stayed to watch the badger's antics with a ball Tom had found for it. Emmet made her way to the field alone to round up the chickens and shut them up for the night. The other dogs followed her and sat patiently, their tongues lolling. Even now it was very hot indeed. The sun was about to disappear between two wooded hills to the west, but light still streamed across the coombe, turning the cornfields pink and the striped shadows that lay on them almost to magenta. Behind them trees swathed other hills in shades of green from viridian to blue-black. It was very quiet; the only sounds were the perpetual moans of the collared doves and the distant thrum of a combine harvester. An Intercity hummed past somewhere behind the trees. Over by the stream, the geese, now settling in and behaving as if they owned the place, honked at a passing car. They would be better watchdogs than the dogs themselves, Emmet thought, as she saw the last chicken safely inside and locked the door.

'All finished?' Barney said, appearing at her side. He was back in his frayed shorts and old check shirt. Wingnut, a rough-haired mongrel with long ears, went to lie on his feet.

'All finished,' she said absently, gazing at a wheeling flock of seagulls who had appeared from nowhere, now joined by swallows. 'They're after the flying ants,' she said, amused. 'It's a bonanza. All they have to do is to fly around with their beaks open.'

They both watched the aerial display. 'Did you enjoy yourself today?' Emmet asked.

'It was wicked,' Barney said. 'Not the sort of caper I usually go to, mind.' He was silent for a moment, glancing at Emmet thoughtfully. 'Funny thing . . . getting married. Promising to . . . what was it?'

'Keep thee only unto her, so long as ye both shall live?'

'That's it. I mean, I suppose you should.'

'I think so. If one possibly can.'

'But if it all goes down the tubes, like with Maurice . . .?'

'I expect we should still have got married even if we'd known in advance how unsuited we were. One always hopes for the best. It just didn't work out. We had different priorities.'

'All the same, kids need a dad, don't they?'

'If at all possible.'

'Now that Maurice has gone off to London it doesn't look like he's going to be much of a dad, does it?'

'I'm afraid he wasn't before.'

'No. Well, look here. I know I'm a bit of a peasant, not quite the sort of fella your family think you should hang round with, but I was thinking . . .'

'Yes?'

'Well.' Barney frowned. He stooped to rub Wingnut's ears. 'I was thinking that we seem to suit each other quite well . . . and was wondering if we could live together, like?' He looked at her quizzically.

'But, Barney, we *are* living together.'

'So we are.' He thought again. 'But I mean like *live* together.'

'Oh, I see. I'm not much of a one for sex and so on, if that's what you mean. It's all right but it's not high on my list of pastimes.'

'That's OK. I can live with that. I'm not exactly a Don Wayne myself. I just fancy the idea of us knocking around together, sort of official. What d'you think? I mean, say if you want to throw up at the idea.'

Emmet thought. 'No. I wouldn't throw up at the idea at all.' She thought again. 'No, I'd rather like it. Do you mean getting married?'

'If you wanted to, yes.'

'OK. That's a deal. You're on.'

'We're an item then?'

'Yeah.' She grinned. Barney stepped over Wingnut and the faithful Earwig, leaned over and kissed Emmet on the mouth.

'Why are you kissing Barney?' Tom said, coming to join them, closely followed by Kojak.

490

'Because we're an item,' Emmet said.

'Oh,' Tom said, pummelling Kojak's stomach as he lay in the grass with his paws in the air. 'I see. Right.'

The restaurant wasn't as pretentious as The Pig in Clover but the food was good and it was quiet. Nell was glad of it. It had been a tiring day one way and another and she had a great deal to think about.

'I'm going to start looking for another flat tomorrow,' she said. 'I decided this morning that I can't stand my bedsit a moment longer. No wonder I've felt sick . . . it was the colour scheme.'

'You've felt sick? Is something wrong?' Hugh looked across the table at her.

'No. I was joking, really!'

'Need any help looking for a new place?'

'Well, if you hear of anything. There's a cottage going next to Mo but I don't think it would be for me. Besides, I think Desna's thinking of taking it. For the time being, that is. Until things get sorted out.'

'I'm so glad she's going to be working with Stevie. Stevie needs help desperately . . . and I think Desna needs Stevie.'

Nell ate some of her lobster salad. 'I can't tell you how relieved I am that Desna isn't going with Roy. I have a horrible feeling that Persis . . . my mother . . . is right about Enrico. You know she spent some time in Italy, she loves it there and she loves the Italians and the Italian way of life. She could easily have heard something about Enrico. I don't think she makes things up.' She smiled. 'In fact, I've come to the conclusion that Persis knows everything.'

'Will you see her again?'

Nell avoided Hugh's inexplicably disconcerting gaze. 'Oh, I dare say she'll descend on us now and again on one of her lightning visits. I may even go to Yorkshire to see her but I can't feel really attached to her in the way I do to Mo.'

'I can understand that.'

Hugh was making a superhuman effort not to show the joy

that was like a fire inside him. He couldn't let Nell see what it meant to him to be sitting here with her, instead of making do with the fleeting glimpses which were what he'd had to be content with until now; and what he would have had to endure if she'd been married to Thorne. What he really wanted to do was to carry her off to Chapel Abbey and make pretty damned sure she forgot Daniel Thorne permanently.

But Stevie said he had to wait; that Nell needed time to get over the disastrous affair. Hugh had shaken his head.

'I don't know, Stevie,' he'd said. 'All the time Nell is alone and that bugger's in the world, I count her at risk.'

'That's a chance you'll have to take, Hugh, dear. If you go crashing into her life at this juncture with your size nines, proposing marriage and so on, she'll turn you down. I can tell you that for a certainty.'

Hugh reckoned he'd waited long enough already but he complied with his sister's advice, reluctantly. He would continue to wait for Nell, until hell froze over if necessary.

'Hugh, there's something I have to tell you,' Nell said when the coffee came.

She immediately had his full attention. 'What is it?' He was ready to believe at any moment that Thorne was back in the picture.

'You'll know sooner or later. I'd like you to know sooner.'

He wasn't sure if he would be responsible for his actions if Thorne was making another attempt to win her back.

'I'm pregnant,' she said before his thoughts could set up any further scenarios.

'Pregnant!' he repeated, astounded.

'Before you ask . . . it's Daniel's, of course.'

'How long?'

'Ten, twelve weeks.'

'You're planning to go ahead with it?'

She nodded.

He took her hands across the table. It would be against Stevie's advice but he couldn't help himself. 'Does Daniel know?'

'No. I don't plan that he should. He would try to take it from me, I know he would. That's how he is.'

Hugh rather doubted that. Thorne didn't seem to be the sort who'd want a young sprog queering his pitch. But he saw that Nell believed it.

'Then we must make plans to see that it doesn't happen,' he said. 'Now you really must let me help you find a place for you both. How will you manage to work when it's born?'

'I'll manage somehow. Others have.'

'There's always a place for the two of you at Chapel Abbey if you're absolutely desperate . . . and even if you aren't,' Hugh found himself saying.

Nell studied Hugh's long face with new interest, a question forming in her head but never asked.

'Stevie said I shouldn't go blurting this out but I can't help it, Nell. I'm just as stuck on you as ever. What's the point of beating about the bush? You may as well know it as not.'

Nell smiled a smile of great sweetness that made his heart turn over. 'Thank you for telling me, Hugh. One day I shall be able to tell you how I feel myself but my emotions are all mixed up. Besides, this baby . . .'

'The baby's neither here nor there . . .'

Nell chuckled. 'I'm afraid it's very much here!'

'And so I am, Nell. I always will be. Until you tell me to sod off.'

CHAPTER THIRTY

Harriet hung the last of Mo's paintings in place; it was the picture of the girl eating cheese on toast. Her portrait, her wedding present. She stood back. The exhibition was complete. The private view was to take place that evening. The wine was ordered, the invitations sent.

The idea for the reorganization and redecorating of the gallery that had taken root in her mind in St Ives had been turned into fact. It was only when they started repainting that Gordon and Toby realized how used to the gallery's slight shabbiness they'd become. The three of them, with some help from Barney, had completed the whole job over a weekend. Now it was all sparkling white, a new sisal carpet had been laid and the lighting augmented. It looked bright, modern and successful, a worthy setting for Mo's work.

These hadn't been the only changes since Harriet had become a partner. She had rationalized Gordon's haphazard publicity and mailing methods, saving them money and making it more effective. With the money saved she had been able to place ads in glossy art magazines like *Painting Now* which had already brought in clients from further afield.

Philip was engaged in much the same activity in the yard. Hindmarch Marine was to be Hindmarch Marine no longer. Roy had been glad to sell out in the end; the marina in Tortola was swallowing up more capital than he'd reckoned on and Bonicelli wouldn't wait. And contrary to expectations, Mount Huish had not yet sold, though there were supposed to be several interested parties. The estate agents had even been forced to lower the asking price. Harriet was surprised at how uninvolved she felt.

She liked living in the small flat in Dartmouth and didn't miss Mount Huish at all; there were too many sour memories attached to the place. Let someone else come to it fresh and create their own good memories if they could.

Persis had provided most of the money to buy the yard; they'd managed to sell off parts of the premises and the moorings had yielded more than they expected. They'd borrowed the rest. It wouldn't be particularly easy, the tiny flat would have to be their home for some time to come.

She climbed the stairs to the office on the floor above. Gordon had gone to fetch some special kind of crisps without which he was sure the evening would not be a success. Toby was in his studio painting, a positive dynamo now that he had been promised a one-man exhibition at Lombards gallery in London. The discovery that Lombards were chiefly interested in his minimal 'drunken spider' efforts, had suddenly renewed his own involvement with them. The daubs on driftwood were abandoned.

Harriet looked out across the river to the small boatyard known now as Emmersons. Philip was on one side of the river, she on the other. Two different spheres. She knew Philip loved her and that she loved him as much as ever; she had anticipated that marriage would draw them together in an indissolubly natural bond, a symbiosis, but she had to admit that it hadn't really happened like that. They were still separate beings sometimes pulling separate ways. All the same, Philip hadn't wanted to possess her in the way she'd seen her mother possessed and reduced to one of the trappings of her father's life, and ultimately disposable. The more she thought of her mother's break with her father the more she admired her and saw how much courage it had taken, after years of being told what to do. What to think, even.

Harriet had kept the grey dress. Every time she opened her wardrobe and saw it hanging there she was reminded of what things had been like before and how they were now. At last she felt as if she was becoming a person; but it had taken some time to get used to going home in the evening without the usual butterflies in her stomach.

At first Philip had wanted to make love to her all the time and she bore it without complaint. She'd even convinced him that she'd enjoyed it. Occasionally, she actually had, to her great surprise. But lately Philip had come home exhausted from long hours at the yard and had fallen like a log into bed.

'We have to make a go of the yard,' he had told her one evening as she sat on the bed unlacing her boots and wriggling out of her jeans. 'And we will, but it'll take time.' He discussed the business at the yard with her in a way that her father had never done with her mother.

'I'm glad Barney can help you now that the season's over. He and Emmet say they're going to open up for B and B properly next year.'

'They'll need the winter to fix up Drake's Farm.'

'Funny, him and Emmet getting together,' Harriet said.

'Funny? What's funny about it? Barney's a damned nice bloke.'

'I know. That's not what I meant. You know she's the only one of the three sisters who had a university education, or part of one, yet in some ways she's by far the most practical and down-to-earth. She never minds slumming it in a way that would drive Mummy or Nell mad.'

'Different fathers, different mothers!' He grinned and tugged at the scarf that tied up her hair so that it undid and spilled a bronzy cascade over her shoulders. 'Your family is a complete dog's dinner.'

'Don't blame me!' she said.

Philip threw off his clothes – he was terribly untidy, Harriet had discovered – and stretched himself on the bed. She didn't worry so much these days about the possibility of his dissolving into the ether. She didn't think about death so much either. Somehow she always seemed to be too busy.

The furniture van drove off. It contained several extra beds destined for Drake's Farm and Desna's set of Cretan pithoi that was to be delivered to a house on the far side of Totnes, the interior of which Nell was currently redesigning.

Desna, Nell and Emmet turned back into the house. There

was no trace of dust or any kind of desuetude about Mount Huish, there were great earthenware pots of daisies and achillea in the hall and potpourri scented all the rooms, but a sense of emptiness was all-pervasive; even the echo of Roy's oppressive presence was fading. Rupert had been packed off to his crammer in Yorkshire, sullen and rebellious after the freedom and camaraderie of Fistral Bay; he was still baffled that his last-minute efforts had failed to win him the success in his examinations he had confidently expected; now he had three re-takes to look forward to.

The three women sought the kitchen where an atmosphere of warmth still remained. Almost automatically Desna made coffee.

'I shall miss coming here,' Nell said, pulling out a chair and sitting down.

Emmet was silent. She couldn't agree. She had always found Mount Huish vaguely intimidating, its presentation too perfect for comfort.

Desna poured the coffee into mugs. No meticulously arranged trays with cups, sugar bowls and matching milk jugs. 'It was a façade,' she said bitterly, 'a sham,' her words echoing Emmet's thoughts uncannily.

'But you worked so hard on it!' Nell said, accepting the mug Desna offered her. 'It's practically a work of art! Things going wrong between you and Roy doesn't mean that what you did here was a waste of time,' she added gently as Desna sat with them at the table.

'No? I think so.' Desna suddenly reached for the sugar and dunked a spoonful in her coffee, stirring vigorously.

'You turned a ruin into a home,' Emmet said. She had her elbows on the table and was twiddling one of her spiralling curls. 'We all watched you do it consumed with admiration. Don't put yourself down.'

'Some home! More like a monument. I thought I was bloody superwoman, didn't I? Why didn't you *tell* me, for God's sake? What are sisters *for* if not to tell the truth?'

'Tell you what?'

'That I was making an idiot of myself, being so totally obsessed with Roy and the house and everything . . .'

'We were too busy making our own stupid mistakes,' Nell said, with a short ironic laugh.

'And besides, I wouldn't have listened?'

'Probably not,' Emmet said. 'But then Nell didn't listen to anybody over Daniel. Sorry, Nell! And I didn't heed the warning signals I was getting from Tom . . .'

'It's so much easier to see what other people are doing wrong. It takes no effort.' Desna held her mug of coffee in two hands, her elbows on the table in an attitude quite new to her. 'Whereas being aware of one's own mistakes involves the need to do something about them, so we try not to see them at all if we can possibly help it!'

There was a long pause while the three of them drank their coffee. The fridges hummed and the distant mew of gulls drifted in through the open door.

'I think we should make a pact,' Emmet said. The other two looked at her.

'What do you mean?' Nell said.

Emmet had stopped twirling her hair and had laid both hands on the table.

'I mean that we should damned well listen to each other.' She grinned. 'Surely our combined wits are enough to cope with most problems if we at least try to share them?'

'It's a nice thought,' Desna said, doubtfully. Sharing problems was something so new to her that she didn't imagine she'd ever find it easy. 'But I think we should at least try it.'

They drank their coffee. Their eyes met in slightly abashed amusement. It was if they were drinking to the idea.

Desna broke the spell abruptly, rummaging in her bag.

'By the way, Rupert sent this. He saw it in the *Yorkshire Post*.' She laid a newspaper cutting on the table.

Curiously, Emmet picked it up and read aloud. 'Risen from the ashes. Artist's new studio rebuilt after the disastrous fire last March which not only gutted the studio but destroyed two years of the sculptor's work. Ms Persis Dane, well known both locally and nationally, says, "It was a great blow but now I can't wait to start work again."' Emmet broke off, looking at the others.

'She never said anything about a fire,' Desna said.

'Or that two years work had been destroyed,' Nell added.

'Poor Persis. How absolutely awful,' Emmet said.

Desna re-read the cutting. 'I wish we'd known. Perhaps we should have tried to be nicer to her. I really wish she'd told us.'

Nell was silent, remembering some of Persis' more obscure comments and blaming herself for her lack of perspicacity or even curiosity about her mother's life. She had not even entertained the notion that Persis might have had troubles of her own.

Mo arrived early for the private view wearing her 'wedding' clothes.

'Your ma said she'd come if she could,' Mo said, helping herself to some of Gordon's special crisps. 'Though she's extremely busy.'

'I'm sure she'll turn up. She reserved this evening ages ago.'

'I heard from Persis.'

'She's not coming, is she?' Harriet looked anxious, well aware of her great-aunt's knack for turning an ordinary occasion into a disaster.

'I don't think so, but one can never tell with Persis. She scribbled me a note to tell me that she's furious about the renovations to her studio. Of course, she still thinks we don't know about the fire. She says she can't work and is thinking of suing the architect.'

'I wouldn't put it past her,' Harriet said. 'Poor Persis.'

'But she sent this so she must be doing something.' Mo took a large envelope from her bag. Harriet drew from it a mounted drawing of the hulk of the *Prudence* that lay on the mud outside Mo's cottage. The lines were dark, powerful and stark, seeming to encompass the whole of the boat's history from the laying down of her keel to her ignominious end. Like a thing that had once been living and was even now continuing to thrust its ribs skywards in a last act of defiance.

'So *that's* how it's done,' Harriet said after a long perusal. It made all her own attempts look cautious and pathetic.

'What did you say?'

'The drawing. It's almost alive, as if it grew.'

'See what she's written underneath?'

'It says, "Here's some window dressing. I've signed it so you can always sell it if you're skint."' Harriet frowned. 'What does she mean, window dressing?'

'She once assured me that that was how she regarded drawing. I never believed her for a minute.'

'She never exhibits her drawings, does she?'

Gordon came over to them. 'Mo, dear! All set?' He stood back to look at Harriet's portrait. 'I love it more every time I see it. It keeps giving me fresh insights; it's positively inspiring,' he said. 'Pity it's not for sale because it's the one painting everybody's sure to want to buy.'

'Well, they're not having it,' Harriet said firmly. 'It was my wedding present.'

'I'm not saying they won't want to buy the others too,' Gordon assured them. '*The Girl with Fish* is a corker, and landscapes always do very well.'

'That evening when you did that sketch of me eating cheese on toast seems an awful long time ago,' Harriet said.

'You're not pining for that time again, are you?' Mo said, looking sharply at her granddaughter.

'Pining! Good heavens, no! Nothing could be further from the truth.'

At that moment Desna and Philip arrived.

'I'm so glad you could come, Mummy.' Harriet kissed her mother. Kissing Desna seemed much easier to do these days. Although Desna was busier than she'd ever been she was more relaxed and far more approachable than Harriet ever remembered. Plumper too. It suited her.

'Naturally I came!' Desna said. 'And I think Emmet and Barney are outside, trying to find somewhere to park the car.' A second later they arrived followed by Nell, now quite obviously pregnant and proud of it. As always these days, she was accompanied by Stevie's brother, Hugh. Harriet glanced at Nell's face as she looked at Hugh. Nell told everyone that she wouldn't even consider marriage again. Perhaps she wouldn't; but Harriet caught a glimpse of an expression on her face that told her quite clearly that Nell, if not exactly falling in love with Hugh, had very affectionate feelings towards him.

Faith bounced through the door.

'Faith!' Harriet cried. 'I never thought you'd come.'

'I had the dosh, so I thought I'd sashay on down and take in a piece of the action.'

'Have you sold some of your work, then?' Faith had managed a Two-one in her degree but Harriet hadn't heard much of her since.

'Christ no! I've got a job in a card shop.'

'So you don't have much time to do your sculpture?'

'Or space. Not much scope in a bedsit.' All the same, nothing seemed to dim Faith's optimism and good humour.

Other guests began to arrive. Mo's work was duly admired, commented on and, some of it, bought. It was one of the Yardarm Gallery's most successful private views that year. Mo felt energy return like an express train; plans for new work were already stimulating her inner eye, tempting her with new visions of form and colour.

The last guests left. Desna and Harriet were helping Gordon and Toby to clear away the glasses and vacuum squashed crisps off the floor.

'I have something to show you,' Desna said to Harriet. 'There's a letter in my bag. I'd like you to have a look at it.' Since her mother had her rubber-gloved hands in the washing up bowl, Harriet fetched Desna's bag and extracted the letter. It was from the estate agent. Harriet skimmed the contents. It mentioned a definite offer for Mount Huish that had been received that morning. It was so near the asking price, they said, that it would be advisable to give it very serious consideration.

'Will you take it?' Harriet asked.

'I shall have to fax your father. But I think we should.'

Harriet studied her mother's face but could find no trace of regret. It was as if Mount Huish was already part of the past. A past with unhappy memories.

'It's not one of those consortiums who want to turn it into a golf club, is it?' Harriet asked sceptically.

'The estate agents say not. They say it's a private buyer. I hope they're right.' Desna put the last glass on the inadequate draining board. She took her hand out of the suds and pulled off the gloves. Then she smiled at Harriet. 'We shall just have to see, won't we, darling?'

In a remote converted farmhouse in the Yorkshire Dales, Persis Dane read a letter that confirmed that her Greek villa and the small house in Tuscany were on the market and that the agents expected an almost immediate sale.

She snorted disbelievingly.

Next to this letter lay another postmarked Devon in which the estate agent assured her that her anonymity was for the moment being respected and that the offer she'd made for a property there was being seriously considered.

'It better bloody be,' Persis said to herself.

If she moved to Devon as planned she'd need help in the studio, someone with some nous. There was that friend of Harriet's of course, whose name she couldn't for the life of her remember. Sculpture student. She might do. She had guts at least.

The outbuildings would have to be adapted to her needs, but meanwhile she'd have plenty of space to work. She liked plenty of space. She needed plenty of space. And privacy.

She dropped both letters on to her untidy desk. It and all the objects on it were covered by a fine film of plaster dust. So in fact was Persis. She fished in her breast pocket for her packet of Gitanes and lit one, chucking the match on to the plaster-dusted floor. Then, remembering, she picked it up again and, cursing to herself, put it into an empty tin that was already half-full of dog ends. With narrowed eyes she surveyed her new studio critically. Although she had seen and approved the plans, the place had somehow turned out to be cramped, sterile and ill proportioned.

Quite impossible to work in, making it imperative to sell and re-locate. She glanced at the collection of small plaster maquettes assembled on an old work table. Later, when she'd hit on the right creative ambience, these would be scaled up to their final size and, later again, transformed by fire and molten bronze into the first of her new series of sculptures. Then they would resemble great split ribcages retaining just enough ambiguity to be seen, alternatively, as the rotting timbers of beached hulks. Much would be written, she had no doubt, on the inner meaning of the new work. 'Total balls, most of it!' she would say, larding her words with the usual vitriolic expletives. 'What do they know?'

But it was quite impossible to go further with her ideas here. She would have to move, and soon.

The morning after the fire she had gazed at the blackened ruins of her studio with a mixture of profound dismay and blazing anger. Amongst the smoking timbers lay the remains of the large plaster sculptures that had been already crated up ready to be transported to the foundry that day. Two years' work destroyed in a night.

And she had no one to blame but herself. The fire officer said that the conflagration had almost certainly been caused by a carelessly discarded cigarette end.

It had been the severest blow in a life that had been practically free of notable set-backs; even two failed marriages did not compare with this. All the same she was not one for self-pity, never had been. She had refrained from telling Mo or Nell about the fire partly because she was afraid of their sympathy but also because they would most certainly come to the same conclusion as the fire officer; that it had been her own fault.

She had had plenty of time to think about her loss, even wondering if the discarded fag-end could have been a sub-conscious act, forcing her to make a fresh start and depart completely from the kind of work she'd been doing for so long. Extreme, but then she'd never gone in for half-measures. A fresh start. There was no doubt that the sight of the dark ribs of the hulks on the Dart had forcibly reminded her of the fire-blackened crates that had opened up like the bars of a cage in the heat. It had started her on a new train of thought altogether.

She could ill afford to lose two years' work but what was done was done. As she'd advised Nell, sometimes one had to count one's losses and start again. Regret was not for the likes of Persis Dane.

Harriet and Philip had gratefully accepted the money to buy the boatyard but it still grated on Persis' feelings that Nell had chosen to be so pig-headedly independent. Helping Nell was supposed to have made up for all the years of her neglect, to square things with both Nell and Mo. Perhaps, after all, Nell's high-mindedness would undergo a sea-change after the baby arrived.

Abruptly Persis got out of her chair and went across to the work table to make a slight alteration to one of the maquettes, her ochre-stained fingers busy with a small knife, cigarette smoke drifting into her half-closed eyes.

One thing was certain, the new work would make her position as one of the leading sculptors of the day even more secure and make her very much richer into the bargain. Certainly rich enough to take the purchase of Mount Huish in her stride.